# Gateway and the Last Priest of the Avatar

# Gateway and the Last Priest of the Avatar

Lawrence Dewyatt Abrams

authorHOUSE

AuthorHouse™
1663 Liberty Drive
Bloomington, IN 47403
www.authorhouse.com
Phone: 1 (800) 839-8640

© 2015 Lawrence Dewyatt Abrams. All rights reserved.

No part of this book may be reproduced, stored in a retrieval system, or transmitted by any means without the written permission of the author.

Published by AuthorHouse   09/11/2015

ISBN: 978-1-5049-3386-5 (sc)
ISBN: 978-1-5049-3385-8 (e)

Library of Congress Control Number: 2015914002

Print information available on the last page.

Any people depicted in stock imagery provided by Thinkstock are models, and such images are being used for illustrative purposes only.
Certain stock imagery © Thinkstock.

This book is printed on acid-free paper.

Because of the dynamic nature of the Internet, any web addresses or links contained in this book may have changed since publication and may no longer be valid. The views expressed in this work are solely those of the author and do not necessarily reflect the views of the publisher, and the publisher hereby disclaims any responsibility for them.

## Special thanks to:

**Paul Ford** – *Photographer*

**Latavia Jones** – *Hair Stylist*

**Charmaine N Mcphee** – *Make-up artist*

# Acknowledgments

It seems sometimes that my writing grows out of the changes of my life. The first was written around the death of my mother, while this one was finished at the tumultuous end of a 13 year relationship. If this has taught me one thing it is that writing can get you through anything.

I felt like humpty dumpty during this process. And I want to thank several people for putting me back together again. First and foremost, I have to thank my father Lawrence Stevenson. He stood up as my dad and taught me about being a man. I have to thank my brother/friend J,T. Anderson who this book is dedicated to. He was my superman and guided me out of the craziness. I love him with all my heart. I have to thank my cousin Starr Butler, for being my besty and confidant. I want to thank Candra Haley and Ms. Melody Haley for giving me tough love when I needed it. Lastly, I want to thank my buddies Steve Blankenship, Robert Saunders, and Paul McIntire for helping me rediscover laughter and friendship.

In everything we do in life we have a partner. With this project my partner was Ms. Carletta Downs. More than an editor, she nutured me through this process. I could not have done it without her. I love her and give all the thanks.

Also I must mention Kontar Mosi. What was broken, 24 years of friendship has begun to repair.

As always I want to thank all my friends and family for their love and support. I also have to mention my ancestors, my blood relatives and all those Black Gay men who dared to write when HIV was stealing their lives.

Lastly, I give all honor and praise to Obatala who has crowned my head for 20 years and guided my life. After all this time, I feel like I am humble enough to truly know you.

See you around the next sentence.

Larry

This book is dedicated to my brother

From another mother

J. Ted Anderson,
you made the impossible possible

v

# PROLOGUE

Idris, the largest sun of Acara, appeared across the early morning sky first. With its appearance, it dispelled the darkness of the previous night. It began to light up a new day. Not long after its appearance Itor, the smaller and hotter sun of Acara, rose to the left of its larger sibling. With the appearance of Itor, heat rained down upon Acara dispersing the chill of the previous evening. The combined heat and light of Idris and Itor beat down on the canopy that covered the countless Lost Islands of Acara, waking the multitude of animals and beasts that made their life there. The morning was filled up with the whoops and hollers of the numerous and varied inhabitants of the Lost Islands stirring under the thick canopy. These signs and sounds of morning greeted a brand new Acarian day.

On one of the smaller of the Lost Islands, partially hidden by the lush foliage, a tall, ashen, brown-skinned man emerged from a small cave. His name was Tori. His tall figure was dressed in rags that still bore pieces of the insignia of the High Queen Mora, remnants of his previous office. The man's hair was as white as the clouds that hung overhead and fell down his back in two long braids. The man's face was deeply lined with the wisdom of his age. A rag was wrapped around his head, covering the empty sockets that once held his eyes. The long ago removal of his eyes blinded him in the literal sense but his other senses were still very strong. He stood tall in front of his cave dwelling with a gnarled walking staff in his hand, barefooted but steady. The staff was almost as tall as the man, it stood shoulder height, and Tori leaned on it heavily.

Tori had long since given up counting the number of days he had been living in exile. He had grown to have an odd sense of peace with his meager existence. It stood in stark contrast to his earlier life when he served as Chief Oracle to the High Queen Mora. He had been groomed for the position from a young age. As a child from the arid, rural Western Region, it was discovered he was gifted with visions and a host of other mental magical skills. Terminus, tKing of the Western Region, paid Tori's family a mountain of gold for him at which time he was transported to Acara City, the capital of Acara. Once in Acara City, Tori was trained by the priests of the Dark God to use his gifts in service of the Acara's High Queen. King Termnus gained favor at Acara's High Court for bringing Tori to the attention of the High Queen.

As a young man in the rugged lands of the Western Region, Tori had been trained to worship the Avatar. Though he had been raised to worship the Avatar – the living spirit of Acara – Tori was conscripted to serve the High Queen and the Dark God. It was a difficult transition for him. However, under the heavy guard of the Royal Guard and the watchful eye of the Priests of the Dark God, he complied. Tori served the High Queen in every way for many years. The weight of the labor aged Tori beyond his years and drained his spirit. The High Queen relied on him heavily. The accuracy of his vision was so much greater than any other in her service. She used him to spy on other members of the High Court and measured the truth of their intentions constantly. Tori found this constant spying on the royals of Acara tedious and draining. It also went against what his mother had told him his gifts were supposed to be used for – balancing out nature. Trapped in the Grand Citadel, he had no other choice but to serve the High Queen or face her wrath. His every move was watched. He was not a ollaborator in her affairs but an indentured servant, barely more than a skilled slave.

In addition to disliking his spying tasks, he was never comfortable with the forced homage to the Dark God. He deplored the constant blood sacrifices to the Dark God that became a daily part of his existence. If the High Queen was not sacrificing some animal on the High Altar of the Dark God, she was shedding the blood of anyone she thought might stand against her. Tori hated to think that his visions were leading to more death rather than enlightenment. Yet he took solace in the fact that he enjoyed a good life at the Acarian High Court and having the favor of the High Queen meant there was no delicacy he could not ask for. Tori hated to admit it to himself but he soon became a frequent user of rare stimulants from the Eastern Region. They gave him high pleasure and dulled his senses after each death that he felt like he played a part. The stimulants were so powerful that it didn't take long for them to enhance his visions and mystical skills. Tori hated to admit it but taking the herbs and powders became a substitute to the meditation he once used to call upon his visions.

All this changed when the High Queen realized that because of her allegiance to the Dark God, as his High Priestess, she had lost the capacity to bare any more children. The dark energies of the Dark God had left her innards barren and cold. After that, Tori was given the sole task of finding her long lost son, Von. Under the guidance of the priests of the Dark God, Tori spent every waking hour searching the known void and the unknown void for Von. However, no matter how he tried, he was never able to find a trace of the lost heir. The location of the kidnapped High Prince was hidden to his visions and sight. Though he felt like the Avatar was blocking his efforts, he dared not tell the High Queen that reason. Unable to locate the lost High Prince, he quickly fell into the disfavor of the High Queen. Over the time he searched for the lost High Price, the High Queen often joked that if he did not find him she was going to take his head. Under this new cloak of fear, Tori searched far and wide for the lost High Price but to no avail. In a fit of rage over his constant failure, the High Queen had taken his eyes taken out as a reminder of his miserable failure and had him exiled to the Lost Islands for the remainder of his days. He had lived there ever since.

As Tori stood in front of the cave he called home, he listened to the sounds of the animals and he felt the energy in the wind. His brow wrinkled and his adrenaline began to pump. He almost fell over himself with what he felt. He had not had any visions since the removal of his eyes. He had long since made peace with the loss of his sight and the other gifts to preserve his own sanity. However, this morning, the world around him was talking to his senses and guiding him in a familiar way. As the white-haired, brown-skinned man stood in front of the cave rocking in the tumult, a four-legged brown-spotted furry being came out of the cave behind him. It had a long curled tail and sentient large green eyes. The creature was called an Opion. The Opions were only one of a few sentient beings that inhabited the Lost Islands. He was Tori's only friend and constant companion. He often provided the sight the man no longer had.

Seeing his friend swaying in the wind and lost in a vision, the small Opion reached up and tugged at Tori's tattered grey pants legs with his five-fingered clawed hand. "What is it that you sense?", the Opion asked in a nasal tone, his crackled voice betraying concern for his friend.

"I am not sure Peku," Tori admitted. "But something is coming. The island is speaking of such a thing. It is all around me." Tori said as he waved his free arm, while steadying himself on his staff.

Peku raised his tiny wet black nose to the air and smelled the wind. He looked back at his companion oddly with a confused expression and twisted his long white whiskers.

"It feels like just another day to me. Forget this feeling you have and let's go find *sweet* foods to eat for today," Peku begged. "Maybe you just have butt vapors! You did eat a lot from the Rotuli tree last night", he recalled.

"No, it is not that," Tori disagreed. "I must go to the veins and consult the waters."

The veins were the names of the myriad waterways that separated all the different Lost Islands. Some of the veins were shallow and ankle deep, while others were wide and expansive as rivers. The veins were as diverse in size as the Islands they separated.

"If I guide you there," Peku began," then can we go get something sweet to eat?" he begged passionately.

Tori smiled at the singular focus of his little friend. "Yes, I promise."

"Then before my hunger gets the best of me, let's go," Peku agreed.

Nothing else needed to be said. Peku struck out in front of Tori, cutting through the thick brush. Tori followed the scent and sound of his companion as they moved through the thick brush toward the shoreline. After some time, they reached a thick vein of water. Tori could feel the spray coming from the water on his face. Some of the veins were peaceful, while others were immense and tumultuous. However, the water in all of them was fresh and sweet to drink. Peku fell back and watched his companion oddly. Tori used his staff to guide him to the water's edge. He sat down at the edge of the cool vein. He placed his staff beside him and dropped his head. He began to recite prayers to the Avatar, the living essence of Acara, as the fresh water rolled around him in waves. It was not long before a presence overtook him. He shook under the grip and power of the energy as it ran up and down his spine. The energy of the Avatar filled his mind. Tori had used his powers in many ways before, but he had never felt anything like this. The feeling of joy and love he felt was overwhelming. It brought tears to his eyeless sockets underneath the dirty bandage.

After a few minutes, the energy subsided. Tori was left sitting in the fresh water of the vein, shaking. He was laughing hysterically.

Watching, Peku approached him slowly and rubbed his furry hide up against him. "What is it?" he asked.

"It was the Avatar," Tori began slowly. "It has touched me. It has spoken to me," he admitted reverently.

"Why did it do that?" Peku asked skeptically as he wrinkled his brow, trying not to betray his skepticism. "I think it is truly butt vapors. You, a blind man living in exile? Why would the Avatar speak to you? You aren't anyone special," he said finally.

Dismissing his words, Tori said, "It did, my dear friend, because the lost High Prince is coming home to Acara." Tori explained as he cleared his throat as he put his arm protectively around Peku and hugged him. "And on top of that, my friend, he is coming to these Lost Islands and we, dear Peku, must find him first," Tori said as he came to his feet. He steadied himself on his walking stick.

Peku looked at his friend oddly. He had known Tori for a long time and he knew that he was full of grand stories about Acara City, visions, and the High Queen. Before Tori, Peku never even thought about such things. Now, his friend was telling him that he had made contact with the Avatar and that it had told him that the lost High Prince was coming to these underdeveloped straits. Peku wrinkled his nose and smiled. It was too much to be believed. However, he loved his friend and kept these thoughts to himself. He still thought it was just a bad case of the butt vapors. Silently, he made himself a promise to keep his friend away from the Rotuli trees.

"Do we have time to find sweet things to eat first?" Peku asked as he jumped around in the fresh water of the veins at Tori's knees.

"I think we do," Tori laughed as he reached down and rubbed at Peku's soft wet fur. "I think we do."

# AFTER BURN

# Chapter 1

Reverend Monroe stood in the ashes of the sanctuary of Gateway Baptist Church. It had only been a day since the fire that had burned down the church. The sanctuary was a charred remnant of what it once was. Surveying the damage, Reverend Monroe could not believe this was once the beautiful church he had built and that he had loved. He kicked at the splintered wood of the pews and made his way through the burned remains of the bibles. There was a knot in his stomach as he took in the devastation caused by the fire that Royal had set using his innate powers. However, he did not blame his surrogate son for the damage. If Royal had not acted so bravely, none of them would have survived the onslaught of the High Queen Mora's assassin cube.

*The assassin cube.*

The words rolled around in his mind as he looked around the scorched walls of the church trying not to remember the battle from the days before. The assassin cube was created by the High Queen Mora and came from the world he was from, Acara. The assassin cube was supposed to kill him and Lethia. It was also supposed to capture Royal and Simon. Though it had not been successful in its principle mission, it had laid waste to all that he and the others had built since coming toEarth sixteen years ago. The church had served as a mask for their presence on Earth. Now, through its violence, the assassin cube had ripped that mask away.

Reverend Monroe sighed and his eyes filled with tears. He had returned to the edifice so quickly after the fire not to mourn burned wood and melted metal, but to get information. He and the Earth-bound survivors of the battle with the assassin cube needed to make sure that Royal and the others had indeed made it through the Gateway under the pulpit and not buried under the weight of the destroyed structure. Reverend Monroe, Purcell, and Simon were lucky that the flames that Royal had set during the battle with the assassin cube had not consumed them. Ben Lee, Hue's father, had successfully pulled them all from the flames. This left the others to the unknown mercy of the Gateway.

Reverend Monroe sighed and a tear formed in his eye as he remembered the bravery of everyone during the battle. Turning his head, he looked over at the empty space where he had seen Tisha and Quan vanish through a Gateway. He was sure they were somewhere on Acara now. He did not want to think what the High Queen would do to the young lady who had risked her life to save them all. A cold chill went up his spine at the thought. He turned his attention to the pulpit area. It was a heap of broken wood and shattered metal. However, he was more concerned with the Gateway that it hid and he hoped that the others had found a way to open it without him as their trusty crystal keeper to guide them home.

After the battle and the fire, he and the others had been too busy with the firemen and the police officers to check on the safety of anyone else. He barely had time to recover from the attack of the assassin cube before he had to deal with the reality of the aftermath of the fire and the civil authorities. While the others hid in Mr. Lee's car, he had the unsavory task of telling the firemen and police that Royal, Tisha, Wisdom, Hue, and Grace (Lethia) had been consumed by the incredibly hot fire. As he looked at the ruined pulpit, it was a lie he hoped to prove false. Reverend Monroe reached into his pocket and removed a jagged crystal. The crystal was no bigger than the palm of his hand. It was yellow and had shards sticking out of it. Reverend Monroe closed his eyes and began to concentrate. The crystal began to glow immediately as it hit his palm. A light from the crystal shot from his hand and fell onto the ruins of the pulpit. The light allowed Reverend Monroe to see beneath the wreckage into the space under the pulpit. He was relieved immediately when he found no bodies there, just the empty archway that had housed the Gateway. The Gateway was still smoldering with the power from its activation.

As Reverend Monroe used the jagged gem to survey the burned out husk of the church, he suddenly realized he was not alone. He quickly covered the light the gem emitted with his other hand and slid the jagged crystal into his pocket. He turned as he watched Ms. Loretta Sims come into the side of the church. The elder woman of the church was dressed in a black dress and her head was hung low. Her usually animated self was dull with grief. Her head that was always adorned with a new wig was simply covered with a dark scarf. She was a shadow of her usual self. It took her a minute before she realized she was not alone also. She looked up and saw Reverend Monroe standing among the debris. She tried to smile at the sight of her pastor, but the pain of the loss she was feeling was too great. For a moment, the two stared at one another over the broken pews; neither of them seemed to know what to say.

"Reverend Monroe," Ms. Loretta began as she cleared her throat". I never thought that when I joined this church it would turn into a cemetery for me or for you," she said as tears began to form in the corners of her eyes.

Seeing the anguish on her, Reverend Monroe crossed the room and went to her. He wished that he could tell her that her grandson, Wisdom, and Tisha - Wisdom's ex girlfriend and the mother of his son - were not dead. However, there was no way he could reveal this to her without having to tell her who he and the others truly were. The heaviness of this lie sat on him like a great weight as he took her into his arms. She was a silent victim of the treachery of the High Queen. Seeing the pain the elder woman was in was a reminder of exactly how much they had all lost with the destruction of the church.

"This is truly a test of our faith," Reverend Monroe began." More than a building we are all going to have to rebuild our lives." he tried.

"I still don't understand what Wisdom or Tisha were doing in the church at that late hour," Ms. Loretta said as she wiped at her eyes." None of it makes me no sense to me." She shook her weary head.

"I guess that would have to be my fault," Reverend Monroe said quickly with a heavy voice". We have been working on opening a youth center in the building across the street. They were here with me working on that". He tried.

"That might explain Tisha being here, but what about Wisdom? He was not a churchgoer" her voice trailed off. "It just doesn't make any sense", she insisted.

"Wisdom," Reverend Monroe began, remembering his gallantry in battle in spite of his life as a drug dealer, "was in the process of having *a change of life*. He wanted it to be a surprise for you and his brother Purcell," Reverend Monroe lied. He thought that it would be something that the grieving grandmother could hear that would ease her pain.

"Lord," Ms. Loretta said as she pulled away from her pastor. She got down on her hands and knees. She began to gather the ashes in her hands. "I knew that boy had some good in him still. I knew he did," she cried out, "I knew he did!"

Reverend Monroe did not respond. He stood back watching her gather the ashes in her hands. He could feel the grief rising off the elder woman in waves. He could not imagine how she felt. He closed his eyes and looked away in spite of himself.

"Look at me," she said somberly as she stood up. "I am so caught up in my grief that I ain't asked you how you are managing with your loss. I may have lost my grandson and the mother of his child, but you done lost your son and your sister, too!", she said as she shook her head.

Reverend Monroe tried not to look too stunned by the question. Quickly, he had to hide his elation that the others had managed to use the Gateway to escape and feign despair.

"The Lord gives and he takes away. Lord knows this is a test of any man's faith," he managed through a scowl of sadness. "Losing a son is bad enough, but my sister Grace too!", he shook his head. "I feel lost with only my prayers holding me together."

Ms. Loretta was at his side instantly. She wrapped her arms around her pastor and let him shed fake tears.

"Gateway Baptist is a strong church," she said as she began to weep again. "We gonna get through this tragedy together. That is what a church family is for. More than for times of good, a real family is for times of trouble."

*Trouble.*

The word rolled around in his head as he held on to her. He looked over her shoulder at the pulpit and truly began to cry. For the first time since coming to Earth, Royal and Lethia were no longer at his side. He knew they were somewhere on Acara, but he was not with them. Though he still had Simon with him, he felt lost without his surrogate son and false sister, Lethia, with him. This realization made him hold onto Ms. Loretta tighter and he closed his eyes trying to shut out the haunting memories the ashes held.

Ben Lee opened his eyes. He was in the master bedroom of his Shirley Avenue, Baltimore City home. He lay in the dark for along time listening to the silence of his house. Sleeping in the master bedroom was something Ben rarely did since the death of his wife, Sylvia. He found the emptiness a constant reminder of his loss and grief. He clicked the light on and swung his legs over the side of the bed. He looked down at his hands. They were wrapped and bandaged, covering the burns from the night before. Slowly, the events from the previous evening began to roll through his mind.

He had gone to the church to retrieve his son, Hue. After giving Hue permission to stay at the church over night, he hade changed his mind when his son failed to answer his calls. He had heard about the explosion across the street from the church on the News and did not feel comfortable with Hue being so close to the damage site. By the time he got to the church, he saw that the sanctuary was also in flames. Living in Baltimore all of his life, he had seen a lot of fires, but he had never before seen a fire like this one. It seemed to be burning impossibly hot and bright. Then there was the way the fire moved. It was unnatural. It was like the fire was alive. He had never been so afraid in all of his life. He saw Tisha, his daughter Sapphire's childhood friend, outside of the church. He tried to find out from her if Hue was still in the church. She failed to answer him, got in a nearby SUV, and drove through the side of the burning building.

Ben remembered being surprised and confused by her actions at first. He stood there stunned for a moment. Then he hurried across the street to the burning building. He followed the wreckage caused by Tisha and the jeep, and peered into the church. Through the flames and smoke, he could see several bodies lying around the wrecked sanctuary. Thinking that one of them might be his so he rushed into the burning church and dragged out all of the bodies that he could get to.

After he had dragged three people out of the fire, he returned again trying to see if he could find anyone else and ~~trying~~ to aid Tisha on her odd mission. As he stood in the wreckage on the side of the church, he could not go any further. The fire was raging out of control and he could no longer continue his heroic acts. However, through the flames he could see Tisha was trapped inside of the jeep. He could also tell that the jeep had a shadowed figure pinned against the far wall of the church. He remembered yelling out to her, trying to get her attention. Then he saw something that he was still having a hard time believing. The shadowed figure took out two long objects. He crossed them over his head causing a flash of light. The light grew and consumed the figure, Tisha, and the SUV. They all vanished. Ben remembered standing there, trying to make sense out of what he saw. At first, he thought the smoke and flames were playing tricks on his eyes. But, after a few seconds, he was sure that Tisha, the figure, and the jeep were all gone.

Ben remembered standing there stunned, unsure of what he saw or what to do next. Reverend Monroe had come up behind him and shaken him out of his stupor. Ben had asked him immediately about the whereabouts of his son. Reverend Monroe had sworn to him that he would explain to him where Hue was if he helped him. Reluctantly, he had agreed. He and the Pastor quickly picked up Simon and Purcell and put them in Ben's car that was parked a block away from the flaming church. They were concealed there just as the police and the firemen arrived. Ben waited in his car as he watched the pastor talk to the police and the firemen. While he waited in his car, he got a good look at both Purcell and Simon. From their wounds, he could tell that they both had been through some kind of battle. They both looked like they had been hurt by more than just the fire.

After some time on the way back to his home, the Pastor had confided in Mr. Lee that he had told the police and the firemen that Hue, Wisdom, Royal, Tisha, and Grace had all been consumed by the flames and fallen rubble. However, he admitted to him that this was a lie and he believed that his son was still alive. As he drove Ben remembered being confused by this, but the Pastor kept telling him that once they got back to his house he would explain everything to him. Ben wrinkled his brow. If his son and the others were indeed still alive, he had no idea why the Pastor felt the need to lie to the police and firemen. Ben felt like the explanation had something to do with Tisha's vanishing act and the wounds he saw on Purcell and Simon. He was sure of it.

Remembering these things, Ben shook his head. He had never been a churchgoer and after his wife Sylvia's death the last thing he wanted in his life was a church. But he had been happy that Hue had joined the church. It seemed like it would be a safe place for his son to connect and spend his free time. Especially with all the secrets he knew that Hue was keeping, having him in the church was a relief. Yet now with all that had happened, he realized he could not have been more mistaken. It was time for them to give him some long overdue answers.

Ben got to his feet and dressed quickly. He turned to leave his bedroom. Before he left, he looked over his shoulder at the unmade bed.

The empty sheets still bore the sting of the loss of his dead wife. Ben still could not believe that she was gone, even after all this time. Now the idea of losing his son was more than he could imagine. It was time for the good Reverend to give him some answers. And principal among the answers he had to render were the whereabouts of his son. Ben did not care if he explained the rest of the strange occurrences as long as he told him where Hue was.

Ben left his room and walked down the hallway toward the steps. He paused for a moment in front of Hue's closed bedroom door. He had a knot in his stomach and adrenaline began to pump through him. He licked his lips. Part of him desperately wanted a drink of alcohol but he resisted the temptation. Whatever truths the Reverend and his comrades had to render, he felt he could best face them sober. He owed Hue that much. His hands began to shake at the thought of a nip of bourbon. He stuck them in his pockets and turned to the steps instead.

He went down the steps and turned into the living room. He found two of his reluctant houseguests awake on the pull-out sofa. The roll-away bed he had bought in from the garage for the Pastor who was noticeably vacant. Ignoring the absence of the Pastor, he turned his attention to Purcell and Simon.

"Now is someone going to tell me what the fuck is going on?", he said flatly as he sized the two men up. "And most importantly, will someone tell me where the hell is my son?", he added.

Looking at the elder Lee, Simon took a deep breath. He would have hoped that the Pastor would have been back before they had this conversation, but he wasn't. Thus, he knew it fell upon him to tell Mr. Lee the truth. With all that Hue had done in aiding them in fighting the assassin cube, at the very least he owed it to him to tell his father the truth.

"You should probably sit down," Simon said softly." What I have to tell you, you may have a hard time believing."

"Try me," Ben said shortly as he crossed the room and sat down in an easy chair. He was getting vexed.

"More than tell you I might as well show you at first." Simon said as he rose.

"What do you mean?" Ben questioned.

"Purcell, let's show him." Simon suggested.

Purcell laid out on the pull-out couch and rolled up his pants leg. It was bloody from the bullet that had ricocheted and devastated his leg. Simon stood up over him and removed a brown crystal from his pocket. It began to glow lightly in his hand to Mr. Lee's surprise. Simon placed the gem over Purcell's shattered flesh. Instantly, the flesh began to mend and the bullet that had been lodged in his leg came to the surface and popped out like a weeble. In a matter of moments, his leg was as good as new except for a slight discoloration where the bullet had entered his skin. Purcell became light-headed under the weight of the healing gem and closed his eyes trying to stay awake. Wide-eyed, Ben looked on in disbelief. His mouth dropped. He had never seen anything like that in all of his life. It was like something out of one of his or his son's comic books.

"Reverend Monroe, Royal, Grace, and myself are not from your world." Simon began slowly. "We come from a planet called Acara. We came to this planet sixteen Earth years ago with a divine mission from the Avatar, a spirit of our world. Our mission was to hide the High Prince of our world from his mother, the High Queen Mora. Unlike us, she worships a Dark God that she has used to enslave our world and its people. We were supposed to keep Royal hidden here until such a time when we would be called home to liberate our people", Simon explained.

"You mean to tell me that you are not really *human*," Ben's voice cracked in disbelief as he stared at the tall young black man before him.

"We are not. I am called a Moritan. I was born with a single purpose. That purpose was to protect Royal at all costs. I was trained since birth to accomplish that task. Until recently, the church served as our disguise. It allowed us to live here as part of your people and keep our true identity hidden. However, unfortunately due to a myriad-of circumstances the High Queen-discovered our whereabouts. She sent an entity called the assassin cube to capture Royal and myself and return us to Acara. The assassin cube was also supposed to kill Reverend Monroe and the person you knew as Grace Monroe. If not for the actions and quick thinking of Tisha it might have succeeded," Simon said flatly. "In the end, she saved us all."

Ben listened to Simon's tale with wide eyes. Then he remembered the way that Tisha had brushed past him in the street and rammed the jeep into the side of the church. He also recalled the way he watched her and the shadowy figure vanish in the flames of the church. If he had not seen it with his own eyes, he might have thought Simon was crazy and kicked him out of his house and called the police. However, his instincts were telling him otherwise.

"Where is my son?" Ben asked candidly.

"Hue, Tisha, Wisdom, and Purcell all volunteered to help us make our escape to Acara", Simon continued. "We did our best to keep them safe as we fought the assassin cube and prepared to leave. Without their help, we never would have been able to survive. Your son volunteered to stay with us through the ordeal. We believe that in the final battle he, Royal, Maximus, the person you knew as Grace Monroe, and Purcell's brother, Wisdom, escaped certain death by passing through a Gateway to our world, Acara."

"A Gateway?", Ben questioned. He was beginning to sweat.

"Yes." She nodded." A Gateway is a portal. It is usually an archway energized by powerful crystals that bend space and time that allows people to pass between different locations or even, in this case, worlds. There was such a Gateway under the pulpit of Gateway Baptist church. In the final battle against the assassin cube, we believe that Royal, Hue, Wisdom, the woman you knew as Grace Monroe, and Royal's pet, Maximus, opened a Gateway and escaped to Acara."

"So hold up a minute," Ben said as he stood up with his hands shaking. 'You mean to tell me that my son is no longer on Earth?" His voice cracked with emotion.

"That is what we believe to be the case, sir," Simon answered frankly as he dropped his head. Reverend Monroe has returned to the church to make sure they passed through the portal and did not get trapped under the wreckage of the pulpit during the fire. That is where he is now."

Listening to this, Ben felt his anger suddenly rise. He rose from where he was sitting and began to pace back and forth. He was fuming with anger. His head ached. He did not know what to do. This was all too much for a simple bus driver from Baltimore City to believe.

"How could you all let a boy get mixed up in any of this?", he snapped. "And isn't Tisha your girlfriend? How could you allow her to be in such danger?"

Simon lowered his head. He, more than anyone else, felt the weight of keeping Royal and their allies safe. Even though they had not been captured by the assassin cube and were still alive, he still felt like he failed them. There was an ache inside of him that he could not describe. He had never been separated from Royal before. Now, they were potentially worlds away from one another. On top of that, the woman he loved was now in the clutches of the High Queen. It was a reality that he could not fathom. If she had not been trying to save him, she would not have been captured. He blamed himself. Simon bit down hard on his lip and lowered his head.

Seeing Simon's posture, Purcell shook off the sleep caused by the healing gem and spoke up. He said, "I know how you feel Mr. Lee. The reason that Wisdom and I got involved was to protect both Hue and Tisha. None of us expected for things to turn out like this," he concluded, trying to share some of the responsibility with Simon.

"So what are you going to do to get them back?", he asked. "It's not like they are across town and you can get on a *bus* and get them home."

Just then, there was a knock at the front door. Ben got up from where he was sitting, crossed the room, and let Reverend Monroe into the house. Reverend Monroe joined the others in the living room and Ben took up the position in the easy chair he had just vacated.

"I guess by now Simon has told you the truth of who we really are," Reverend Monroe said frankly.

"He has," Ben said evenly. "It is all still hard to believe," he admitted as he shook his head. He had gone from wanting a drink to feeling like he needed a pain reliever of some kind.

"I assure you it is all true," Purcell interjected. "I would not believe it myself if I had not seen it all with my own eyes," he added as he rubbed at the space where his leg had just been healed. "And I am a police officer, I would never lie to you sir."

"Well, the good news is, I can assure you that the others were able to open the Gateway without me. I scanned the rubble and there was no sign of them. They are all on Acara now." He announced to the relief of the others.

Reverend Monroe got up from where he was sitting and went over to Simon. He took the healing crystal from him and went over to Mr. Lee. He bent down next to him and unwrapped his burned hands. He slowly began to pass the glowing crystal over the charred flesh. Mr. Lee looked on with surprise as his hands began to mend. He immediately began to feel light-headed and sleepy, but did his best to shake it off.

"What are you going to do to get my son back?" Ben asked Reverend Monroe. "Can you make one of those Gateways and bring him home?"

"Building a Gateway is not a simple thing. You need to have the right crystals and/or a particular space to make one. Right now the only space where I know that I could make one is buried under the rubble of the church's pulpit! On top of that, I do not have the crystals that I need to form one anyway. Right now, Simon and I are stranded here and your son, Tisha, Grace, and Wisdom are stranded on Acara." He explained as he released Mr. Lee's hands and fell back to his knees.

"That is as unacceptable to me as this whole fucking situation!" Ben said as his anger exploded. "I trusted you all with the care of my son. Now you expect me to believe that you can't bring him home! I lost my wife. I can't lose my son too", he said as his voice cracked and his eyes filled with tears.

Ben jumped to his feet and stormed out of the room.

"I will go and talk to him," Purcell said as he slowly rose to his feet. He was slightly unsteady on his recently healed leg and he was still light-headed from the effects of the healing crystal. "I understand how he feels. I want my brother back as much as he wants his son back, trust me."

Simon and Reverend Monroe sat in silence as they watched Purcell limp after Mr. Lee.

"What are we going to do?" Simon asked as he turned to Reverend Monroe.

"We are going to do something that might prove to be harder than fighting the assassin cube," Reverend Monroe began. "We're going to have to find a way home and a way to rescue the others."

"Is such a thing possible?" Simon wondered out loud.

Feeling an ache for his absent surrogate son, Reverend Monroe took the healing crystal and began to treat Simon's wounds. Then he said, "It is going to have to be."

Old Ben Anderson pulled up in front of the Sims' family residence on Monroe Street. He had the cab take its time as it went up the block. He consulted the address on the tattered piece of paper several times to make sure he was at the right place. He paid the driver and got out of the cab carrying one of the duffle bags Wisdom had left with him. He stood on the sidewalk for a minute and straightened his suit. He stared at the row house for a long time, getting his nerve up to knock on the front door. Since he first started selling drugs for Wisdom, he had dreaded the day that he would have to make this visit. Wisdom asked him along time ago to perform this task for him in case something ever happened to him. He had asked Old Ben to take a bag of money to his grandmother's house and tell her that there was another one hidden in the house's attic if something ever happened to him. He knew that Wisdom did not trust anyone other than him to perform this task for him. For Old Ben, it was a tragic honor.

Finally, Old Ben got up the courage to approach the front door. He took his time and walked steadily up the steps. He tapped lightly on the front door. Ms. Loretta opened the door after a few minutes. Old Ben took a step back as he looked at the woman. He could see Wisdom in the features of her face. Her eyes were red and her hair was slightly disheveled. Normally, Ms. Loretta would have been wearing one of her pricey wigs. However, with the day's events her head was bare. She stood in the doorway with a head filled with grey cornrows. Old Ben could tell that she had been crying. He had been crying over the death of Wisdom, too. However, he guessed his tears were not as long as hers. Ms. Loretta was not surprised by the knock on the door. Family and long time friends had been coming through all day since the news of Wisdom's death. However, she was surprised to find a stranger standing in her doorway.

"Yes, may I help you?" she asked cautiously as she sized Old Ben up.

"Good afternoon," Old Ben said as he cleared his throat. "You don't know me, but I was a friend of your grandson's." he explained as he felt the weight of the bag that he was carrying. His words felt heavier on his tongue.

"It sure nuf is the truth that bad news spread faster than good," Ms. Loretta said as she shook her head leaning on the doorframe.

"That is the truth," Old Ben laughed. He found himself having an immediate affection for the woman. Looking at her he could tell she was near his age. "I got something for you," he announced.

"Something for me?" she repeated with surprise.

"Yes'um," Old Ben said. "Your grandson dropped off something for me to give to you if something ever happened to him."

Ms. Loretta nodded simply as she eyed the bag that he was carrying. It was full and almost as big as this old man in her doorway. She stepped aside and invited Old Ben inside the house. Old Ben was impressed by the immaculate decor of the small Monroe Street house. He looked around and could almost imagine Wisdom growing up here. He smiled. The house was warm and inviting like an old friend. He waited in the foyer until she motioned for him to follow her into the living room. Old Ben almost tripped over himself as he moved into the room after her. He sat down on the worn couch, while she sat down in a chair on the other side of the room near the entranceway. Old Ben was glad to see that she was being careful with receiving a stranger into her home. He smiled widely. She was a smart old woman. She was definitely Wisdom's kin.

"Now, what is this that you have for me?" she asked suspiciously.

"My name is Benjamin Anderson but everybody calls me Old Ben. I guess you could say that I worked for your grands," he explained.

Ms. Loretta stiffened immediately at the man's explanation. She knew the kind of work Wisdom did and she was having a hard time believing that a man of Old Ben's age had anything to do with that mess. She could not believe that he was a drug dealer, too. She found herself wondering who she had let into her house.

"I see," was all she managed to say. She looked away at a picture of Jesus on the wall.

"Well," Old Ben cleared his throat." He told me if something happened to him to give this to you. He also wanted me to tell you that there is another one like it buried somewhere up in your attic," he said as he shoved the duffle bag across the floor with the tip of his good shoes. It came to rest at Ms. Loretta's feet. She stared at the bag curiously for a minute, then she turned her attention back to Old Ben.

"I guess I should say 'thank you', I think," she managed.

"I'll be getting out of your way then," Old Ben said as he stood.

Ms. Loretta led him back out to the foyer and opened the front door. He paused for a minute as he passed over the threshold.

"I really loved your grandson," he said before turning to leave. "No matter what he did, he was like a son to me, too."

Ms. Loretta simply nodded and ushered him out of her house. She stared out of the peep hole, watching the old man vanish down Monroe Street. She made sure her doors were locked and returned to the living room. She sat down where she was before and simply looked at the duffle bag for a long time. She lifted it. She could barely manage it. She was immediately surprised by its weight and sat it down on the coffee table. She waited a minute longer then yanked back the zipper.

"Dear Jesus," she said as she saw the volume of money in it. The bag was filled with rolls of tens and twenties wrapped in multi-colored rubber bands. Her hands immediately began to shake and she fell back in the chair where she was sitting. Her eyes began to well up with tears as she looked at the bag and she felt an ache inside. More than the money, she would have preferred the rattle and hum of Wisdom down the hallway of her home. No amount of money could replace that feeling for her. Though she felt the stirring of her twin grandsons upstairs, she felt horribly alone. It was an ache she couldn't shake as she plopped down on the couch in her Monroe Street home. As tears welled up in her eyes, the pictures of generations of relations mocked her from the wall across the room.

# Chapter 2

Tisha woke up to a sweeter smell than she had ever smelled before. She lay still for a long time with her eyes closed, taking in the fresh aroma. For a moment, she thought that she might be dead and had gone on to heaven. However as she shifted her limbs, she realized that she was horribly sore; especially, in her lungs. In spite of the sweet smell that permeated the air, Tisha was having trouble breathing. She guessed that her lungs were burnt from the smoke and fire in the church. She stirred slowly and opened her eyes. To her surprise, she found herself lying on a bed that was draped with the finest covers she had ever seen. Her normal clothing had been removed and she was dressed in lavish yellow robes. Looking down at her self, she felt silly. She thought she looked like a doll from an antique collection.

As she stretched her limbs under the weight of the new gowns, she reached up and touched her neck in a panic. She sighed in relief as her fingers grazed a familiar object. The crystal arrowhead that Simon had given her was still there. Yet, to her surprise, there was something else around her neck. She looked down at it quickly. A green, oblong crystal on a black cord had been placed around her neck. She touched the new relic slowly and felt a faint glimmer of power. This shocked her. Tisha tried to remove the implement from around her neck, but no matter how hard as she pulled, the cord would not break. She sucked her teeth as her hand finally fell away from it. Strange clothing and a crystal yoke of some kind, she shook her head and wrinkled her brow. She didn't like this at all.

None of this made any sense to her. She guessed that she had been sucked through the Gateway that Quan had created back at the church. The little that she knew about crystals and making Gateways, she had been led to believe that you needed a particular locale to form such a wormhole. For Quan to create a Gateway at will like that meant that the crystals he carried were far superior to any Reverend Monroe had described to them.

Nonetheless, with her actions she had expected to wake up in a dungeon or worse, not in the lap of luxury. Tisha searched her memory, but she could not remember anything after vanishing into the Gateway with Quan. Tisha came to her feet and crossed the candlelit chamber. The stone floor was cold to her barefeet. She went to the window and looked out at Acara City for the first time. Her mouth dropped. It was like no city she had ever seen or imagined before. It reminded her of something out of the Middle Ages or a bad movie. She stared at the torchlit edifices for a long time. A knot curled up in her stomach. She supposed that she was lucky to be alive. Yet, she felt lost inside. She was separated from her son, her family, and Simon. She sighed out loud and bit down hard on her lip. She did not know what she was going to do.

Tisha returned to the bed and curled up in a human knot. She wrapped herself around a pillow and began to sob lightly trying not to draw attention to herself. After some time, she must have drifted off back to sleep, because when she opened her eyes she realized that she was not alone. She looked up from her bed and was surprised to find a woman standing in the curtain-draped doorway of her small room. The newcomer was taller than any woman she had ever seen before. She had an alabaster complexion and long red hair that was knotted behind her back. She was dressed in lightweight armament and had a sword at each side. The woman also had a dark tattoo across her face that matched the one that Quan wore. The two women stared at each other for a long time without speaking.

"What is it that they call you?" the woman asked.

Tisha's mouth dropped. She was surprised that she understood the woman's words. As the woman talked, she felt the new crystal tingle.

She guessed it had something to do with her new ability to understand Acarian.

"Tisha," she introduced herself. "And what is it that they call you?" Tisha mimed back with more sass than she really felt at the moment.

"I am called Ela," she introduced herself, looking down on Tisha. "I had to lay eyes upon you," the warrior woman said finally. "I needed to see the woman that was responsible for besting my mate, Quan, and capturing my son's heart."

Tisha was surprised by the woman's words. She could not believe that she understood her and what she was saying. She opened her mouth to speak, but her mouth fell silent.

"I can tell that my words have left you in dismay," the newcomer explained as she crossed the room. "It is the second crystal that you wear which allows you to understand my words. One of the seers or priests of the Dark God would have placed our language in your mind, but coming through the Gateway left you dull. In that condition, it is not good to play in your mind. From my mate, I understand that you do not have such crystals where you hail from."

Tisha reached up and touched the second crystal that she found herself wearing and nodded her head yes. Of course, she had an application on her tablet that she used to help her with her Spanish homework, but it was nowhere as powerful or as efficient as this.

"So, you are Simon's mother?" said Tisha, her mouth dropping open.

"I am," she agreed as she bowed her head. "I am second to my mate, Quan, in leading the Moritan, the Royal Guard of the High Queen Mora," said by way of further introduction.

"So I am a prisoner here. . .," Tisha surmised.

Ela laughed as she looked around the room. "Our worlds are not that different. Truly, if it were up to me, you would be buried under the weight of the Grand Citadel but our High Queen has seen fit for a different fate for you…..," she explained as her voice trailed off.

"What do you mean?" Tisha quizzed.

"Simply put," Ela began as she came over to the bed, "You carry in your womb the rightful heir to the Moritans."

"Excuse me?" Tisha's voice cracked as her hand fell to her stomach. She was shocked by Ela's words.

"The High Queen felt the presence of your offspring the moment that you arrived in the temple of the Dark God. For that reason, she had you brought here to these rooms in her Grand Citadel instead of the dungeon and placed you in my care," Ela explained.

"I am going to have *another* baby," Tisha found herself stumbling over her words. It was far too much to be believed.

"No my dear, you are not going to have *any* baby," Ela explained. "You are going to have the heir to the holy house of the Royal Guard. I cannot say that I think much of the vessel that my lost son has chosen for his seed," she said as she looked Tisha up and down. "But if my husband is to be believed there is more to you than meets the eye," Ela snickered with a wink.

"I've been told that before," Tisha said trying to sound brave in the shadow of Ela's stature.

Ela did not say anything at first. She simply kept an eye on Tisha. She was measuring her worth before she spoke.

"I do not expect you and I to become friends. I think that is too much to ask for. However, we have much work to do in the coming Suns," Ela announced.

"And that work is?" Tisha sucked her teeth trying to look strong.

"Worthy, child, worthy." Ela said as she rose to the fullness of her height. Looking at her, Tisha swallowed hard; the woman must have stood over seven feet tall. "It is the command of the High Queen that you be made worthy to be the mate of my lost son. So when he returns with her heir, you can take your full place at his side and match the arrow you wear. I must teach you the ways of the Moritan," Ela explained.

"And what makes you think that Royal and Simon will ever return here to take a place with your High Queen?," Tisha said trying to sound brave in Ela's immense shadow.

Ela laughed at Tisha's bravado. "You are truly an off-worlder. You do not know the will and power of our beloved High Queen. However, over time I hope you always stay in her favor," Ela warned. Her words were ominous.

Tisha did not know what to say to this last statement. She did not remember encountering the High Queen since coming to Acara. Listening to Ela's words, she found herself dreading the notion of laying eyes on the monarch. Tisha swallowed hard.

"Rest for now off-worlder," Ela invited. "If you need anything the maidens outside this chamber will see to your needs. At next Sun, you and I will come together and I will begin to discuss with you the ways of the Moritan."

"I guess I don't have much of a choice, do I?" Tisha said sarcastically and sucked her teeth.

"No you do not," Ela agreed as she turned to leave. Quietly, she was trying to mimic the sound Tisha made each time she sucked her teeth. It was bizarre to her, but endearing.

Tisha watched Ela leave. Once again she sat alone among her covers. She drew the blankets up around her and hugged her legs. She was unsure what to feel. Since she had found out the truth about Simon and the other Acarians, things had been happening so fast she could barely keep up. She was in a state of shock. Now she not only found herself on the planet that her beloved Simon came from without him, she was pregnant with his child as well! Tisha rubbed at her stomach unconsciously for a moment. She guessed that she was not alone after all.

Tisha leaned back among the covers and closed her eyes. She let herself enjoy the aroma of the scents she first smelled when she woke up and the lavish texture of her robes. She had no clue what tomorrow would bring and the idea of spending any time with Ela at all scared the living daylights out of her. Tisha had a hard time believing that that cold, impenetrable figure was Simon's mother. Not to mention the fact that she was a white woman of all things. She would have never guessed Simon was biracial or if that even mattered here on Acara. However, she had no reason not to believe her. The reality that she was on another planet began to solidly sink in for Tisha for first time. She was a simple Black girl from inner-city Baltimore. How had she found herself here of all places? She guessed that she would do whatever she had to in order to keep herself safe; especially now that she knew she was pregnant. She would be smart. Fortunately, before Simon, she had been Wisdom's girl and he had taught her a few things about the art of the hustle. Tisha knew she was going to have to have game if she ever expected to see those she loved again. In the meantime, she would do whatever Ela, the towering white woman, said or asked of her until either Simon came for her or she saw an opening for escape.

She reached up and wrapped her hand around the arrowhead around her neck. She held onto the trinket and she took solace in the fact that she could feel Simon even though they were worlds apart. And she knew that if she could feel Simon, he could feel her. She sighed in relief, believing that no matter the distance or obstacle, Simon would find her. It was the last thought she had before she drifted off to sleep with aching lungs full of Acarian air.

Quan stood alone in the chambers of the High Court before the green crystal throne of the High Queen Mora. She had summoned him. Quan looked around at the empty room and sighed. The usual members of the Royal Guard that guarded the High Queen had been dismissed for this briefing. Quan knew instinctively that whatever the High Queen Mora had to say to him, it was for his ears only. Since his return, he had barely seen a glimpse of her. Once he appeared in the Grand Temple of the Dark God without Simon and Royal at his side, she had left him alone to contemplate his failure of her.

He looked down at himself, his dagger like arm and his wolf arm. He had been horribly changed to achieve this mission. He still felt the echo of the other souls that were now a part of him. He would never have expected that he would have failed. Normally after a mission, he would have immediately returned to the High Queen's side. However, since his time back she had not requested him. This was unheard of. He was her Royal Guard. He was bonded to her. He knew that her lack of summoning him was a sign of her disappointment in him. He lowered his head in shame and regret.

Quan waited alone for what seemed like forever before the High Queen appeared. She entered from the right side of the chamber and swept into the room in long, lavish, flowing, purple robes with a collar made of similarly colored flowers. Her head was covered by a hood and she did not immediately give Quan her attention. She ascended to the height of her throne and sat down. She sat there for a long time looking out at the room. Her gaze finally fell upon Quan and she waved him forward. He moved immediately to the edge of the throne and prostrated before his monarch and charge.

"Quan, you failed me," she said simply as she looked down at him. Her voice was soft but it somehow reverberaterd through the entire hall. The weight of the statement washed over him and he felt his stomach sink. Quan opened his mouth to speak but he could not find his voice.

"In all the years that you have been by my side, you have never failed me. There is no one I trust more than you," she continued. In the darkened room, it almost looked like she was tearing but it may have been the light of the candles.

"I am aware." Quan agreed. "I am ready to receive whatever punishment you see fit," he offered and meant it.

The High Queen laughed, "To punish you would be like me punishing myself. The weight of my disappointment in you serves as punishment enough I think. It will plague you long after any punishment I could come up with had subsided," she insisted.

"That is true," Quan said as he lowered his head.

"Then with that you will return to myside immediately as my Royal Guard. Your second son, Elric, served me well in your absence, you should be proud of him. But I long for your familiar presence at my side," she commanded.

"As you wish," Quan said happily as he slowly ascended the stairs toward the throne and disappeared into the shadows behind the seat of power of Acara. He felt relief immediately as he took up this familiar position behind the throne.

"In your absence, old friend," the High Queen began in whispers, "rumors have reached this High Court of those who would stand against me."

"You are the rightful monarch to sit on the throne. They would not dare. . ." Quan's voice trailed off.

"Yet they do dare," she interrupted. "And without my rightful heir to stand next to me, they think I am weak." She chuckled as a bit of dark fire flared from her fingers.

"Weakness is not a character trait that you suffer well," Quan observed.

"True," she agreed. "Now come close to my ear and whisper to me about your adventure to this Earth as my assassin cube. Leave out no details. Nothing may be too small for me to know in the days to come if I am going to recapture my son," she instructed.

Quan leaned in and began to tell her about his journey to Earth, his confrontation with Royal and his supporters. He left nothing out. He told her about the abandoned building where he appeared and all the elements of his attacks. He was sure to give her the details of her son's power and the power of his protectors as well. He was sure to describe to her the exploding weapons that Royal's allies used in their defense of him. The High Queen Mora took in the aspects of the tale with a blank expression. She took an odd pride in hearing about her son and how he stood up to Quan. He was turning into a true heir for her throne. Now all she needed was to find him, get him away from his kidnappers, and turn his energies to the direction of the worship of the Dark God. Once he was lost among the stars, she too believed like Quan that he was here on Acara. She smiled to herself. While they were somehow able to keep him hidden from her when he was not on Acara, it was just a matter of time before she found him now. In her long battle against those who worship the Avatar, it was very often the goodness of their character that made them easyfodder for her plans. Though Quan had failed, he had brought her back invaluable information. With an heir at her side raised on such an odd planet as Earth, there was no reason why it, too, could come under her reign. If not that, then she would make sure it became a permanent part of the void, nameless space. The High Queen Mora smiled to herself in quiet anticipation.

Underneath the Grand Citadel of the High Queen Mora was a maze of tunnels, chambers, and catacombs. This area of the Grand Citadel was referred to as The Bottoms. Unlike the majority of the citadel, these caverns were barely used by the majority of the inhabitants of the royal dwelling. It was here that the High Queen Mora's uncles, the elder High Princes, first introduced her to the worship of the Dark God. Even after all these years, they still met and conspired in the shadows of these ruins. Burton, the High King Roman's middle brother, made his way down one of the dimly lit corridors. Unlike his elder brother, Roman, Burton was not an attractive man. He looked worn for his cycles of time. He was a deep chocolate brown with a fading hairline. In terms of his body, he was stout with short limbs. His forearms were large and protruding; the thick hide-like skin bore the markings of too many years of battle. However his bed was never empty because of his royal heritage and his wealth, not because of his demeanor. Secretly, Burton kept his own private brothel hidden within Acara. It was there he often retreated to address his frustrations with his life. Unfortunately, this meant the person who ran his private playpen had to keep refreshing his supply of playmates, both male and female, of all ages.

He was flanked by his Royal Guard, Ilson, as he moved beneath The Bottoms. They turned a corner and came upon a huge ornate metal door. Outside of the door stood Bilk, the Royal Guard of Holi. Holi was the youngest brother of the late King Roman and uncle to the High Queen Mora. Upon seeing Burton and Ilson, Bilk tapped lightly on the door and stepped aside. Burton barely noticed Bilk as he moved past him. He opened the door and stepped inside the darkened sanctuary of his younger brother.

The room was like a cave. It stretched back far into the shadows. Holi stood behind several tables filled with bottles and bubbling vats filled with different colored liquids and powders. Unlike his brother, Burton, Holi was considered "pretty" by most. He was tall and slim with long, reddish-brown hair that he kept in a braid down his back. Holi tanned easily under the weight of Acara's twin suns. However, since he usually stayed tucked away in the recesses of his lab, his skin remained a mellow yellow. Though Holi looked more like his elder brother, the late King Roman, he too had grown up in the shadow of the heir to the throne. Thus early on, he grew fiercely close to Burton and was known to follow him into any dubious folly. Though Holi found attraction in women, he rarely indulged in experiments of the flesh. He found people to be too complicated. He preferred the perfectibility and mysteryof his experiments.

Watching his brother tinker, Burton frowned. Burton never took an interest in his brother's interests in the natural sciences. Ever since Holi was a child, he was taken by the mixing of chemicals. Before Mora was born, Holi was third in line for the High Throne. Thus he was left alone and he entertained himself with his diverse interests. Burton was not so lucky. He was trained to be King if something happened to his elder brother. He had high hopes that it would happen one day, since

Roman was a risk-taker with dangerous habits and wild fancies. Burton hoped that his brother would find his end on the edge of a scavenger's sword or that he would not return from one of his long trips. Yet all that changed when their father, Menton, passed of old age and Roman ascended to the next High King. Burton watched as his brother's habits changed and he became married to the life of the High Court.

And for years, Burton bowed his head to the throne and served his brother who was the rightful High King of Acara. Burton was more than a fixture at the High Court. He often did the jobs that the "beloved" High King Roman did not want to do or knew about. As Roman aged and did not marry, he was sure that his older brother would leave the High Throne to him. Then in his later life, High King Roman was taken with a sand princess from the Western Region. Soon, a royal wedding was held and the princess Jezell joined him on the High Throne.

Burton's dream to be High King was not immediately lost after his brother's marriage. For as much as the High King Roman loved the High Queen Jezell, it seemed her womb would not hold a child. It was not until her last pregnancy that with her lasttbreath she gave her dear Roman a child and blood heir. It took her life to deliver the baby, but the High Princess Mora was born. For as much as the High King Roman loved his daughter and heir, he missed his beloved wife more. Just as before his rise to power, Roman went back to his wandering ways, leaving the High Court, as well as the care of his infant daughter, to Burton.

It wasn't until Mora had seen ten cycles that he returned to embrace his responsibility as High King and father. However, by this time, Mora was as attached to her uncle as she was to her father. With Roman's return and the birth of Mora, Burton knew he would never sit on the High Throne if he did not act. Knowing the High King Roman's devotion to the Avatar, the living spirit of their world, Burton used his influence over Mora to direct her toward worship of the Dark God. Burton knew that if he could convert her, she would dispatch her father. He also knew that if he pushed her as a High Priestess of the Dark God she would be barren. Tending the Darkness at its highest level consumes a woman's womb and a man's seed.

His plan had worked out better than he had ever dreamed. Mora had taken to the teachings of the Dark God, gotten rid of her father by slow poison, and become the Dark God's High Priestess. The only thing that happened that he had not foreseen was the birth of her son before she became High Priestess. Mora had him before she assumed the mantle and power of High Priestess of the Dark God. The birth of the child was a surprise to Burton. Upon the birth of the child, he thought his plan to finally assume the High Throne was thrown into disarray. Burton blessed the day that Mora's son was kidnapped away not just from the High Court, but from all of Acara as well. Burton believed that the High Throne was to be his at last. Now, Quan was back with news of the heir after all of these cycles. Burton shook his head as he looked at his younger brother. He wished sometimes that he could be like Holi and lose himself in random interests. However, he had devoted his life to the High Court and he swore to himself that before he died he would be High King of all of Acara.

"You look troubled, dear brother," Holi said as he finally looked up from his powders and potions.

"Quan has returned," Burton said. "He is meeting with Mora right now with news of her bastard son."

"You worry too much," Holi said simply. "She greatly weakened herself with the making of that insane assassin cube. You should know this. I am sure that Quan has returned with more rumors than substance. The heir is as lost to her as ever. Continue on your road and I am sure it will lead you to the High Throne."

"How can you be so sure? You have not consulted an oracle or cast a crystal," Burton said shortly as he began to pace the room.

"Time is a science unto itself, dear brother, and the time we have put into this plan has not gone unnoticed by the Universe, no matter which God you worship," he said simply.

"I wish I could be as sure as you are," Burton said.

"People think me strange as I labor over my powders and potions, but I find certainty in them. They give me comfort. I suggest you find something of a similar ilk to find comfort in until our time comes," Holi said with finality as he turned his back to his brother.

Burton knew that was all he could expect from Holi. At the very least, he knew that he was still on his side. That would have to be enough for now. Burton turned and left the room. He moved down the corridor away from Holi's chamber with a heavy heart and a weighted head. He stopped in midstep and turned around to face his Royal Guard, Ilson. As always, Ilson's towering presence stood ready to be commanded.

"I sense grave days ahead for us, old friend," Burton said, "and I may need to call upon you to do me a yet another dark favor."

"Anything for you my High Prince," Ilson assured.

"If Quan has indeed found the High Queen's heir, I may need for you to get rid of him." He spoke flatly sin whispers, knowing he was suggesting treason at the highest level.

Ilson touched his sword at his side and nodded his head. "As I have done before, my blade is sharp and ready to be commanded by you. Even if that means shedding royal blood."

Burton shook his head and continued to make his way down the tunnel. Silently, once again, he made a promise to himself. He would be High King no matter what it took and no matter whose blood had to be spilled. He took a deep breath. He had waited this long. He could wait a little bit longer.

"Send word into the city," Burton commanded Ilson, "tonight I got to my special place. I am in need of diversion," he admitted with a wrinkled brow.

"Is there anything they should prepare for?" Ilson asked carefully.

Rubbing his hands together and thinking of his young nephew, Burton said, "Young, inexperienced, disposable, and fragile," he insisted.

Ilson touched the scar that ran the length of his face and simply nodded before vanishing into the shadows to do his master's bidding, leaving Burton alone to contemplate his next steps among the shadows where it had all begun.

# Chapter 3

Royal stood at the edge of one the water veins. He let the water roll over his bare feet. The cool water tickled his small, light brown toes. He bent down, daring to take a drink. To his surprise, the water was almost sweet to the taste. It quenched his thirst instantly. After several mouths full, he sat down on the shore. It was the first time since his arrival on Acara that he had a few minutes alone to sort out his thoughts about all that had happened to him. He still could not believe that he was supposed to be the savior of a world he did not know. In fact, until a few days ago, the only world he ever knew that existed was Earth. Now, he had been transported to this new world. As Royal looked around at the landscape, it reminded him of a brochure of the tropics. It definitely didn't feel like another planet.

He had no idea what was expected of him now that he was on Acara. All he knew was that he was supposed to somehow dethrone a mother he never knew. The thought raced through his brain like wild fire. He had spent most of his life wishing for a mother. Now that he had found her, she was supposed to be an evil monarch that worshiped the Earthly equivalent of the Devil. He shook his head as the water ran over his tender toes. He grabbed his head. It was too hard to believe.

On top of that, he had these new powers. He could do things that he never imagined. He could set fires. He could fly. He could control others. The thoughts sent a shiver up his tender spine as he looked at his little hands. He was raised as a Christian to believe in miracles, but he never believed that he could cause them or make them happen.

However, over the last few days he had done exactly that. He looked down at his small, tender brown hands and sighed. He wondered what else he could do and if it would be enough to stand up against an evil mother he never knew.

"I know you must have a million questions," avoice said from behind him.

Royal turned. Lethia was standing a few feet away from him. She was still dressed in the armament that she wore to face the assassin cube but her stomach was bandaged with tattered rags and she leaned heavily on a branch to stand. Her wounds at the hands of the assassin cube were severe; Royal knew she was lucky to be alive. Looking at Lethia, it was hard for Royal to believe that this woman had been his Aunt Grace in disguise. For the majority of his life, Lethia had worn a warping crystal to hide her true self from everyone. Royal had loved and confided in his Aunt Grace. It was still hard for him to believe that she was gone and it had all been a lie. Lethia and his surrogate father, Reverend Monroe or Arkon, had kept so much from him that he still found it all hard to believe. Royal came to his feet instantly and walked over to her to lend aid. She raised her free hand to stop him.

"I am home now," she said. "Healing these wounds will take no time. As I told you before, I am trained in land magic. Once we have concealed you, I will bury myself in the ground and the Avatar will see to my healing."

"Where are we?" Royal asked.

"We are on the Lost Islands the very end of Acara. The Lost Islands are a body of islands that are separated by veins of water. They are shrouded by a mist of mystical fog called. The Haze distorts their location. It's the perfect place for us to hide. We will not be easily found here. The Avatar was indeed wise in bringing us here," she explained as she tried to smile through the obvious pain.

"Won't the High Queen, I mean my mother, be able to find me here?" Royal asked quickly.

Lethia smiled, "Acara is made up of many beings. Most of them are still sacred to the Avatar. I have summoned some of them to help us."

"I don't understand," Royal said frankly.

"Look," Lethia pointed her walking stick into the water. For a second, the waves looked the same to Royal then all of sudden he could make out shapes in the waves. They reminded him of mermaids but they weren't solid, they were made out of pure water.

"These are the Sylphs. They are the spirits that live in these veins. They are the sprits that give sea witches and water bearers power. Their magic dates back to the beginning of our world. They, too, are sacred to the Avatar. They are on our side. All you have to do is bath among them and they will make sure that you stay invisible to the Dark Queen's prying eyes," Lethia assured.

Royal looked at the fish-shaped creatures with astonishment. He could feel them calling out to him. They gave off a reverence that reminded him of being baptized back at Gateway Baptist. Trusting Lethia and what he felt, he stripped down to his under shorts and waded through the water. He opened his arms and invited the beings close to him. They jumped and pranced all over his body. As they touched him, they eased the pressure and the sourness of his wounds. They also secreted a fine film that covered Royal, making him invisible to most magic.

As Royal swam with the Sylphs, he felt like a little boy again. All the troubles of the last few days seemed to vanish. Royal had never drunk wine or touched any drugs before but being with the Sylphs made him wonder if this was what it was like to be drunk. He licked his lips happily. If Royal could have, he would have stayed in the water with the Sylphs forever. After some time, the Sylphs began to recede, leaving him alone in the waves with a slight chill. Royal was about to rejoin Lethia on the shore when he felt a tug at his leg. He turned to find a huge wave coming toward him. For a moment, Royal was afraid. Then the wave transformed into a huge aquatic figure. The figure was riding a fish-like creature and wore a crown.

Looking at the majesty of the creature, Royal was moved to bow. The King of the Sylphs smiled and bowed to him as well.

"I am King Carolyn. I bring you greetings from the waterways of Acara," he heard a voice say in his head. "As long as you stay pure and true to the Avatar there is no waterway that will stand against you or that you will not be able to cross," he swore. "And our other minions of the deep will be there to protect you, too."

*"Other minions of the deep…"*. The phrase rolled around ominously in Royal's mind but he did not dare say a word about it.

"I thank you," Royal said inside his mind as he tried to take in the majesty of the figure.

"No, it is we who thank you, young High Prince," King Carolyn assured as he vanished among the waves.

Royal stood still for a moment unsure of what to do next. Then he made his way back to the water's edge where Lethia was waiting. He was about to open his mouth to speak about what just happened when she raised a hand forbidding his speech.

"Royal," she began as she rested heavy on her staff, "you will soon have to learn that there are things that you know that you must keep to yourself, even from us. There is only one person that you can find confidence in all the time and that is your Royal Guard," Lethia explained.

"But Simon is not here," he found himself stuttering as he put on his clothes.

Lethia smiled as she waited for Royal to dress again. "The Avatar is indeed wise and all knowing. I think you will not be without the confidence and support of a Royal Guard until Simon is at your side again."

Royal did not say a word. He simply put his clothes back on and followed Lethia back toward their makeshift campsite. Bathing with the

Sylphs had left him refreshed and he felt renewed; especially after the battle with Quan. However, he would have felt better still if Simon was at his side. Simon had been with him all of his life and he trusted him more than he trusted anyone else. Though the waters had refreshed him, he was still having a hard time reconciling all of this with his ministry training. He had been trained to believe in a Savior, not in a crowned water spirit; he only hoped he could find a way to reconcile the two in the days ahead.

At the campsite, Hue was finding a way to make himself useful. He organized their packs and gathered wood for the fire. With Lethia and Royal gone, Wisdom and Maximus had both drifted off into an odd silence at either end of the camp. Wisdom was whistling. He was taking his time and cleaning his guns of sand, while Maximus took a nap under a nearby tree with his head resting on his paws. Staring at the bulk of the two men, Hue felt oddly useless around them. He did not feel like he had any particular purpose that he could point out. Thus, he busied himself with making their new home tidy. He kicked off his sneakers in the rich white sand, rolled up his pants legs and set up camp for everyone. On top of that, he found himself missing his father and his sister, Sapphire. In agreeing to help Royal and the others, he never imagined that he would be separated from his family. Hue swallowed hard. He did not know if his family even believed if he was still alive. His father and sister had already lost their mother to cancer, he could not imagine what they must be going through if they thought he was dead, too. Hue tried to put the thoughts out his mind and make himself busy instead.

Upon his third trip back into the wilderness around the beach, his foot got tangled in an odd thick branch. At first Hue, thought nothing of it. He kicked at the branch and continued to gather wood. However, the branch reached out, inched up his leg, and grabbed him. It curled up his leg and tightened around his calf. Hue dropped the wood he was carrying and tried to remove the branch-but it would not budge. It had him entangled. He was stunned. Then all of a sudden, the branch began to pull him further into the odd tangle of trees. Hue was dragged across the woods by his leg. He began to scream. The branch pulled him toward a large open-mouthed flower. Hue looked on in horror as the branch tried to stuff him down the center of the carnivorous bud. Hue grabbed onto a tree and held on for dear life.

"Help!" Hue screamed as he felt his grip begin to loosen around the tree limb.

Hue's grip was just about to wane when Maximus appeared through the trees. With one giant swipe of his paw, he tore the branch from Hue's leg. Then Wisdom appeared through the trees on the other side of Maximus. Wisdom leveled a double-barreled shot gun at the flower and began to unload it into the deadly foliage. The plant screeched as it shot sap in all directions.

"What kind of fuckin' place is this?" Wisdom murmured as he reloaded his gun and lit a cigarette. He went over to the plant and kicked at it with his brand new sneaker. The sap from the destroyed predator ruined the sole of his shoe.

"Aw come on," Wisdom sucked his teeth as he tried desperately to clean his sneaker, but to no avail. He had spent a small fortune for them at the Mall before all of this began. He hadn't even had the chance to sport them on the Avenue back in Baltimore yet. He looked around angrily. He couldn't find anyone to be pissed off with but himself.

"Are you alright?" Maximus asked Hue as he licked at the young man's scrapes.

Hue was dirty. He was cut. He was bruised, but he was no worse for the wear. Looking around, Hue found himself wondering again what he had gotten himself into. He was used to the outdoors from cruising the parks of Baltimore for intimacy, but nothing he had experienced prepared him for this. He knew how he secretly felt about Royal, yet that was not enough for him to risk his life over and over again. Was it?

"I think we all need to stay close to the camp until we find out more about where we at," Wisdom offered as he kicked at the exploded flower with his ruined sneaker. Wisdom put his gun over his shoulder, took out another cigarette from the pack and began to smoke. As Wisdom smoked, he secretly held on to his gun's hilt. Like Hue, he was having a hard time believing that he was on another world. He had agreed to help Royal and the others more as a favor to Tisha, the mother of his son, than anything else. Now, he found himself on another world fighting creatures that were something out of a bad dream. In addition, he had no idea if his brother, Purcell, or Tisha were still alive. Silently, he prayed that they both had survived the fire in the church. On top of that, since they had arrived on Acara no one had mentioned anything to him about the possibility of them returning to Earth. Granted, as a drug dealer, he did not have much to return home to, but silently he found himself wondering if he would ever lay eyes on his son or Grandmother again. Wisdom took a deep drag of his cigarette and watched the smoke rise. Wisdom promised himself that if he ever got the chance to see his family again he would not take them for granted ever again.

Listening to Wisdom, Hue nodded his head as he sat up and wiped at his torn clothing.

"And you, little friend," Maximus began in his canine voice, "you should stay especially close to me. I will make sure nothing will make a meal out of you," he promised as he cleaned splinters from his paws.

Prior to them coming to Acara, Hue knew Maximus as Royal's loyal pet. As it turned out, he was more than that. As far as Hue could tell, Maximus was a cross between a dog and a werewolf. Now that the secret was revealed, instead of remaining in his all-canine form, Maximus stood upright and talked. He was also much more vicious than Hue would have imagined. During the fight with Quan and the assassin cube, Maximus had held his own. Now that they were on Acara, Hue had no idea what kind of dangers they would face. He was definitely going to stay close to the big canine for his own protection. At least he found some security in that.

"Thank you," Hue said." I think."

The group made their way back through the underbrush to the shore. By the time they arrived, Lethia and Royal were sitting around the fire Hue had built. Hue was happy to see his friend. Royal looked oddly renewed. There was a shine to him that had not been there before. He looked good to Hue, like new money. Looking at Royal, Hue began to blush. He immediately looked away as not to reveal his attraction. Strangely, as renewed as Royal looked, Lethia looked weak. She could barely sit up. Without Arkon's crystals to heal her, she was relying on her own strength to keep herself going. Hue ran over to her immediately and checked her bandages. At first she resisted his care, but then she allowed the young man to tend her wounds.

"What happened to you?" Lethia asked as she looked down at Hue's cut up face, dirty clothes, and chafed hands.

"Let's just say I was almost dinner for another one of your amazing flowers," Hue said sarcastically, remembering the blossom that was a part of the assassin cube.

"I should have warned you," Lethia said gravely. "Beautiful as the Lost Islands are they contain many dangers. We must be at one with nature and the Avatar to truly avoid these dangers, "she explained.

"Now you tell me!" Hue said, sucking his teeth. "We're going to have to do something about this," Hue said as he turned his attention back to Lethia's bandages. He looked at her with concern. Hue was no nurse, but he was used to changing dressing from his mother's bout with cancer. He could tell that Lethia's wounds were getting infected. "I don't suppose there is an emergency room around here."

"Don't be silly," Lethia snapped.

"What can we do?" Royal said hurriedly as he came to her side. Since Lethia revealed her true self to him, she had seemed unstoppable. She was so very unlike Royal's Aunt Grace, the woman she had pretended to be for most of Royal's life. Without her warping crystal she may have looked different but Royal was beginning to see she was still very much the same person. Lethia was still the woman that had raised him alongside Reverend Monroe.

"I know," Lethia agreed with Hue. "I am going to have to go into the ground and let the Avatar and the Logos, the land spirits, tend to my wounds," she explained." It is the way of the CODA."

"Then let's be about it," Wisdom said as he sat down by the fire. He picked up a handful of sand and let it fall between his fingers.

"It is not that simple my friend. I am going to have to go inland from here to find the perfect spot to commune with the Logos. And I will need at least three suns to regain my full strength," she explained.

"I don't think we have much of a choice," Royal chimed in. "If we are going to survive any of this we are going to need you."

"I'll go with you," Wisdom volunteered. "Maximus can guard Royal and Hue while we are out and about. You might need my quick draw while you convalesce."

Lethia thought about Wisdom's offer for a moment; part of her wanted to protest. Looking around at those assembled she knew it made sense. Now that Royal had the protection of the water of the veins and Maximus, he would be safe. She also knew about the pact that Wisdom had made with Simon to be Royal's Royal Guard in his absence. This would give her a chance to measure the man's worth and teach him a few things he would need to know.

"Okay then, we leave at dawn," she said as she rose and limped back to the cove, leaving the three males alone around the fire. For a moment, no one talked and simply chewed on the rations that they had packed. Wisdom came to his feet first and went over to one of his armament bags. He took out a box of shells and a small handgun and waved at Hue to come over

"This is how you load it," he said demonstrating. "And you take the safety off here, you hold it with both hands, then you aim and then you shoot. It's that simple; the worst thing you can do is hesitate. You will miss your target and fuck ya'self up. You got me?" he said as he handed Hue the gun.

Carefully, Hue went through the smechanics of loading and unloading the small .22 handgun. He eased his finger over the trigger and let the bullet slide into the chamber.

"That's it and then you shoot," Wisdom explained. "And around here, I say we shoot first and ask questions later. Tomorrow, before I leave, I'll show you how to shoot it. Tonight just make it yours. Get used to the weight. You feel me?" he concluded as he drifted off to his bedding in the cove leaving Hue, Maximus, and Royal around the fire.

Hue was slightly shocked to receive the gun. He had never shot a gun in his life. He knew that if they were going to survive this trip, they were going to learn to do a lot of things they had never done before.

"Are you alright?" Royal asked him

"I'm going to have to be," he said glibly as he curled up next to the fire and drifted off to sleep.

Royal looked at Hue with concern. Unlike, the others he did not have the battle experience they had or any special powers. He was a novice in the war that was coming. Royal was afraid for him. He hated to think that being his friend meant being in such danger. As if reading his mind, Maximus came up behind him and placed a heavy paw on his shoulder.

"Do not worry, my High Prince," he assured him. "I will watch the youngling and I defend him with my life," he swore, "as I watch over you as well."

"I hope that is enough, Maximus," sighed Royal, "I hope that is enough."

"Enough?" Maximus growled as he transformed before Royal's eyes. He shape-shifted to full beast. He danced around the fire comically and spun around. "I am Maximus the great, the slayer of the assassin cube. None may stand against me!" he growled.

Royal found himself laughing in spite of himself. He rubbed the fur behind Maximus' ear as he always had done at home in the Rectory and the beast purred in spite of himself.

"Now you get some rest," Maximus insisted. "I will take the first watch," he volunteered as he galloped into the underbrush leaving Royal alone with the fire.

Royal turned from his canine protector and lay down next to the fire. Sleep did not come easy to him. He had a lot on his mind. The band of heroes that were supposed to defeat the High Queen Mora was now split between two worlds. On top of that, his so-called Royal Guard was not at his side to advise and protect him. Even though he still held anger at his surrogate father, the Right Reverend Monroe (also known as Arkon), he had come to rely on him and his crystals and he was not there, either. In addition, Lethia was gone to recover from mortal wounds that were incapacitating her. Now all he could rely on was a drug dealer and his previous pet for his defense. A chill went up his spine. And yes, the Sylphs had promised to hide him from the High Queen, but he really did not know what that meant.

Royal closed his eyes and took a deep breath. He wrapped his hand around the cross-hanging from his neck. He wanted to pray, but he found himself stuck. He did not know to whom to pray. For the first time in his life his faith was challenged. He always took solace in praying to Jesus but now there was the Avatar to consider. Without the help of the Avatar, they would not have survived or escaped to Acara. Surely, it was worthy of his prayers too. Carefully, Royal began to pray to both his Savior and the Avatar. Royal removed his bible from one of his packs, placed it under his head, and laid down. After some time, he drifted off to a restful sleep.

While in the past Royal had dreamed of Acara now all he did was rest. At some point during the night, Royal felt the familiar presence of the Avatar invade his sleep. Through his haze of sleep it simply said: *"Help is on the way"*.

# Help

# Chapter 4

Ulfast was a small fishing village on the Northern Coast of Acara's largest land mass, Sandor. It was made up of small wooden and mud brick houses. Most of the people in the village made their living off the sea by fishing. Those that dared try their hands at farming usually put in more than they gained from the dry, arid land. Whether by crops or by fish, the majority of the bounty of Ulfast went to Lord Grimhold. Like all Flasion nobility, Grimhold had yellow skin, the color of foodstuff on the stalk. He was a rotund baron who poked his nose into all aspects of Ulfast life. He was born of lesser noble blood so he was often excluded from the High Court of Acara. This fact never left his mind. In his meager halls, he often talked about the few times he had been to Acara City and how he had refused to bond with the shadow-like warriors known as the Royal Guard. In his "great" hall, he would boast over the huge meals that were prepared for him that he was strong enough by himself, that he did not need a Moritan on his heels.

Thus, Grimhold was surprised when he saw a regiment of the finest Flasion horsemen make their way through his gates led by a black-robed priest of the Dark God. He immediately sent for his finest robe and his simple crescent crown. He alerted the kitchen to visit the villagers and take what they needed for the preparation of a feast in honor of their guests. Ulfast rarely saw soldiers from the High Queen, but a priest of the Dark God was unheard of in these parts. Surely if they were coming to Ulfast a huge feast was in order. Grimhold met the captain of the regiment and priest in what was taken for a great hall. The twenty riders did not dismount their brutish hairy mounts before entering the large room that made up the center of the great hall. The dirty hooves of the mounts grating the stone floor of the great hall was a slight toGrimhold. The chief among the armored riders was a tall Flasion man whose skin was the color of yellow flowers in bloom. He raise his hand to Grimhold as a sign of modest respect but did not bow his head. Grimhold took in the gesture and rolled around in his odd seat of power.

"Well met Grimhold of Ulfast. I bring you greetings from your cousin Queen Enora of Blinow and I speak with her authority," he said carefully as he held out a rolled up scroll.

Grimhold listened carefully to the captain's words. It was rare that he heard from his distant cousin, the Queen of Sandor's greatest city-state, on any matter. He knew if the guard and a priest of the Dark God were here it had to be of the greatest importance. Grimhold rubbed at his hands thoughtfully. Helping these guards would be a way to gain favor with his distant cousin and, perhaps, an ambassadorship to the High Court itself. With a wave of his hand, he had one of his manservants accept the scroll from the chief rider.

"I am sure I can carry out any deed my good cousin has set before me. But before we get to all that, let us water your mounts and prepare banquet in your honor," Grimhold offered.

The captain of the regiment thought for a moment and glanced back at his party. They had been chasing signs of Etera, the escaped slave, for the better part of six suns. The taste of hot food on their tongues would be a welcomed change from the dried rations they had been eating. He looked at the priest for confirmation. The captain dismounted and the others followed. The priest moved last.

"I am Captain Holidor," he announced as he approached the throne. "And this is the Priest of the Dark God, Agar."

"Well met Grimhold," Agar said as he stuck out his gloved hand. It bore a dazzling dark gem ring that signified his station.

Looking at the ring, Grimhold swallowed hard. He hated formalities but he liked his life more. He rose from his small throne, bent before the priest and kissed the large gem in his ring. As he kissed the ring, he found himself thinking he could feed his entire kingdom for an entire cold cycle on what the ring was worth. As the thought passed through his head, he was quick to dismiss it. He knew that the priests of the Dark God were quick to read your thoughts. He would have to be mindful of that while they were here.

"And I am afraid what we have to tell you is for your ears only," Agar said as he looked at the meager court that buzzed around them.

"Then let's make it so," Grimhold said as he clapped his hands.

In seconds, a boy servant appeared to take the soldiers and their mounts away. The youth led them and the other members of the small court out of the great hall. When Holidor and Agar were sure that they were alone, they approached Grimhold on his rickety seat of authority.

"Some time ago," Agar began in whispers," you suggested the girl, Etera Korner, to your cousin and the High Queen as a servant."

"Yes. Yes. I do recall," Grimhold wrinkled his brow as he tried to remember her face. In truth, over the years he had sent countless folk for hard labor. "She was from a long line of Sea Witches if I ł remember correctly," he said as he scratched his receding hairline.

"Ah, you do recall correctly that she was given a golden ticket to serve the High Queen Mora," Agar continued. "She spat at the idea. She spat at the High Queen's offer and mumbled about visions of the lost High Prince and the Avatar instead. Though rude, these visions of hers did increase her value to the High Queen," Agar recounted.

"Pure blasphemy," Grimhold cursed. "And wasn't she given a sentence at hard labor at one of the camps in the west of Sandor?" he inquired.

"Yes, indeed," Holidor agreed. "But she showed no special abilities while there. Even the priests of the Dark God could not understand the nature of her waterpowers and their relationship to the Sylphs. So she was sentenced to spend the rest of her days at hard labor or until such a time as she was willing to serve our High Queen and share her visions of the lost heir," Holidor said.

"And such a pretty thing," Grimhold remarked beside himself as he rubbed his overflowing belly through his robes. As they spoke of Etera, his mind remembered her well. Before the notion of sending her to the High Court became a possibility, he had designs on tasting the nectar that flowed from between her legs. He often dreamed of riding her into submission.

"She was a pretty young thing," Agar remembered. "But looks can be deceiving. She escaped from the mines almost ten Suns ago. We have been chasing her ever since."

Grimhold looked on with surprise. He silently laughed to himself. When he delivered Etera to his cousin in shackles he had warned her not to underestimate the young girl. His hold on her had been her fear that he would have her grandmother and twin brother killed. He had told both his cousin and the High Queen to take major precautions. However, they had relied on the arrogance of miner bindings from the Dark God instead. He chuckled to himself. Now that they had lost her, they had come back to him seeking his aid in her recapture. This was more than ironic to the Lord of Ulfast.

"Do not worry, dear Captain," Grimhold assured. "On the morrow, we will go to her family farm and take her relatives captive. Surely Etera will reappear once her brother and grandmother are in hard irons."

"Are you sure she will go to her family?" Holidor questioned.

Remembering Etera, Grimhold said, "She is joined to her grandmother and her twin. Rest in my keep tonight, we will strike out at first light and I guarantee you we will find her there."

Holidor shook his head. This time he bowed to Grimhold. It was an act of respect. The Queen Enora had given him the task directly to return the young Sea Witch to the mines. He knew that failure would mean a loss of rank and possible death. It had been under his watch that Etera had vanished. He desperately needed to redeem himself in the eyes of the ruler of Blindow. He did not like placing his future in the hands of a lesser royal like Grimhold but in this case he had no choice. They had lost Etera's trail. She was using the wind and the rain against them. Even with Agar in their company, her where abouts had been lost to them.

The boy who had taken the mounts and led the soldiers away returned. He led Captain Holidor and Agar out, leaving Grimhold alone with his thoughts. He knew that Etera would seek out her family now that she was free of hard labor. However, he also knew that capturing her would not be as easy as he made it sound. She was a fifth generation Sea Witch born of Ulfast's waterways. Who knows what kind of powers she had grown into in her time away from Ulfast. Then there was her brother to consider. Though rumor was that he had no magic, he was believed to be a more that worthy swordsman. And of course there was her grandmother, Anna Beth, to consider. She was an elder Sea Witch. They had only been able to capture Etera while her grandmother was away on one of her mindless missions. He had no idea what the old woman would do if attacked in the open. A chill went up his spine. For a moment, Grimhold wondered if risking his life was worth securing his cousin's and the High Queen's favor. Grimhold removed his crescent crown and sighed. His eyes drifted to the window and the dull terrain beyond. Anything had to be better than his exile on the Northern Coast of Sandor.

"Dark God," Grimhold began, "give me strength."


On the outskirts of Ulfast, Tildon Korner tended the land. He was a tall boy for his age, muscled from farming, and deeply tanned from being out in the suns. Unlike his fraternal twin sister, Etera, Tildon looked like his father. His skin was the color of dark moonstones and his hair speckled with the color of the sandy shores. On the bitter outskirts of Ulfast, there was only one road that led to the Korners' farm. On the other side of the farm was a cliff face that dropped steeply into the sea from which the women in the family drew their powers. While Tildon worked the land, his grandmother sat on the porch of their mud brick home humming and playing a wooden flute. While Tildon worked and his grandmother, Anna-Beth, played her flute, there was an odd peace between them that represented this daily ritual.

Long before the stranger came into view, Anna-Beth felt a familiar stirring in her spirit. She put her flute away and took out her divining board. Tildon watched his grandmother begin this ritual as he approached the house. He stopped working the field and headed toward the house. Individuals came from far and wide to have Tilden's grandmother tell their fortunes. It was more from her divining board, than from Tilden's tilling the land that they made money to live. Anna-Beth began to burn herbs to clean her divining board as she watched the person approach in the distance. She removed a tattered pouch from around her neck and cast out the animal bones in front of her and looked at the pattern in shock. She picked up the bones and cast them again. She got the same pattern.

"Tildon!" She called as she came to her feet almost knocking over her divining board, spilling bones. "Tildon!"

Hearing his grandmother's shrill cry, Tildon came to the door with his long sword in his hands. He looked at the small stranger in the distance with dismay. He knew that Grimhold tolerated his grandmother's presence more out of fear than anything else. He would not be surprised if he sent a dark practitioner or an assassin to test her mighty powers. Grimhold had already captured his twin sister, Etera, and spirited her away, That happened when he was still an apprentice and his sword skills were not yet honed. However, that was a long time ago. Though barely a man, Tildon stood tall with his weapon in defense of his family home. He would not allow anyone to harm his aging grandmother or to take her away from him. She had nurtured both him and Etera since the death of their parents at the hand of pirates. She was the only true parent he and Etera ever knew.

"Put your sword away," Anna-Beth recommended as she found herself fighting back tears. "We have nothing to fear from this visitor," she assured him as she watched the weary straggler approach.

Tildon looked at his grandmother suspiciously. It took a lot to rattle Anna-Beth Korner and she was clearly disturbed by the appearance of this stranger. Tildon watched the person approach with a wrinkled brow. His hand tightened on his blade as he looked from his grandmother to the newcomer. He was unconvinced. He let his long sword fall to his side, but he did not put it away just yet. By this time, the interloper had reached the edge of Tilden's crops and he still could not make out the face of the person under their cloak. However, judging by their size in relation to his crops, he was sure he could take them in combat if magic was not involved. Anna-Beth came to her feet and put on her shoes. Slowly, she came down from the porch. Then she surprised Tildon by breaking out into a full run. Leaving Tildon on the porch in shock, she ran up to the figure and caught the stranger in her arms. She unwrapped the person's head from the cloth hood that concealed it. The person fell into Anna-Beth's open arms. She cradled the person in her arms and wiped at the person's dirty face through her own tears. Tildon came down off the porch slowly and approached his grandmother. He looked down oddly at his grandmother and the stranger. Seeing the person's face for the first time in years, he was surprised to see a mirror image of his own features. His mouth dropped open and he fell to his knees on the dirt path.

"It is your sister, Tildon! It is Etera!" Anna-Beth cried. "Your sister has come home."

Tildon and Anna-Beth lifted Etera from the ground and carried her into the house. They laid her out across an over-stuffed golden sitting chair. Anna-Beth laid her hand across her granddaughter's head and closed her eyes. She could tell that Etera was both starved and exhausted but luckily still in good health. Anna-Beth could tell that Etera had spent herself using her skills with the Sylphs to hide from those chasing her. The elder Sea Witch could not believe the stamina of her granddaughter.

"Bring me food, my bag of herbs and a glass of water," Anna-Beth commanded Tildon. However, he failed to move. His eyes were fixed on his sister. He had given up cycles ago that he wouldever see her again. Now she was here. He could not imagine all she had gone through to get there. "Tildon move!" Anna-Beth commanded stirring him from his stupor.

Tildon turned and left the room.

"Grandmother," Etera said through her delirium. "I did not know where else to go, "she mumbled.

"My dear you were right for coming here. We will take care of you," Anna-Beth declared through her tears.

Tildon returned with rations, a large satchel of herbs, and a large vat of water. Anna-Beth looked through the herbs and placed several in the vat. She covered them with her hand and said a prayer over them. Then she lifted Etera's head and forced her to drink the bitter brew. Etera choked on the mixture before falling into a deep sleep. Tildon placed a blanket over her and sat down beside her. He could not take his eyes off of her. He had not seen his twin in several full cycles. Though he had never mentioned it to his grandmother, he had given up all hope for her return. Now that she was back, Tildon did not know what to feel. Part of him was overjoyed, but another part of him sensed the danger that she represented in being in their home. Tildon kept looking out of the window, unconsciously expecting Grimhold or the High Queen's men to be coming down the road. He rubbed the hilt of his sword nervously. He knew he was more than a match for any of Grimhold's men one-on-one, but they would strike in numbers. A sinking sense of hopelessness overtook him.

For a second, he resented his sister for disturbing the peace he and his grandmother had created in her absence. But when he looked down at how frail she was,–he quickly dismissed the thought. More than anything else, he felt the need to protect his twin. While Tildon watched over his sister, Anna-Beth ran upstairs. Her slippered feet creaked on the steps as she moved. After a few minutes, she came down in a long, brown, hooded traveling cloak. Tildon looked up from his vigil over his sister at his grandmother with confusion and surprise. Tildon came to his feet instantly. His grandmother had not gone out alone since Etera had been kidnapped when she was away doing divination. Now, all of her clients came to their house where she was strongest and Tilden's sword was sharpest. Tildon rose to his feet ready to follow his grandmother out of the house. She shook her head no.

"Tildon I need you to stay here and watch over Etera," she directed. "I will be fine, "she assured him. "I have to make some arrangements. I will be back before morning."

"Arrangements?" Tildon questioned with a wrinkled brow, unsure of what to make of his grandmother's words.

Anna-Beth reached up and placed a reassuring hand on her grandson's face. There was no time for explanations now. It was a time for action. Her enemies had caught her off-guard once. She would not let that happen again.

"Trust me, Tildon," she said simply as she removed her comforting hand from his face and turned toward her hastily planned mission.

Tildon walked his grandmother out to the porch. Day had yielded to night. Tildon watched his grandmother pass through the top of the crops and vanish down the road toward Ulfast. She walked slowly at first with her cloak pulled tightly around her. As she got closer to the center of town, she avoided the eyes of those she passed. She hastened down several dark alleyways and finally came upon a tavern called the Dark Opion. She looked through the dirty, fogged over window of the tavern. Through it, she could not make out any faces, yet she could tell it was full. After waiting outside for some time, she decided to enter the swinging doors. No one took note of the elderly woman as she sailed through the tavern. She went up to the bar counter, waited a moment for the barkeep to notice her before clearing her throat to get his attention. He was a tall, swarthy man with a cut across his face that had been stitched badly. Pus still ran down from the recent wound. He wiped at it hastily with a dirty cloth as he came up to her.

"What can I get for ya?" he asked as he looked Anna-Beth up and down.

"It is not what you can get for me but *who* you can help me find," she said as she slid a yellow coin across the counter. "I am looking for the one who sails the *Lucky Lady*. I am looking for Captain Sarison."

The barkeep looked at her oddly for a moment. Then he took her money and pointed her toward the back of the tavern to a shadowed area. Anna-Beth thanked the man and headed in the direction he pointed. There were several men arm-wrestling surrounded by a group of onlookers. Hastily, Anna-Beth made her way through the crowd. Captain Sarison was one of two men arm-wrestling on a wobbly table. Captain Sarison was a tall man of dark complexion with huge arms. His long black hair was braided and he sported a trimmed beard. His arms were large and painted with the stories of the journeys he had made. His light armor was full of short daggers and he had a heavy blade at his side. He looked up from his battle and caught sight of Anna-Beth. She took off her hood and faded to the back of the crowd. Captain Sarison rose from the table where he was fighting, picked up his winnings, and joined Anna-Beth in the back of the crowd.

"I never thought I would see you in a place like this," he said to Anna-Beth as he ushered her over to a nearby table.

"I, too, thought I would never need to be in a place like this;." she chuckled. "But I find myself in a position where I need a favor from you."

"A favor from a piece of the sea like me?" Captain Sarison said with surprise. "This is a change. Usually it's me coming to you for a favor of some kind. You still reading aren't you?"

"Yes I am," Anna-Beth said. "And it is because I see so much that I need to ask you for a favor."

Captain Sarison sat back in the chair and looked at the woman gravely. Then he laughed," With all the trouble you have kept me out of over the years. You can ask me for a limb and I would give it to you." He said earnestly as he waved to a bar maiden for a drink.

"I need you to take my grandchildren far away from here. "Anna-Beth said bluntly." I need for them to be safe." She concluded.

Captain Sarison wrinkled his brow, "What about you?" he asked.

"I am an old woman Sarison. For as strong as I am, I have too much water in my bones. I am anchored here. This is my home. I can do better by staying here than going with you to protect them," Anna-Beth explained. "I have money." She said as she pulled a pouch out of her cloak.

Captain Sarison leaned forward, looked at the pouch and pushed the money back toward her with disdain.

"Your money is no good here good woman." Captain Sarison snapped." I will guard your grandchildren with my life. I am due to take my ship to the Lost Islands at first light. There is no place further away from anywhere than that." He assured.

"I want to thank you Sarison and I pray you a safe voyage," Anna-Beth sighed.

"I think I have taken as much of these rogues money as I can get." He said as he drank down his ale." I will have the Lucky Lady behind your house when Idris and Itor first sail the horizon."

"They will be waiting for you." Anna-Beth said as she rose.

"May the Avatar be with you," Captain Sarison said as he watched her leave.

Anna-Beth turned and smiled, "It always is my friend. It always is."

Tildon stood on the porch of his country home holding his sword on guard. He could not believe that in the last few hours his life had changed. His twin sister that was kidnapped several cycles ago was now asleep on a chair in his livingroom. On top of that, his grandmother who never left the length of land they owned had vanished. Tildon shifted his long blade from one hand to another. More than protecting his home, he found comfort in the familiarity of the blade. His sword teacher, an old man who came to his grandmother for readings, told him that when life got hectic his sword would always be there to rely upon. He was taught that there was truth in the metal of the finely crafted blade. Tildon began to do a form with his sword up and down on the porch. As he moved, the edge of the sword it caught the candlelight. He was so lost in his form and the glow of the blade, he forgot about the presence of his sister as she appeared in the open doorway.

"I thought I would never live to see my brother hold a sword." Etera admitted as she leaned against the doorway weakly.

"And I never thought I would see my sister *ever* again," Tildon said as he came up to Etera and wrapped his arms around her." It has been too long good sister."

"I cannot tell you the heart ships I have endured to get here, but I made it none the less." Etera said proudly as she stretched and yawned.

"Grandmother always told me to keep the faith. I have to tell you for a long time I didn't." He admitted as he ran his hand over her fine face.

"I have to tell you that it was you, grandmother, and my visions that kept me going." Etera admitted as she pulled her robes around herself.

"What visions did you have? Did you see the Avatar?" Tildon asked quickly.

Etera shook her head, no. "I visited with the lost High Prince. I saw him more than once in my mind travels. He comes to rescue us all."

Tildon wrinkled his nose and drew his sword. "I do not believe in High Monarchs. I prefer to believe in cold metal." He swore.

"Do not be so short sighted brother. It is the Avatar that sends for him to liberate us all." Etera assured.

Just then, Anna-Beth appeared at the row of crops that led to their home. She was moving quickly toward her grandchildren. Upon reaching the porch, she waved them inside the house. She removed her traveling robes and sat in her comfortable chair. She put up her feet and Tildon began to massage them slowly. Anna-Beth took comfort in his familiar touch and waved her granddaughter over to her while Tildon cracked her toes.

"It is good to see you," she began," I can die now knowing that the two of you are safe and back together." She said.

"Grandmother, do not speak of such things, "Tildon whined. "Your suns are many and long to come." He swore.

"I serve the will of the Avatar. When it is my time, it is my time. But you and your sister must leave Ulfast. Your destinies lie beyond these shores." Anna-Beth explained.

"Does it have to do with the High Prince? "Etera asked. "I have visited with him in my mind travels."

"I believe it does." Anna-Beth agreed." Besides, Grimhold will not allow you to stay here in peace. I have been a thorn in his side enough over the cycles, but I am an old woman. You are young and just beginning to understand what you can do." She explained.

"I will not leave you," Tildon insisted as he stopped rubbing her feet and playing with her toes." Let him and his men come. They will taste the edge of my blade," he swore.

"Tildon," Anna-Beth began." You are mighty with the sword. That is why you must go with your sister and be her protector now."

"But I have just gotten here," Etera cried as she reached out to her grandmother, "I do not want to leave so soon."

"My sunshine," Anna-Beth smiled as she reached out and touched Etera's face." I do not want you or your brother to leave. But I have read it in the bones and they do not lie. You know this. If they are correct, we will see each other again. Let's spend tonight loving each other and with good cheer; because at the dawn you and Tildon will leave these shores."

Tildon looked from his grandmother to his sister. He knew that there was no arguing with his grandmother once her mind was made up. He got up from where he was sitting, and went into the kitchen. He began to go into their stores. If this was going to be their last night together he would make sure it was a feast.

In the Great Hall of Grimhold no one could remember a feast like this one. He provided provisions and entertainment for all of Holidor's men and the dark priest Agar. Everyone ate until they were full and Grimhold bedded the regiment down well for the night. After the merriment of the feast were done Grimhold, Agar, and Holidor retired to his private study for fruits and ale. The three sat by the fire basking and burping in the afterglow of the meal.

"Well met Grimhold," Holidor began. "I will be sure to tell the Flasion Queen that we were well received by her cousin."

"Indeed," Agar chimed in," Such a feast was worthy of more noble boots than my own."

"It is the least I can do, "Grimhold said as he drank his ale." After all, it was I that brought the worrisome wench to the attention of the High Queen."

"Do not be so hard on yourself new friend," Holidor assured." It was under my watch that she slipped through our fingers. I have never lost a slave before and I do not plan to lose one now." He swore.

"I am here to simply assure her capture," Agar said as he drank." Sea witches can be a nasty and unpredictable bunch." He said as he waved his bejeweled hand and created a slight purple glow around his hand.

"Indeed, "Grimhold agreed turning his head from Agar's magic uncomfortably." I have dealt with her grandmother's witchcraft and water works for more cycles than I can count. It was no wonder we were able to steal the girl away from her at all."

"And you tell me the boy is a good swordsman?" Holidor asked.

"He is rumored to be so," Grimhold agreed." He was supposedly taught by one of the elder sword's masters from the East."

"Good," Holidor said." My blade has not been tested in along time. I can't wait to test it." He assured.

"Hold your vigor old man the morrow will give you much sport." Grimhold assured as he stared into the fire. "But good friends riddle me this?" He began again. "Rumor has it that the lost High Prince has been found."

For a second, no one spoke and the air in the room got heavy.

Agar broke the silence. "It seems that rumors have even reached this far out in the realm." He began. "I can assure you that it is true. The High Prince has been found. Yet what the rumors do not tell you is that the High Queen has taken every precaution to apprehend both him and his captors. You need not worry yourself over such things," Agar assured as he turned his ale around in his hand.

"I think we have drunk enough for one night. Much more can make a man stiff in the saddle," Holidor said as he stood. "We leave at first light."

"At first light it is," Agar said as he stood.

Grimhold did not move. He let the others take their leave. He was not one for idle gossip, but it occurred to him that the presence of an entire regiment and a priest of the Dark God were a lot for a simple runaway slave even if she was a Sea Witch. They had to have a reason. Grimhold sipped at his ale. He wondered what insights the little witch had to the lost High Prince, if any. He shook his head. Only time would tell.

As the suns rose over the banks of Ulfast, the Lucky Lady appeared on the horizon. The Lucky Lady was a tall wooden air ship that was powered by both ores men and mystical silken sails. The sails allowed it to fly through the sky powered by the water's wind, while the ore's men allowed it to move smoothly across the water. At the head of the ship was a beautiful winged Sylph made of metal. Captain Sarison liked to say that it was her magic that had gotten him and his crew out of the situations he had found himself in over the cycles. He was unsure about taking on passengers, but Anna-Beth had broken a horrible curse he had been under several cycles ago. He was literally wasting away before she tended to him with her herbs, powders, and enchantments. Since then, he made it a habit to stop by and let her read bones for him whenever he was in Ulfast. He was sometimes unsure of the messages he received from her, but they always seemed to play out in one fashion or another.

Now he was headed to the ends of Acara, the Lost Islands, on a scouting mission for a treasure he had won a map to. He only hoped her grandchildren stayed below deck and did not cause him any trouble. Captain Sarison stood on the helm of the great ship and turned its wheel. The ship veered into a small cove that was behind Anna-Beth's lodging. Through a looking glass, he could see three figures on the beach. She had been true to her word. Captain Sarison gave the signal to his second in command to lower the small boat over the side and retrieve their passengers.

Anna-Beth, Etera, and Tildon were standing on the shore. They all wore long traveling cloaks. Anna-Beth had packed them each fresh bread and provisions for their voyage. There was a somber mood over the Korner Klan. Tildon did not want to leave his grandmother's side. He knew Grimhold would come for her and he wanted to be there to protect her. Etera felt remorse for even coming home in the first place. She felt like this was all her fault. Anna-Beth was the saddest of them all. She was sending her only family out into the world without her. She trusted Captain Sarison, but anything could happen to them along the way especially at sea. She prayed to the waves and the Avatar that they would be safe.

As the small boat neared, Anna-Beth swept Tildon and Etera into her arms. She held them both firmly and covered them with a parent's kisses.

"This is not goodbye," She swore as she pushed them out toward the cold looping waves. "We will see each other again. I believe the Avatar will keep us until that time."

"Avatars and Dark Gods, I am sick of the lot of them." Tildon swore as he picked up his pack and headed to the small boat.

"Etera," Anna-Beth said as she pulled her granddaughter's ear close." I think before this thing is all over you will play a role in our liberation that you can't imagine. It is for this reason I can so easily let you go. "She explained." Keep your brother close and rely on your mind travels they will show you the way." She added.

Etera did not know what to say to her grandmother's words. She simply hugged her back fiercely and followed Tildon into the small boat. Anna-Beth stood on the shore and waited until the small craft was pulled upon the Lucky Lady. She watched as Captain Sarison waved to her from the deck of the great air ship. She waved in return and spoke to the morning sea air. It lifted the sails of the great ship with a huge gust and pushed it out to sea. Anna-Beth stood there until she could not see the Lucky Lady anymore before she turned toward her home. She climbed the stairs that led from the beach to her small home. She sat down on the porch as she had a million times before and cast the animal bones on her divining tray. She looked at the pattern and nodded her head. The pattern warned her that company was coming. She smiled to herself as she sank back into her robes. She hoped they knew they were not facing a defenseless old woman.

Grimhold was up before the dawn. His servants dressed him in his finest armament. Grimhold patted his sword at his side as he looked at his reflection in the looking glass. He and the old witch Anna-Beth had tolerated each other at best for more cycles than he could recall. Rumors and tales of her magic had reached his ears. He knew this was not going to be a simple battle, even with the power of the dark priest at their sides. Once he was dressed, Grimhold made his way to his great hall. Holidor, Agar, and the rest of the regiment were preparing their mounts and sharpening swords against stone. Little was said between the men as they prepared. They let Grimhold take the lead as they rode out of Ulfast to the Endings, the outskirts of Ulfast and the Korner homestead.

By the time morning was full and after along ride over rugged terrain, the regiment had reached the Korner farm. They turned down the crop filled path toward the house. Anna-Beth stood on her porch tall in full defiance of the interlopers. Her long ashen hair hung down her back and caught the morning breeze as she stared down her attackers. Her worn face showed no emotion. It was stone like with age. A squire came to the fore of the regiment. He marched down the length of the fields toward the house. He stopped short of the porch and unrolled a parchment and began to read.

"By order of the right and almighty High Queen Mora, "He began." By order of the just and true Queen Enora. By order of the good Feudal Lord Grimhold, you will return to this officer the personage known as Etera Korner. She is claimed as the property of the High Queen Mora." The Squire went on." Any other action will be met with death."

"Gone! Anna-Beth said simply with a sly smile." She is gone from here. And if she was not, I would not allow you to take her from this house anyway." She said sternly as she looked past the squire at the regiment.

"Enough of this posturing," Agar interjected as he came to the fore of the regiment. "Search the house. And if Etera is not here, kill the old woman and be done with it! "He directed.

Holidor motioned for his first line of men to dismount and enter the house. As they neared the house, Anna-Beth looked at Grimhold and smiled. In one sweeping motion, she raised her hands and a thick fog blew in from the sea. It covered the house completely and the small farm. The mounts of the interlopers choked on the fog and struggled to keep their riders aloft. Then marsh critters by the dozens rose from the sand around the farm. They used their sharpened claws to nip at the legs of the mounts and the men of the regiment. The men fell from the back of their mounts. Agar managed to stay aloft and charged the porch. He raised his hand and dark fire cut through the fog where Anna-Beth had been standing. The bolt did not make its target. She was already lost somewhere in the fog.

After a few minutes, the fog lifted and the marsh critters receded. The only thing that remained was Anna-Beth's empty house and the rows of crops. Grimhold smiled to himself as he came to his feet. He knew the old witch was not to be toyed with. Yet the out-landers, were so sure of themselves. If they would have asked him, he in no way would have attacked Anna-Beth directly. He would have devised some clever ruse to lure her away and then come for her granddaughter; but what did he know. He was just a low level royaland a Feudal Lord, consigned to a sparse piece of land at the edge of his cousin Queen Enola's grand kingdom.

"I want this place torn apart, "Agar ordered." The stench of that young witch is still in the air. And if you find the old one leave her to me." There was acid in his voice.

"Might I suggest a more indirect approach," Grimhold said feeling full of himself.

"And what do you suggest? "Holidor asked as he replaced his sword in the scarab.

"I suggest you leave Anna-Beth to me," he volunteered." She and I have been playing this game for years and we know each other well. I can assure you when she reappears I am best suited to dealing with the old croon."

Grimhold could see both Holidor and Agar thinking over his suggestion. He tried to show no expression at all, not trying to betray his confidence.

Finally Agar said, "I give you two suns. If you do not find her and the young witch by then I will raise this land and you as well." He threatened.

"Such nastiness, "Grimhold said as he turned back toward his meager dwelling with the others in tow. As he rode off, he knew exactly in his mind how he would handle the dear sea witch Anna-Beth. It had worked in the past and he was sure it would work again in the future. All she needed to hear was that the regiment was at bay and he would come by himself for a reading of sorts. She was married to those bones as he was to his next breath. Once he engaged in the reading he would find out the whereabouts of the lousy little witch and her brother. He was sure of it. Now all he had to do was keep this regiment and this dark priest content till then. He shook his head. He did not know if there was enough wine in Ulfast to accomplish that task.

# Chapter 5

Tisha grew tired of the small suite of rooms that had become her personal prison. It was just like Ela said. There was no delicacy that she could think of that her group of handmaidens would not bring her. They kept Tisha full of all sort of drinks, fruits, and cheeses. Pretty soon, out of shade and pure mischief., Tisha began asking for things that she knew those in her service could not possibly acquire. She wanted to test the resolve of these kindly servant women. She wanted to see how serious they took their duties.

"Dear Miss," Tisha kindly began as she stuck her head between the curtains. The handmaidens jumped to their feet and ran over to her with full smiles waiting to be commanded. I need something." Tisha whispered coyly with a sly grin, knowing full well she did not need what she was about to ask for,

"Anything my dear, "Dilga replied. Dilga was a doughy colored lass that seemed in charge of the others "What do you need?'

Tisha could barely hold in her pranking. She lowered her head and looked up to make sure she had all of their attention, then she cleared her throat and said," I need a tampax with wings for a heavy flow."

The servant women looked at each other with loss.

"Oh I am sorry, "Tisha began." Let me explain that to you in terms you may understand."

The handmaidens leaned in and clung to Tisha's whispers and graphic details. Before she was finished, they had all turned a dark shade of red. Tisha could not help but laugh to herself.

"Normally, I would run down the road with a dollar and get me one, but you see I can't do that here. Be a dear and work that out for me before I leave a trail." She said as she vanished back into her room leaving the women dumbfounded. After a few minutes, Tisha heard the women scurrying from the room like mice when you turn the ligh ont.

"Ah!" Tisha smiled." My work here is done."

Tisha soon realized that though she was living in the lap of luxury, she was no less a prisoner. In addition, for as advanced as Acara seemed to be they had no television or radio. Tisha would have given anything for some mindless soap operas, music videos, or reality shows to help her pass the time. When she asked for a television, all the handmaidens did was giggle and bring her parchment to write with, old books to read, and crystals to stare into. Tisha sucked her teeth. Even when she was in school, she did not fancy reading and writing. This had not changed since she had come to Acara. Tisha tossed the parchment aside and thumbed through the books absently. Tisha soon found that the crystal she wore also allowed her to read Acarian script. As she thumbed through the books, they seemed to be a history of the Acara's High Court from the beginning and the tales and deeds of the Moritans, the Royal Guard, Simon's people.

At first, the books on the Moritans caught her eye. She was giving birth to Simon's baby. At the very least, she would learn something about the man she had promised herself to. In one of the books, she caught a picture of the arrow that she wore. It seemed that Simon had truly given himself to her when he bestowed the trinket on her. As Tisha read about it, she realized it was more like an engagement ring than anything else. She also realized that it connected her to Simon across time and space. This lightened her spirits. She had never meditated before, but she found herself spending at least an hour a day with the crystal in her hand meditating on Simon. And soon enough, she realized that for as much as he was able to feel her she could also feel him.

It was a relief at first. Yet, it too soon became a burden as she realized how angry and hopeless Simon was growing about their current situation. She could tell that Simon blamed himself for her exile to Acara and her separation from her son little Wisdom. These realizations were the hardest of all. They served as a reminder that she was away from her bouncing toddler and her family. She could not imagine what her mother was going through. For all she knew, they might even think she was dead. These were the gravest times of all for Tisha. Tisha found herself pacing her suite back and forth. She wanted to scream. However, she held it inside. She knew intuitively that for as much luxury as these rooms afforded, she could imagine what the prisons must be like. She was not going to do anything that might tempt her hosts to toss her in a dungeon and throw away the key; especially, being pregnant she knew she had to be careful.

On the fifth night of her captivity, Tisha decided to test the boundaries of the handmaidens that tended to her needs. She looked out the window of her chamber at the three moons that rose every evening on Acara. She waited until Acara's moons were full up in the sky, she slipped on something she had been provided with and a cloak and headed for the doorway of her suite of rooms. In the evening, she was tended to by only one handmaiden by the name of Stula. The woman had a sunny disposition, but she did more sleeping than tending to Tisha's needs. Tisha waited until the woman was in full snore, then she slipped past her out into the hallways outside her suite. Looking left and right, Tisha did not know which way to go. The hallway looked the same in both directions. Then the sweetest scent caught Tisha's nose. It was the smell of flowers she was sure of it. Pulled by the smell, she turned right down the hallway and followed her nose down a row of back stairs. She emerged in a small courtyard that was full in bloom with the whitest flowers she had ever seen. Just beyond the garden was a high wall that looked impenetrable. Tisha did not let that dampen her spirits. It was enough that she was outside and in this beautiful garden.

Slowly, Tisha walked through the garden. She took off her sneakers and let her bare feet intermingle with the soil. Drunken on the dew of the flowers, she laid down among them dreaming of Simon's touch. She held onto the crystal he gave her. She was sure that he could feel her even though they were worlds apart. After a few minutes, Tisha soon realized that she was not alone. She got up from where she was lying in the flower bed and looked around. Sitting on a small boulder near the doorway to the garden was a single figure wrapped in the most beautiful purple robes Tisha had ever seen. Still remembering her status as a prisoner, Tisha approached this figure carefully. The figure did not move. At first Tisha was unsure if the person even saw her. However, as she got closer the hooded figure waved her over.

"How are you enjoying the rooms that I provided for you?" the woman asked carefully.

The question shocked Tisha as she approached. Then she looked into the face of the woman and she saw Royal's dark features staring back. This had to be his mother, the High Queen Mora herself. More from traditions she had seen on television than anything else, Tisha bowed her head to the High Queen.

"Your Majesty," Tisha said softly.

As if not hearing the young woman at all the High Queen continued to talk, "These are moon buds. They are one of Acara's rarest flowers. When I was born my father used to call me his moon bud, since I was such a nocturnal creature." Mora reminisced as the women stood side by side.

Looking at her, Mora did not look like the terror that she had been described as being. In fact, she looked no older than Tisha's own mother. However, Tisha reminded herself that this was the woman that had sent the assassin cube after them and nearly killed them all. Yet, Tisha found wondering if Little Wisdom or the baby she was carrying were ever lost to her what steps she would be willing to take to get them back.

"I will leave you to your garden," Tisha said as she bowed again and tried to move past the reflective monarch. As she passed, the High Queen reached out and grabbed her arm. She had a vise like grip that caused Tisha to halt immediately. Her hand was cold to the touch. It astonished Tisha and made her blood run cold. She was stunned for a moment.

"Looking at that contraption that you used to best my Royal Guard, I cannot imagine what a world of them would be like. They seem so cold and un-alive. You must tell me its secrets." It was not a question, but a commandment.

"Yes, your highness," Tisha agreed, remembering the way she had used Wisdom's SUV to pin Quan against the wall of the burning church.

"Good. I will have Ela bring you to me in a sun or so, so you can teach us all about this wonderful machine that bested my most able Royal Guard."

Tisha simply nodded.

"And I think I will have Ela take you out into Acara City. Perhaps you will find that our world is not so different from your own." The High Queen offered.

"That is most generous of you, "Tisha said as she bowed her head again.

"Yes and I will let the handmaidens know that this garden is open to you at any time. Come smell some of the sweetness of Acara. It may not be home for you, but it can be no less sweet." Mora offered.

"Thank you, "Tisha said shyly.

Then moving faster than anyone should have been able to move the High Queen Mora was at her side and placed her hand on Tisha's stomach. It lingered there a few minutes then she pulled it away.

"You will give birth to a strong Moritan child. In fact, he will one day be the center post of the next generation of Royal Guards. Guard him well off-worlder. In the things we do in life, sometimes so precious a thing as having a child can be overlooked until it is too late. "Mora said grimly.

*Another boy.* Tisha was shocked at the thought. Little Wisdom will have a brother. And it would not just be a brother it would be an alien child. She was going to be giving birth to Simon's son. Tisha had no idea what this would truly mean. She reflected on the arduous delivery that Little Wisdom had put her through. Silently, she began to wonder if having Simon's baby would be any different considering he was not fully human. It was a scary thought.

"We have kept you locked up far too long." Mora said matter –a-factly." I will have Ela take you on a tour of our fine city. It is important for you to see the place that you will call home." Mora insisted.

*Call home.* The words rolled around in Tisha's head. She had never given a thought to the possibility that she would never see Earth again. The idea left a sinking sensation in her stomach. She reached up and grabbed the arrow that Simon had given her for comfort. It made her think of home. As Tisha stood in the dark gripping the arrowhead, the High Queen Mora receded into the darkness of the doorway that Tisha had used to find the small garden.

Tisha was surprised by the countenance of the High Queen. She did not know what she expected a "High Queen" to be, but the woman she met in the shadows of the garden was not it. Most of all, Tisha was surprised at how normal Mora appeared to be. She was also surprised at how much thought Mora had given to her situation. Surly a woman with an entire world to rule over had more pressing matters to think about than her captivity. However, it did not matter to Tisha. Tisha would be happy to get out of the tower for a while. She had seen the city from her bedroom chambers and it left her in wonder.

Carefully, Tisha picked a flower from the garden. She smelled it. It had the sweetest scent she had ever smelled before. As Tisha headed back into the tower, she took the white speckled flower with her. Its sweetness comforted the parts of her that longed for home.

The next morning Tisha was awakened with the suns by her handmaidens. They had prepared a scented bath for her. Though she resisted, her handmaidens stripped her of her clothes and washed her from head to toe. They took a long time with her hair. With disdain, they carefully untangled the fake hair from Tisha's real hair. This alone took several hours since they really did not know what they were doing. Once it was done, they finally took a razor to her head and shaved it clean; this left Tisha in shock. Her hair had never been very long, but she never imagined herself being bald.

After they were done, they led Tisha back to her bedchamber. Her Earthly clothes were gone and had been replaced with a suit of light hide armor. Tisha dressed quickly in the armament. She caught site of herself in the mirror in her room. In the armor and without her braids, she barely recognized herself.

"You are looking more and more like a Moritan each day," Ela said as she came into Tisha's bedchamber without knocking.

"This is not me," Tisha protested as she shifted in the armor.

"Nonsense," Ela protested." You look like a woman that my son Keyton would be proud to call his mate."

"I am more than *Simon*'s mate. I love him." She corrected.

Ignoring her words, Ela came fully into the room. She picked up the flower from the pillow on Tisha's bed and smelled it.

"I hope you are well rested," Ela began." We have a long day ahead of us." She explained.

"I am," Tisha assured her.

"Then let's go see about getting you a gorda. "Ela said quickly as she rose to leave Tisha's bedroom chambers. Tisha followed Ela out of her chamber. Unlike the night before, the hallways of the tower were filled, bursting with life. People and beings of all sorts were making their way through the tunnels as Ela and Tisha passed. Tisha tried to keep her head down so she would not stare at the different beings that she passed in the hallways. However some were so exotic in their look they took her breath away. After a few minutes, Ela led Tisha through a set of wooden doors to an open field behind the tower. Tisha's eyes widened and her mouth dropped at what she saw. There were rows and rows of Royal Guards tending to what looked like huge lizards. These green scaly animals looked like a throwback to Earth's dinosaurs.

"These are the gorda. They are the official animals that the Moritan ride upon. Their nature is usually gentle, but they are fierce in battle. Once one has chosen you, he or she will become your responsibility. It will be necessary for you to get him or her a stall and see to its daily needs. Ela explained.

"You mean you ride upon these things, "Tisha protested in shock. She was intimidated by the sight of the gorda.

"I assure you little flower the gorda are harmless here, but once you have made a connection with one they would lie themselves down for you in battle." Ela explained. "It is one of the secrets of the Moritans. It is said that when the first High King was chosen and he was joined with the Moritans the gorda bore witness to this sacred union and have guarded it ever since." Ela explained.

"How does the picking work?" Tisha asked as she scratched at her newly baldhead. "Do you choose one for me?"

"You have it all wrong, little flower" E la explained. "It is written in the annals of the Moritan that the gorda choose us, we do not choose them."

Tisha could hear Ela's words, but they were falling on deaf ears, since she was captivated by the sight of the green creatures. At home, she had a cat named Mittens that she loved but taking responsibility for a gorda was a very different thing all together. She could not imagine what it would take to take responsibility for such a creature. It seemed like an awesome responsibility. On Earth, Tisha remembered riding a horse when she was a child once or twice at summer camp in Druid Hill Park back in Baltimore. The gorda were bigger than any horse. She could not imagine actually riding on one.

"How do they choose you" Tisha asked timidly as she looked at the pin of gorda grazing in an open field under the light of Acara's two suns.

"You simply walk among them and the one that is yours will make himself or herself known to you." Ela explained.

"You mean I've got to go in there with them?" Tisha said as she held onto the fence that surrounded the field a little bit harder.

"I know this is a lot, but I can tell by the contraption that you used to defeat my otherhalf you are not a coward. Besides, while the gorda do not talk they do have a strong sense of empathy and telepathy. I cannot tell you how many times my dear Rambian aided and saved me in battle. And while we sit here talking, I'm sure one has already chosen you." Ela explained.

Tisha cleared her throat. She was not convinced by Ela's words. Once again she silently wondered what she had gotten herself involved in. In the back of her mind she saw herself being trampled by the herd of huge beasts and eaten alive. Her blood ran cold. Sensing her fear, Ela entered the pin first. She reached out and took Tisha's trembling hand and guided her over the fence and into the pin filled with gorda. The gorda looked up from where they were grazing and met eyes with Tisha with indifference. Ela nudged her forward. Tisha moved from the edge of the fence awkwardly tripping over her nervous feet.

Tisha felt stupid standing among the gorda. She was unsure of what to do next. Tisha was about to return to the gate when one gorda caught her eye. He was slightly smaller than the rest of the gorda, but unlike the others he was covered with an exo-skeleton. Two long horns framed its mouth and jagged bones protruded from its back and tail. Slowly, it ambled its way toward Tisha. For as dangerous as it looked to Tisha, she looked into its large blackeyes and she felt an instant connection. It surprised her as a sense of calm and relief over took her.

"By the Dark God," Ela mumbled under her breath as she watched the odd gorda come up to Tisha.

Tisha did not know what to do as the odd looking gorda approached her. Tisha thought about what she had learned on Earth about dogs, so she simply stuck out her hand toward the animal. The gorda stuck out the horn that protruded from its forehead toward her hand. An odd pink glow appeared around her hand and the gorda's head, cementing their bond. Tisha led the gorda back to where Ela was sitting on the fence.

It took a lot to surprise this mother of the Royal Guard, but this joining had surprised her. It was very rare for a gorda to be born with horns. In fact, you could go a lifetime and never see one. Gorda with exo-skeletons were so rare they were said to be omens of war. Ela knew that one had been born as part of this herd, but she would have never expected it to join with an off-worlder. As she stared at Tisha and her oddly shaped gorda, she was at a loss for words. Yet while she did not know what to say, she did know what she had to do. She definitely had to tell Quan about the joining, so he could inform the High Queen. She would definitely need to know about this. In addition, Tisha would need to go through the *birthing* immediately; faster in fact than Ela had anticipated. It was the Moritan way.

"This gorda looks different from the rest," Tisha commented as she rubbed at her gorda's head.

"He is very different from the rest. In fact, you do not see a gorda like this but once in a lifetime, if at all. It is a thing of legends." Ela commented as she reached out to touch it to make sure its horns were real. "What shall you call him?"

Tisha ran her hand over his head and looked deep into the animal's eyes. The gorda rubbed its head against her armored chest. Tisha looked deep into his eyes and felt the connection. It was warm and comfortable. It felt like nothing she had ever experienced before. Then she felt a name enter her mind.

"His name is Aspion that is his name." Tisha announced, "Aspion."

"Then Aspion it is! That is a fine name." Ela said as she came to her feet. "As we look at the city, I will have him fit for riding gear and a stall prepared for him."

Ela called over to a group of the Royal Guards. They opened the pin and led Aspion out. Reverently, they took Aspion from Tisha and led him down the row of stables. Tisha immediately felt an odd sense of loss as she watched the Royal Guard take Aspion from her. Tisha had never felt anything like this before. She had had mittens for most of her life, but she never felt the kind of connection to her beloved cat that she instantly had for Aspion. Seeing her reaction to the immediate separation, Ela placed a reassuring hand on her shoulder.

"You will have plenty of time with him later. Now we will see Acara City," Ela explained as a wagon pulled up being driven by a stable boy. The wagon was being pulled by two feisty hairy mounts. Ela waved for Tisha to sit up front on the wagon with her. "Hold on little flower," Ela said as she directed the wagon under a huge ornate archway. "Let's ride!"

The archway led to the cobble stone grounds that surrounded the Grand Citadel. For the first time Tisha realized that the Grand Citadel was surrounded by several smaller grounds like the pin for the gorda and the garden of white buds. All of the grounds that surrounded the Grand Citadel were enclosed by a hauntingly high wall. The wall separated the Grand Citadel from the rest of the city. The wagon then passed across a bridge that was over a moot that joined the grounds to the rest of the booming city-state.

"Acara City is the largest city on Acara. Over a million souls make their home inside and outside of its outer walls." Ela explained as she led the wagon through one of Acara City's many districts. Tisha was surprised at how normal the people looked to her as the wagon transversed the cobble stone streets. After some time, Ela came upon a dark domed building. She brought the wagon to a halt outside. Tisha looked up at the countless steps that led up to the door of the building in wonder. "This is the second largest building in Acara City. It is the temple of the Dark God." Ela explained as she climbed down from the seat in the wagon. Tisha hesitated for a moment then she did the same.

Slowly, the two climbed the stairs and passed through the ornate doors of the Grand Temple of the Dark God.

Tisha felt small as she stood among the pillars that held up the dome. The huge room was empty except for a huge black oblong block that sat in the center of the room. She stared at the main alter of the Dark God in wonder. It was made of the darkest stone she had ever seen. Though the stone alter was still it seemed to be vibrating with power. As Tisha stared at it, she felt her head get light and she got sick to her stomach. Going to church, Reverend Monroe and Reverend Royal had described evil to the congregation countlesstimes. Tisha had supposed evil existed but she had never felt it before, until now. Tisha immediately found herself covering her stomach with her hands, trying to shield her unborn child from this dark power.

As they stood in the empty room, several dark robed men appeared from the rear of the room. They did not look at Tisha and Ela as they formed several lines in front of the dark alter. They began to prayto it as she and Ela surveyed the chamber. The priests did not move as Ela led Tisha over to one side of the room. There was a large thing under a tarp on the side of the room. From the shape, Tisha knew immediately it was Wisdom's SUV, her weapon of choice in the battle against Quan.

"You are going to have to show me and the High Queen how to use that weapon." Ela said as she pointed at the tarp.

"It is not a weapon," Tisha tried to explain." It is like a wagon that moves without animals pulling it."

Ela squinted and wrinkled her brow, "You mean to tell me that my mate became the assassin cube to be bested by a wagon!"

"It is more complicated than that," Tisha snapped as she remembered using the SUV to pin Quan against the wall of the burning sanctuary of Gateway Baptist Church.

"When we meet with the High Queen I would choose my words well as you describe these complications," Ela snapped as she headed for the doors of the temple. Tisha followed her quickly as she looked over her shoulder at the main alter of the Dark God. The presence of the altar alone scared Tisha. Staring at it made Tisha sick. She was glad to leave this place.

Once they were outside, Tisha asked, "Do people practice any other religions here?"

"There was a time when that was so, "Ela said as she climbed back into the wagon," But with the rise of the High Queen Mora the worship of the Dark God has become the sole religion of Acara and her people." She explained.

"Where I come from people are allowed to practice many different religions," Tisha said as she climbed into the wagon.

"It is not the way of the Royal Guard to question any edicts of the High Queen. It is written that the Moritans are born to protect and serve the High Monarch." Ela explained as she brought the wagon back onto the cobblestone streets.

Tisha looked at Ela oddly as she thought about her last statement and many others she had made. She did not like the way the woman sounded. She made being a Moritan sound like being in a cult. It was beginning to sound like Jones Town on Earth. And she was definitely not going to drink the cool aid. As they moved through the different districts, Tisha found herself thinking of Royal. He was a not only a Christian, but an ordained minister. Tisha guessed that in addition to fighting his mother, he was going to have to fight a prescribed way of life. She wondered how he would be able to get a people conditioned to have one faith to become open to another way of living. Silently, she hoped that this Avatar that had appeared to him would give him the strength and direction he needed to make that kind of change.

They rode down the cobblestone streets for sometime until they reached a U shaped building. Once again, Ela got down from the wagon and Tisha followed.

"I see that you wear the heart stone," Ela explained.

"You mean this?" Tisha said as she pointed to the arrow around her neck.

"One and the same," Ela agreed. "I am sure that my Keyton is basking in every feeling that you are having as you venture here."

"It's not like with words. It is more like with feelings. Each time I touch it, I feel him and he feels me." Tisha said.

"That is ancient Crystal Keeper magic," Ela explained as she led Tisha through the doors of the U-shaped building. "This is the Crystal Hive the center of learning for Acara"

Tisha was stunned by what she saw. From the floor to the ceiling were rows of crystals of every color and size. There were men and women sitting at candle lit tables tending the crystals. Tisha took note of the ones that resembled the ones that looked like the ones that Quan had used to create the gateway that brought them to Acara. She made a mental note of where the Crystal Hive was in relation to the palace and she began to wonder if she could make it to these doors without being seen. Tisha sighed to herself. Even if she made it here, she would not know which crystals to use to get her back to Earth. There were rows and rows of everywhere. In addition, even if she was able to locate the gateway crystals she would not know how to use them. Silently, she wished that Reverend Monroe would have given them more of a lesson of his sacred craft.

"These crystals are not only used for transportation, healing, storage of knowledge and warfare." Ela explained. "Their major use is storing and documenting the collective history of the peoples of Acara."

"So more than creating gateways these crystals are like books." Tisha surmised.

"Exactly," Ela agreed, "Someday you will be allowed to come here and experience the true history of our world as it has been recorded by these crystals not in words but in images."

All Tisha could say was, "She was looking forward to it."

"Come little flower there is more for you to see, "Ela said as she led Tisha from the Crystal Hive.

After some time of riding, they reached the market square of Acara City. People parted to make room for the wagon as it passed numerous vendors.

"Wait here," Ela said as she climbed down from the wagon leaving Tisha alone to watch children playing in the street. Ela returned with two meat cakes and some fruit. She handed one to Tisha and they ate them under the awning of an empty vendor's station. In the distance, Tisha caught sight of a stage where several people were milling around.

"What is that for?" Tisha asked as she devoured her meat pie.

"That is the slaver's block," Ela explained." People buy and sell slaves there."

Tisha choked on her next bite. She was African American. Her ancestors had been enslaved by the European settlers of the Americas. She could not imagine how any culture could accept such a thing. She believed that if Royal did defeat his mother, this would be one of thethings that he would have to put a stop to immediately. As they sat there, Tisha watched in horror as several people were dragged across the stage and auctioned off to the highest bidder. At the very least, it did not seem that those conscripted to slavery were not just Black. They were all colors, ages, and sorts or beings One of the enslaved could have been no more than ten years old. As the young girl was being sold, she stared directly at Tisha. Tisha felt a sinking sensation in her stomach. She was truly powerless to do anything about it.

"What would you give me for this fine specimen?" the slave trader asked as he pushed the girl forward. The man locked eyes with Tisha as he went about his business. It made Tisha sick to see how much the man was enjoying his work. She almost threw up her lunch.

Seeing the effect the slave trade had on Tisha, Ela said, "I think we have seen enough of Acara City for one day,"

"Amen," Tisha felt like she was going to be sick, "Amen."

"However, before we return to the citadel there is one other thing I think you should see before we return." Ela said as she finished her meat pie.

"Great," Tisha sucked her teeth and sighed.

Ela brought the wagon around and guided it through the market square. Then Ela led the wagon through districts of mud and wood houses. The wagon reached the edge of the city and the huge wall that surrounded the entire city. Ela brought the wagon to the great gates of the city-state. Tisha looked at the huge doorway in awe. It was huge, ornate, and guided by complicated locks. Tisha watched as four guards slowly opened the doorway. The doors ran on a track as they opened it.

Ela led the wagon through the doorway. The cobblestone streets gave way to a winding dirt road that separated a lush green valley. Once on the road, Ela pushed the mounts from a walk to a run. Tisha held on to the side of the wagon as it trans-versed the countryside outside the gates of the city-state. The terrain quickly transformed from a fertile lush valley to a dry arid dirt plane. In the distance Tisha caught sight of three huge mountains that rose from the planes. As they got closer and closer to the mountains, Tisha could tell that the mountains were riddled with open caves that covered the front of all three mountains.

Ela stopped the wagon at the edge of the road that led to the narrow path that led to the mountains. There was a huge rock gateway at the edge of the path that led to the mountains. The gateway was covered with crystals and odd carvings. A wind came down off the mountains that whistled as it passed through the archway. As Tisha looked at the mountains and the archway, she had an odd feeling that she was looking at a holy place.

"This is the Valley of the High Monarchs," Ela explained." Since the time of the first High King all the monarchs of Acara are buried in the recesses of these mountains. One day the High Queen Mora will be laid to rest here and her son will assume the High Throne. It has been that way since the beginning of Acara's recorded time."

Tisha looked at the mountain tomb in awe. She found it hard to believe that generations of Royal's relatives were buried there. She knew that Royal once believed that his mother was dead. Now that he knew she was alive things were definitely different. Tisha wished that she could show Royal this place, so he would know where he came from and where he would finally be laid to rest.

"Only the High Queen Mora and Quan are allowed to venture past this point." Ela explained. "It is said that she is allowed to commune with the spirit of the dead High Queens and High Kings. It is rare that she comes here." Ela remarked." It is a place that she uses in dire consequences."

Looking up at the burial mound Tisha realized that it was not guarded. One thing she had definitely learned about Acara City was that it was well fortified. She found it hard to believe that such a sacred place would be left unguarded.

"Why are there no guards here?" she asked carefully.

Ela laughed as she reached down, picked up a hand full of sand, and let it run through her fingers. The sand seemed to glow as she touched it "The very ground and each burial mound is enchanted heavily to protect the remains of the fallen High Monarchs and their treasures. In all the time Acara has existed, no one has been able to pillage this sacred place."

"Have people tired? "Tisha asked. "I mean to rob the tombs."

"Yes they have, "Ela admitted." And their bones litter the walkway of this sacred place"

Looking up at the huge burial mound Tisha asked, "Why have you shown me this place?"

Ela smiled." You can be a Moritan and Royal Guard by birth or by being made into one. As the mother of the next generation of Moritans, it will be your responsibility to impart this knowledge unto your son. Besides, this is the place where the High Prince will find his history. It is important that both you and Keyton know this place."

Tisha nodded and rubbed at her stomach absently. She studied the huge tomb with both fear and admiration. It was hard for her to believe that Reverend Royal's ancestors were buried here. It was such a grand and ominous place. Royal was simple and understated. She had a hard time connecting him with the history of this place. She even had a hard time connecting the High Queen Mora with this place. She did not seem like she would require such a place for her final resting place.

Besides that, Tisha did not like the feeling the place gave her. Like the Grand Temple of the Dark God, there was something electric in the air in here. Though this was a place of death, things felt remarkably alive here. It sent a chill up Tisha's spine, made her blood run cold, and left her joints aching. Once again, Tisha found herself wondering what kind of place she had found herself and what it meant for the baby she carried. She knew that her unborn son would be a Moritan because that was what his father was. And she knew that Ela was doing everything in her power to seduce her into being a Moritan as well: cutting her hair, changing her clothes, giving her a gorda, and showing her around Acara like it was some kind of Disney Land. However, Tisha made a silent promise to herself that no matter what she would do her best to make sure that her unborn son held on to his humanity. Tisha never thought that being from Baltimore could be so valuable. However, facing all the things she had seen in Acara City today, she was learning to quickly value her heritage.

Seeing Tisha's discomfort Ela turned back toward the wagon. "Come little flower," Ela said as she led her back to the wagon." The suns are beginning to hang low in the sky. I think we have seen enough for today."

"Amen to that," Tisha mumbled to herself as she got back into the wagon. The two headed back to the walls of Acara City. Like before, Ela made the two mounts that held the wagon run. Tisha held onto the side to steady her as they passed through the countryside and back into the city-state limits. As they neared the capital of Acara, Tisha watched the huge Grand Citadel rise out of the city center in the distance. She sighed to herself. She had been happy to be out of the Citadel, if only for one day. However, she was not looking forward to returning to the silence and loneliness of her chambers. Though she was supposed to be able to tend her gorda now and have access to the garden of the moon buds, none of it made up for her not being home or her longing to see Simon and her family.

As they passed through the doors of the city, Tisha found herself reflecting on all she had seen that day. She prayed to herself that she would not have to raise her and Simon's baby in a place like this. She could not imagine bringing a child up in a world where there was slavery and they worshipped a Dark God. What kind of place was this?

By the candlelight's of the houses of Acara City, Ela led them back toward the Grand Citadel. As Tisha passed under the archway that led to the citadel's outer courts, she reminded herself to be nicer to her handmaidens since they were probably slaves as well. Ela brought the wagon back by the gorda pins and the two dismounted. Tisha thought that she was going back to her rooms, but Ela directed her back to a field adjacent to the gorda pin. There were towering Royal Guards fighting against one another using all manner of weapons. Tisha guessed it a training field of some kind

"Why have you brought me here?" Tisha asked.

"It is the role of every Royal Guard to protect members of the High Court," Ela explained. "That means each member of the Royal Guard has to have a weapon that they specialize in. You need one." Ela said.

"But I'm pregnant," Tisha protested.

"Yes you are," Ela agreed." That is why I want you to practice with a weapon that you can use to protect yourself and your unborn child from a distance."

"You have got to be kidding me," Tisha protested. This was too much to be believed.

"Do I look like I kid?" Ela snapped.

Ela led Tisha over to a table away from the other Royal Guards. It was filled with a host of hand held throwing weapons and a target stood several lengths away.

"I want you to practice using these tools every day, until you master them," Ela commanded. "You can use these tools, be pregnant, and still learn to protect yourself and your unborn child."

Tisha walked up to the table and let her hand run across the numerous throwing weapons For a second, she had the crazy thought to use these to fight her way out of here. She dismissed the thought immediately. She had never used a weapon before in her life. Besides, where would she go? The Crystal Hive? Even if she made it there, she would not know which crystals she could use to make a Gateway to get home. She lowered her head. She was trapped. All her hopes rested on Royal and Simon. The only way she would ever get home would be if they came for her.

Tisha ran her hand over the metal throwing tools. As she looked at the target, she imagined the face of the slaver she had seen earlier. She was filled with frustration at her current situation. It fueled her. Tisha picked up one of the tools slowly. Then she began throwing them at the target. Her first few shots missed totally. The cold metal vanished in the distance of the fading day and landed on the soil. Ela laughed out loud.

"You have to focus little flower," Ela said. "I know that you have more power in your upper body than that."

Tisha looked at Ela and sucked her teeth. In high school she had been and fair athlete. She was many things, but she was not weak. Tisha picked up one of the tools, looked at the target, and squinted. Then slowly, with much concentration, she began to hit the wooden target until it was covered with cold metal. Ela smiled to herself. She was surprised Tisha was turning out to be a natural born warrior. Perhaps Keyton had not chosen badly after all. Ela stopped Tisha from throwing the last of the throwing tools and guided her hand away from the table.

"You will have plenty of time to practice here," Ela said." Now I want you to rest. We still have one more stop to make before this day is over." Ela said as she looked up at the setting suns in the Acarian sky.

Tisha replaced the throwing tools back on the table and followed Ela back into the Grand Citadel. After a long day of touring Acara City, Tisha was glad to take dinner alone in her chambers. As she ate, she reminisced over the sights and sounds that had filled her day. Acara City was nothing like she had ever seen before. A part of it was very simply, but other parts of it appeared deadly. On top of that, Tisha noticed that there were troops everywhere. It was like the people of the city went about their daily lives under the threat of constant armed guards. The majority of it reminded her of something out of the middle ages.

However, there were several buildings that Tisha had seen that had astounded her. In particular, she remembered the Grand Temple of the Dark God that was as large as a sports stadium, the Raven's arena in Baltimore. Tisha remembered the fear the dark altar struck in her. There was something evil emanating from that oblong black block that truly scared her. Just being in the room with it made her blood run cold. Her hand absently covered her stomach as if she could shield her unborn child from the energy. She could not imagine what kind of being resided there and she did not care to meet it.

She also remembered the Crystal Hive of the crystal keepers and how it promised with any luck a way home. There were literally thousands of crystals there and the guard seemed to be particularly heavy there. Tisha did not know how, but she knew she had to unlock its secrets if she was ever going to go home. Tisha did not know how, but if she was ever going to unlock its secrets she was going to need help. Then there was the slaver's stand. As a Black woman it had disgusted her and left her livid. She was haunted by the look of one of the girls that was quickly wisped away in exchange for coin. It reminded her of how it must have been for her ancestors of Earth generations ago. If Royal was ever going to make this world civilized this part of the culture would definitely have to go. Lastly, there was the visit to the Valley of the High Monarchs. Memories of the space, sent chills up her spin. She had visited cemeteries before when her relatives had died, but she had never felt anything like that before. For as much as these Monarchs were supposed to be entombed they felt alive to her. At times, she felt like she could almost reach out and touch them. It had left her wigged out and wanting to run away.

Tisha remembered that the people of Acara City parted the wagon that carried her and Ela as they passed. Many people dropped their heads as they passed in both fear and reverence. Tisha recalled that there were troops everywhere that seemed to keep the business of the city flowing. Tisha could tell that between the Royal Guard and the other troops, the High Queen kept things in the capital city under her tight control. She wondered if the rest of the planet was that way as well.

After the tour, Tisha was led back to her chamber and left alone to eat. By herself, Tisha took some time to meditate on her arrowhead. She could feel Simon's presence instantly and she did not feel as alone as she was. After she ate she took some more time to meditate on Simon. It was nighttime now, and the three moons of Acara were sending light into her small chamber along with the candlelight.

As Tisha looked at the moons, she soon realized that she was not alone. She looked up from her empty plate half expecting to see one of her handmaidens or Ela. She was surprised to see a Royal Guard standing there. He was slightly smaller than Ela and Quan, but bore a striking resemblance to them. Looking at this young man, Tisha knew that he had to be related.

"Forgive the intrusion my lady," the man began as he bowed his head. "But I had to meet you." He said.

"Who are you?" Tisha asked.

"I am called Elric." He introduced. "I am the younger brother of Keyton. The one you know as Simon." He smiled.

Tisha smiled as she looked at him. She could tell he was around her age and he reminded her instantly of Simon. She could not put her finger on it, but there was something instantly likeable about him. Tisha felt an ease with him that she did not feel with Ela, his mother.

"My mother tells me that you carry my nephew in your womb," Elric announced.

"I am told that, "Tisha giggled.

"We have never had a Moritan that was not directly born from the tribe in generations. You will be the first," he explained.

"I don't know about all of that. All I know is that I am from Baltimore." Tisha joked.

"Bal-ti-more," Elric pronounced." I would very much like to hear about this place called Bal-ti-more where my brother grew up." It was a request not a commandment.

Tisha took an instant liking to Elric. It was nice to be talked to, not directed, or commanded. Besides, she would very much like get to know Simon's younger brother, her unborn son's uncle.

"Anytime," Tisha invited.

"Then I will come again, "Elric agreed." Especially, when my mother is not so thick on my heels." He said as he began to fade into the curtains.

Tisha sucked her teeth. She would have rather spent the evening talking to Elric about the Ravens and Druid Hill than another session with Ela. She sighed to herself. She guessed that was not to be. After a few minutes, Ela came back into her chambers. She was wearing a long black traveling cloak and had another one in her hands.

"You are to put this on," Ela said as she handed the other cloak to Tisha, "There is another place I must show you."

Tisha did not question Ela. She put on the traveling cloak. The two women made their way through the dark citadel and out back near the pin of the gorda. There was a young Royal Guard standing there holding the reins of both Rambien and Aspion. Ela mounted her Rambien with ease. Tisha was happy to see Aspion again. She rubbed at his forehead instinctively. He responded gladly to her touch and nuzzled close to her.

In spite of their closeness of him Tisha said, "You can't think that I am going to ride this thing."

Ela laughed as she brought Rambien around to face her. "I don't expect you to walk little flower. You have to learn to trust your gorda. There is no time like the present."

Tisha rolled her eyes at Ela and looked at Aspion with suspect. Then she summoned her courage, placed a foot in the stirrup, and threw her weight on top of her gorda. She was surprised that she felt comfortable in the saddle. However she still held onto the reins tightly for dear life. Silently, she said a prayer that she would not fall off the horned beast and break her neck or lose her baby.

-I will not let you fall, Aspion whispered to Tisha's shock somewhere in the recesses of her mind.

"I can hear you!" Tisha thought with a flushed face.

-I was born for you," Aspion assured as he walked up next to Rambien.

"Born for me?' Tisha questioned.

-ll will be made right in time," Aspion assured her as his voice faded and left her with the first true feeling of hope she had gotten since arriving on Acara.

Looking at Tisha, Ela could tell that Aspion was communicating with her. She found herself wondering what the odd gorda was telling the off-worlder.

"Let's ride," Ela said as she led Tisha under the archway of the Grand Citadel again for the second time that day. The two rode through the night along the darkened streets of Acara City. Ela led Tisha to the wall that surrounded the city and through the giant doorway. Once they had passed through the doorway, the two riders led their gorda across the open planes until they reached a forest. Ela slowed her gorda down as they came to the thickest part of the trees. Ela stopped her Rambien and Tisha managed to do the same with Aspion. Silently, the two passed through the trees into the mouth of an open cave that lay hidden among the tangled growth.

"Why are we here?" Tisha asked.

"It is time I must show you one of the greatest secrets of the Moritans." Ela explained.

Ela led Tisha down into the darkened tunnel. She picked up a torch, whispered a word to it, and it burst into flames. Ela led Tisha down the tunnel along time until they reached a silent pool of water that was surrounded by seven large statues.

"Those are the visages of the first Moritans. The first Moritans that were chosen to watch over the High King and members of the High Court. Since their time, every Moritan child is brought here to swim under the eyes of our forefathers and receive the mark of the member of the High Court they are supposed to watch over. When I saw your gorda today, I knew I had to bring you here for the birthing. Aspion's external bones show that he is marked for war, now it is time for us to see who you will be fighting for." Ela explained.

"But I am not a Moritan child," Tisha protested as she remembered the markings on the faces of all of the Moritans she had seen.

"But you are carrying a Moritan child and you are promised to the son of the king of the Moritans." Ela explained. "You are carrying the one that is supposed to be the heir of the Moritans. That makes this ritual even more important for you." Ela explained. "I want you to swim through the water to the other side of the pool and back." Ela paused. "Undress and immerse yourself into the water." Ela directed.

Tisha looked at the pool and squinted. She was unsure about this. But looking at Ela she felt like she had no choice. Tisha sighed. Tisha slowly peeled out of her armament and stood at the edge of the pool. The water tickled her toes. She was surprised at how warm the water was. Then without thinking, she waded into the water and began to swim the length of the pool. Tisha had always been a good swimmer. She had learned to swim at summer camp at the local YMCA in Baltimore. However, she found it hard to move through this pool. The water was thicker than any water she had ever been in before. As she moved through the pool, she felt a burning sensation on the side of her face. Tisha swam the length of the pool, touched the wall on the other side, and made her way back to the edge of the pool. Tisha got out of the water and looked at her reflection in the water. Like the rest of the Moritans, she had a mark on the right side of her face. However, the one that she wore was different than any of the others she had seen.

Ela looked at Tisha and her mouth dropped. Tisha wore the marking of the High Prince Von. Ela had seen it many times in her travels throughout the Grand Citadel. It was even on the side of the High Prince's rocker that lay still and dusty in the High Queen's quarters.

Most of the Moritans wore the general symbol of the house of the High Queen Mora. It was only Quan that wore the sign as her personal protector. They all knew that Keyton or Simon was the personal protector of the High Prince. It was unheard of for another Moritan to bear the same sign. However, Tisha wore it prominently. It could only mean a conflict of epic proportions was clearly coming that would split the fiercely loyal Moritans apart.

"What is it that you see?" Tisha asked as she pulled on her armor. She felt horribly fatigued after her swim.

"The future dear girl, "Ela said," The future."

# Chapter 6

The funerals were over. It was time to rebuild and time to look forward.

Reverend Monroe sat silently in his office in the rectory. It still smelled of smoke from the fire in the sanctuary. Though the sanctuary had been a complete loss, the rectory still stood strong. In front of him, on his desk, was a single oval crystal. He picked it up and held it in his hands. An image of Royal appeared in the crystal as he cradled it. Tears came to the old crystal keeper's eyes as he looked at his lost son. He felt as if he had failed him. Yes, he had been able to create the gateway that allowed Royal and the others to escape to Acara, but he was not at his side to advise and to protect him. Although he knew he was not Royal's real father, he had raised him and he felt like Royal was his real son. Lethia was gone as well. He hated to admit it to himself, but he had grown fond of her surly nature over the years and he looked to her for guidance. He even missed her constantly saying that she was going to snap his neck. These were the memories that made them a unique family of sorts.

Reverend Monroe got up from his desk and went over to his bookshelf. He opened a secret compartment and brought out a bag of crystals. He laid them all out on his desk before him. He had not decided which of these gems he was going to part with, but he knew that all he had to do was to sell one to rebuild the church. Gateway Baptist would rise from the ashes bigger and better than it was before. He promised himself that. He may not have Royal's power anymore to fuel his sermons, but he would give the people of Baltimore a true cathedral within which to worship. It was the least he could do for the sacrifices that Wisdom, Tisha, and Hue were making in their journey to Acara.

Carefully, he picked up a long, clear crystal and held it to his forehead. This was the crystal that held the information he had used to build the first Gateway Baptist Church. It contained the history of a traveler who had come to Earth and been captivated by its temples of worship. Reverend Monroe never knew who the traveler was, but he had left a load of images of churches to choose from. As Reverend Monroe surveyed the images, he got a nagging feeling that he was missing something. Again and again he went over the images of the churches he saw. Then, when he came to the last one, he almost dropped the crystal he was holding. The final image was of a priest standing in front of an altar. The priest had two elongated crystals in his hands. They were gateway crystals, he was sure of it. Seeing this image his heart began to race franticly and he almost dropped the precious device. Now all he had to do was find this priest, obtain the crystals, and he could make a gateway home. Reverend Monroe's hands began to sweat with this realization. It seemed like who ever this traveler was, he had left an extra set of gateway crystals with a minister for safe keeping.

Reverend Monroe locked the image of the man in place and rose from his desk. He left his office and climbed the stairs of the rectory still smelled of charred wood and twisted metal. He went up to the room that had been Grace Monroe's and knocked on the door. He did not get an answer. He was so filled with excitement he pushed the door open and entered the room. It appeared empty with all of Grace's meager possessions still in order, as she had left them. Her warping crystal was still by her bedside, but the closet door was slightly ajar. Reverend Monroe knew that Simon was in her war room practicing. Since the others had gone to Acara, Simon had spent all of his time there practicing. Reverend Monroe had tried to get Simon to talk about what he was feeling, but to no avail. The same way Simon had left him to his crystals, he had left Simon to his swords.

Reverend Monroe went over to the closet and pushed past Grace's clothes. He opened the door to the war room to find Simon there.

Simon was sitting on the floor holding onto the arrow that he wore. He had a long curved blade resting on his lap. The only times that Simon felt alive these days were when he was practicing his swordsmanship or holding on to the crystal arrow that connected him to his lost love, Tisha. Reverend Monroe looked at Simon sadly; for as badly as he was feeling, he could not imagine what Simon was going through. His soul was bonded to both Royal and Tisha and both had been taken away from him. More than his silence, he had to be in unspeakable pain. However, it was a pain that he now believed he could relieve.

"Simon!" Reverend Monroe called as he came into the war room.

Simon looked up from his meditation at the Reverend and then looked away. At that moment, he lost in the intimacy he shared with Tisha and he did not want to be distracted. He did not like all that he was feeling from her. The images were coming in too quickly at times for him to process. However, he was getting the gist of what Tisha was going through. Beyond the sites of Acara City that were being sent to him, he was learning a lot about being a Moritan. Through their connection, he had learned more about being a Moritan than Grace had ever taught him. On top of that, he had learned that Tisha was carrying his male child. More than anything else this truth was overwhelming him. He desperately wanted to talk to someone about it but Grace had always been his confidant.

Then there was Royal to consider. He was his Royal Guard. It was his job to protect Royal with his life and be his confidant. He felt that he had failed him. Yes, he had been able to protect him from the assassin cube but he had failed to make the journey with him to Acara. He had made a pact with Wisdom to be his second if he failed to be there for Royal. It seemed like a good idea at the time; especially when he was facing his father, Quan, as the assassin cube. But now, he found himself second-guessing his decision. How could he have thought that a common drug dealer could take on the holy task of being the Royal Guard to the High Prince of Acara? Simon shook his head and looked up at the elder Reverend.

"What is it, old man?" Simon asked as he reluctantly released the crystal he was cradling in his hands.

Reverend Monroe came over to Simon holding the oblong crystal in his hand that he had been gazing into in his office.

"Look at this," Reverend Monroe insisted.

"I do not have time for your crystals right now," Simon snapped as he came to his feet, "unless they have found a way for us to get to Acara.".

Reverend Monroe smiled in spite of himself. "That is just it. I think I have found what we need to make a gateway to Acara," he announced proudly.

"Do not toy with me, old man," Simon warned.

"I was looking for designs in my archives for a new church and something caught my eye. The priest in this last image is holding two gateway crystals. If we find him, I can use the archway under the church to make us a way home," Reverend Monroe explained.

Simon's mouth dropped. He went over to the elder man and took the crystal from him. He held it to his forehead. And sure enough, Reverend Monroe was right. The priest standing in front of the church was holding two gateway crystals. Simon almost dropped the crystal with excitement. Reverend Monroe reached up and steadied his hand.

"Do you know what this means?" Reverend Monroe asked.

"We can go home now," Simon said as his hand brushed happily against his own crystal arrowhead. He was surprised that he was referring to Acara as home. Though he had never seen it before, the fact that both Royal and Tisha were there was redefining it for him.

"Now let's not put the cart before the horse," Reverend Monroe warned. "We still have to find this church, this priest, and the crystals. Looking at the church, it is none I recognize from Baltimore."

"This is when we have to use the tools we have at hand to aid us. Purcell is a police officer. He has excellent deductive skills. I am sure if you showed him the image, he might be able to figure out where the church is and who the priest is as well," Simon suggested.

"I am sure you are right," Reverend Monroe smiled as he turned to leave, "I will call him immediately."

Simon raised his sword over his head for what felt like the millionth time. Slowly, Simon went through a warrior's form again. He moved through Grace's war room swiftly. As he moved through the room, he felt the blue arrow he wore tingle. It was Tisha. He was sure of it. He knew she was alive and she was thinking about him. Simon dropped his sword. He fell to his knees and took the arrow in his hand. He concentrated with all of his might on her and sent his love out into the universe toward her. Where as before he could only project hopelessness, he now found himself projecting hope.

As he had done each day since the mass funeral, Purcell Sims brought his police cruiser over to Patterson Park. He stopped on one of its tree-lined streets and surveyed the houses. His Sergeant had suggested that he take off more time since the death of his brother, but he had declined the offer. The job gave him something to do and he was tired of sitting in his house mourning a brother that was not really dead. He got out of his car and approached the Williams' residence. Laura Williams, Tisha's mother, opened the door before he knocked. As always, the elder woman fell comfortably into his arms and invited him inside the house. Purcell stepped into the living room which had been transformed into a paradise of toys and playthings for Little Wisdom. Purcell knew that keeping Little Wisdom busy was the only way that his grandparents could prevent him from asking about his absent mother, Tisha.

"Hey, little man!," Purcell said as he picked him up and cradled him in his arms.

"Uncle," Little Wisdom tried to say as he rubbed at his shiny shield.

Ms. Laura stood at the head of the steps shaking her head, with tears in her eyes, as she watched Purcell with Little Wisdom. Since the "death" of her only daughter, Tisha, she had hardly slept. She had taken to pacing the house into the early hours of the morning and drinking too much coffee. Her husband, Tyler, had found it impossible to comfort his wife. He took solace on the road between hauls as a trucker. Oddly enough, Ms. Laura only found comfort when Purcell visited. There was something about having him in the house that quelled her grief and reminded her of her lost daughter.

"I swear to God I don't know what I would do without you and your grandmother," Laura complimented. "Tyler had to go back out on the road. I don't know how he is managing to stay focused. Lord knows I'm glad I'm a nurse. I told them I wasn't coming back till I was good and ready. And I still ain't felt none too ready, "she admitted.

"I know how you feel. It is times like this that you have to rely on family. We are all we got, "Purcell said as he placed Little Wisdom back on the floor with his toys.

"You hungry?" Ms. Laura asked. "I got enough food in here to feed a fleet. "People really have supported us through this tragedy," she said, shaking her head.

"No, thank you," Purcell said. "I had a break and I just wanted to check in on the two of you," he admitted.

"Just holding on," Ms. Laura admitted as tears welled up in her eyes. "Just holding on."

"Well, I am here if you need anything. Do not hesitate to call me, day or night." Purcell offered.

Ms. Laura wrapped herself around Purcell again and pulled on his strength.

"Thank you for that, ya hear? And the same thing goes for you," she said.

"I know," Purcell said as he walked toward the front door.

Ms. Laura picked up Little Wisdom and they waved goodbye to his big uncle. Purcell got back in his police cruiser and he drove away. He was angry. He hated to see what this situation was putting the people he loved through. It was hard enough burying empty caskets and putting up headstones when he knew that folks were still alive. Yet they had no choice. In the absence of the others, there was nothing else they could do. Just then, his cell phone rang. He recognized the number immediately. It was the phone number to Gateway Baptist Church. He pulled the police cruiser over and opened his phone. He answered after the third ring.

"Yeah?" Purcell answered.

"It is me, Arkon. Reverend Monroe."

Purcell could tell that there was excitement in the man's voice.

"What is it?" he asked.

"I may have found a way to get us to Acara," he said bluntly.

Purcell almost dropped the phone. He was astonished.

"How?" he asked.

"It is too complicated to explain over the phone. Can you come to the rectory this evening, say around 6:00 pm, and I will give you all the details?" The pastor asked.

"I'll be there," Purcell assured as he aimed his cruiser back toward Patterson Park.

Ben Lee stood in the kitchen of his Shirley Avenue home. He was dressed in his bus driver's uniform and he stood at the sink. On the side of sink were countless half-filled bottles of bourbon and other miscellaneous alcohol bottles. One by one he poured them down the drain. While the loss of his wife had driven him to drink, it was the absence of Hue - his son - that was making him sober. Ever since the night he found out that Hue was actually not hurt and on another planet, he had not been able to touch any alcohol. He needed to have all of his wits about him if he was going to figure out a way to get his son back. His decision to stop drinking had even brought his daughter back home. Ben did not know what he would have done if Sapphire had not moved back to their family dwelling from Morgan University where she was in school. Soon after the funeral, the walls had been closing in on him.

Sapphire sat at the kitchen table watching her father complete the ritual of emptying the bottles.

"Dad, you don't have to do that for me, you know. I will still live here," she promised.

"Cupcake, I'm doing this for me and your brother. Maybe if I were sober, things between us could have been different and none of this would have happened," he said grimly as he emptied the last bottle.

Sapphire got up from the table where she was sitting. She was a slight thing with dark eyes and long hair. She was dressed in a pair of tights and a sweatshirt from her University, Morgan State. She looked more like her long lost mother, Sylvia, than her father or Hue. She hugged her father from behind and held him gently. It had been a long time since she had been home. She left after the death of her mother. However, the death of Hue, her younger brother, had brought her running back to her roots.

She had been surprised by her father's reaction when she returned home. When her mother died, her father had been totally desolate. He was unable to function after the death of her and Hue's mother. Sapphire had had to hold things together. With Hue, however, her father was totally driven. It was more like he was going through the motions of grieving than truly grieving. She tried to talk to him about his behavior, but he shut her out. Sapphire was secretly committed to finding out the secrets that she believed her father knew about her brother's empty coffin. Then, on top of that, she was grieving over the loss of her childhood friend, Tisha. They had not been close in recent years but Sapphire still considered her a dear friend. There were pictures of them as children that still adorned the mirror in her upstairs bedroom. She had not gotten the energy to go see Little Wisdom yet. She thought it would be too much for her.

"I can't believe they are all gone; Mommy, Hue, and Tisha. It does not seem real or fair," Sapphire said leadingly.

"It really doesn't," he said biting his tongue about all he knew about the gateway and Acara. He hated keeping secrets from her, but there was no other way.

"Are you going to be okay going cold turkey?" Sapphire asked frankly.

"I've got through it once before. I'll do it once again," he said as he kissed Sapphire on the top of the head.

Just then, the phone rang. Sapphire got to it first. She called for her father.

"Who is it?" he asked.

"He said his name is Officer Purcell."

Ben took the phone immediately. He said very little and took in the entire conversation. The last thing he said was that he would sure be there, too.

"What is it, Dad?" Sapphire asked suspiciously.

"It's a meeting at the church that I need to go to. You don't have to worry about a thing. I will be right back," he assured her as he went to the foyer to get his jacket. Sapphire watched her father leave. She came out on to the steps of their home, sat down, and held her legs. She rocked back and forth. She hated being alone in the house. It held too many memories.

At dusk, the men arrived at the rectory. Purcell was the first to come into the Pastor's study. He joined Reverend Monroe and Simon. To their surprise, Ben Lee came knocking at the door next. Simon and Reverend Monroe looked at each other knowingly. The reason the Monroe's had not called him was because of his drinking. However, as he stood there in his bus driver's uniform, they could tell he was clean and sober. He joined the others in the Pastor's study gladly.

"Now how do we get them back?" Ben asked as he sank into a comfortable chair.

"It's not that we get them back, but we go get them," Reverend Monroe explained. "I was going through the crystals looking for ideas for the new church. When I got to the last image, I realized the priest outside of a church was holding two powerful gateway crystals. It is a long shot that he may still have them after all this time, but it is at least a plan."

"Okay," Purcell said as he began to pace the room. "Where is this priest?"

"That is where you come in. I don't recognize the priest or the church. I thought maybe if I showed it to you, you could figure it out." He \tried.

"I'm game," Purcell said.

Reverend Monroe handed the elongated crystal to Purcell. Purcell held it up to his forehead and he felt a tingle. Then his consciousness shifted into the image in the crystal. More than seeing the image, he was inside of the image. Purcell noticed immediately that the clergy person was not a minister at all but a Catholic priest. He could tell from the vestments. Sure that the man was a Catholic, Purcell began to look at the iconography of the church. The Father was standing in front of an altar in a Catholic church that was adorned with images of the Sacred Heart of Jesus Christ. As Purcell studied the images, he realized the man was not white but Latino. Adjusting his vision to see all that the image contained, he glimpsed a sign with the numbers "115" on it outside of a window of the church. By the color and shape of the sign, Purcell knew the church had to be in New York City.

"I think this church is in New York, perhaps in Spanish Harlem or the South Bronx. The man in the image is not a minister at all. He is a Catholic priest and I think the church may have something to do with the Sacred Heart. I'd stake my badge on it," Purcell assured.

"Then we have a destination," Ben said, gladly.

"But Reverend Monroe, those crystals are years old," Simon said. "How do we know that priest is still there?"

"We don't, but at least we have a destination," Reverend Monroe said. "We have taken so much from you all. We would not dare ask you to do any more."

"Try leaving us behind," Purcell said. "I want my brother back as well as Hue and Tisha. Plus, I got a score to settle with Quan and that damn High Queen, too. You don't come into my city and my kidnap folk, yah know. I have worked too hard to keep all of us safe."

Reverend Monroe smiled to himself. He had grown fond of Earthlings in his time among them. These were proving to be the best he ever met.

"Then we leave at dawn. We'll take the church van," Reverend Monroe said as he dismissed the meeting.

"And my only condition with that is that I drive the van." Ben said. "I can drive anything." he said boldly.

"No arguments from me," Reverend Monroe agreed. "None at all."

"Me, neither," Simon said. "Me, neither."

After the meeting was over, Purcell was about to leave. He had to tell his sergeant that he was going to take some immediate family leave. He was about to leave the Rectory when he caught Simon on the stairs. Simon gave him the eye, so Purcell followed him up the stairs to Grace's room and into Grace's her old war room. For a second, the two stood among the weapons in silence looking at one another oddly. Then Simon took off his warping crystal and stood full-bodied at his almost seven feet. Purcell could not believe how big he really was. He felt small before him. He found himself stepping back unconsciously.

"I just need someone to talk to," he admitted as tears brimmed in his eyes. "I am getting overwhelmed by images of Tisha on Acara and thoughts of Royal."

"Are they both safe?" Purcell asked quickly.

"For now, I am sure they are. They are both doing better than we could have imagined. But that could change at any time," Simon said nervously. "And being here, there is nothing I can do about it. My connection to them is making me crazy! I am afraid it is throwing me off balance and I could be a liability in battle."

"I have seen you in battle Simon. I doubt that anything could throw you off especially thoughts about those you love and care about," Purcell assured him.

"I have to be honest with you, my friend. There is a new development that I have not told anyone about yet."

"And what is that?" Purcell asked. He was scared of what it could be. He shook his head. After finding out about the true nature of the "Monroes" and fighting the assassin cube, nothing could surprise him.

"Tisha is pregnant," Simon admitted. "I can feel my son growing inside of her."

Purcell was shocked. He did not know what to say. He wanted to be happy for Simon and Tisha, but this was the worst possible time for such a development. On top of that, he had no idea what Simon really was and how his DNA would combine with human DNA. He shook his head as he wondered what kind of child it would be. The thought conjured up visions from Sci-fi movies of babies with multiple heads or Jurassic Park-like entities. He tried to dismiss the thoughts and looked at Simon with a smile.

"My God," Purcell said. "I mean congratulations! Are you scared for them?"

"It seems the Dark Queen has taken particular interest in my unborn child." Simon explained. "I have surmised that much. I really do not know if that is a good or a bad thing. It scares me though," he confessed.

"I can't imagine." Purcell shook his head as his eyes drifted to the weapons on the wall. It seems that Little Wisdom, his nephew, was going to have a little brother. And on top of that, his little brother was going to be at least half-human and half-Moritan. Purcell shook his head. He was having trouble wrapping his head around all of this. They had several incredible tasks ahead. They had to rescue his brother Wisdom, Hue, and Tisha from Acara. They had to find a way to get Simon and Arkon to Acara. They also were supposed to help Royal take the throne from his evil mother. On top of that, they now had to protect Simon's unborn child. To Purcell, it seemed like a laundry list of impossible tasks. Purcell found himself wondering how he had gotten himself into all of this.

"I did not mean to burden you, my friend," Simon admitted. "I just needed to share it with someone."

"I don't mind," Purcell said as he reached out and took Simon's large hand. "We are all in this together."

Purcell shook his head as he watched Simon pick up one of the weapons and begin to go through a meticulous ancient kata. Purcell knew one thing. If they were going to survive this they would have to rely on each other in the same way they relied on one another to defeat the assassin cube. He guessed that what they lacked in individually they made up for as a group. As Purcell felt the weight of the long, clear crystal that Reverend Monroe had given him to study, he knew what he had to do. He turned to leave Simon to his practicing and headed for the one place where he could always feel comfort.

Ms. Loretta Sims had just finished fighting with the twins in the bath and got them down to bed, when there was a wrap at her front door. She checked the clock. It was after 10:00 pm. She had no idea who would be coming by her house at this hour. Carefully, she approached the door and looked through the peep whole. She was surprised to see Purcell, her grandson, standing there on her porch in his starched uniform. She opened the door immediately.

"Boy, you okay?" she asked as she invited him in.

"I'm more than okay. Sorry for stopping by at such a late hour, but I need a favor from you."

"You know what I got you got." She meant it.

"I have to go on an undercover mission for a few days so I won't be around for you and the boys," he lied.

Ms. Loretta looked at Purcell squarely in the eye. She could tell that there was more to what he was saying than his words betrayed. Ever since he was a boy, he could not lie to her.

"Well, boy, I will hold you up in prayer and I know the Good Lord will bring you back to me unharmed," she insisted. Ms. Loretta began to say a silent prayer. She had just lost Wisdom. She was in no space to forfeit another loved one.

Purcell smiled, "While I'm gone I want you to hold this for me," he said as he handed her his badge. Ms. Loretta really didn't like this, but she took the shield from his quivering fingers.

"Why you leaving your badge with me?" she asked as she looked down at the police shield.

"I'm leaving it with you for luck," Purcell said.

Ms. Loretta wrinkled her brow as she felt the weight of the shield in her hand. She did not know what to make of Purcell's behavior. It did not make any sense. However, none of what was happening lately made any sense to her.

"I'm gonna wear it around my neck with my lucky cross close to my heart till you come back for hear? And you will be coming back for it," she stressed.

"And if things go the way I want, I may be bringing home a miracle," Purcell smiled as he kissed her on the forehead.

"What do you mean?" Ms. Loretta questioned. Her faith was strong and she believed in miracles. One right now would surely brighten her day. Ms. Loretta looked at her grandson funny.

"Now you hold on," she said as she vanished into the kitchen. She came back with a thick envelop filled with money.

"I can't take this," Purcell protested.

"All God's children need traveling shoes. And these days, shoes ain't cheap. Besides, your brother done took real good care of these old bones. And I have a feeling that whatever you doin', it ain't gonna come cheap. Sometimes miracles cost a penny or two!"

The two shared a nervous laugh. Purcell had no idea where this leg of the adventure was going to take him and his small band of heroes. He hadn't thought about the cost of things, but this way, things would be covered. Purcell shook his head. Even after all these years, his grandmother was still taking care of him. He said a silent prayer to himself. He was going to bring Wisdom and the others back home to her no matter what the cost.

"Okay," Purcell said as he took the thick envelope. He hugged his grandmother and turned to leave.

"Do me one favor," she asked as he opened the front door.

"What? "Purcell asked.

"You come back alive, ya hear?" Ms. Loretta insisted. "Alive."

"I'll do my best, Grandma. I'll do my best," Purcell said as he vanished into the night, leaving Ms. Loretta alone with her prayers.

# Chapter 7

With his senses to guide him, Tori continued to drag wet logs down to the shore of the Lost Island he inhabited. He lined them up one by one and used thick seaweed to bind them together. Peku stood off in the distance eating sweet fruit and sucking his teeth. As Tori worked Peku was good for an occasional joke at his friend.

"What are you doing?" Peku asked.

"I'm building a raft," Tori said for what felt like the hundredth time. "I am sure that the High Prince is here on the Lost Islands. I can feel him."

"Are you sure that is not just gas or have you been in the suns for too long? Peku quipped.

"My little friend I am as sure of it as I am my own name and I am also sure that I need to find him before anyone else does," Tori continued.

"Oh yes," Peku said sarcastically. "Why don't you just leave those people alone? It already cost you your eyes and your sight. Next time they may take your balls!" he scolded.

"Peku, I cannot expect you to understand, but this is some thing that I must do." Tori said finally.

Peku thought for a moment, then sighed. He walked over to the raft and used his small fingers to tighten the bindings between the logs. The two worked in silence for the greater part of the day until the raft was complete.

"Now what do we do?" Peku asked. "The Lost Islands number in the hundreds! How are we supposed to find him?"

Tori smiled. "We ask for a little help."

Tori waded into the water until it was knee high. Then he began to sing a melodious song. It was odd to Peku's ears, but he wss surprised to see effect on the water. Suddenly, a man with a crown rose from the waves right in front of Tori. The man was made totally of water. Peku knew who it was immediately: Carolyn, King of the Sylphs. Peku and Tori bowed their heads to the monarch of the Sea and Water Elementals.

"Well met, Tori," the king bellowed in a voice that filled the beach.

"Well met, your Highness," Tori replied, shivering before the King's waterspout.

"Why is it that you summon me?" he asked bluntly.

"I believe that the High Prince of Acara has come here to these Lost Islands and I have valuable information to give him. I am a man without eyes, but I still know things and see more," he said humbly.

The King looked at Tori thoughtfully and read his intentions well.

"Then bring your raft to the water and my children will carry you to the High Prince," the Sylph King commanded.

"Much thanks, your Highness," Tori said as he stumbled back over to his raft and began to pull it toward the water. The struggle was not as great because Peku joined in and led him from the shore into the waves.

"Peku, I cannot ask you to come!" Tori cried. "Who knows what dangers we will face?"

"Fiddly doo," Peku said as the raft reached the water. "I am as good as your eyes and handy with a knife. Where Tori goes, so do Peku!" he insisted.

The two climbed onto the raft as the Sylph's image sank back into the water. All around the raft they could see small Sylphs pushing them forward. After being permanently exiled to the Lost Islands by the High Queen, Tori felt that it would these actions that might set him free.

Under the watchful eye of Maximus, Hue and Royal played in the sand and swam in the veins. It was a welcome relief for them as they waited for Wisdom and Lethia to return. Hue found himself growing more and more fond of his friend as they splashed water on one another and ran along the beach. For Royal, it was like a vacation from all he had gone through with the assassin cube. Though he still held some guilt about bringing Hue to Acara, it did feel good to have a friend alongside him.

"The water here is so sweet," Hue remarked as he fell upon the beach.

"It is, isn't it?" Royal agreed. "I have never been in water so warm and so rich. This is better than the Caribbean."

"I still have a hard time believing that I am on another planet," Hue admitted.

"Me too," Royal agreed, "But those two suns make it hard not to believe it."

As the two young men sat talking, Maximus made his way down to the shoreline and settled behind them. They laid their wet heads on his fur and used him to dry off. Royal was still having a hard time believing that Maximus was his old boxer that once lay at the foot of his bed, but seeing Maximus in this form he felt safe. Hue and Royal dozed off on the beach listening to the waves. It was Maximus who first caught sight of the small raft coming toward them.

"Up," he growled. "Up!" he repeated as he shook the boys awake.

"What is it?" Hue asked as he wiped the sleep from his eyes.

"Maximus, is everything okay?" Royal asked as he felt the fire begin to boil inside of him protectively.

Maximus came to his feet. He used his great paw to point at the raft that was coming directly towards them.

"You two go back into the trees," he commanded, "while I see what they want."

Without questioning him, Hue and Royal ran up the beach into the trees. Royal's hands began to glow with fire. Hue fished the gun that Wisdom had given him out of his shorts and they watched as the raft made its way toward Maximus. They watched as a tall, greyish man pulled the raft to shore as his small companion bounced around in the water. They met Maximus on the edge of the veins and engaged him in conversation.

"Too bad your powers don't include super hearing," Hue said, nervously trying to adjust to the feeling of the small gun in his hand.

"I wish it did, too," Royal agreed as he watched the two interlopers confer with Maximus.

After sometime, the two newcomers settled on the beach. Maximus rose and went into the bushes where Hue and Royal were hiding.

"You can come out now," Maximus said as he called toward the trees where Royal and Hue were hiding. "The old man and his pet are no danger to you. I could swat them both with a wave of my hand," he said proudly.

Royal came to his feet. His hands were still glowing. Carefully, he came out of the bushes and let Maximus lead him down the beach toward the strangers. Hue followed them uselessly trying to look over Maximus' massive shoulder.

"He is here! He is here!" Peku said as he jumped up and down and danced in a circle.

Tori used his walking stick to get to his feet. He could feel the small group getting closer. Once they were upon him, he fell to his knees and bowed. Royal looked at the man oddly. He had never had anyone bow to him before. He turned to Maximus and asked him to tell the man to get to his feet. Maximus slowly pulled Tori from his knees. He was trembling. He sat cross-legged in front of Royal. Royal sat down in front of him and did the same with his legs. With one withered finger, he touched Royal's forehead, then his own, as well as Peku's tender brow.

"I never spoke another language before," Peku said as he danced some more uttering his first words in English. "I'm smart!"

"Easy, Peku," Tori said as he tried his English on. "Or we mays care our new friends."

"Okay," Peku said as he curled up close next to Tori.

Tori reached out and ran his hands over Royal's face. He let his fingers linger there for a long time. He wanted to make sure he was indeed in the presence of the High Prince. Once he was sure of it, he exhaled and tears formed in his eyes.

"Your Highness, you have to forgive an old man's insanities," Tori began," It was because I could not find you that my eyes were taken from me." Tori explained.

"Are you serious?" Royal said with disbelief and wide eyes.

"Quite," Tori agreed. "I was the High Oracle to the High Queen Mora. I was the person she came to in all things magical. When she realized that because of her worship of the Dark God she could not bear any other fruit, it became my sole mission to find you. And once I proved that I could not, she took my eyes from me and exiled me here to die alone," he explained.

Royal was horrified. He hated the idea of another person suffering because of who and what he really was.

"But he was not alone," Peku chimed in. "He found me!"

"Yes, my dear Peku," Tori laughed. "If not for your constant companionship, I do not think I would have survived to this day."

"I am truly sorry," Royal said earnestly.

"It is not your fault," Tori corrected. "You were a child when you were taken and by my count you are barely a man now. I am just glad I have survived all these years to be in your presence," he said reverently.

"You mentioned to Maximus that you know who my true father is?" Royal asked carefully. I *must* know."

"Yes I do," Tori assured, "and if you can spare an old man a bit to eat, I will gladly tell you the story of the last priest of the Avatar."

"Not a problem," Hue said. "We have plenty."

Hue and Royal helped Tori to his feet. They led him back through the trees to their camp. They made sandwiches for him and the Opion. Everyone ate in silence as they enjoyed the new company. Hue and Maximus went into the woods to get fuel for a fire as day turned to evening. As they built the fire, Tori sat off by himself meditating, as if he were gathering facts. Once the fire was at full height, Tori moved close to it and called everyone near.

"What I know," he began as he cleared his throat," is because I bore witness to these things and I was given the rest of the details through my fore-sight. It was less than twenty cycles ago that there was a Great Reckoning. Your mother was in the process of killing all the priests of the Avatar and turning Acara into a world that was dedicated solely to the Dark God. Though many of us were against such a thing, there was no one powerful enough in the High Court or in the ranks of the Avatar to stand against her. Blood covered the streets of most of the City-States of Acara as the priests of the Avatar fell one by one. Little did she know that in the most holy place of the Avatar, it most senior priest hadmade a pact with the Avatar. He would shed his red robe and appear to be a noble from afar and seduce the High Queen. While his brothers died across Acara, this man came to Acara City with eyes the color of amethyst. He instantly found favor at the High Court. And though your mother tried her best to resist him, he soon became her lover and a Royal Heir was conceived," Tori explained.

"What happened to him?" Royal asked hurriedly

"Once you were conceived, he vanished. It is rumored that he went to the place where the priests of the Avatar have their most holy shire, the Red Desert. If he still lives, it is there you will find him," Tori continued.

Royal immediately remembered the red robed man from his dreams and the way the man said he was waiting for him. In that moment, Royal knew where he had to go and what he had to do. He had to go to the Red Desert and find his father. In addition, if the holy shrine of the Avatar still existed in its sands of the Red Desert, he had to find it as well. More than his dreams and his power, there had to be something there strong enough to defeat her.

"So you see my young friend, you are not only the son of the High Queen and the last priest of the Avatar, but of the Avatar itself. To keep your father hidden during his time at the High Court, he was joined with the very spirit of our world, the Avatar" Tori concluded.

Royal swallowed hard at this last bit of information. He actually jumped. This last piece was more than he could believe. Tori was telling him that he was not only mortal, but born of the Avatar itself.

"This is why you have so much power," Tori explained. "Probably more than you know or realize. This is why you and you alone can defeat the High Queen Mora."

Royal did not know what to say to this last statement. It was just as he had feared earlier in coming to Acara. He had the sneaky suspicion that he had more miraculous powers to discover. This was too much to be believed. He really wanted to avoid this realization. Having so much power went against his humble nature.

"My father," Royal began as he cleared his throat," What was his name?"

"He was called Jul during that time," Tori announced." I do not know if he has another name."

"Do you know where the Red Desert is?" Royal asked.

"It is far far from here," Tori answered," You will need a ship with swift sails to carry you to the shores that lead to the Red Desert or crystals to create a gateway there," he said.

Royal was overwhelmed by the conversation. He wrapped his arms around himself and rocked by the fire. Hue came over to him and put his arms around him for comfort. Royal did not struggle against him, he let himself be held. Maximus drifted behind them both and pulled them close.

"I think that is enough for one night." Maximus said as he felt Hue and Royal rest against his rich fur.

"I do agree," Tori said as he laid down next to the fire. "My words were never meant to be a burden for you, Royal, only a doorway, "he assured them.

Royal did not respond. All of the information that the old man said was swimming around in his head. He had a birth father that was still alive. He was sure of it now. The story of the old man only confirmed his dreams. Now he knew where he had to go and find him. Once Lethia and Wisdom returned, they would have to figure out away off these Lost Islands and a means to get to the Red Desert. With Hue and Maximus close, Royal closed his eyes and tried to sleep. This night he dreamed of red sand dunes and rock formations.

Wisdom took the lead as he and Lethia marched inland on the Lost Island. Though her wounds were severe, Lethia's mind was still sharp. She gave directions to Wisdom as if she knew where she was going. For two days, they marched all day and rested at night. They said little to each other as they traveled. On the third day of their travels, they reached a rocky hill and Lethia abruptly sat down. Confused by her actions, Wisdom stopped his forward motion and sat down beside her. He placed his gun close by, as he listened for interlopers in the distance. Hearing nothing, Wisdom leaned back, took out a cigarette and began to smoke. He looked down at the pack and frowned. He only had one other pack left. He was used to smoking at least two packs a day. He had no idea what he was going to do when he ran out. It wasn't like he could run out to a local store and get a fresh pack. He sighed out loud as he exhaled a stream of smoke.

"We are here," Lethia pronounced as she looked around weakly. "We are at the spot that I need to heal and be re-born."

Wisdom looked around thoughtfully. All he saw was more forest. However, he had no reason not to believe her.

"Just through those trees is a cave I can use to heal myself," she explained as she pointed.

Wisdom looked off in the direction that she pointed. He did not see a thing. He began to wonder if the woman had lost her mind, but he did not say anything.

"Are ya sure?" he asked with a wrinkled brow.

"I am," she said. "And I leave you here until I return with a single assignment."

"And what is that?" Wisdom asked.

"Break down that tree." She directed as she rose. "Do not use anything other than your hands and arms to do it," she instructed.

Wisdom looked off in the distance at the tree she was talking about. It was absolutely mammoth. Wisdom frowned as he took a long drag of his cigarette. He had no idea how she expected him to break down a tree of that size with nothing more than his hands and arms. Lethia rose from where she was sitting. She reached up and pulled some leaves from a tree overhead. Carefully, she wrapped Wisdom's arms in the leaves and tied them in place with vines.

"By the time you make that tree fall, I will return," she assured him as she began to move off into the flora.

"Wait!" Wisdom called, but she did not turn around. She kept on moving through the trees leaving Wisdom alone with his impossible assignment. Standing there with his arms covered with leaves, Wisdom went up to the tree. He pushed it. To his surprise the bark gave way. Slowly, Wisdom began to beat each side of the tree with his arms. Its bark began to splinter; in the places where he hit the tree, his arms were covered with a rich, sticky sap. As Wisdom beat at the tree, he found himself wondering what the fuck he had gotten himself into. He was a drug dealer not a hero. This was the work for his brother, Purcell, or Royal's cousin, Simon. He had survived the assassin cube, only to be left in the jungle with an impossible task. He shook his head. There had to be a better way.

Lethia moved on through the trees leaning heavily on a wooden walking stick. Her senses had not lied to her. There was a cave a few feet in land from where she had left Wisdom. She entered the cave swiftly and with her bare hands she dug a hole in the soft ground for herself. As she lay in the rich earth of Acara, she pulled the dirt in on top of herself. Unsure whether she passed out from the effort of digging, or if she fell asleep from pulling the ground, Lethia closed her eyes as she mumbled prayers to the Logos, land divinities, and the Avatar. Seconds later, she was lost in a deep healing sleep, resting in the arms of the Avatar.

# Omens

# Chapter 8

Deep within the recesses of the Grand Citadel were the quarters of Quan and Ela. It was late in the night when they both found their way home. Ela had left Tisha in her residence and Quan had left the High Queen in her chambers. Once they were in the safety of their rooms, they discarded the armor of their daily duties and drew close to one another. The two touched immediately as they came into the inner recesses of their sleeping rooms. Ela did not shy away from the changes the assassin cube had made in her mate. If anything, she honored his sacrifice and loved him more. The two fell into bed with one another and drew each other close. Their lovemaking was hot, feverish, and familiar. Their bodies came together as one. After their lovemaking was complete, they sat silently in the shadows enjoying the familiarity of each other's company. Ela was the first to break the silence.

"Quan, there is much I have to tell you," she said. "I have spent the day with the one called Tisha. A gorda has picked her and she has gone through the birthing."

"Those are wonderful things," Quan insisted. "They are preparing her to give birth to a Moritan prince."

"If it were that simple, my heart," Ela interrupted him. "Her gorda bares the bones of war and after the birthing she came from the pool with the mark of the High Prince Von," she explained grimly.

Quan looked at her with utter surprise. One of these omens would have been bad, but both of them meant war was coming to the High Queen. Quan did not say another word. He put his armor back on and left their room. Swiftly, he moved through the tunnels of the citadel until he reached the quarters of the High Queen. The Royal Guard that were at her door, stepped aside for him as he passed. Once inside her chambers, he dismissed her handmaidens and stood outside of her bedroom door waiting to be summoned.

"Quan," the High Queen called as she noticed him, "you may enter."

Quan came into the room and bowed to her. Since they were alone, formality was something they did not suffer. He quickly gave her the report that Ela had given him. The High Queen listened to him carefully, betraying no emotion. Once his report was completed, she moved across her chamber and dressed in the robes of the high priestess of the Dark God. She raised her hands and turned into a pillar of dark smoke. On the night wind, the smoke moved through the streets of Acara until it reached the Grand Temple of the Dark God. As she became solid again, Quan was making his way down the street on his gorda. The two climbed the steps and entered the Grand Temple of the Dark God together.

At this hour there were no priests afoot, leaving the main altar vacant for her prayers. The High Queen Mora went directly to the dark altar as she had so many times before and she prayed to her dark father for guidance and protection. Normally, she would have left it there, but for the first time she felt something move inside of her. The altar erupted in black flames and pulled Mora close to it.

--Mora, the voice said to her,-- I am here for you.

Mora began to sway back and forth as the energy of the Dark God over took her.

--You have sacrificed so much in my name. Now it is time, I give back to you, the Dark God said to her.

"Oh yes, dear father," Mora managed with tears in her eyes.

--I will send my marauders after those that have wronged you and seek to bring war to your reign. They will bring your son back to you and kill those that have stood against you.

"Oh yes dear father," Mora cried out. "I am yours to command."

--Once your son is at your side, nothing will stop us from making Acara all mine. And once we have taken Acara, we have worlds to conquer!

The High Queen Mora shook with the power of the Dark God. The huge altar began to resonate with power. It hummed and erupted in flames. The flames in front of her formed two pillars. Each pillar slowly took the form of two huge dark beings. They were identical and deadly looking. Each one stood almost as tall as the pillars that held up the dome. They were shadow beings with large heads with jagged edges. Each one had nine devil hounds tethered to them. The dome of the temple opened and they each took to the night sky. As the fire on the altar subsided, the High Queen Mora fell back into Quan's arms. He cradled her for a long time until she gathered her strength again. The High Queen Mora came to her feet slowly. She was dripping with sweat and her robes were drenched.

"Quan," she cleared her throat, "ready the Royal Guard and the troops. Have torches lit all around the walls of the citadel and the city. The forces of the Dark God will not be denied. Let us prepare our great city and our people for war."

"As you command," Quan said as he bowed his head. As Quan held onto the High Queen, he found himself thinking about his son, Keyton, the one that was called "Simon". Yes, he had been able to overcome the power of the assassin cube, but now he had to face creatures given birth from the dark matter of the Dark God itself. A shiver went up his spine. He wondered whether his son and Royal would survive if they continued to stand against the High Queen.

It was two suns after the attack on Anna-Beth's house. Grimhold was growing tired of the presence of the regiment and the dark priest in his small hall. They were eating all of his food and taking to all his concubines. However, he knew he had to wait to act if he was going to get the information out of Anna-Beth that he needed. On the third set of suns after the attack, he took off by himself at dawn and went into town. There he slipped silently into a merchant's stand and waited to be tended to by the keeper. An old crystal keeper came into the vender's booth. He was dressed in rags and his face was lined with age. It had been so long since he had been to the Crystal Hhive he was considered a legend or at least long dead, Grimhold smiled at the familiar man casually. They had done much successful business in the past.

"Well met, Skrill?" Grimhold said as he greeted the old man.

"Well met," the older man repeated as he sat down across from Grimhold at a small table. "Why do I deserve this visit for today my Overlord ?"

"I need to visit the sea witch Anna-Beth and I need you to once again disguise me to her powers," Grimhold demanded.

"A powerful warping crystal is what you need, "Skrill replied. "It will conceal you from her magic and make you lovely to her prying eyes," said, laughing.

Grimhold reached into his robes and tossed the old man several gold coins. The old man took the money without counting it. He reached into his robes and removed a beautiful crystal bracelet. Grimhold took hold of it immediately and placed it on his wrist. As the man promised, Grimhold's image began to bend and he looked like a fine, red-skinned, young noble. Grimhold picked up a hand mirror and looked at his reflection. He did not recognize himself. He smiled devilishly.

"Speak to her in soft tones and she will not be able to resist you," Skrill explained as he rubbed his gnarled fingers together. "She will have no idea who you are."

As Grimhold looked at his distorted image in the mirror he said, "You are truly a craftsman." He laughed.

"I try, my Overlord," Skrill responded smugly, "I try."

Grimhold shook his head and left the man's vending station. He left his mount at the man's booth and switched to a beautiful white steed. He immediately mounted the new onea nd headed out toward Anna-Beth's home. He had no way of knowing if the sea witch was still there, but ~~hei~~if she was, he would be able to seduce her. He reached the edge of her farm by mid-day. He reached down and picked a hand full of wild flowers that were growing at the edge of the road. He dismounted his steed and walked up to the house. The small house was quiet and looked unlived in. Grimhold sighed. At first, he was sure that she was gone then the door opened to meet him. Anna-Beth looked him up and down. For a moment, Grimhold wondered if she could see through his disguise. However, she smiled at him and invited him onto her porch with a wave of her hand. Grimhold smiled and handed her the flowers. Anna-Beth blushed.

"Are you here for me to read the bones?" Anna-Beth asked as she looked down the road to make sure the beautiful young man was alone.

"Yes," Grimhold said as he bowed his head. "I have traveled many miles to be read by you. Your reputation precedes itself," he flattered her.

Anna-Beth smiled as she smelled the flowers. She could not remember the last time someone had given her flowers. She invited the young man to sit down at her divining table with a gesture and sat across from him. Seeing how hypnotized she was, Grimhold smiled slyly to himself. He had her just where he wanted her.

"Yes," Grimhold said quickly as he slid several gold coins across her divining table. "I am looking for someone and I hope you will help me find them."

Anna-Beth took her bones in her hands and said a prayer. She cast the bones across the board several times before she answered.

"Those that you seek have gone far from here," she said, in spite of herself in a spirit filled voice.

Excited by her answer, Grimhold gave her another coin. "Where have they gone to?"

Compelled by the spirit of her own divination Anna-Beth said, "Those you seek have gone to the Lost Islands. There you will find them."

Grimhold smiled to himself widely. He stood without saying another word and left Anna-Beth with her bones. Anna-Beth watched the stranger leave in disbelief. All of her senses were telling her that he was indeed a stranger, but there was something in the man's manner that made her uneasy. She cast the bones several times as the man left, but the reading was unclear. She sat back in her chair and said a silent prayer to the Avatar that she had not somehow revealed something that would bring danger to her grandchildren or the High Prince they were destined to encounter.

In the Grand Hall of Grimhold, Holidor and Agar waited for his return. They had grown impatient with his unspoken plans and were ready to strike out again in search of Etera. As they waited for Grimhold to appear, they began to prepare their mounts for journey. Just before Holidor called for his men, Grimhold entered the hall on his white steed. Holidor immediately drew his sword upon seeing the newcomer.

"Hold fast!" Holidor said as the man came closer.

Grimhold dismounted and laughed at the captain's bravado. He held up his hand, removed the warping crystal and his true form was revealed. Seeing the man for who he was, Agar laughed loudly and clapped his hands.

"I have gone to see the sea witch," Grimhold said. "And in spite of herself, she has revealed to me where Etera and Tildon have gone. You cannot reach them by land but by sea. Their destination is the Lost Islands."

"Well done," Agar said as he clapped his hands again. "Well done!"

"Why is it that they go there?" Holidor asked.

"That much I do not know, but I will make my fastest sea ship available to you and your men. You should be able to catch them before they reach their destination," Grimhold offered.

"Then let us waste no time," Holidor said, "We shall have that young sea witch back in our grasp before she knows it!"

Grimhold said nothing else. He had done his part and that alone would bring him favor with his cousin, the Flasion Queen. He would give them his fastest sea ship and his best men to sail it. He knew it would give them the ability to overcome most ships on the waves or in the air. However, when it came to recapturing the young sea witch he knew it would not be as easy as they thought. He had gleaned from the sea witch's reading that they were going to the Lost Islands for a divine purpose. With such forces working against them, he knew it would take more than a fast ship and the singular magic of a dark priest to overcome them.

# Chapter 9

Wisdom sat silently by himself in the woods. This was the first time he had been alonesince they had come to Acara. He was having a hard time believing that he was on another planet. However, the extreme tropical nature of his environment made him believe it. The plants and the animals that ran around him were all unfamiliar to him. It was like he was in a National Geographic episode that someone else had scripted. Besides that, he was waiting for Lethia to heal herself by going into the ground. He had no idea what that meant, except he had a picture of her buried up to her neck in his mind. The thought made him feel sick as he envisioned worms and bugs crawling over her skin.

She had given him an impossible task to perform while waiting for her to come out. He was supposed to knock down an odd-looking tree with nothing more than his bare hands. At first he thought she was crazy. However, as time passed, he found the bark of the tree malleable to his constant touch. For the majority of the time, he spent his time working the tree from either side. As the bark gave way, he found himself covered from head to toe in a thick invisible sap that seemed to soak into his skin. By the third day, he was covered in the gooey substance and the tree was ready to fall. With one mammoth blow he knocked it down and a splash of the sap coated his face. He sat down next to the broken stump to survey the wreckage he had made.

More than felling the tree, he realized that Lethia had wanted him to get covered with the sap. His light-brown skin now seemed to have a permanent glow. His skin felt odd to the touch. As he sat waiting for Lethia, he tested his newfound complexion. He tried to cut himself with a knife he had. His skin would not break Wisdom eyes widened at the sight. He felt the pressure but nothing more. He stuck his fingers in the fire that he used to cook his food, but they did not burn. By the fourth day, Wisdom was feeling adventurous and cocky. He turned one of the guns he was carrying with him against his chest. While he felt the pressure of the bullet when he shot himself, his skin did not break. .

"What the fuck ?" Wisdom said in amazement he marveled at the skin covering his hand.

Wisdom looked down at the remains of the tree in wonderment at the gift it had given him. Now he knew he could handle any situation this world could throw at him.

"That's right!" he sang out as he raised his arms over his head, "I'm bad. A real gangsta now!"

On the night of the fourth day, Wisdom ate alone and was resting by the fire. He lit a cigarette and leaned back. He found himself wondering about Tisha and her safety. A chill went up his spine. She was the reason that he was herein the first place and he could not imagine what she was going through at the hands of the High Queen Mora. He was definitely not in love with her any more, but she was still the mother of his son. He needed to know she was safe. Though he did not reveal it, he was happy that she was with Simon. He was definitely a brother filled with honor, a nerd for sure, but honorable nonetheless. He knew that he would never do her wrong the way that he had. Wisdom sighed to himself and smoked his cigarette. He leaned back and prepared to go to sleep. As his eyes began to get heavy, he noticed the fire shift in color. He sat up immediately. Wisdom pulled out his gun and looked out intothe forest around him. It was still. He was about to lie down when an apparition appeared on the other side of the fire. As the figure's shape became clear, the cigarette fell from Wisdom's lip He was astounded. He recognized the face of the ghost immediately. It was Malik Jones.

"Hello, Wisdom," he said from the other side of the fire.

"What the hell," he began with a quivering voice. "I must be dreaming," Wisdom added as he looked at Malik's shifting figure hollow through the fire. Back on Earth, Malik Jones was Wisdom's mentor in the drug game. He had taught Wisdom all he knew about the making and distribution of crack cocaine. Wisdom was just a boy when he met his more flamboyant mentor. They had drawn blood together when Wisdom overheard some other brothers planning to take Malik out. Wisdom shook his head. The memories were harder than the reality. Eventually he and Malik had a falling out over drugs and money. Wisdom had killed Malik in cold blood, a bullet right through the head, and assumed his operation. Wisdom had hid Malik's body in his workroom as a reminder of what would never happen to him. Seeing his dead mentor across the fire was more than a surprise for him. Wisdom's mouth dropped along with his gun.

"You ain't dreaming, muthafucka," Malik said. "And I know I taught you never drop ya gun! I taught you better than that," he snapped. "I'm really here. In fact I beeen with you this whole time," he said as he moved from around the fire. "Man I wish I could have one of those smokes. Being almost dead sucks."

"Almost dead?" Wisdom questioned nervously.

"Yeah, more dead than alive though, not quite crossed over yet." Malik tried to explain. "I don't know man. I don't pretend to understand all this shit, but it's me, for sure."

With all Wisdom had experienced as of late, seeing a ghost seemed to make odd sense.

"You haunting me?" Wisdom asked. There was a chill in his voice.

"You could say it has been something like that. On Earth, I was with you ever since you took my life," Malik explained as he pointed to the bullet hole in his head.

"You've been watching over me?" Wisdom asked.

"Nigger you killed me!" Malik snapped. "The last thing in the world I wanted to do is look out for your Black bitch ass."

"Then why are you here?" Wisdom wondered out loud.

"You ain't the only one that has been given a second chance. This is my second chance, too. I am going to be here to help you to protect Royal as best I can." Hr swore." Where on Earth you couldn't see me, but on Acara, you can. It has something to do with that Avatar thing I guess. I do't know." He hunched his shoulders eyeing Wisdom cigareet. He was dying flor a puff.

Wisdom shook his head as he watched Malik's frame shimmer back in to the fire. He could not believe that he was actually talking to the ghost of Malik. This was the strangest thing that had happened to him personally since he got to Acara. In addition, Malik was saying that he was going to help him to protect Royal. Wisdom shook his head. Malik was a ghost, how did he expect to help him? He could not shoot or anything. He shook his head, a bull shiter in life snd in death; yet, then he had a thought.

"Can you travel anywhere?" Wisdom asked quickly.

"I pretty much can," Malik said. "I don't know my way all over Acara, but I think if I focus I can get pretty much anywhere."

"Good," Wisdom said. "Then I want you to find Tisha and make sure she is alright."

The fire erupted at the request. Malik shook his head and he began to pace back and forth

"I'm supposed to stay close to you and Royal and help you out if I can. That is the only way I am going to cross over." Malik explained told him. "I don't think I'll get there by looking for ya baby mama."

"Come, on man, I need to know how she is doing," Wisdom pleaded.

"You always was pussy whipped," Malik mocked as he faded into the fire.

"Hey Malik!" Wisdom shouted to him before he faded.

"What?" Malik turned around in the flames.

"Sorry for how things went down," Wisdom said. He had never stopped regretting their last encounter.

"Fuck you, man," Malik said as he faded.

Wisdom was alone again under the watchful light of the three Acarian moons. He leaned back against a log. He could not believe that Malik was with him. It was too much to imagine. Wisdom took out one of his cigarettes and began to smoke. More than the appearance of Malik, he found himself thinking about what he said. He said that this was a second chance for the both of them, on taking over the care of Royal and being his Royal Guard, too. Wisdom had guessed that this was a second chance for him to move past his drug dealing roots. Wisdom swallowed hard and smiled as he thought about his new indestructible skin and his new ghostly reluctant guardian angel. This time he would be the hero. His grandmother would be proud of him the way she was proud of his brother Purcell. He hoped he would live long enough to get to see her smile again.

On the morning of the fifth suns that they had been away from Royal and the others, Lethia opened her eyes. For a moment, she had forgotten where she was and what she was doing. Then, as her eyes adjusted to the half-light of the cave, she remembered her wounds at the hand of the assassin cube, her journey back to Acara, and her need to heal herself by going into the ground. She had been mortally wounded having been impaled by Quan. She knew that Quan was Simon's father. However as she thought of her wounds, she smiled oddly. Yes, she would fulfill her duties to Royal. But the next time Quan was in sight of her he would feel her wrath. This was personal It had taken all of her will to keep herself alive until she found this resting place in her own land. Once she was cradled in the arms of her own world, she was able to weave a spell that had healed her wounds. It had taken longer than she thought it would, but she was alive and back up to full strength. It felt good.

Reverently, Lethia made her way from the ground saying prayers to the Logos and the Avatar as she went, thanking them for restoring her strength. She stood tall in her armor as she emerged from the cave. She made her way through the trees to where she had left Wisdom. He was sleeping by a low fire and did not hear the Queen of the CODA coming. He woke with a start as he saw her towering over him. Lethia laughed at his surprise as she sat down next to the fire and found something to eat. Wisdom watched the woman move as she fed herself. Her walking stick was gone and the wounds appeared completely healed. He had no idea what she had done, but it had definitely benefited her.

"I see the tree has fallen," Lethia said as she continued to consume volumes of food, not taking her eyes off of Wisdom's glowing skin.

"Yes, it hasWisdom said as he stuck his f," ingers in the fire and wiggled them around playfully. They did not burn. He thought about telling Lethia about Malik, but he thought better of it. It was a secret that he wanted to keep to himself for now.

"The CODA teaches us that there is only one tree like that in a thousand which a person can take down with their bare hands, only to be made stronger than the tree," Lethia explained. "It is a blessed gift from the Avatar. You are a true minion of the land now."

"I see," Wisdom said as he looked down at his hands. He wished he would have had something like this when he lived in Baltimore. It would have made him less afraid of the guns that he knew were constantly pointed at him. As he looked at the broken tree, he felt a level of responsibility for the gift it had given him by its demise. He would use it wisely in the service of the thing they called the Avatar. And he knew that it meant keeping Royal safe, especially since Simon was not around. Wisdom nodded his head as he remembered the promise he made to Simon to keep Royal safe.

"Simon showed you the way. Now I have given you the tools Wisdom, and it is time for you to walk the walk," Lethia said as she brushed up against him, testing the strength of his skin. It was firm to the touch.

"I will. I promise you that," Wisdom said as he brushed back up against Lethia. She did not budge. In the early morning light, the two predators from different planets looked at each other across the fire with renewed respect.

"Now let us go see how our chargees have faired in our absence," Lethia said as she finished the last of her food.

Wisdom waited patiently for Lethia before they turned back toward the shore. As he followed her through the jungle, there was a lightness in his step. For the first time, he felt prepared for whatever they might confront.

Royal stood on the edge of the waters of the vein. He let the water wash over his feet and it tickled his toes. After the meeting with Tori, he had stayed to himself. He had taken his meals with the others but then slinked off to be on his own. He was having a hard time taking in the fact that he had a real father who was still alive and that the Avatar was also his parent. And he knew from his dreams that this red robed man was waiting for him. It was frustrating to think about. Now that he knew that his birth father was alive, he was frustrated that he had no way to get to him. He felt trapped on these islands.

"Do not be so heavy, my High Prince," Tori said as he came up behind him.

"I feel trapped here," Royal admitted. "I feel like I need to get to my father. I feel sure that he can fill in some of the gaps in my life."

Tori walked up to the High Prince and put a caring hand on his shoulder. "Do not worry; the Avatar has brought you too far to leave you now. You have to believe it."

"To be honest, Tori," Royal began "I feel a war is coming and I do not know if I am prepared to fight it."

"The war has already begun," a voice said from behind them.

Both Tori and Royal turned around to see Lethia and Wisdom standing there. Royal saw a healed Lethia and he burst into a smile.

"Wisdom! Lethia!" Royal screamed out their names announcing their presence. He ran up to her and threw his arms around her. Lethia hugged him back uncomfortably and pushed him away. Royal then turned to Wisdom and to his surprise he hugged him as well.

"Okay," Wisdom mumbled. "Let go nigga," he laughed as he rubbed Royal's hair. "I wish I would have packed some clippers. You're gonna need a haircut soon," he remarked absently, while Lethia walked up to Tori.

"It has been a long time since I have seen you," Lethia said to Tori. "And I am happy to see you on our side."

Tori laughed, "It is you, Queen of the CODA, that I am happy to see alive and well. It makes me believe we can actually win this thing."

"Tori has told me that my father is still alive in the Red Desert. He also told me that the Avatar is my parent as well," said Royal shaking his head. "He also told me that my father maybe the last priest of the Avatar left alive."

Lethia looked pleasantly surprised. She shook her head as she took the information in. "I guess he did not tell you that to get to the Red Desert you have to go through the Plains-controlled by the CODA. I am still their rightful Queen and if we need an army, it can start there."

"No," laughed Royal. "He did not tell me that."

"It has been a long time since I assumed my rightful role as leader of the CODA. It is nowtime for that," she declared. "But first, we are going to have to put our minds together to get off these Lost Islands. I fear that challenge may be the greatest hurdle of all," she said as she kicked the sand at her feet.

"Do not fear, Queen of the CODA," Tori began. "I believe that the same way I was brought to you, the Avatar will make a way for us."

"I hope you are right, Tori," Lethia said as she looked out at the waves. "I hope you are right."

"How is it that he speaks English?" Wisdom asked Lethia as he looked up and down at Tori.

"Tori has many gifts," Lethia said simply.

"Shit, I could have used him in school," Wisdom quipped as he remembered the way Tisha kept pushing him to get his GED.

"You are a fool," Lethia said with a grin as she turned away, shaking her head.

The others left Royal alone on the shore with his thoughts. He continued to watch the water as it came in waves. He thought about the Avatar being a parent to him. It seemed hard to believe. How could a person have three birth parents? He supposed with all that had happened to him, nothing should seem impossible at this point. As Royal stared at the water, he began to pray to the Avatar. He did not know what form his prayers should take, but he simply spoke from his heart. After some time, he felt a familiar presence creep near. He knew immediately it was the Avatar.

--I hear you, my High Prince, the Avatar said.

"You are one of my parents," Royal said. It was a statement.

--Yes, I am, the Avatar responded. --I am a part of you as you are a part of me.

"Exactly what does that mean?" Royal asked hurriedly.

--It means that you must have as much faith in yourself as you do in me, the Avatar responded.—All that you need dwells within, the Avatar said as its presence faded.

Royal sucked his teeth. He was happy that the Avatar had come to him but the visitation had left him with as many questions as answers. In addition, he did not get a chance to ask about his birth father or abouthow they were going to get off the Lost Islands. It seemed far too easy to say have faith and believe in yourself. It had gotten him this far, he supposed it would have to get him a little farther. As Royal sat thinking, he did not hear Wisdom come up behind him. Wisdom settled down in the sand next to Royal. Though they did not say anything to each other at first, Royal felt an instant sense of comfort arise between them. It was not as strong as what he felt with Simon, but it was similar. It surprised Royal, but he was thankful for it. Unconsciously, Royal leaned back against Wisdom. At first the gesture surprised Wisdom, but he did not withdraw. Instead he put a tender arm around Royal and the two stared out at the water together.

"How you doin'?" Wisdom asked casually.

Without thinking, Royal began to tell Wisdom all that Tori had revealed to him about his birth and his visit from the Avatar. He also expressed all of his fears and doubts about what lay ahead and what was expected of him. He also told Wisdom how much he was missing Simon and Arkon, his surrogate father. In addition, he expressed how happy he was that Wisdom and Hue were with him and how much of a steadying force they were for him.

"You know, I'm trying to look brave in the face of all that has happened, but it is actually scaring the hell out of me," Royal admitted as tears appeared in his eyes. "I mean until a few days ago, I thought I was only human, and young at that!"

Listening carefully, Wisdom pulled Royal a little closer. "And it is real easy to say "have faith and trust in yourself" when you ain't scared. Man that sounds like a fucking cliché. I don't care whose god that it is coming from."

"Exactly," Royal laughed in agreement.

The two shared a nervous laugh.

"How was your journey with Lethia?" Royal asked.

Wisdom thought about it for a minute. Then he reminded himself that he was Royal's Royal Guard and the last thing that they ever needed between each other was secrets. Wisdom guessed that, more than the spiritual stuff and duty, trust had to be the basis of their relationship. Wisdom exhaled and told Royal about the trial with the tree that Lethia had put him through and how the sap had changed appeared yo make him indestructable. Then he told him about his encounter with the spirit of Malik Jones and how he had asked the entity to check on Tisha.

"I've told only you about my encounter with Malik," Wisdom confided.

"Why is that?" Royal asked.

"I guess. . .No I am kind of ashamed to admit why he is haunting me," Wisdom said carefully.

"Why is that?" Royal asked with a wrinkled brow.

Wisdom sighed heavily and proceeded to tell Royal about his entree into the drug-dealing arena as Malik's protégé. He told him about their friendship and brotherhood as they went about their illegal trade. Then he carefully explained how things between them went sinister, and how that led to him putting a bullet between Malik's eyes and how he had buried Malik's remains in the basement where he housed his product. Wisdom left nothing out. He was exhausted when he finished speaking.

He could not remember the last time he had told someone the entire story of his journey with Malik.

Royal listened without judgment. He could see that what Wisdom was telling him was not easy for him. Though he had guessed that Wisdom was a murderer when he first met him, it was different to actually hear him talking about it. However, it did not change the growing affection that Royal was beginning to have for him. He did not feel that he could judge Wisdom for his past. All he could do was judge him based upon the time he had known him. And since then, Wisdom had proved himself to be nothing but homorable and an asset. He would leave the hudging up to God.

"It will be good to find out about Tisha," Royal agreed, as a breeze went up his leg.

"Yeah," Wisdom agreed. "I know she is Simon's lady now, but she is still my son's mother. I got to know how she is doing and look out for her."

"She risked a lot for all of us," Royal agreed.

"Sure nuf," Wisdom agreed as he watched the waves, "Sure nuf."

# Chapter 10

The *Lucky Lady* made her way through the sky on her silken sails. Captain Sarison stood tall at her helm, steering her toward the Lost Islands. As he guided the ship, the captain perused an animal-skin map that he had won in the Dark Opion. The map showed a clear trail to a lost treasure that he swore he would find. The man he had won the map from was a notorious fellow. However, Captain Sarison did not know him to be a liar. He believed the man when he told him that at the end of the map was more riches and gems than he could carry. Captain Sarison believed that if he and his mates captured this bounty, they could all retire to a good life in some forgotten place

Below the deck of the *Lucky Lady*, Tildon looked toward his sister Etera. They had been given a small cabin to share. Etera did more sleeping than anything else, leaving Tildon alone with his thoughts. Happy as he was to see his lost twin sister, he was equally distressed to leave his grandmother alone to face the forces of Grimhold. While he knew the old woman could take care of herself, he would have preferred to have his sword backing her up.

Etera woke from a daze and stretched her aching limbs. Tildon came to her bedside and wiped her hair out of her face. He smiled at their similar features.

"We are being followed," she assured him with an anxious yawn.

"What do you mean?" Tildon asked with concern.

"Those that were in pursuit of me have taken to the waters. I saw them in my dream. They are coming for us all now, in a swift sea ship," she assured him.

Tildon wrinkled his brow. He was not gifted with the visions that led his grandmother's and sister's life. However, he had learned over time to follow them.

"Then we must tell Captain Sarison!" he said sternly.

"I believe we must," she agreed.

The two younglings gathered their cloaks and left their chamber. They walked down a dank hallway and up a set of stairs that led to the deck of the flying ship. They passed by a host of scalawags that were tending to the sails of the ship. They walked to the helm of the ship where Captain Sarison was steering the huge vessel. He turned to greet them with a grunt as he took a pause from spinning the ship's massive wheel.

"What can I do for you?" Captain Sarison asked with an annoyed expression. He was not used to having passengers on his vessel or on his helm. The *Lucky Lady* had been with him for more cycles than he could count as was most of her crew. And the last thing he wanted was to endanger his crew or his vessel; especially now that they had finally found a true treasure to go after. Yet, he had given Anna-Beth his word. And more than anything else, he lived by that.

Etera did not speak at first. She was intimidated by the hulking captain of the flying vessel. In the absence of her voice, Tildon spoke up.

"We are being followed," he told Captain Sarison.

"And what brings you to this conclusion?" he asked dismissively.

"My sister has had a vision of them overtaking us," Tildon stated.

Captain Sarison did not say a word. He ran to the stern of the ship and took out a looking glass. Sure enough, on the horizon he caught site of another vessel on the gale. He shook his head. The *Lucky Lady* was a fast ship. He prided her on that. If this was a vessel from Ulfast, it had to be moving exceedingly fast to catch them. He would not have been surprised if their sails were fueled by dark magic. It was the only way that another ship could so quickly overcome them, and she was coming up fast! He put his finger in his mouth and measured the potency of the wind. It was weaker than he would have liked it to be. It was not strong enough for them to outrun the vessel that was following them. He ran back to the helm of the vessel and spun the wheel.

"You two get back down below," he commanded. "This is my fight now," he assured them.

"My sword is sharp and I am able to defend both me and my sister in a fight!" Tildon cried.

"Let's hope it does not come to that," said Captain Sarison, as he laughed with a wink at the young man's bravado. "But the *Lucky Lady* is filled with a host of tricks of her own! I promised your grandmother I would keep you two safe. I am a man of my word if nothing else. Now do not defy me and go below."

Seeing no reason to argue with the captain of the ship, Etera and Tildon returned to their bunks below deck.

"Lower the sails and bring out the oarsmen!" Captain Sarison commanded as he watched the new ship quickly close in on them from afar. As the crew drew in the silken sails the huge ship fell from the sky and took position on the open sea. On either side, oarsmen lowered their oars into the water and began to row the ship forward. Captain Sarison had no idea what kind of vessel was trailing them. He hoped the speed of his own oarsmen would be enough, so he would not have to rely on his weapons.

Agar and Holidor stood on the helm of the vessel pursuing the *Lucky Lady*. It was a fast sea ship called the Wind Jammer. Holidor looked at the captain of their ship. He was a tall, gaunt, yellow-skinned Flasion man. He had a scar across his neck that was a medal from his years in battle. A patch covered the space where his right eye used to be. The man's name was Thorn. As Thorn caught the look from Holidor, he signaled the men to lower their sails as well. This was a battle that they would have on the water not in the air.

"I see that our prey seeks to out run us," Agar said as he watched the *Lucky Lady* sink onto the drink. "Let's see how they do if the very sea they rely on turns against them," Agar said as he raised his hands and looked at the calm ocean. The dark priest uttered a few words at the ocean and it began to churn viciously. The waves began to fight against the oarsmen of the *Lucky Lady* as it made Agar's ship move even faster. Soon the two ships were in eye length of each other, with nothing but the cruel sea between them.

"They are getting close," Etera moaned as she walked up and down the length of their small cabin. "They are using dark magic." she explained to Tildon. "I can feel it! We have to help them."

"What can we do?" Tildon asked.

"More than sitting here and waiting to be captured," she said as she headed to the door with Tildon on her heels. Once again, they reached the deck of the *Lucky Lady*. Members of the crew were busy steadying the boat in the wake of the sea's tumult. The ship that was following them was almost in long weapons' range. Captain Sarison was at the helm of his ship, holding the wheel steady, refusing to give an inch to the storm and choppy water around them. Etera glided past him and placed her hands on the helm of the ship.

"What are you doing?" Captain Sarison said as he watched her come on deck. "I thought I told you two to stay below!" he snapped.

Ignoring his words, Etera summoned her power. The boat immediately began to steady in the waves. The oarsmen picked up on the reprieve and pushed the *Lucky Lady* forward.

"She is fighting me," Agar said with a taste of acid in his voice. He was surprised at her strength.

"Ready the forward Longs!" Holidor commanded while they still had the *Lucky Lady* in their site.

The men began to fire the Longs at will. Their ammunition missed the wooden deck of the *Lucky Lady* but it slowed them down.

"Men, arm your selves!" Captain Sarison ordered as he swung the boat around and brought it up to ramming speed. With Etera guiding the helm of the ship, the missiles from the other vessel continued to miss their deck.

"Prepare to board them! "Holidor roared as his legion of soldiers came onto the deck of the Wind Jammer, fully armed and ready for battle.

"There are too many of them," Tildon said as he brought his own sword to bear as he counted the bodies on the deck of the approaching ship. They were outnumbered.

"Nonsense!" Captain Sarison laughed with the wind in his hair as he watched his crew hand out armaments as the two ships came side by side. Now they exchanged shots that exploded against both of their decks. Men from both ships clung to lines as they swung back and forth between the two decks. In moments, both ships were covered with dueling pairs of pirates and soldiers. Tildon hung close to his sister as the fighting broke out. He made quick work of several invaders that tried to reach the young sea witch. Then through the fray, he caught sight of Holidor. He knew the captain immediately by the uniform he wore. Tildon did not hesitate. He took the fight to the older man. Back and forth they fought, with neither of them losing ground. Then Tildon brought up a shattering blow that knocked the captain from his feet and into the water.

Etera still clung to the head of the *Lucky Lady*. She was using all of her will to steady the giant ship. As she stood there, a dark robed figure made his way through the crowd of fighting men toward her. Agar reached out with all of his might and caught Etera by the throat, astonishing her. She fell to her knees instantly and rolled around in pain. Seeing this, both Captain Sarison and Tildon tried to get through the masses to Agar and Eterato no avail. As Etera felt the last bit of air draining from her lungs, she called upon all of her power with all of her might. She prayed to the Sylphs for help. Suddenly, deep beneath the two ships, a presence stirred, awakened by her call. A huge multi-legged sea creature emerged from the waves. It began to crush the interloper's vessel with huge swipes of its tentacles. Agar cursed loudly in fright of the creature as he tried his best to fight off the young sea witch's call. However, she was proving stronger than him. As the monster splintered the deck of the interloper's ship, its men fell into the drink and were quickly consumed by the giant water beast. Seeing an opening, Captain Sarison rallied his men aboard his ship. They immediately unfurled the silken sails and prepared to take to the sky.

"You will never be rid of me witch!" Agar swore as he continued to choke Etera.

He was so fixated on the young witch that he never saw the blow coming from behind him. Tildon ran him fully through. He pushed his sword up into the dark priest to the hilt. Agar fell back against the side of the ship, his body wrecked from the blow. He raised his hand again to summon a spell but a tentacle of the sea monster grabbed him and he disappeared beneath the waves. Etera crawled to the side of the ship, struggling for air. Tildon was at her side immediately. He was bruised and cut from the fray, but his hand was steady. He helped his sister to her feet.

"I'm all right!" Etera said as she took to the helm of the ship again, steadying the great ship as it leaped to the sky.

"Unfurl the sails," Captain Sarison said as he took to the great wheel once again. The captain of the *Lucky Lady* was barely standing from the fight. He was cut and bleeding in countless places from the fight. However, his gaze was certain and he was no less in command of the vessel.

As the members of his ship discarded the last of their invaders, they once again took to the ocean gale. As they moved out to sea, they fired their weapons and sank the last of their attacker's vessel, leaving the survivors to the attacker's vessel, leaving the survivors to the mercy of the sea and her creatures. As the *Luck Lady* made her way through the sky, the crew quickly-doused random fires and secured its splintered decks.

"I knew that having you two aboard was dangerous," Captain Sarison said, "but I never thought it would be like this," he grunted with a sly grin.

Tildon did not say a word. He simply tended to his sister who was weak and barely standing after the onslaught. Tildon sighed to himself. He believed the worst of their journey was over now that Holidor and Agar were off their tails. Now, as the way opened up before the *Lucky Lady*, he looked forward to an easier ride.

It was late in the evening hour. Tisha had found that she was unable to sleep. She informed her night maiden, Stula, of her plan. She was going to go down to the stables and spend some time with her gorda, Aspion. Dilga smiled at her when she passed, then faded back into a deep slumber. Tisha walked through the Grand Citadel slowly. As she passed beings in the hallway, they nodded to her and looked at her with respect. She was dressed like a Royal Guard, she wore the markings of the High Prince on her face, and she had been joined with a gorda. They had even trusted her enough to begin to train her on how to use weapons. Granted, the simple throwing weapons in no way gave her the idea that she could go busting out of there. At the very least, she gave them the illusion that they controlled her. The picture was definitely deceiving.

Tisha made her way down to the stables. She walked quietly to the stall that held her Aspion and she smiled at him. More than anything else, her joining with Aspion had been the most spectacular thing that had happened to her since she had come to the Grand Citadel. Now that she was joined with him, she had no idea where she began and he ended. Tisha got a bucket of fresh protein and another filled with water. She sat down on a small stool and gave Aspion his midnight treat. The horned dragon-like animal purred deeply as it ate. Tisha sat back on a stool stroking Aspion's cold, scale-like skin, when the hair on her neck stood up. She looked around quickly. The stables seemed silent, but she felt like she was not alone and being watched. Tisha reached into her leather armament and removed a throwing dart. The weapon felt strange in her hand, but Tisha knew she had to protect herself and her unborn child.

-Do not worry Tisha, Aspion said in her mind. —It is a friend.

"A friend?" Tisha said out loud as she wrinkled her nose. Beyond a friendly conversation with Simon's brother, Elric, she would not have counted anyone she met as a friend.

Tisha was about to leave the gorda stable when something in the corner of the pen caught her eye. She froze stock still. There was a shimmer in the air in the corner of the pen. As Tisha watched, the shimmer took shape. And she found herself facing a vaguely recognizable yet opaque figure. Before the figure became clear, Tisha held the throwing dart in front of her protectively. As the figure became clear, she hesitated and lowered her weapon. She was surprised to recognize the ghostly figure. It was Malik Jones, Wisdom's former mentor and friend.

"Malik?" Tisha said with surprise in her voice as she lowered the hand that held the weapon. "Is that you?"

"Yes you might as well say it is. What's left of me!" Malik laughed as he raised his hands.

"What are you?" Tisha asked with surprise and confusion.

"I am a ghost, of sorts," he exhaled.

-Actually, a shade, Aspion corrected in Tisha's mind.

"I been following Wisdom ever since he left Earth and came here. He was able to see me once we got to Acara," Malik explained. "I think it has something to do with the Avatar. I don't know." He was tired of telling the story.

"You mean Wisdom is here on Acara?" Tisha's voice lit up.

"Yes, he is. He made it through the Gateway with Lethia, Royal, Hue, and Maximus. Right now, they're stranded at the end of Acara on the Lost Islands. Wisdom sent me here to check on you and make sure that you awright," Malik explained.

-I will take care of you, Aspion assured her.

"Quiet, Aspion," Tisha said quickly.

"Who you talking to?" Malik asked as he looked around.

"It is a long story," Tisha sighed.

"I guess it all is," Malik chimed in. The two shared a nervous laugh.

"You can tell him that I'm okay. I am being treated well and trained like a Moritan since I am now carrying one, having Simon's baby," she explained.

"You are?" Malik gasped. "But he ain't human!"

"Yes I am," she sucked her teeth. "You can tell Wisdom they won't dare hurt me because of the child I am carrying. You tell Wisdom that I need him and the others to get me the hell out of Acara City and back to them!" she scolded.

"I will get the message back to them immediately," Malik said as he began to fade.

"Malik, I hate to ask you but I have one more favor," Tisha said quickly. "Are you able to move between worlds?" she asked, thinking on her feet.

"Yes, I believe I can," Malik said slowly. "It may take all the energy that I have but I believe that I can do it," he explained.

"Then will you go to Earth and let Simon know that I am alright? I mean I might look different, but I'm still his girl, ya know. He can feel me through the arrowhead that I wear, but a direct report may sooth him more," Tisha pleaded.

"You are asking a lot," Malik said cautiously, as he folded his arms in front of him.

"I realize that I am. But I need for him to know that I and his unborn child are alright," Tisha begged.

"No you ain't playing the baby card!" he shook his head.

"I am," Tisha admitted.

"I must be the only half-dead ghost errand boy sucker on this rock," he said as he laughed out loud.

Malik stared at Tisha thoughtfully, then nodded his head yes.

"I will do my best," Malik agreed.

"That is all I can ask," Tisha smiled.

Malik's image faded. Tisha sighed in disbelief. Things were happening so fast she could not keep up. Ghosts? Shades? She shook her head and turned her attention back to Aspion.

-You worry too much, Aspion laughed.

"I guess I do," Tisha agreed as she continued to stroke him. It felt good not be alone after all.

She hummed to herself as she stroked and oiled Aspion's scaly skin. She sighed to herself. She was happy to know that Wisdom, Lethia, Hue, Maximus, and Royal had made it through the Gateway. She felt good that she had played some minor role in helping them escape. It took her a few minutes before she realized that she was not alone again. She looked up and saw Ela standing in the doorway of the stall.

"And who were you talking to?" Ela asked suspiciously as she looked around the stall. Ela took a deep breath trying to catch the scent of anyone that might be around her charge.

-Just say me, Aspion directed.

"I was just talking to Aspion," Tisha said quickly.

Ela smiled widely and shook her head, "You do not lie very well, Little Flower. You do not lie well at all."

Tisha did not know what to say to this. Instead of speaking, she continued to stroke Aspion's scales under Ela's stern gaze. Ela did not believe that Tisha was talking to Aspion. There was the faint presence of another being. It was not a scent she recognized. Ela prided herself on being able to recognize most of the beings on Acara by their scent alone. The fact that she could not make out this scent troubled her greatly. As she looked at Tisha, Ela wondered what she was hiding. She guessed only time would tell.

# Chapter 11

Royal rolled over in his blankets. Since he had come to Acara, he had been blessed with restful sleep. The insomnia and nightmares that plagued him on Earth were gone. As frustrating as the experience had been so far, the one blessing from it for Royal was the fact that he was sleeping normally. It had never been something that he could take for granted. Now he felt like a normal person since he was able to sleep. However, this particular night, he found himself tossing and turning just before dawn. Deep within the darkness of his slumber he felt a familiar presence. Then he found himself in a beautiful garden near a still pond.

He approached the pond and sat down beside it. He looked at his reflection in the pool and ran his hand over the water. The water was cool to the touch. Royal was lost in the pool for a long time, before he realized that he was not alone. He looked up and Etera was standing next to him. Royal smiled immediately and invited Etera over to him by the edge of the pool. She sat down beside him and took his hand.

"It is good to see you," Etera said with a smile.

"It is good to see you too," Royal said as he found himself lost in her almond colored skin and dark eyes. "What is this place?" Royal asked.

"It is my meditation space. It is the place I go inside of myself when I need to get away from the world. It was my salvation when I was a slave in the Flasion mines," she explained.

"Why have you invited me here?" Royal asked.

"I want you to know that I am coming for you," Etera assured.

"What do you mean that you are coming for me?" Royal asked anxiously.

Etera smiled and reached out and touched Royal's face. "I am coming to the Lost Islands to get you. I am on the way with my twin brother and a great sea ship. We are coming to rescue you and take you wherever you need to go. I know this now. I am sure of it," she explained.

"When will you get to the Lost Islands?" Royal asked hurriedly.

"In a few suns or less," Etera assured him. "The Sylphs are pushing our sails faster than can be imagined so that we may get to you quickly."

"How will you find me? There are so many Lost Islands."

Etera smiled, "The Sylphs will guide me to you. I am a sea witch. They will show me the way. Now you rest, my High Prince. I do not know that the suns ahead will be as restful."

Royal nodded his head as Etera's meditation space faded. Royal once again was lying thick in the arms of restful slumber. Royal slept for a few hours more. He was awakened by the smell of cooking bacon and laughing voices.

"I can't believe that you can't cook," Hue said as he tended the bacon over the fire.

Lethia was lying back against her pack smoking a cigar. "I can kill a man in a thousand ways, preferably by snapping his neck. Tending to food was never a skill I picked up. Even when I was Grace Monroe, I found it better that you men cook for yourselves than to have me accidentally poison you," she joked.

"It will be good to have hot meat again," Tori said as he licked his lips. "It has been a long time."

"Now what is this meat called?" Peku asked as he danced around the fire.

"It is called bacon," Hue said as he flipped the slab in the pan, "*Bay*-con."

"I like it better raw," Maximus growled as he tore into a raw slab of bacon and began to devour it. He drooled all over the meat as he ate.

Wisdom watched Maximus in disgust as he ate. He still had a hard time believing that he was once that old boxer that slept at the end of Royal's bed. He sat and lit a cigarette. As he looked at the smoke, he found himself wondering where Malik was and if he had seen Tisha yet. He had no way of knowing. He was going to have to wait and be patient.

Royal came up to the small group and picked up some food. Hue smiled at him and handed him a bottle of water.

"I had a dream last night that I need to tell you about," Royal said as he sipped at his water.

"What did you dream?" Lethia asked as she sat up, floating in a ring of cigar smoke.

Royal explained to them about the garden he had visited and the fact that he had met Etera there. He told them that she was on her way to the Lost Islands with a ship that could take them wherever they needed to go.

"I told you that the Avatar would provide," Tori said as he slapped his leg.

"She told me that the Sylphs would lead her to us," Royal concluded.

"Do you believe that you can trust her?" Wisdom asked suspiciously.

"Yes, I do," Royal said.

Royal explained to the group how she had first come to him. He also explained to the group that Etera had described herself as a sea witch that had been enslaved by the High Queen because she failed to serve her and how she spoke of the High Prince's return.

Lethia stood up abruptly and began to pace back and forth.

"We need to be ready to go once she comes. It is time we go the Red Desert." She announced.

Royal came to his feet. He suddenly began to get very nervous. He remembered the man from his dream dressed in the red robe. He also remembered that the man had said that he was waiting for him. Royal found himself shivering. He had always thought that Reverend Monroe, or 'Arkon', was his father. Now, he was going to go and meet his true father. He did not know if he was ready for that. In a panic, Royal came to his feet and headed to the forest behind the encampment.

"What is wrong with him?" Peku asked as he did a flip, before reaching for the hot bacon.

"I do not think that seeing his father is going to be as easy as we might think," Lethia said.

"I never knew my father," Wisdom said, "so I can just imagine what he is going through."

"And his father is the last priest of the Avatar," Tori reminded them. "That is a lot for an Acarian child. It must be even more for a young man born off-world."

"I will go after him," Maximus volunteered, as he finished off the last pieces of his bacon.

"No." Hue said as he handed the pan of bacon to Wisdom. "You eat. I will go after him. Maybe he will talk to me," he added as he rose to follow Royal.

"I think that is a good idea," Lethia said as she settled back to continue smoking her cigar.

"Hue!" Wisdom called before the boy got too far.

Hue turned to face him.

"You have what I gave you, right?" Wisdom asked.

"Right here," Hue assured him as he patted the gun at his side.

"Good," Wisdom said as he took out another cigarette and began to smoke.

The small group watched Hue vanish into the woods after Royal. They each silently worried about the young High Prince and what the journey was asking of him.

The High Queen Mora woke up and opened her eyes. Light came through the windows of her chamber to greet her. She lay in bed along time without moving. There was an unfamiliar presence in her room that was holding her attention. For a moment, she thought to call to Quan and the Royal Guard to sweep through her chambers but she thought better of it. She was about to move when she watched a shadow form near the window. She sat up in bed immediately. She raised her hand and summoned her dark powers to her. However, before she struck, she watched the shadow take the form of Agar. As she recognized him, she knew immediately he was a shade. She bit down hard on her lip. She had sent Agar and Holidor to find the runaway slave, Etera. Sea witches were rare beings and she did not want Etera to slip between her fingers. Seeing him in this form, she knew that he had failed her. The

High Queen sighed to herself. Quan had failed her, now a trusted dark priest as well. She hated incompetence.

"Death would not prevent me from serving you," Agar said as he bowed to his monarch.

The High Queen crept from her covers slowly. She slid into a long green robe and sat on the edge of her bed. She stared at Agar coldly and waited to see what he had to say.

"It is with great pain that I have to tell you that the young sea witch has slipped through our fingers," he began slowly. "We all gave our lives in pursuit of her."

"That much I can tell," The High Queen said coldly as she watched the wraith shift in the morning light.

"However, I have used the last of my dark gifts to break through the seal of death to bring you information of value," Agar smiled.

"And what information is this?" the High Queen asked as she leaned in curiously to hear Agar's words.

"We fought to capture the young sea witch at sea. It was there that she called upon a monster that was beyond our ability to kill. However, as Holidor and his men were sucked into the bowls of the drink, I saw that she was on her way to the Lost Islands." Agar explained.

"Of what value is this to me? The Haze there is too great for any to see." The High Queen asked. "The Lost Islands are at the end of Acara, as well," she added with a huff.

"In my drowning moments, I was able to see that Etera goes there to meet with those who kidnapped the High Prince. While I could not see him, I felt the presence of the off-worlders there. If they are indeed there, then the High Prince must be with them or they have knowledge of where he is," Agar said flatly.

The High Queen Mora was out of her seat before she knew it. She smiled to herself widely. Though Agar had failed her on one level, he had brought her vital information that she needed to get young Von back at her side. Immediately, she knew what she had to do.

"Your sacrifice was admirable, my dark priest," the High Queen began. "I assure you that it will render a blessing that will resonate all through Acara," she swore.

"Your words comfort me as I face this new life," Agar said as he bowed.

"Your service to me is indeed not over yet," the High Queen said as she raised her hands. Immediately, the image of Agar began to shimmer and darken as she infused him with dark essence. "You will stay close to me and be available for command," she commanded as she used her power to anchor Agar to this life.

Agar looked down at himself. He could feel the energy of the Dark God flowing through him anchoring him to the land of the living. Agar smiled to himself. The High Queen reached up and rang the bell for her handmaidens. They rushed into the room, tripping over themselves to serve their mistress. Their eyes widened as they looked upon the wraith-like presence of Agar, but they quickly gathered themselves and turned to their mistress for direction. Without speaking, she motioned for them to dress her. Quickly, they brought her royal vestments to her and assisted her in dressing.

With Agar floating behind her, the High Queen made her way through the Grand Citadel to the throne room. She climbed the stairs to her throne and took her seat of power.

"Quan," she said softly.

Seconds later, her Royal Guard appeared at her side. He looked down from the throne at Agar with little expression. He turned to the High Queen and waited for direction from her.

"Bring my uncle, High Prince Burton, to me," the High Queen commanded Quan.

Quan nodded his head and vanished behind the high throne. While the High Queen waited for her uncle to appear before her, she reached out with her mind and called the two Marauders to her. The creations of the Dark God appeared before the monarch with their nine hellhounds tethered to them. Burton appeared from the left side of the chamber with Ilson, his Royal Guard, in tow. He stopped short as he beheld the sight of the Marauders, their hounds, and Agar. A shiver went up his spine under the weight of the dark energies at the control of his niece. He took a step back and almost tripped over Ilson. Ilson placed a reassuring hand in the middle of his back and eased him forward.

"Your Highness," Burton said as he bowed, trying to regain his composure and shield his thoughts of apprehension.

"Information has reached me that the High Prince and his allies maybe on the Lost Islands," the High Queen Mora began. "I want you to take one of the Marauders and a regiment of men to retrieve them. Go to the crystal hive and make a Gateway there with much haste," she commanded." And I will provide you with what you need to find them since you will be on the otherside of the haze."

"It will be done," Burton swore.

". . .And before you go," the High Queen interjected, "I want you to take Quan with you to the crystal hive and send the other Marauder to Earth to retrieve Keyton. This matter has gone on too long. Now, by the will of the Dark God, I would see it done," she said flatly.

"By your command," Burton echoed as he turned to leave the great hall with Ilson, Quan, and the Marauders on his heels.

"Uncle," the High Queen called behind him. He paused and turned to face the great throne. "Do not fail me," she said menancingly.

"On my life," Burton swore as he turned to part with the others, leaving the High Queen alone in the great hall with Agar. The High Queen was about to leave when Ela appeared in the throne room. She came to the foot of the throne and bowed.

"Your Highness," Ela began, "may I have your ear?" she said candidly as she caught sight of Agar's ghostly apparition.

"Speak, Ela!" the High Queen commanded.

Carefully, Ela began to tell the High Queen about her encounter with Tisha from the previous evening. Though she was unclear about with whom Tisha had been talking, she was sure that she had been speaking with someone or something.

"So it seems our Little Fower has been busy," the High Queen joked.

"If I may," Agar began to speak, "I feel that Tisha may have been visited by a shade from afar. I can sense the presence of another of my kind around the Grand Citadel."

"Continue to watch her," the High Queen directed Ela. "Agar, you have my permission to haunt these halls and let me know if you sense another of your kind. If you do, I empower you to destroy the interloper."

"By your command," Agar said as he faded from sight.

"Well done Ela," the High Queen complimented. "We will have to work hard to reign in our Little Flower; especially before she bares Keyton's son."

"Thank you, your Highness," Ela said, bowing her head. "I will continue to work with her. I promise you, we will seduce her to our level of understanding." Ela said as she receded from the room, leaving the High Queen alone with the echoes of her edicts.

Simon stood on the deck outside the double windows of what had been Aunt Grace's room. It was well after midnight. He was lit up under the light of the moon. Over the time that the others had been away, Simon had grown greatly. He now stood over seven feet tall, when he was not disguised by his warping crystal. His body was lean and muscled from all of the practicing that he had been doing in Grace/Lethia's war room. He held on to the arrow that connected him with Tisha. He felt the surge of their connection. He knew instantly that she was alright; a little depressed, but okay. He sighed to himself. As he held onto the arrow, he could also feel the new life that was growing inside of her. It was strong and it was definitely a Moritan heart. Simon smiled to himself.

He was just about to go inside when he saw a shimmer in the center of the room. Simon immediately drew a dagger from his side and crouched in a defensive position. The shimmer lingered for a long time and slowly became solid. Simon found himself standing face to face with the ghost of Malik Jones.

"What business do you have here?" Simon said carefully. "Has the High Queen sent you?" he said as he raised his dagger.

"No!" Malik said as he raised his hands. "I'm from here! Or at least I was when I was alive. I was a friend of Wisdom Sims. I was here with you through your battle with the assassin cube. I escaped with the others as they fled to Acara. Somehow, once I was there, I was able to take form and be seen. I'm not sure but I think it has something to do with the power of the Avatar. All I know is that I'm here and I can move between worlds. This shit is a trip!" he shook his head." Wisdom asked me check on Tisha and she asked me to come to you to let you know that she's alrigh;. Bald as shit, but all right," Malik told him.

"You have seen Tisha!" Simon exclaimed as he sat down on the bed. He smiled in relief.

"I've seen her. And she asked me to come here to let you know that she was okay. I guess I am just that kind of guy. Mail man and shit. Anyway, she sends her love to you as well, blah blah, and all that tender shit. They are doing their best to try and change her, but she remains true to herself," Malik said.

"What of Royal?" Simon asked hurriedly.

"He is well. They are hidden away from the High Queen on the Lost Islands. Wisdom is doing his best to be there for him, but he struggles," Malik said candidly.

"I can imagine. That is truly my job," he said as he lowered his head. "I am just glad that they are all alright," Simon said, half to himself as he stretched out on the bed.

Malik shook his head and his image began to fade.

"I don't know how this ghost shit really works," he admitted, "but somehow my energy is tied to Wisdom. This trip to Earth took all I had and I am being drawn back to him. Is there anything you want me tell the others?" he asked. "Say it quickly!"

In his time with Malik, Simon had almost forgotten about their quest to find the Gateway crystals that they had seen in the image in Reverend Monroe's archives.

"Let them know that we may have found a way to get to Acara. There may be a set of Gateway crystals here on Earth left by an earlier traveler. Purcell and Arkon are doing everything in their power to locate them," Simon explained.

"That is good news, my Brother," Malik smiled, his gold tooth caught the light in the room. "I will pass it on," he swore. "See ya."

"Also," Simon called frantically using his will to hold onto Malik's fading image, "if you can, let Tisha know I love her and that I am coming for her."

"No problem. I'm getting used to this errand boy shit," Malik said as he vanished, leaving the young Moritan alone in his room. Simon immediately got to his feet and went downstairs to the rectory. He went over to the pastor's study and knocked on the door.

"Come in," Reverend Monroe said from the other side of the wooden portal.

Simon opened the door. He was surprised to see Purcell and Ben Lee there with the pastor. They were all carefully studying the image that the archival crystal was casting on the wall. The image was of a clergyman standing before a huge, ornate altar with two Gateway crystals in his hand. Purcell and Mr. Lee were standing in front of the image discussing the particulars while the pastor sat behind his desk, plucking away at the computer.

"How many times have you gone over this picture?" Ben asked as he squinted at the image.

Purcell laughed. "It seems like it's all I've been doing since I took this time off," he admitted.

"What have you come up with so far?" Ben asked. "Tell me again slowly," he said hopefully.

"Well, first of all looking at the altar it, definitely isn't Baptist. You see all the stained glass and the saints? I think it's Catholic. I don't know a lot about liturgical clothes, but the pastor feels that the clergyman in the image is wearing something a Catholic priest might wear," Purcell explained.

"Makes sense," Ben smiled anxiously.

"Look carefully at the face of the man. Look at his features and hair." Purcell began as he pointed. "He definitely is not white. He looks Latino, either Puerto Rican or Mexican perhaps," Purcell concluded.

"I see that," Ben agreed.

"And the image that appears most in the background is the Sacred Heart of Jesus Christ. So I'm thinking that we're looking for a Catholic church that maybe called the Sacred Heart of Jesus Christ in a Latino community," Reverend Monroe concluded. "The traveler who left these images of Earth for me on Acara did so with no time stamp. So I have no idea how old his catalog of Earth churches is. This image could have been taken a hundred years ago for all we know," Reverend Monroesaid gravely.

"Let's hope not," Ben said trying to be the voice of optimism in the group.

"And even if we locate the church and the priest is there, there is no telling if he still has the crystals," Purcell added.

"I like to believe that he will," Ben said firmly as he studied the man's face. "The priest who the crystals were left with, probably kept them safe in case the traveler would ever need them."

"I would like to believe that," Reverend Monroe said as he sat back in his chair and wiped at his eyes. He was not particularly good at using computers. All the church work that had to be done on them he had always left to Royal or one of the deacons. Now he was having to sharpen his skills on the fly as he searched the internet for churches that fit the description.

"How many churches have you found so far that fit the profile?" Simon asked as he came into the room.

"As well as I can tell, at least seven across the country," the pastor announced. "I will start making calls to them in the morning." he exhaled.' As I search, I believe this parish to be in New YorkCity." It was a guess. "My intuition is usually good."

"It's someplace to start," Purcell said as he tried to smile.

"I have news," Simon announced.

"We know that you can feel Tisha through your crystal arrow head," Reverend Monroe reminded the group.

"No, it is more than that," Simon began as he sat down in the chair across from the pastor.

"What do you mean?" Ben said hurriedly.

Quickly, Simon began to tell the group about his visit from the shade of Malik Jones. He left nothing out about the details of the visit. The three men looked at Simon in shock, awe, and disbelief.

"Wait a minute!" Ben said as he threw up his hands. "Aliens are one thing. Now you're telling me that ghosts are real too!" he said silently remembering about his dead wife, Sylvia.

"On Acara, such things are rare but not unheard of among its many peoples," Reverend Monroe said. "What we believe is that we are all parts of the Avatar and when we die, we simply become something else, another form of energy," he explained. "Those spirits that linger close to us are usually those that have some unfinished business they have to do or they may have something to make up for."

"Wasn't Malik a criminal?" Ben asked.

Remembering Malik's criminal record Purcell said, "Yes, he was. A lot of nickel and dime bullshit And like my brother, he was a career criminal."

"It would make sense that he would linger," the pastor interjected. "He may have things to atone for before he goes on to his rightful place in the afterlife."

"Can we contact him?" Ben asked hurriedly. "I want to ask him about my Hue," he said as tears brimmed his eyes.

"I cannot," Simon said. "He is attached energetically to Wisdom."

Ben hung his head.

"Be encouraged, Mr. Lee," Simon said as he rose from his chair and placed a hand on his shoulder. "Malik made it clear that the entire group had crossed over safely. I am sure that Hue is safe.".

"But how long will that last?" Ben snapped.

No one had an answer.

Hue put on his hoodie and followed the tracks Royal had left in the sand. He followed him inland as the trail turned toward the jungle. Hue marched forward for several feet. He looked around, scared. He did not take his hand off the gun that Wisdom had given to him. He eventually reached a grotto with a waterfall not too far from the shore. Hue paused. Caught in the light of Acara's duel suns, the grotto was one of the most beautiful things he had ever seen.

Royal was sitting on a rock near the stream thumbing through his bible. He was looking for any words of comfort that he might glean from the text. Hue approached him cautiously, not wanting to disturb his reading and concentration. Carefully, Hue came and sat down next to Royal. The two sat silently for a long time, enjoying each other's company. Royal was the first to break the silence as he closed his bible.

"I wish I had never come here," the High Prince confided.

"You don't mean that, Royal," Hue scolded him lightly. "You knew you had to come."

"I know Hue, but this is all so confusing. Now I have three parents - the High Queen, the priest, Jul, and the Avatar. Not to mention that I really still feel like Reverend Monroe, or Arkon, is my father. Sometimes, I do not know if I am coming or going, just going through the motions." he admitted as tears began to form in his eyes.

Watching him cry, Hue's heart went out to him. He did not know what to do at first. Then, impulsively, he put his arms around Royal and drew him close. Royal did not resist the gesture. He let Hue hold him. It seemed like the two stayed that way for a long time before Royal reached up and touched Hue's face. Hue jumped as he looked down into Royal's eyes. His heart was beating fast as a familiar heat was rising in him as he looked at the young High Prince.

"You are a good friend, Hue," Royal said softly as he stroked his face.

"I care about those I love," Hue said before he realized what he had said. He blushed as the words came out of his mouth.

Royal sat up and he turned to look at Hue as if he was seeing him for the first time. He was shocked by his words.

"You love me?" Royal repeated as he stared into Hue's eyes.

"Do you think I would have gone through all of this, if I didn't?" Hue asked sarcastically as tears blurred his eyes. He punched Royal's shoulder playfully.

The two shared a nervous laugh.

"Come with me," Royal said as he began to strip down to his boxers.

Hue hesitated for a second and then did the same. He placed the gun that Wisdom had given him on top of his clothing so it was in easy reach. Royal went into the water of the grotto first. It was cool to the touch. He reached back and took Hue's hand and guided him into the water. Hue's heart was beating fast in his chest. Hue could not believe what he was seeing. He let Royal lead him deeper into the grotto's waters and the two swam beneath the waterfall. As the water cascaded over their young bodies bathed in the suns' lights, they faced each other and kissed for the first time. It was a long, lingering kiss that brought the two of them closer than ever before. It made Hue feel closer to the young High Prince than he had ever. For Royal, it was a tender comfort from all of the confusion he was feeling. Royal felt like Hue was someone he could really trust and he needed that.

As the two kissed under the falling water, holding one another, Maximus patrolled in the distance, securing the perimeter. He was not asked to, but he felt as though he needed to protect the two younglings from any unseen dangers. He was happy to see the two of them bonding so intimately. It could only serve them in the days ahead.

The elder High Prince Burton moved down through the tunnels of the Great Citadel. He was attired in full armor and held his helmet under his arm. As always, Ilson followed him a few steps behind. He reached the door to his younger brother Holi's, workroom. Holi's Royal Guard, Bilk, stood in front of the door with his sword resting in both hands. At the sight of his master's older brother, Bilk stepped aside and opened the door. Burton moved in past Bilk without acknowledging him. Ilson took up station next to Bilk outside the door. The two Royal Guards sealed the workroom and gave the two brothers their privacy.

As Burton came into the room, he expected to see Holi at work with his mixtures, powders, and potions. However, he was surprised to find his brother at the far end of the room sitting on a lavish couch, drinking a dark wine from a decorative decanter. Burton approached him slowly. Though the two brothers looked alike, there was a stark contrast as to how they were dressed. Burton's armor was glowing in the candlelight of the workroom. Holi was dressed in rich layered fabrics that covered his lean form. Holi did not react immediately to his brother's presence onto the fact that he was dressed for war. Instead, he gave more attention to his wine and his thoughts drifted back to a new healing powder he was working on for the Infirmary. When Holi finally acknowledged his older brother, he put down his glass and invited Burton to sit with him. For a moment, the two brothers sat in silence enjoying the familiarity of their contact. Holi was the first to speak.

"I see that you are ready for battle," Holi began. "Like the torches that now burn day and night on the walls of Acara City, you are ready for war."

"I am, my brother," Burton agreed. Then he launched into an explanation of the High Queen Mora's plan that he had been commanded to lead. He left nothing out, not even the appearance of the ghost, Agar, or the presence of the Marauders. There was excitement in his voice as he laid out the details. He was happy that he was being moved from the shadows of the battle to the fore. It was the perfect position for him to put his own personal plan into action.

"She expects me to capture the young High Prince," Burton said as he leaned back on the sofa. "But I swear to you, he will not leave the Lost Islands alive."

"All kinds of accidents happen in battle, especially with a Maruader around," Holi said as he poured them both a drink of wine. Things can be unpredictable," Holi smiled.

"You have read my mind," Burton said with a great deal of satisfaction.

"And to insure that outcome, I have the perfect thing for you," Holi announced as he stood and returned to his mixtures and powders. He finally found a small vile of greenish-colored liquid and gave it to Burton. "This is called Aldam. It is the most lethal poison on Acara. It is not even of this world. Apply it to your small blade and when you scratch him, he will be paralyzed. If you stab him, and this gets into the blood stream or a major organ, he will die a slow, agonizing death."

"Is there a cure?" Burton took the vile and smiled anxiously.

"None," Holi said confidently.

"Thank you for this gift, brother," Burton said hurriedly. "When I am on the Green Throne, you will not be forgotten."

"I do not worry about that, brother," Holi assured. "You and I have been through a lot together. I trust you with my life."

"And I trust you with mine." Burton agreed. "We leave for the Lost Islands within moments. Will you come see us off?" Burton asked.

"I would not miss it, dear brother," Holi promised.

"Good," Burton said as he stood to leave.

Once he was on the other side of the door, Ilson fell in behind him. They made their way through the familiar catacombs slowly and spoke in whispers. As they turned a corner, Burton handed the vile of green liquid to Ilson. By the look of the it, Ilson could tell that it was some kind of poison. Silently, he waited for further instructions.

"Hold fast to this, my dear Royal Guard, and in this upcoming battle, let us coat our blades so we will see the young High Prince dead," Burton explained happily. He was exuberant with himself and his gift from his brother. He could taste that the Jade Throne within his reach, and he would not be denied.

At dusk, the streets of Acara City saw a rare sight. From the Grand Citadel of the High Queen, a procession appeared at the gateway of the enclosure led by the High Queen, Mora, herself. She was riding a magnificent white mount and was dressed in flowing crimson robes and a spectacular golden crown. Behind her followed the two High Princes, her uncles Burton and Holi. They, too, rode white mounts and were dressed in silver armaments. Directly behind the High Royal family were their three personal Royal Guards, Quan, Ilson, and Bilk riding their individual gordas. The sound of the hooves of the mounts of the Royal family and their Royal Guards was drowned out by the howling of the hounds of the two massive Marauders that followed them through the streets of Acara City. The citizens of Acara City shrank back at the sight of the twin carnivorous dark beasts. Bringing up the rear of the procession was a regiment of twenty troops. The troops followed their monarch on foot. They were dressed in light armor and were fully armed. They were an imposing sight to the regular citizens of Acara City as they passed.

The High Queen Mora led the procession through the streets of the capital until they reached the Crystal Hive. The entire litany of crystal keepers were assembled outside of the huge u-shaped structure. They were all dressed in the green dress robes of their station. Lancer, the senior crystal keeper, came to the fore and bowed to the procession. The other crystal keepers followed in the same way.

"Have you prepared the way?" the High Queen asked as she dismounted her steed.

"Yes, I have, your Highness," Lancer said quickly as he led the procession through the doors of the Crystal Hive.

Lancer led the members of the procession past the countless rows of crystals. He led them to a set of ornate crystal doors. He removed a decorative key from his robes, unlocked a heavily gilded door and led the procession down a set of winding stairs. After several minutes of descent, the stairs gave way to an enormous earthen catacomb filled with row after row of huge archways. Lancer led the procession to a huge archway on the first level. It was encrusted with glowing orange oblong crystals. Lancer reached into the Gateway and removed a leather pouch that contained two matching crystals.

"Your Highness, I have personally prepared this Gateway to the Lost Islands to your specfications," Lancer said proudly. "I will activate it to send the mission to the Lost Islands. All your uncle needs to do is make a cross with the crystals in this pouch to return," he explained.

The High Queen Mora turned her attention from Lancer to High Prince Burton.

"Bring my son back to me," she commanded.

The High Prince stepped forward and bowed to his niece. He shot Holi a knowing glance before he stepped toward the Gateway.

"It will be done," he swore as he turned to rally his forces.

Ilson waved and the regiment of troops stepped forward. They were followed by one of the two marauders and its hounds. Lancer led them over to the huge Gateway. He bowed his head as he handed Burton the pouch with the crystals in it. He removed a tuning fork from his robes and touched it to the side of the Gateway. The Gateway began to glow as it was activated. The High Prince Burton led his regiment of troops and one of the Marauders through the Gateway and they vanished.

"Your Highness, the Gateway to the place you call Earth was not easy to create. We used some of our oldest and most powerful crystals to send Quan there the first time. However, I was able to create a way there for your Marauder and for it and it's captives to return," Lancer explained as he led the remaining members of the procession into the bowels of the catacombs. They came upon a smaller archway encrusted with black oblong crystal fragments. Lancer once again picked up a pouch that contained similar crystals and waited to be commanded.

The High Queen turned to the Marauder and its hounds.

"You are the creation of the Dark God," the High Queen began. "I send you to do that which my own trusted Royal Guard could not. Bring Keyton back to me and do not spare the lives of any who stand in your way," she commanded.

The remaining Marauder let out a blood-curdling scream that resonated throughout the catacombs. Its hounds responded with yelps of approval as they strained at the reins that tethered them to it. The huge creature lurched forward toward the Gateway. Lancer shrank back in fear of the dark creature. As it passed, it snatched the pouch and went up to the Gateway. Carefully, Lancer used his tuning fork to activate the Gateway. It glowed-in response. The Marauder bent down and passed through the archway. It vanished instantly, as well.

"You have done well, Lancer," the High Queen Mora smiled. "For as long as I have lived here, I never knew that such a place as this existed," she admitted as she gestured to the catacombs.

"It is the Crystal Crypt," Lancer explained. "It is only known to the crystal keepers of the highest order. When I received your orders, I thought it prudent that you know about this. With these Gateways at your disposal, we shall find your son," Lancer swore as he led the remaining members of the procession out of the catacombs.

The High Queen Mora passed through the lines of crystal keepers and remounted her mount. She was followed by Holi, Bilk, and Quan. As the High Queen Mora traversed the streets back to the Grand Citadel, she smiled to herself. It was the first time since assembling the assassin cube that she felt like her victory was at hand.

Etera woke from her dream with Royal. She got to her feet immediately and dressed quickly. She crept from the bowels of the ship and came on deck. It was nighttime. One of Captain Sarison's officers was at the wheel of the ship. The *Lucky Lady* sailed high over the seas. The large silken sails caught the breeze sent by the Sylphs and the sea ship moved forward faster than it ever had. Tildon was standing at the bow of the ship looking out at the sea. He was bandaged from their fight earlier with Holidor and Agar. Etera walked up to her brother slowly and placed a hand on his shoulder.

"How are you?" she asked

"I am alright." Tildon said without taking his eyes off the sea. He was thinking about their grandmother, Anna-Beth. He was wondering if she was indeed alright. He was happy that his twin sister was back. But, ever since she had returned, nothing had been the same. His simple life had been turned upside down. He did not want to blame her for this, but he was having a hard time not resenting her.

"You are not a very good liar, brother," Etera laughed. "You forget that we are twins and that I am a sea witch, as well. I can sense your ambivalence about me being here," she said sadly.

"It is not that. I am happy that you are free, but things are so different now. I also miss our grandmother," he admitted.

"I can understand that," Etera said as she leaned over the edge of the boat and let the wind blow through her unfurled hair.

"But I have you," Tildon smiled, "and we will get through this together."

"I hope so," Etera said. "But there is something else that we have to discuss."

"What is that?" he said with a wrinkled brow.

"The High Prince is on the Lost Islands," Etera announced.

"He is!" Tildon cried. "What is he doing there?"

"He has come back to Acara to liberate us from the High Queen, I am sure of it. And we are supposed to help him," Etera explained.

Tildon laughed. "I am just a farmer. Yes, I am good with a sword, but I am no more than that. Liberating a whole world is far beyond my reach. I was made more for tending crops."

"Believe in yourself, Tildon Korner. Before this is over you will prove yourself more valuable than even you imagine," Etera predicited.

"I don't know about that," he laughed. "But we have to tell Captain Sarison so he knows what he is walking into."

"I agree," Etera said.

The two walked from the bow of the ship and made their way to the Captain's quarters. Captain Sarison was sitting in his quarters drinking ale. Greedily, he was looking at the treasure map he had won. Etera and Tildon knocked on the door. They waited until Captain Sarison answered.

"Enter!" he commanded in a gruff tone, clearly annoyed to be disturbed.

Etera and Tildon entered his dimly lit quarters. They stood before the Captain, awkwardly shifting back and forth. Captain Sarison looked up from what he was doing and sat back in his chair.

"What can I do for you now?" he asked plainly, sizing them up.

Tildon turned to Etera. Carefully, Etera explained to him her dream about the High Prince and the Lost Islands. The Captain of the *Lucky Lady* listened with little expression. He simply shook his head.

"Thank you for bringing this to my attention," he said. "We will be ready. The men of the *Lucky Lady* are a stern bunch," he assured them as he returned his attention to his map. Etera and Tildon did not wait to be dismissed. They left the room quickly, leaving the Captain to his map. Captain Sarison continued to look at his map absently until they were gone. He thought about what the twins had revealed to him. He sighed out loud. He had the sneaking suspicion that somehow, on this trip to the Lost Islands, he may not get to his treasure after all. He had to laugh to himself at this thought as he put the map away. He found himself thinking about Anna-Beth and her bones. He began to wonder if the old woman knew about all of this when she approached him about the twins. He laughed out loud as he reached for his ale. She was a tricky old woman.

# LOVE
# &
# WAR

# Chapter 12

Peku dozed in the fading light of the day. Tori sat next to him on the shore playing a hand-held flute. Lethia and Wisdom watched the waves that filled the veins of water between the Lost Islands. They were looking for the ship that Royal had promised was coming for them. No one was talking but there was tension in the air. They were all ready to go. In addition, they were all silently worried about the young High Prince. He had vanished earlier into the woods with Hue and Maximus. It was clear that the experience was taking a heavy toll on him.

As Lethia and Wisdom watched the water, there was a shift in the air near Wisdom. Lethia immediately moved into a defensive stance and drew her blade. Wisdom turned to see what she was looking at. Instinctively, he drew a gun from under his hoodie. He stepped away from the shifting air just as Malik appeared.

"By the Avatar!" Lethia said as she stared Malik down.

"Lethia," Wisdom said softly, "you don't have to worry about him. This is the ghost of Malik Jones. He has been with us the entire time. When you went into the ground to heal, he came to me for the first time. I asked him to go check on Tisha for me," Wisdom explained.

Lethia looked from Wisdom to Malik and sucked her teeth.

"And when were you planning to tell me that you had a shade following you?" Lethia snapped.

"I was not trying to hide it. I just didn't know how to bring it up," Wisdom said as he dropped his head.

Lethia laughed. "I could snap your neck! This is why I hate working with men. You keep too many secrets that are not necessary. If you would have told me, perhaps I could have explained why he was haunting you."

"I didn't think about that," Wisdom admitted as he blushed.

"No, you did not think," Lethia said sarcastically. "Now let us hear what your shadow has to say," Lethia said as she took out a cigar and began to smoke it.

Carefully, Malik began to tell them about his visit to Acara City and his conversation with Tisha. He revealed to them how much they had changed her in her time with them. He also told them about the child that she was carrying. Wisdom was shocked at the news. Then he told them about his journey to Earth and his meeting with Simon. He made it clear to them that there was a sliver of a possibility that they had found a way to make a Gateway to Acara. Lethia smiled widely. Silently, she knew that Arkon would not let anything keep him from his son.

"You have done well, Wisdom," Lethia said as she exhaled a puff of smoke. "And you, too, Malik. I hope your actions help clear the way for you to escape this in-between-ness and you get to the other side."

"I do, too," Malik said as he began to fade. "If you need me Wisdom, I am just a whisper away," he promised. "After all this globe-trotting, even a ghost gotta rest!"

"One more favor," Wisdom interjected quickly.

"Ah man," Malik yawned. "Okay. What?"

"Before you rest," Wisdom said, "go to Tisha and let her know we are coming for her."

"I will do that," he said as he faded.

Lethia turned to Wisdom and hit him squarely in the chest. Wisdom was shocked by her action. He stared at her grimly. He did not know what to do.

"You have inherited a shade," Lethia said. "It is a rare occurrence in the life of a true warrior. Many warriors kill and go into battle for a lifetime and never gain what has come to you. I guess there is honor somewhere buried deep within those drug-dealing fingers."

"Thank you. . . I think," Wisdom muttered. He did not know how to take Lethia's words. Once again, things were moving too fast for his comfort. He was used to being in control and nothing that was happening gave him that sense of security. On top of that, he had just found out that Tisha was pregnant. She was going to bare Simon's child. Though he thought Simon was cool, he did not know how he felt about the fact that Simon wasn't even human. He did not know what kind of child he and Tisha would have together. The thought sent a chill up his spine. All he kept seeing was reruns of "Aliens" running in his mind. He was slightly ashamed.

Just then, a dot appeared on the horizon. It was still far out, but a ship was definitely coming. Lethia smiled and put out her cigar. She turned back up away from the beach with Wisdom on her heels. Seeing them move, Peku gathered up Tori and the four moved inland toward their makeshift camp. By the time they got there, Royal and Hue were sitting casually by the fire eating. Maximus was nowhere to be seen.

"Thank the Avatar for your dreams, Royal," Lethia said as she sat down. "I spotted a ship on the horizon."

"Etera is coming," Royal said, trying not to betray his excitement. Hue looked at him oddly, then looked away.

"We have more news than that," Wisdom said as he sat down.

"What news?" Hue asked as he regained his composure.

Carefully, Wisdom recited all that Malik had told them from his visits with Tisha and Simon. Royal was as surprised as Wisdom to hear about the pregnancy. As Wisdom was speaking, Royal could tell the news of the preganancy had unnerved him and that he was trying not to betray himself. Royal was overjoyed to hear that Arkon and Simon might be joining them soon. Though he felt safe with those who were currently surrounding him, there was no replacing his connection with Simon and Arkon. Silently, Hue said a prayer of thanksgiving to both his Savior and the Avatar. He might see his father yet, drunk or not.

Listening to Wisdom tell his tale and explain about his shade, the now unseen member of their party, Hue was relieved to hear that Arkon and Simon might be joining them soon. If they could get to Acara, then there was a chance that he and Wisdom could go home. He could not imagine what his father and sister, Sapphire, were going through. Unconsciously, Hue licked his lips where he and Royal had just touched. For the first time in a long time, Hue felt hope. He exhaled.

"Let us break camp and go to the shoreline," Lethia commanded. "I will also have Tori guide your heads so we may all speak Acarian."

"I can do that," Tori agreed gladly as he held up a wrinkled finger.

"Good," Lethia said.

Quickly, the others began to gather their packs and provisions. They did so fastidiously with little conversation. Tori sat off to the side playing his flute with Peku resting by his side. He was about to start another song when he suddenly stopped and dropped his flute. The others did not notice it, but Tori quickly grabbed his walking stick and came to his feet. He turned his head from right to left listening to the wind and the animals of the Lost Islands. A chill went through him. He swallowed hard. Immediately, he did not like what he felt. Just then, Maximus came galloping in from the foliage at full speed. He was in his full canine form and his hackles were up. Royal caught sight of him and dropped his packs immediately.

"They are here," Tori said softly. His throat had gone dry.

"What do you mean?" Lethia said as she drew her sword.

"A Gateway has opened on a Lost Isle close to here," Tori announced.

The others froze at the announcement. Royal lifted his pack over his shoulder

and let his hands burst into flames. Wisdom took up position next to him with an ominous looking black bag swung over his shoulder, a sawed-off machine gun in his right hand and a magnum in the left. Lethia scanned the jungle with her bird-like eyes, searching. Hue shrank back from the group and took out his .22. He could barely see over the others. He felt small in comparison. His adrenaline made him feel ready nonetheless. He began to shudder.

Lethia stepped out from the group and began to march up and down.

"It does not matter who is here," she snapped. "We must stick to our plan. So finish getting our supplies together and let's get to the vein to meet the sea ship."

"I will go to the trees and see exactly who they are," Maximus offered as he stood up suddenly, blotting out the suns.

"Easy big fella," Lethia said as she steadied him. "We may need you to stay by the High Prince."

"But we need to know with whomwe are dealing," Maximus growled.

The others looked at each other oddly. She ignored the stare of the others. Lethia

turned to face Wisdom. Looking at each other, their eyes met with mutual understanding.

"Malik," Wisdom called out to the fading light.

Instantly, Malik made his ethereal presence known.

"Brother from another planet here" he joked. "What can I do for you?"

Wisdom immediately filled Malik in on the situation. He nodded to his old friend and vanished.

"While Malik figures out who these newcomers are, we'll make for the beach," Lethia-ordered as she boosted several packs over her shoulder and turned for the veins. The others followed her silently in a single file. Everyone was in deep thought, but nobody knew what to say as they marched on.

Several islands over Burton, Ilson, the Marauder and his hounds, and the regiment of troops appeared under a natural archway in the jungle. Burton stood still for a moment taking in the scenery and surveying the land with his battle-tested eyes. They weren't here, but they were close by. He could feel it. Burton licked his lips in anticipation. Ilson came up behind him and waited to be acknowledged.

"Yes, Ilson?" Burton asked.

"Remember this," Ilson whispered as he handed Burton the vile of poison that Holi had given him in the Citadel. The aldam glowed in the sunlight.

"Yes, indeed." Burton smiled.

Secretly, he and Ilson put on gloves made of Gorda intestines to protect their skin. They carefully applied the poison to their blades.

"Your Highness," one of the troops said as he came up to Burton and Ilson-bowing his head.

"The Marauder and its hounds are pointing to an Island two over," the officer explained. "There we will find our prey."

"Good. Get the men in march formation," Burton commanded.

As High Prince Burton and Ilson made their way through the foliage, they were hardly aware of the shade of Malik Jones that was haunting them in the distance and taking in their every word. As they moved toward encountering Royal and his comrades, Malik vanished to go back and report to his friends.

Wisdom, Lethia, Tori, Peku, Hue, Royal, and Maximus stood on the sandy beach of the island. Tori had finished his work with each of them, permanently installing Acarian in their minds. He was a little unsteady after the effort. Peku steadied his longtime companion. The sea ship that they were waiting for looked larger in the distance. Its large masts were obvious on the open horizon now. A small boat had been lowered from the side of the ship and oarsmen were rowing toward the beach where the small party stood. Captain Sarison stood at the helm of the small boat. Etera and Tildon were seated in the middle of the boat surrounded by several oarsmen, his best men. The Sylphs pranced invisibly around them guiding their motion.

"There they are!" Etera said as she pointed to the group on the beach.

Captain Sarison removed a long looking-glass and spied the group on the shore. After looking at them, he put the scope down. He shook his head.

"I knew that when Anna-Beth asked me to take you all on that this would not be a simple venture," he laughed. "But I had no idea that I would be bringing the entire wrath of the High Queen down upon me," he snapped.

"Are you scared, Captain?" Tildon asked sarcastically.

The Captain of the *Lucky Lady* turned to his passenger and winked.

"Few things sc are me boy! Poverty and an evil woman!" he said, laughing.

On the beach, Malik reappeared. He waved Wisdom over and spoke to him in whispers before vanishing again. Wisdom had a grave look on his face as he re-approached the group. He carefully explained to the group the detailed report that Malik had given him. He was quick to describe to them what the interlopers looked like and what weapons they carried. Lethia listened attentively. She showed no signs of fear or weakness. She lit a cigar and began to smoke. She turned to Royal and began to speak.

"It would appear, young High Prince, that you are about to meet one of your uncles."

"My uncles ?" Royal questioned.

"Yes. It appears the person leading this party is a High Prince. There are two in the realm besides you. I doubt that your uncle Holi would ever leave the capital. Therefore, the man leading this attack would be High Prince Burton. He is known for doing the High Queen's bidding. In addition to him, he travels with a regiment of troops and a creature of Dark Magic that I do not know."

"What does the creature look like?" Tori asked hurriedly.

Wisdom quickly described the nine-foot beast and its dark hounds to Tori. As he began to describe the monster to Tori, he began to shake his head knowingly.

"It is a Marauder. They are conjurations of the Dark God himself. They are lethal creatures that are known to eat and to destroy men in a variety of ways," Tori said, as he shook his head. "Surely doom has come to these Lost Islands."

"I need a nap," Peku quipped.

Just then there was a rustle through the trees. Burton, his men, and the Marauder seemed to come out of nowhere and fill the beach. The Marauder let out a blood-curdling howl which made everyone freeze. It was about to charge in on the small party when Burton raised his hand. He caught sight of Lethia and smiled. They were old friends and adversaries. Each drew their swords without taking their eyes off the other.

"It has been a long time, Queen of the CODA," Burton laughed.

"Not long enough, High Prince," Lethia responded as she exhaled a mouthful of smoke.

"I suppose that is my nephew," Burton said as he motioned to Royal. "He favors my dead brother."

Royal went to step forward. Wisdom stopped him from advancing and Maximus came around in front of Royal, bore his claws and began to growl. The members of the troop drew their weapons. Ilson drew his tainted blade and eyed the young High Prince. For a second, no one moved.

"They are under attack!" Captain Sarison yelled from the small boat. He drew his sword and leaped over the side.

"Wait here," Tildon said as he turned to Etera.

"No, I must go," she said as she leaped in the water after Captain Sarison.

"Etera!" Tildon called as he followed her into the drink.

The three of them began to swim toward the impending battle on shore. Several of Captain Sarison's oarsmen followed their captain into the water, ready to fight. Royal turned and watched them as they came. He whispered a silent prayer to the Sylph and the water creatures responded. They lifted Captain Sarison and his party on waves and drove them into the shore. Silently, Royal smiled to himself.

As Royal turned, the first of the troops were advancing. Maximus did not wait for them to get close. He transformed into full canine form and banged into the front line of them. Their armor proved little defense against Maximus' claws. He tore past the thick hide armor and cut into skin. Wisdom came up next. He began to fire his double-barreled shotgun into the throng of troops. Those that advanced on Wisdom and his party scattered instantly. The sound of the gun and the power of its projectiles startled them. The bullets brought several of them down and they began to scatter. Lethia moved like a cat through the fallen troops straight for Burton, Ilson and the Marauder. She drew both of her blades and crashed into them. Burton and Ilson held their ground and began to duel with her fiercely. The Marauder and its hounds eased past them and advanced toward Royal and the others.

Hue stood up infront of Royal and began to shoot at the Marauder wildly. He struck it several times but the bullets seemed to have no effect to Hue's horror. The Marauder released its hounds and the nine huge beasts charged Royal and the others, leaping over the fallen troops. Royal pushed Hue out of the way and raised his hands. He called up the energies within him and produced his flames. They shot out from his fingers in all directions, scattering the hounds. As the hounds ran for cover, Ilson moved through the smoke, his blade dripping with poison. He moved with great stealth and got very near to Royal. He raised his sword to strike the young High Prince when another blade blocked it. It was Tildon. He had made it out of the water first. He engaged Ilson in battle without hesitation and pushed the huge Royal Guard back with all of his might.

The troops began to regroup in spite of Wisdom's constant barrage of bullets. They created a line across the beach and began to advance just as Captain Sarison, Etera, and his men got out of the water. They quickly formed a line in front of Hue, Tori, and Peku-and began to advance under the leadership of their Captain. The Marauder was advancing on Royal. His flames proved useless against it. The Marauder was breaths away from grabbing him. Royal bent down and was about to take to the air when the Marauder grabbed his leg and pulled him back to the ground with a hard thump. Royal tumbled across the beach. Several of Captain Sarison's men tried to get between Royal and the

Marauder. However, the Marauder screamed and tore through them. The Marauder began to advance toward Royal. All of a sudden, Etera appeared between the two. She reached down and picked up a handful of sand. She blew at it. From her hand, the sand began to swirl. It turned into a huge spinning twister. It grew from her palm and encircled the Marauder. It fell back totally disoriented by the attack.

Lethia and High Prince Burton were locked in desperate combat. Neither of them was giving ground. They eyed each other across the sands and they charged at each other. Lethia lifted the High Prince Burton's blade with her sword, swung around, drew her short blade, and stabbed him squarely in the chest. The High Prince of the realm of Acara fell. Out of the corner of his eye, Ilson saw his master fall. He charged Tildon, knocked him down, and nicked him with his sword as he went. Tildon began to shake uncontrollably before falling still on the beach. Wisdom was out of bullets and his bag of ammunition was not closeby. He lifted a sword from the sand and stood his ground. He met the onslaught of the Marauder's hounds head first. They bit and tore at his skin. It did not break. With all his strength, Wisdom used the blade to push the hounds back. He was able to push them back down the beach. Seeing their master fall, the remaining troops charged to his side to surround and protect him.

Seeing the break in the battle, Captain Sarison rallied his men.

"To the waves," he commanded.

Royal and the others, as well as Captain Sarison and his men, ran into the sea and began to swim toward the awaiting boat. As they swam, Royal called upon King Carolyn to protect them. The High Prince Burton managed to get to his feet, he was bleeding profusely but he was alive. He commanded his men to go in the water after them. However, the waves proved too powerful and pushed them back. As Royal and the others got into the boat, they could hear the Marauder screaming at them from the shore as it regrouped its hounds.

Captain Sarison turned the small boat back toward the *Lucky Lady* and the oarsmen quickly began to row, powered by the Sylphs. The others settled into the small boat and began to lick their wounds. Royal looked around and said a small prayer of thanks that his entire party had made it. He looked at Etera. She was crying softly. She was cradling her brother in her arms. He had gone pale and was shaking slightly. Lethia and Captain Sarison had gone over to him and were checking his wounds. They led Tori over to him and the blind old man let his fingers linger over each of the boy's scratches. Finally, his fingers lingered on a scratch on his neck. He bent down and smelled it.

# Chapter 13

Reverend Monroe sat in his office with Purcell, Ben, and Simon. Reverend Monroe was on the phone making calls to the various churches he had found on the internet. The other three men were waiting with bated breath for the outcome. Reverend Monroe was speaking to people on the phone in a mixture of Spanish and English. Ben and Purcell were surprised at this fact.

"I didn't know that the Reverend spoke Spanish," Purcell said with surprise in his voice.

"Arkon speaks most of the languages spoken on planet Earth. It was one of the qualities that made him perfect for coming to Earth," Simon explained.

"The Reverend is full of surprises," Ben said as he watched the pastor staff the phones.

"Yes, he is," Simon agreed looking at the old man, too. As he looked at him, he realized how much he had devalued the man over the years. He had grown up so close and under the sole guidance of Lethia, he had had little contact with the crystal keeper. As a result, he took for granted all the things he could actually do. Yes, Lethia had trained him as a master warrior, but there was more to life than swords and knives. He made a mental note that he would appreciate his surrogate uncle more. At the very least, it would make him more awell-rounded person. This would help him be a better Royal Guard for Royal and better father.

In that way, he would be able to offer the young High Prince and his child more than just his sword.

They waited patiently as Reverend Monroe went through the list, church by church. In each case, he asked to speak with the priestwho was responsible for the particular parish. As a fellow pastor of a church, he got through to them immediately. He asked each of the gentlemen he spoke with about a church heirloom that one of his church members may have left with them for safekeeping. Most of the men were polite but did not know what he was talking about. He got to the second from lastchurch before someone recognized what he was talking about. He spoke with a priest who was the pastor of a Catholic church in Spanish Harlem in New York. It was just as Purcell and the pastor had surmised. The father was new to the post but seemed to remember a crystal church relic that the previous father had left behind.

"Father Benedito," Reverend Monroe said with excitement in his voice, "would it be two long, red crystals that might be bound together?" he asked

"Si," the Father said across the line. "I seem to remember something like that from the journals of the previous Father of this parish. Let me speak with the church secretary, Isabel, about this. She has been at the church for years: if anyone knows if it is here, she would know. Hold on please," he said.

"Thank you so much, Father!" Reverend Monroe said as he stood up in anticipation. He gave the other men in the room an excited thumbs up. They looked at the Reverend expectantly and came to their feet. Over the phone, Reverend Monroe heard the Father have a conversation in Spanish with someone who he assumed to be the church secretary. He could hear that she knew exactly what he was talking about. After several minutes, Father Benedito returned to the line. He was holding a bound, brown paper package in his hands. He opened it carefully and revealed two gleaming Gateway crystals. Over the phone, Reverend Monroe could feel the pull of the crystals across even that great distance. They were still strong and fully charged.

"Si, yo los tengo. I think I have them Reverend," Father Benedict said as he began to read the note that the previous priest had left with thecrystals. "They were left in the care of the previous Father of the parish, Father Francisco. The note he left with them says that one day someone would come for them. Do you know the name Roman?" he asked.

"Yes, I do," Reverend Monroe smiled. He was shocked. "That would be the name of my church parishioner," he said, stretching the truth.

"I see no reason why I can't send them to you. I can send them overnight mail," he offered. "Like too many things in this parish, they are sitting around and collecting dust," he joked.

"No," Reverend Monroe said quickly. "I would prefer to pick them up in person. They may not look valuable, but they are fragile. An old member of the church that is dying has requested them back. I would like to handle this personally," he lied. "You understand."

"Si senor. Yo comprendo. I understand. When will you come?" Father Benedict asked.

"I will come tomorrow," he said.

"I will see you then," Father Benedict said. "May God keep you until then," he added before hanging up.

Reverend Monroe fell back in his chair. He was smiling ear to ear. He sighed to himself and looked at the others happily.

"It seems we have found our Gateway crystals." he announced to the group.

"Where are they?" Ben asked nervously.

"They are in a church in Spanish Harlem in New York City," Reverend Monroe told them. "The priest there said he would send them to me, but I thought it better if we pick them up ourselves."

"I told you!" Purcell chimed in. He felt satisfied about his deductive reasoning.

"I agree," Simon agreed. "They are too valuable to be left to chance. We can take the church van."

"I will drive," Ben offered. "I can drive anything and it will give me something to do."

"No," Purcell insisted. "This might be dangerous."

Ben shook his head, no. "Hue is my son. No disrespect, but I have left him in your hands and he wound up on *another* planet. I'm going to go get him."

Simon, Reverend Monroe, and Purcell looked at each other knowingly. Then they shook their heads reluctantly. They could tell that there was no use in arguing with him.

"Okay, we all leave tomorrow morning together," Reverend Monroe offered.

"Good," Ben exhaled.

"I also learned something else from the good Father," Reverend Monroe recalled.

"What did you learn?" Simon asked.

"The traveler who originally came to Earth was the High King Roman, the father of the High Queen Mora. He was known for going on long journeys. I never imagined that it was him who came to Earth. He came this faraway. He left the Gateway crystals. I suppose he left them in case another traveler came here and got stranded."

"We are certainly stranded!" Simon laughed nervously.

"Isn't the High Queen supposed to be evil?" Ben asked.

"Yes, she is. But her father was nothing like her. Unlike her, he worshipped the Avatar not the Dark God. He died too young, leaving his daughter to Fate," Reverend Monroe explained as he went to the window and stared out. He was looking at the building across the street from the church when he saw a flash of light. Reverend Monroe would know that light anywhere. It was the sign that a Gateway had just opened. It had to be a powerful one to occur without an archway. It could only mean, the High Queen. His jaw tightened as the perimeter crystals around the church began to ring in his ears. Reverend Monroe had almost forgotten about them. He had laid them down before the assassin cube came to Earth to attack them. He had not had time to gather them up with all that had happened. The perimeter crystals were an alarm system uniquely attuned to Acarian energy. Reverend Monroe's mouth dropped and he stepped back from the glass.

"What is it?" Simon asked as he went over to the window and looked out.

"A Gateway just opened across the street," Reverend Monroe said seriously as he returned to his desk and began to fumble with his own crystals.

"Do you think it is one of our folk?" Ben said hopefully.

Reverend Monroe took out a tuning fork and tapped it lightly. The fork began to vibrate, reading the energy in the immediate area. He turned toward the window and stared at it grimly. He scrunched his face up like something smelled.

"It is a dark force," Reverend Monroe said grimly. "It is even darker than the assassin cube. Where there was some humanity in that, I fear there is none in this."

Purcell looked at Simon and the two nodded at each other.

"You two wait here," Simon commanded as he and Purcell left the room.

"What do we do?" Ben asked as he nervously began to chew on his fingernails.

"We wait," Reverend Monroe said as he looked through the blinds with Ben anxiously looking over his shoulder into the fading evening.

Simon ran up the stairs to Grace's old bedroom. He took the stairs three at a time. He burst into the room and glided into the closet that hid her war room. In seconds, he exchanged his clothes for heavy armament. He took several swords from the wall and returned to Grace's outer room. He went down the steps and out of the rectory. As he came out into the evening air, he met Purcell at his car. Purcell had removed two double-barreledshotguns from his trunk and put on a bulletproof vest. He snickered to himself as he looked at his weapons. Even as kids they were Wisdom's favorite.

"It seems we have been here before," Purcell smiled at Simon, then winked.

"But, I fear nothing like this," Simon said grimly. "And it is just you and me this time. I would give anything for Maximus' claws and Lethia's blade right now."

"We will make due," Purcell said as he pump-loaded both of his guns.

They turned to the rubble of the building across from the church, just as the Marauder appeared out of the building with its hounds. Towering over nine feet in the air, it made Simon look small. It let out a howl that filled the night air. It chilled Simon and Purcell to the bone. Simon drew both of his blades. He had never seen anything like the Marauder before. Silently, he wished that Lethia was here by his side. She would know what to do.

"You!" the Marauder growled as it pointed one dark-nailed finger at Simon. "Keyton, son of Quan and Ela, you come with me," it directed.

For a moment, Simon thought about it. At the very least, he would be back on Acara near Tisha, and maybe he could get to Royal faster that way. Simon took a slight step forward and lowered his blade.

"What are you doing?" Purcell asked with a gasp. "Are you really going to trust this thing? Think Simon!" he demanded.

"I don't want anyone hurt on my account," Simon said sincerely. There was a tear in his eye. "It might be easier this way," he stuttered.

"Easy, Simon," Reverend Monroe said as he came out of the doorway of the rectory. "There are things on Acara you simply do not understand. Do not be so quick to place yourself in the hands of the Dark Queen, even if motivated by the love for your High Prince and your woman."

"Then, what do you propose I do?" Simon asked as he raised his swords again defensively, looking from Reverend Monroe to the Marauder.

"You do what Lethia trained you to do," Reverend Monroe said as he removed two crystals from his pocket and crossed them, making them glow. "You fight!"

Reverend Monroe did not wait for the Marauder and its hounds to attack. He shot a burst of light into the Marauder and its hounds scattering them. Purcell followed without hesitation. He lowered both of his guns, anchoring each one under an arm and began to fire. His bullets hit several of the hounds. They yelped as they exploded in a cloud of black smoke, before reforming again. The Marauder lurched forward and came for Simon. Simon met him squarely in battle. The Marauder hammered at Simon's swords with its claws and arms. It was strong. It was even stronger than Quan was as the assassin cube, but Simon was more focused and sure of himself now. He used both of his blades to push the massive dark beast back. From behind Purcell and Simon, Reverend Monroe continued to fire bursts of light at the hounds after Purcell's bullets. The pastor's weapon seemed to stun the hounds and confuse them. They were not able to shift back into form as quickly.

Carefully, he fired around Simon into the belly of the Marauder. It staggered back against the power of the crystals. Simon saw the opening and crossed his blades. He whispered a prayer to the Avatar and the blades began to glow red-hot. He charged the Marauder and sliced into its chest. The Marauder howled as it dissipated in a huge cloud of black smoke. Its hounds seemed to scatter aimlessly without their master's direction. They seemed to go berserk and bump up against the parked cars on the street.

"Let's get out of here," Reverend Monroe shouted over the howls of the hounds.

As the pastor shouted, the church van came screeching around the corner. It ran into several of the hounds and they vanished under the bumper in a burst of smoke. Ben was behind the wheel of the van. He honked the horn several times. For a second, the three of them looked at each other dumbfounded. Then slowly the Marauder began to re-form. Purcell, Simon, and Reverend Monroe did not wait. They ran over to the van and got inside.

"Can you drive this thing?" Purcell asked as he strapped himself in.

Ben smiled. "I can drive anything," he declared as he put the van in reverse and backed down the street and began to drive away from the church. "What was that creature?" Ben asked nervously as he looked into the rear view mirror to see if they were being followed.

"It is called a Marauder," Reverend Monroe explained. "I have never seen one before but I have studied them in my crystals. It is a creature of pure dark energy. I don't know how to destroy or kill it, but I do know that it is an exceptional tracker. It is going to keep on coming."

"Then where are we going to go?" Simon asked.

"I think we go straight to New York to pick up the Gateway crystals, get back here, create a Gateway and go to Acara," the pastor said firmly.

"Sounds like a plan," Ben agreed as he turned the van toward the turnpike.

"But we don't have any money with us," Simon interjected.

Remembering the envelope his grandmother, Loretta Sims, had given him Purcell smiled. "I think we do," he said as he directed Ben toward his Federal Hill home.

On the way East, the *Lucky Lady* ran into a huge storm. Rain poured down upon its deck in sheets. The nature of the storm forced Captain Sarison to lower the ship from the air and let it make way on the tumultuous sea. He ordered the oarsmen into position and they began to row against the heavy waves. The huge air ship strained under the weight of the storm but it still made its way across the seaways. The Captain even asked Etera if she could do something about the storm. She tried to intervene, but the Sylphs told her the storm was a natural occurance not to be tampered with. When she told Captain Sarison this he wrinkled. What gtood was having a sea witch on board if she couldn't quiet the sea.

As Captain Sarison thought about the passengers stowed below, he realized that the storm was the least of his worries. He shook his head as the rain washed over him and he spun the ship's big wheel. Thinking about the High Prince below in his ship, he wondered what had he gotten himself into. He laughed to himself. He had lived so many lives in his lifetime, he wondered if he had anymore saved up for what lay ahead.

Beneath the deck of the *Lucky Lady*, Captain Sarison had distributed his guests among the empty cabins that remained. Etera was in a cabin tending to her fallen brother, Tildon. Peku was with them. Tori had shown her how to extract the secretion from his gland that slowed the poison that was slowly taking Tildon's life. Tori shared a cabin with Lethia. The two senior members of the party were strategizing about the group's next steps. Wisdom was in a cabin with Maximus. They took turns guarding the cabin that Royal and Hue inhabited.

While Maximus slept, curled up in a hammock in his cabin, Wisdom sat outside of the one that Royal and Hue inhabited. He sat on a small stool with a shotgun across his lap. Silently, Wisdom was playing back the encounter with Burton in his mind. He looked down at his enhanced skin. He shook his head. Without the tree sap that had soaked him, he would either be dead or in a similar paralysis toTildon. Silently, he said a prayer of thanks for Lethia giving him this gift. It had served him well. He felt that he had made a difference for the first time in his life. He had also kept his word to Simon by keeping Royal and the others safe. Then he thought about what Lethia had said to him about him having a shade and it being because he was a man of honor. He would have thought many things about himself, but not that. He supposed this journey was indeed full of surprises.

In the cabin that Wisdom was guarding, Hue and Royal were rolled up together in bed, cuddling. They were watching the rain through a small window, curled up in each other's arms. Hue stroked Royal's hair tenderly. Royal pushed back against Hue, enjoying the warmth of his tender embrace. All Royal could think about was Tildon falling. Throughout this situation, he had faced many life and death circumstances. However, this was the closest that anyone had come to dying in their desire to protect him. Royal had been raised a pacifist. All of this violence and bloodshed was beyond him. He also found himself thinking about the troops that had died at the hands of his protectors. They were only there following the orders of his mother. If any of them were as honorable as Simon, it was a true waste of life. Royal shook his head. This was madness.

"How are you holding up?" Hue asked as he continued to stroke Royal's hair.

"I don't know," Royal admitted as he turned around in Hue's embrace. "All this violence seems so unnecessary to me. I wish there could be another way," he said despairingly.

"I know what you mean," Hue agreed. "I never held a gun before this experience with you. It is kind of crazy to think that people take life so lightly."

"And I am afraid that before this is all over a lot more people are going to die on my behalf," Royal said, shaking his head as he stood and put on his shoes. "I just hope it is not for nothing."

Hue got up from where he was laying and wrapped his arms around Royal. Royal let himself be held, then hugged Hue back. The two young men looked into each other's eyes and smiled. Before they knew it, their lips were touching. The kiss was gentle and familiar. For Royal, it was good to have someone so close to comfort him. He had given little thought to what was happening between him and Hue. He was just happy that he had it. Hue was nervous about letting himself become intimate with Royal. There was more to his attraction to Royal than the physical. He truly liked him and his heart was opening to him; however, he knew that Royal was supposed to become a High King. He wondered where he could possibly fit into the life of someone like that.

"I am going to go check on Etera's brother," Royal said. "I mean, my god, I barely know his name and he could be dying because of me."

"I think that's a good idea," Hue agreed.

"Will you wait up for me?" Royal asked timidly as he headed for the door.

"I will," Hue agreed as he sat down on the edge of the bed and watched Royal leave.

Royal opened the door. Wisdom looked up from his post. He and Royal nodded at one another but did not speak. Royal went across the hallway and knocked on the door. Peku came to the door and opened it from the other side with his tail. The Opion smiled at Royal before running back across the room to a small table filled with sweet fruit. The Opion did not give the other people in the room any attention. All he did was fill himself with the tray of succulent delicacies. He burped loudly as he continued to eat.

"Good eats," he said as he wiped his mouth and burped again.

Etera was seated at the bed wiping sweat from Tildon's brow. Upon seeing Royal, she came to her feet and bowed to him.

"Your Highness," Etera said.

Royal laughed as he came up to her and made her stand.

"I don't know about all of that," Royal insisted. "And I know is that here on Acara I am supposed to be some glorified High Prince, but where I come from, I am like everyone else. So please, no bowing, okay?" Royal asked.

"I will try," Etera agreed.

For a moment the two stood awkwardly in the middle of the room looking into each other's eyes. Royal felt an intense heat begin to build in him as he looked at Etera. Without thinking he reached out and touched her face. Her skin was soft to the touch. Royal smiled.

"How is your brother?" Royal asked.

"He is the same," Etera said with a sigh. "Thanks to Peku's enzymes, the poison has not progressed, but it is far from a cure. I fear that his only hope is what the CODA can offer him."

Royal went over to the bed where Tildon was laying down. He looked just like Etera, except that his complexion was pale and he was sweating profusely. Royal could sense through his enhanced senses that he was in the grip of a deadly toxin. He wrinkled his nose. He did not like how he smelled He smelt lke rotting flesh. Royal sat down on the edge of the bed next to Tildon and picked up his hand gently. He was hot with fever and stirred slightly at the High Prince's touch.

"What does yout brother like to be called?" Royal asked Etera.

"He is called Tildon," Etera said. "He is my twin. I fear that he would not be in this space if not tried to come home in the first place."

"No!" Royal cut her off. "If it is anyone's fault, it is mine. He would not be in this space if he had not been trying to save me. I want to thank you and Captain Sarison for coming when you did. If you hadn't, I don't think that we would be sitting hernow," Royal admitted sincerely.

"I was just following the will of the Avatar," Etera said candidly. "I only wish the cost was not so great."

Royal thought about what Etera had just said. Then he looked back at Tildon. Since finding out about the Avatar, he had never really asked it for anything. He knew that it was supposed to be omnipotent. Surely, it could handle a simple poison. Besides, the Avatar was supposed to be one of his parents. He had been trained in his ministry that one had to approach God like you were a child and ask for what you wanted. Royal sighed to himself. He hoped this truism worked with omnipotent, omnipresent divinities of other worlds as well.

Royal closed his eyes and began to pray to the Avatar. After a few minutes a wind swept through the small chamber. Peku, who had nodded off to sleep in the corner, fell off his chair and scrambled under the table. The wind put out all the candles in the small chamber. Then, an amber light formed around the bed where Royal was tending to Tildon. Etera gasped she felt the power of the Avatar fill the room.

-I am here because you called, the Avatar said.

"Thank you for coming," Royal said sincerely. "Tildon risked his life in order to try and save me. Now he is dying from a poison called Aldam. There is supposed to be no cure. But I believe that you can save him."

-Aldam is a substance that is not supposed to exist on this world. It is a product of science gone wrong. I have no cure for it, the Avatar said.

At the utterance of these words, Etera fell to her knees and began to sob uncontrollably. Royal looked down at her and began to shiver. He shook his head. For all that he had discovered since finding out about Acara, he refused to believe that there was no way that Tildon could be cured. There has to be something that we can do," Royal pleaded. "Please!"

-Aldam is a poison that corrupts every cell of the body. The only thing that could possibly save him is to get him to the CODA. They tend a spring of water that gives eternal life. Wash Tildon in that spring and he may be rejuvenated, the Avatar explained as it began t to fade.

Royal stood up from where he was sitting. He knew that the CODA did not have room for men in their society, but Lethia was their Queena and he wasthe High Prince of Acara. He had to believe that between the two of them they could get the CODA to make an exception to the rules of their culture. Royal walked over and lifted Etera to her feet.

"You must have hope," Royal said as he sought to comfort her. "We will get the CODA to help us."

"Royal, you do not understand," Etera sobbed. "The CODA are a reclusive group and they abhor anything that has to do with men. There is no way they are going to help us," Etera said grimly.

Royal put a finger to her lips and smiled.

"You have to have hope, my dear," Royal said softly. "The same hope that got you from the mines and home again will help us save your brother."

"I will try," Etera said. "I will try."

"That's my girl," Royal said.

The two of them embraced and held onto each other for a long time. As they separated, the pair looked into each other's eyes and smiled. For a moment, Royal was about to kiss her when he thought about Hue.

Royal kissed Etera on the forehead and excused himself from her room, leaving her alone with Peku to tend her fallen brother.

Lethia sat in a window of her cabin, watching the rain and smoking a cigar. She was thinking about her homeland on the Eastern plains. She had not seen them since her last visit to the capital awhen she had been tasked with taking Royal and Simon to Earth by the Avatar. In retrospect, it was the hardest decision she had ever made. It went against all of her teachings as Queen of the CODA to help men. The CODA was a society set up for women outside of the world of men. It was a world set up for the female spirit to thrive in conjunction with the Avatar outside of the oppressive world of men. Except for ritual procreation, the CODA kept themselves separate from all interaction with men. It was the central tenant of the CODA and it was absolute. Even though Lethia was their Queen, it was her responsibility to embody the tenets of the CODA, not make changes to them. She had no idea how she was going to get them to help Tildon. She shook her head and watched the smoke drift up in the air.

On the otherside of the room, Tori stirred from where he was sleeping. He grabbed his walking stick and went over to where Lethia was sitting. For a moment, the two senior members of the party simply sat with one another, listening to the rain. Tori broke the silence first.

"So what are you going to do?" he asked.

Lethia turned to Tori and shook her head.

"I do not know. The ways of the CODA are absolute. I do not know how I am going to get them to help this child. The CODA would rather die than have anything to do with men. Even as their Queen, I cannot change CODA law. It is my duty to uphold the ways of the CODA, not change them. Only the elder mothers of the tribe can change CODA law and over the eons, they have made few exceptions," Lethia explained.

"Is there any hope?" Tori asked.

Lethia laughed and said, "There is always hope, my friend. However, one thing that we have not discussed is the presence of the poison at all."

"What do you mean?" Tori questioned.

"It is the goal of the High Queen to capture her son, not kill him. I do not think that she had any knowledge of its presence. I fear, the young High Prince may have enemies other than the High Queen who want him dead by any means. This is something I had not foreseen," she admitted.

"Are you going to tell Royal?" Tori asked.

Lethia shook her head, no.

"Royal has enough on his plate. I will inform the others, so that we can be even more vigilant of him. In the short term, that is all we can do."

Back at the Grand Citadel, High Queen Mora sat comfortably in her private study. She was sitting in front of a stack of parchments. They represented the entire set of business that would be handled at the next meeting of the High Court. The High Queen sighed to herself. She tired greatly of the petty issues that brought the royalty or their representatives to the capital. While dealing with the issues of royalty and their respective lands kept her in power, she preferred her role as the High Priestess to the Dark God. It was much more gratifying to her personally. She enjoyed her constant flirtation with the dark energy and all that it offered her.

The High Queen was about to return to her work when Quan came in the room. She looked up from her papers and waved for him to approach.

"My High Queen," Quan began, "Ela would like to speak with you."

"Do you know what it is about?' she asked.

"She said she would prefer to speak with you in person first," Quan replied.

"Send her in," the High Queen said.

Moments later Ela came into the room. She bowed to the High Queen and moved close to her, so that her words would be for her ears only. Carefully, Ela explained about Tisha being visited by the shade the previous evening. She told the High Queenabout how Agar interceded and used his dark power and described to her how Tisha was immune to its effects. The High Queen looked up at her in surprise. This was a development she had not foreseen.

"Bring Tisha to me," the High Queen commanded.

"Yes, my High Queen," Ela agreed and vanished from the room.

The High Queen went over to a small chest and opened it. She removed a golden tiara and placed it on her head. She sat down next to the fire in the room and waited for Tisha to be brought to her. Moments later, Ela returned to the room with Tisha by her side. Tisha caught sight of the High Queen in the light of the fire and swallowed nervously. The High Queen looked up from where she was studying the fire and smiled at Tisha. She motioned for her to sit in the chair across from her. Tisha cautiously bowed and sat down. For a moment, the two women sat still in the warmth of the fire.

"I had no idea whether holding you here would make you one of us," the High Queen said without lifting her gaze. "However, I hoped that by making you one of us, Keyton's adjustment to the Royal Guard would be easier," she explained.

"I do understand," Tisha said meekly.

"However, you have proven to me that I have invited more into my house than even I had anticipated. You conspire with shades and you even prove immune to the dark touch that makes me who I am. What say you to this?" the High Queen asked.

Tisha thought for a moment before she spoke. She did not know what to say. After some time, she cleared her throat and began to speak.

"You have not been anything but kind to me," Tisha began, "and I thank you for that, more than I can say. It was not my intention to conspire against anyone. I just needed to know that those I love were okay. You can understand that?" she paused. "And the reason why the dark stuff didn't hurt me is as much of a mystery to me as it is to you."

The High Queen looked at Tisha with no expression. Then she raised her hands and said a prayer to the Dark God. A fine black mist poured from her fingers. It curled through the room and wrapped itself around Tisha's chair. However, as it neared her it was summarily cast away. From deep inside Tisha the High Queen could feel her unborn son resisting the energy. It seemed to glow with an energy that the High Queen did not recognize. She lowered her hands and smiled. This was an unforeseen development. She would have to go to the Dark Temple and ask the other priests of the Dark God about this.

"Go to your chambers, Tisha, and rest. We will talk more of this at a another time," the High Queen declared. "Ela!" she called.

Ela came into the room and met Tisha at the door. She informed the High Queen that her uncle was at the door to her chamber waiting for her. The High Queen looked at Ela in surprise. She had not been informed of his return from the Lost Islands. She squinted, trying not to show emotion. She knew that if her uncle was coming to her here, at this time of night, the news must not be good. She sighed and told Ela to send him in and she returned to her fire.

The High Prince came into the study and waited until Ela and Tisha were gone before approaching his niece. The High Queen rose from where she was sitting. She looked at Burton and saw his wounds. He had not even gone to the crystal healers to be healed before coming to her. He showed her respect in that way. It softened her reaction to him. Ela went over to the table and poured a goblet of wine for herself and her uncle. She offered him the cup and returned to the fire. She waved for Burton to join her. He sat down across from his niece and began to drink. For a moment, the two sat without speaking. It was a rare moment for them both.

"I gather that news from your quest is not good, my uncle?" the High Queen inquired.

"I have failed you, my High Queen," Burton said as he drank.

Carefully, he recited the news from the quest to recapture Royal and return him to the High Queen. He did not leave anything out except for the presence of the poison he hoped touse to kill his on grandnephew. He also told her that the only reason for his delay in coming to her was that he wanted to investigate the name of the ship that had rescued Royal from the Lost Islands. During the battle, he had seen the markings on her sails. Upon taking the Gateway back to the capital city, he had gone to the ships'registry amd found the markings of the vessel. He told her that her son and his champions were passengers on the *Lucky Lady* and that it belonged to a man listed as Sarison. The High Queen took the information in with little expression. Carefully, her mind calculated her next move.

"Uncle, go and see about your wounds," she directed him. "We will talk more of this later," she assured him.

"Again, I am sorry that I failed you." Burton said as he lowered his eyes to his empty cup.

Carefully, the High Queen reached out and touched her uncle's face then pulled away. She cracked a rare smile.

"Failure is something neither you nor I have ever tolerated well from others, but we are family. Our code must be different for one another," the High Queen said carefully.

"True, my High Queen," Burton chuckled.

"Leave me now," the High Queen directed. "I have much to think about."

Burton rose and bowed to his niece, leaving her alone with her thoughts. The High Queen paced the room for some time thinking about all that had happened. Tomorrow, the capital city was to see the opening of another High Court. Royalty and representatives from all the lands of Acara were in Acara City. She had hoped to have Von at herside by now.

"Quan!" she called as she removed her tiara and placed it back in the box. The High Queen's Royal Guard came into the room. Quan bowed to his mistress. The High Queen went back over to the fire and sat down. She was wearier than she thought. She waved Quan over to her. His mere presence soothed her. She smiled at Quan and touched his hand. Carefully, Mora began to recite to her loyal Royal Guard all that had happened. Quan listened carefully to the re-telling of the tales and took it all in.

"May I make a suggestion to you?" Quan asked.

"Of course, old friend," the High Queen said.

"I would suggest that you go to the Valley of the Monarchs and retrieve the Scepter of the Monarchs. Present it at the convening of the High Court. It is a show of unmitigated power and your right to lead. Also, send word to all of the members of the High Court about the presence Captain Sarison's ship, Make sure that there is no safe place for it to harbor anywhere on Acara," Quan suggested.

"As always, your counsel is wise. In the morning we will go retrieve the scepter and I will send the command about the ship," she said. "But, this time when we locate the good High Prince, I will be there to capture them. It seems that I am the only one who has the power to reel him in," the High Queenshe lamented. "I guess it is destined to be so."

"I fear that you may be right," Quan agreed as he lowered his head. "I fear that you may be right."

# Chapter 14

On the way from Baltimore to New York, Ben stopped at Purcell's house. While the others waited in the van, Purcell ran upstairs. He retrieved the envelope of money that his grandmother had given him. He also took a bag of guns and ammo he had in his house after the assume clubs first take, On the way out of his house he looked at the picture of himself, Wisdom, and his mother. He reached out and touched the faces in the photo. He said a silent prayer to his mother that he would do whatever he had to in order to bring his brother home. Purcell locked up his small apartment, turned on his heel and did not look back.

He returned to the van where Simon, Reverend Monroe, and Ben Lee were waiting. Once he was inside the van, Ben put the van is gear and turned ttoward the highway. The sun was beginning to set as Ben reached the Maryland Turnpike. Ben turned on the radio as he drove. The music calmed his nerves as he tried not to think about the attack of the Marauder from hours before. He had accepted the fact that his son was on another planet and that off-worlders were real. However, confronting the Marauder was the first time he had actually faced any of the dark forces that he had been told could come from there. As he thought of the Marauder, a shiver went up his spine. He wondered what kind of dangers his son, Hue, was facing on Acara.

As they drove, Simon looked aimlessly out of the window. He was still dressed in his armament and carrying his swords. He carefully reached into his vest and pulled out his warping crystal. His image shifted and bent, disguising his true form and vestments. Next to him on the chair were the two swords he had used in his battle against the Marauder and its hounds. They were the only weapons he had with him. If he had had more time, he would have packed several more. He realized that in fighting creatures formed of dark energy his steel was not the best weapon. He had been successful in summoning some of his own life force to best the creature in battle. It was a tactic that Lethia had taught him to use sparingly. He was feeling a weariness in him from using it that he had never felt before. He did not know if he could easily do it again. However, as he looked around at the members of his party he swore to himself that he would do whatever he had to keep them safe. He had not been able to protect Royal, Tisha, and the others in their fight with the assassin cube. He would not make that same mistake again.

Reverend Monroe watched the signs on the turnpike as the van went down the road. He was more nervous than he wanted to let the others see. First of all, he was not used to being outside of the confines of Baltimore. It had been his home for the last 16 years that they had been on Earth. Secondly, he was away from the cadre of crystals that he was used to having at his disposal. Yes, he still had the ones that had proved effective against the Marauder and its hounds in his pocket. He reached into his pocket and fumbled with them unconsciously to make sure they were still there. However, he knew more than anyone else how vulnerable they were to attack away from the perimeter crystals that protected the rectory. The Marauder was a creature of pure dark energy and was surely hunting them now that it had their scent. He only hoped they would be able to retrieve the Gateway crystals and get back to Baltimore before they fell prey to the power of the Marauder.

Burton and Ilson hurried through the tunnels beneath the Grand Citadel to his brother's, Holi's, workroom. Bilk looked up from his post at the door as Burton approached. He did not say a word but stepped aside and let Burton pass. Burton was tired from his visit to the crystal healers. He was freshly healed and needed to sleep. Buthe felt the need to see his brother and let him know that their plan had not been successful and to seek his advice. Burton burst into Holi's lab and came into the room. As usual, Holi was at the large table in the middle of the room tending his potions and powders. He looked up long enough from his work to wave his brother over to him with a smile.

"Are you here to celebrate the death of our grandnephew?" Holi asked. "Let us toast the way we toasted at the death of our brother," he invited.

Burton went over to the couch in the middle room and sat down. He stretched out his legs and stretched. He yawned deeply.

"If only that were the case, my brother," Burton said wearily. "The young High Prince and his companions proved stronger than even I would have foreseen. They were more than a match for me, the regiment of troops, the Marauder, and the poison you prepared."

Holi stopped what he was doing. He was clearly shocked. This was a development that he had not foreseen. He was certain about his brother's intentions and the tools at his disposal. He found himself wondering how someone so young was proving to be this elusive. He found himself wondering how young Von had managed to escape both the trapping of his niece, the High Queen, and his brother. He wrinkled his brow as he sat down next to Burton. For a long time the two brothers sat side-by-side deep in thought, each assessing a plan they had laidout and put into motion countless cycles earlier.

"Where is he now?" Holi asked.

"That I do not know," Burton said. "He and his companions were taken out to sea by a flying ship. On the morrow I will consult the oracles, but I am not hopeful that they will lend me much more information than they have historically given our niece. I fear that Von is truly tapped into energies that we may not be able to overcome."

"Do not doubt, my brother," Holi said hopefully. "Let us pull back and wait like the great Helios monster before we strike again. I am sure that we will find an opening for our plans and maybe then we will be able to get rid of Von and Mora in one grand motion."

"You remain faithful to our cause even after these failures," Burton said, yawning as his eyes began to close.

"Just rest, my brother," Holi said softly as he rose and returned to his potions and powders. "After all, we have done I assure you that you will be the next High King and hold the Scepter of the Monarchs."

Royal stood on the deck on the *Lucky Lady* looking out to sea. It was nighttime and he was looking up at the dark sky. He was surprised at the light the stars and the moons reflected off of the water. It was a beautiful sight to behold. Royal appreciated this moment of peace in his journey. Behind him, Captain Sarison directed the ship and its huge sails by glancing up at the stars. Since Royal had been on board, the Captain had said little to him. Though they did speak the same language with Tori's intervention, to Royal it seemed that the Captain was avoiding him altogether. This did not bother Royal. The large captain scared him.

Thin king of Tildon below, Royal knew that time was of the essence. He had no idea how far it was to the Eastern Region, but he knew they had to move faster. Carefully, Royal looked at the darkened waters and began to pray. He called out the name of the King of the water Sylphs, Carolyn. Almost immediately, he could see the shapes of the Sylphs surround the huge air ship. Then at the head of the ship, he saw the image of King Carolyn appear. The monarch nodded to the High Prince.

"King Carolyn," Royal called from the deck. "I have a favor to ask of you."

"Anything, my High Prince," the water monarch responded quickly.

"We need to get to the Eastern Region as soon as possible. Can you help us?"

"That is a simple request," the King responded. "We will carry your ship on the sea as well as through the sea air faster than any boat has been carried before," he swore.

Immediately, Royal felt the current pick up and a harsh wind filled the *Lucky Lady*'s sails. The deck hands had to hold on to the main masses as the ship picked up speed.

"Steady as she goes!" Captain Sarison said as he struggled to keep hold of the huge vessel as it accelerated, fueled by the unseen power of the Sylphs. The Captain turned from the wheel of his vessel long enough to nod at Royal. He did not know what the young monarch had done but he could tell that he had done something. The *Lucky Lady* was a fast ship, but she had never come close to the speeds that she was traveling at right now. The wood of the ship whined under the weight of the movement and its sails billowed harshly.

"Easy, girl," Captain Sarison said as he patted the wheel of the vessel. "Easy."

With the wind in his hair, Royal continued to look blankly out at the rolling waves. He was happy that he could do something to support their sojourn East, Yet he found himself nervous in thinking about entering an Acarian City. He did not know what to expect from such an experience. Now, he realized that he had seen Acarian Cities in his dreams and he hoped those dream visions would be enough preparation for the real thing. Feeling the weight of his thoughts, Royal bowed his head.

Concerned about the uptake in the ship's speed, Wisdom came up on deck and stood behind Royal. After the attack on the Lost Islands, he rarely let Royal out of his sight. Wisdom needed to know where the young High Prince was at all times. Though he did not disturb him, he was learning to be like a shadow to him; always around and available to him. Wisdom nodded at the Captain at his wheel as he stood behind one of the *Lucky Lady*'s large masses. A gun was at his side, cocked and ready in case of attack. Wisdom scanned the horizon for possible attacks. His vision was met only by the silence of the Acarian oceans.

Wisdom was about to return below deck when Royal turned to his Royal Guard, smiled, and waved him over. Wisdom approached him casually.

"How are you?" Wisdom asked.

"I feel alone," Royal admitted. "I feel lost here. I can see the beauty in this place, but there is so much violence here and that is not who I am. I am not used to this," he whined. "I have been a minister all of my life and a High Prince for just a few days. And the two are definitely in conflict. I mean, I am not used to people laying their lives down for me; even people who I do not know, like Tildon. I am scared that he is not going to make it. I don't want anyone dying for me," Royal began to cry.

Seeing the tears roll down his cheeks, Wisdom walked directly up to Royal and smacked him across his face. The blow was so hard that it stopped his tears. Royal held onto his face and stared at Wisdom in surprise.

"What did you do that for?" Royal asked angrily, his red cheek glowing in the moonlight.

Wisdom walked up to Royal and pulled him to the head of the ship, so only they would be able to hear each other's words. Royal resisted slightly. Wisdom turned around to make sure no one was listening before he spoke.

"Listen, Royal, and listen well, muthafucka. None of this fair, it ain't been fair to any of us since this thing started. You trying to spin straw into gold here and it just ain't happening. Boy, you got to suck it up. You are the High Prince and may one day be the next High King. It means that a lot more people are going to die before this shit is all over and you are going to have find the strength to deal with it, ya hear?" Wisdom said sharply.

Royal looked at Wisdom. He was stunned by the clarity of Wisdom's words. They shook him out of the space he had found himself. He had to admit it. He felt better. Royal said nothing to Wisdom. He simply reached out and put a hand on Wisdom's shoulder. Royal walked away and went below deck, leaving Wisdom and Captain Sarison alone to contemplate the stars and the Acaraian moons. Once he was below, Royal stood in the small corridor between the room that he shared with Hue and the one where Etera and her brother slept. Royal sighed out loud as he looked at both doors. For a second, he did not know which one he wanted to enter. It wasn't that he felt that there was anything wrong with entering either door. His surrogate father, Reverend Monroe, had taught him that love in any form was sacred. It was the fact that he found a profound attraction for both Hue and Etera pulling him that was troubling. Both feelings felt natural to him.

"You look lost, my High Prince," Maximus said as he appeared out of the shadows. Without his warping crystal, the huge canine stood in his true form, looming over Royal.

"I find my heart moved in two directions, my friend," Royal said softly. "Right now, I do not know where I want to go."

Listening to his master, Maximus laughed and rubbed his fur up against him.

"You two legs have too many rules," Maximus said. "We of the Manda do not worry about such things. We let the joy of our private parts lead us. From your scent, I can tell that you are still too young to decide on your true joy. Instead of choosing a room, let's sit and have wine!" Maximus suggested, baring his huge teeth.

"But I do not drink," Royal protested.

"Blah!" Maximus howled. "Sometimes the joy of the drink chills the pull of the flesh," he explained.

Royal did not protest anymore. He pulled up a stool in the hallway and rested his head against the wall. Maximus ran down the hall on all fours and returned with a jug of wine between his teeth. Royal smiled at the sight of his former pet with the jug of wine between his teeth. As the *Lucky Lady* rocked back and forth among the Acarian high seas,

Royal sat back in the shadows of its hallways with his pet, drinking wine. Somewhere in the darkness, he found a modicum of peace in all that was haunting him.

Idris and Itor rose high above the capital of Acara, Acara City. The High Queen met the coming of a new day dressed in her traveling clothes. She wore fine, deep purple leather armor and a flowing black cape. Once the suns reached their apex, Quan appeared at her doorway. He wore a long green hooded cloak that covered his transformed body, made different because of the assassin cube. Quan stood in the doorway waiting for the High Queen to acknowledge his presence.

"Are you ready?" the High Queen asked her Royal Guard.

"I am," Quan responded as he bowed his head.

"Then let us go and get it," the High Queen said as she turned to the door, moving past Quan and out of her chambers. The two moved swiftly through the Grand Citadel and out into one of the open-air arenas around it. The High Queen mounted a huge whitesteed, while Quan mounted his gorda. It was called Enox. Enox was twice the size of a regular gorda and was heavily armored. The Royal Guards opened the door to the compound and let it fall over the moat that surrounded the Grand Citadel. Quan spurred his Enox on in front of the High Queen's mount. They galloped together through the streets of Acara City. Soon, they reached the outermost gates of the great city-state. Quan waved at the guards and they opened the gates. Quan and the High Queen passed through the walls of the city and out into the open plains. They rode for half of the day. The fertile plains slowly vanished and became arid land, full of dust. In the distance, three mountains appeared looming high over the dry land. Wind off the mountains seemed to be inviting them as they neared. Quan led the High Queen to the carved archway that led to the Valley of the High Monarchs.

Quan dismounted Enox and helped the High Queen down from her mount. The two walked up the long winding path that led to the tombs in the mountains. The High Queen Mora passed by the resting place of her grandparents, their royal guards, and finally the tomb of her parents. The High Queen Mora took off her shoes and entered the tomb where her father, the High King Roman, rested in a crystal sarcophagus. Quan took up his position at the mouth of the tunnel as the High Queen entered. The High Queen looked down at her father through the lid of the ornate coffin. The former High King was dressed in full royal splendor with his crown and the Scepter of the Monarchs in his hand. In the Acarian way, his body was perfectly preserved. He did not look dead at all, but merely asleep.

The High Queen Mora looked down at her father with a disfavor that had not faded over the years. She still hated him for leaving her alone with her uncles for all the years he was away. While she understood that he missed her mother, she did not understand how he could leave her. The day her mother died, she had not only lost a mother but a father, too. While her mother did not have a choice in dying, he did have the choice in leaving her alone. Out of her space of loneliness and in search of comfort, she had found her worship of the Dark God. If not for that, she would have surely lost her mind. Her father's leaving her had been the poison of their relationship. It had made it easy for her to, literally, poison him years later and take power from his idled hands.

As Mora stared at her father, she was reminded of how much she hated weakness of any kind. Silently, she renewed a promise to herself that she would not show any mercy to those who had stolen her son from her. They had taken advantage of her in a moment of weakness. They had waited to seize him in the hours after she had given birth when her body was healing. Not to mention the fact that they had played on her emotions and the innate loneliness of her position by presenting an ideal lover to her. As the High Queen looked down at her father, she tried not to remember her time with Jul. It had been some of the best times of her life. He seemed to love her and understand her in ways no one ever had before. Thus, his betrayal and duplicity had been even more hurtful and unforgiveable than her father's actions. The shadow it left over her soul was everlasting.

The High Queen touched the top of the beautiful crystal coffin where the mark of the High King Roman was engraved and the top vanished. The High Queen reached inside and removed the Scepter of the Monarchs from her father's timeless hands. The Scepter was as long as the High Queen's arm. It was adorned lavishly with the finest and rarest jewels of Acara. At the bottom was a yellow gem as big as the palm of the High Queen's hand. The top of the scepter was crowned with jeweled arms that were curved into a globe which met at a huge, red stone. The scepter had been formed at the moment the covenant was struck forming the High Court of Acara. Besides its symbolic power, the scepter also magnified the power of the person wielding it. It was traditionally displayed at holiday functions of the High Court and used as a weapon in cases of war among the Acarian city-states. Now, the High Queen was going to use it at the annual meeting of her court to affirm her power.

As the High Queen took the scepter from the hand of her father, she immediately felt her own dark energies begin to amplify. It took her a few minutes to catch her breath as she adjusted to the intoxicating power of the scepter. The High Queen turned her back on the gravesite of her father and the past that it represented. As she moved away, the top of the coffin was restored and her father, the good King Roman, was left to rest in peace. Leaving the tomb of her father behind, the High Queen could feel the pull of her ancestors trying to speak to her. The High Queen ignored their call as she took the holy scepter from its resting place. Quan bowed his head to his mistress as he went down the path from the Valley of the Monarchs.

The two left the Valley of theh Monarchs with their prize. It was late in the evening when Quan signaled for the gates of Acara City to be opened for him and the High Queen. With his High Queen in tow, Quan led the way through the candle-lit streets of the capital. Making her way toward the Grand Citadel, the High Queen noticed that the inn sof Acara City were filling up. Members of the royalty of Acara had been arriving from all over the world for the commencement of the High Court. A sense of dread crept into the High Queen at this realization. She hated the petty business of the High Court as well as its members. The High Queen felt it a useless but necessary element of her position.

On the way to the Grand Citadel, the High Queen stopped her mount at the Grand Temple of the Dark God. She removed the Scepter of the monarchs from her saddlebag and handed it over to Quan. He accepted it with reverence, wrapped it in leather, and bound it to Enox.

"Take the Scepter to my quarters and wait for me there," the High Queen directed. "I must confer with the priests of the Dark God on a matter."

"As you direct," Quan said as he bowed his head, watching her leave. As he watched her, he could hear his Enox whispering in his mind.

-Do not trust them with her, Enox warned gravely.

"I never have old friend," Quan said as he turned Enox toward the Grand Citadel.

The High Queen waited until Quan was out of sight before she climbed the countless steps to the Grand Temple of the Dark God. She passed through the doors and stood before the High Altar. She said a small prayer to her divinity and passed behind the altar to the catacombs beneath. The High Queen went into a small meeting room with a long, black table. She sat at the head of the table and rang a bell that was on it. Slowly, several dark-robed, hooded figures filed into the room and took seats at the table. They all turned to their High Priestess and waited for direction from her.

"We have a new development in our battle against the Avatar," she began. "I come to you for advice."

"What is this development, your Dark Holiness?" one of the priests asked.

Carefully, the High Queen described to them what Ela had told her had happened with Agar and Tisha. Then, she told them how she tried to look into Tisha with her dark gaze and was summarily and easily rebuffed.

"I have never experienced anything like this before," the High Queen admitted as she rose from the table. "I come to you seeking your wise council."

The priests all looked at one another and engaged in whispered chatter. Finally, a priest at the end of the table raised his hand. It was Fildis, the oldest and wisest of the dark priests. He had been a priest of the Dark God long before Mora had taken up the religion. Prior to Mora becoming a High Priestess of the Dark God, he had been the most senior and most powerful among his devotees. Now that Mora had taken charge at the Grand Temple, he barely spoke and kept his own council. The High Queen was surprised to see Fildis' hand. She nodded at him and signaled for him to speak.

"Your Highness, I believe there may be a new power that we have not seen before. The Moritans are scared to Acara and aligned with all the energies of the planet whether light or dark. Now that Keyton has sired a child with an off-worlder, we maybe encountering a new set of forces we have not seen before," Fildis explained.

"So you think that this child maybe more powerful than the average Moritan?" the High Queen asked as she raised her eyebrows.

"That is hard to say until it is born. At the very least, from what you have described I would say that it is definitely *something* different," Fildis conjectured.

"Thank you for your wise counsel," the High Queen said as she turned to leave the room. As she left the Grand Temple, the High Queen Mora was glad that she had not assigned Tisha to the dungeons beneath the Grand Citadel. It seemed that her child may be a tool she could use in her war against the Avatar and her son. At the very least, she knew that she could use it as another tool to wipe out any dissension she faced. With a smile on her face, the High Queen transformed into a pillar of dark mist and headed toward the Grand Citadel, leaving her mount to roam the streets behind her and find its way home.

In the meeting room beneath the Grand Temple of the Dark God, the priests remained seated around the table. As they discussed the presence of the hybrid child, Fildis rose from the table and locked the door. He looked at the door and closed his eyes. A dark glow enveloped the door and the room, sealing the sound of the priests' voices in the room. He returned to the table and rapped his knuckles on the table top, getting the attention of the priests. They all turned to face the senior priest.

"Brothers," Fildis began, "we must move carefully. I believe that this child maybe a tool that we can use against Mora and her son. If I am right, we may be able to use this child to rid ourselves ofthe High Queen and High Priestess once and for all."

"What you speak of is treason," one of the priests said.

"No," Fildis disagreed, "what I speak of is liberation from the High Monaches so that we, the brotherhood of the Dark God, can take our place as the rightful rulers of this planet once and for all!"

The priests began to beat upon the table in agreement as they summoned their collective power of the Dark God and it filled the room making the very temple shake.


Far within the Eastern region of Acara was the Red Desert the most inhospitable area on the entire planet. nothing but stretches and stretches of red sand that defied life to flourish. Here the twin suns of Acara aligned perfectly in the sky, creating a sweltering heat that withered most living things. Aside from the red sand, huge rock formations rose in all directions making it impossible to cross the featureless and constantly twisting terrain.

As the wind blew, a single figure made his way through the endless sand dunes. He had been living here longer than even he could remember. He had learned to over come the odds and live where so little did. Despite the sweltering heat, he still wore the hooded crimson robes of the station of his previous life. His name was Jul and he was the last priest of the Avatar.

Trudging through the sand, Jul turned his dark brown face up toward the Acarian suns. With the suns shining in his face, he looked up at the clear sky searching for his sole companion. Suddenly on the horizon, a speck appeared in the distance. Jul stopped and waited until it got closer before he moved. Eventually, the speck on the horizon turned into a huge, dark-brownbird that circled over Jul's head. From its beak, the bird dropped a small animal at Jul's feet. He smiled to himself. His companion, a huge fire roc named Bly, had provided him with the nourishment he needed for another day.

Jul bent down and picked up his meal with Bly circling overhead. He tripped over his sandaled feet as he made his way back through the red sand. After walking for some time, he came upon a particular rock formation that was jutting out of the sand. The rock cast some shade away from the impenetrable heat of the day. Jul dug his hand into the sand and removed a small gourd. He ran his hand over the dry rock several times and whispered a prayer to the Avatar and the Sylphs. The rock began to sweat water and he filled the gourd. Jul sipped from the gourd and replaced it in its hiding place in the ground. Then he dug a small pit and said another prayer to the Avatar and a small fire erupted, as the Etos, the fire elementals came to his aid.

Jul was about to build a spit to cook his food when he felt the fire tug at him. Jul turned to look at the fire and its color changed. The fire shifted from red to white. Jul looked down at the fire with wide eyes. He felt the power of the Avatar wash over him through the fire.

-Your son is coming, the Avatar said simply. And he is not coming alone.

After uttering these words, the fire returned-to normal. Jul sat for some time in the shade of the rock, unsure of what to do. Then a tear formed in the corner of his purple eye and it began to fall down his cheek. He could not believe after so long that he was going to lay eyes on the child that he had sired for what seemed like a life time ago. Alone in the desert, his faith had been tested in ways that he would have never imagined. Now, after so long he was going to see the fruit of his labor. No matter what, he felt that his vigil would soon come to an end and he could die in peace.

Overhead, Bly circled and let out a guttural cry. Jul crept from the shade of his enclosure and held up his arm. The huge Roc swooped down and landed on his arm. Jul reached down and fed him a bit of the animal that he had provided his master.

"We will have visitors soon," Jul said to Bly with a smile as he looked up at the twin suns. "There is much we have to do," he added as Bly took from his arm and vanished in the bitter daylight.

Tisha sat down on the bed. She looked at the table near the window. It was filled with books and crystals. She was tired of reading and looking at the images the crystals provided her. She would have done anything for the internet, an I-pod, or a television set. The novelty of being on a new world was quickly fading. She wanted to go home. On top of that, she missed Little Wisdom, Simon, and her parents more than she could say. As she thought of them, tears formed in her eyes. She got up from the bed and went over to the table. There was a bowl of red and green fruit on it. She picked one up and looked at it. She sniffed it and sucked her teeth. She would have given anything for a cheeseburger and fries.

Tisha was about to return to her bed when there was a familiar shimmer in front of her. Seeing it, she rushed to the window and closed the curtains. She went to the door and looked into the anteroom. Dilga was fast asleep. Tisha pulled the curtains in front of the door. She turned around just as Malik came into view.

"It is good to see you," Tisha whispered as she rushed toward Malik. She almost forgot he was ghost and wanted to hug him. Remembering, what he was, she stepped back.

"I do not have much time," Malik said quickly as he looked around. "There is a different presence here," he said as he looked around.

"What do you mean?" she asked as she looked around at her empty room. She was confused by his statement.

"I don't know," Malik said as he shuddered.

"How are Simon and Little Wisdom?" she asked hurriedly.

"They are well. Making plans to create a Gateway to get here. Simon wanted me to tell you that he is coming for you," Malik recalled.

"Thank you," Tisha said as more tears formed in her eye. "How areWisdom and the others?"

"Them I am not so sure about," Malik admitted. "When I left them they were facing an attack from the High Queen,"

Tisha felt her stomach drop.

"A what?" she asked.

"An attack," Agar said as he appeared near the door of her room out of the nothingness.

"Did you think you could have such a visitation and we would not find out?" Ela said as she walked through the curtain.

Malik and Tisha froze in surprise. Agar raised his hands and dark fire appeared in his fingertips. Malik went to vanish but found that he couldn't. He looked at Tisha in distress. Agar was about to unload, when Tisha stepped in front of Malik. Ela screamed out, trying to stop Agar. However, it was too late. The dark fire shot out from his fingers. It went across the room and squarely hit Tisha. Tisha raised her arms to protect herself and her unborn child. She screamed. Instead of being burned bythe dark fire, it bent around her and dispersed. She was somehow shielded from it. As the dark fire dissipated, Malik found that he could move again. He vanished instantly.

"I am sorry," Agar said sheepishly as he bowed to Ela and vanished.

"Well, Little Flower, it seems that we need to talk," Ela said as she sat down at the table and poured herself a glass of nectar.

The High Queen Mora sat silently in her chamber. She was waiting impatiently for the return of her uncle's party and the Marauder she had sent to Earth. She said a silent prayer to the Dark God for the success of their collective missions and the return of her son and Keyton. It was long overdue that they had been at her side. Silently, she was tiring of the distance and the failures of those who she had commanded to help her. She went over to her bed and took off her robe.

The High Queen Mora was about to retire for the evening when a low bell rung throughout her chamber. The High Queen got up from her bed and put on her robe. She went over to the far wall of her chamber and ran her hand across the bricks. She found a loose stone in the wall and pressed it. As she pressed it, a hidden doorway opened in the wall. Mora stepped back and allowed a shadowed figure to come into her room. The figure was tall and wore a dark cloak. Mora smiled at the stranger in spite of herself. She went up to the stranger and removed his hood. She revealed a blue skinned man with pointed ears and sharp, yellow, bird-like eyes. The man was tall, lean, and oddly muscled. Under his cloak, he wore a sword on each side. Looking at the High Queen, the young man smiled widely, revealing sharpened teeth.

"It has been a long time, Prince," Mora said as she moved back to her bed. She removed her robes and undergarments. Nude, she sank into the covers and looked at the stranger.

"Far too long, my High Queen," he said with a smile as he removed his cloak and began to remove his armor.

"How was your journey from the north, Gregor?" Mora asked as she rubbed at the fine linen shirt that was under his armor. There was an emblem with two birds on the front, the seal of the Royal family of the North.

"Too long," Prince Gregor sighed. "The passage from the North is becoming more perilous. Bandits continue to inhabit the mountain passes. My father remains too soft on them."

"When you are King of the great city-state of Nelp, that will all change," Mora said assuringly.

"One day," Gregor laughed as he leaned across the bed toward Mora. "How do things fare here?"

Mora exhaled. "It is a challenge. I am surrounded by failures, but I have found my son," she announced.

"So, these rumors I hear bear some truth," Gregor said gravely.

Mora shook her head, then said, "I want my son at my side more than I can say. The world, the capital, is a lonely place even for a High Queen who seems to have everything," Mora admitted.

"I wish that I could be here all the time for you. But the royals of the North are a treacherous breed. I must guard my future throne," Gregor admitted as he reached out and touched Mora's face. She smiled and kissed his taloned hand tenderly.

"You know, your father would never have that. I would have to lay siege to the North, if he knew about us," Mora laughed.

"It would be worth it," Gregor murmured as he slid into bed next to Mora and stroked her face. "I would love to be able to give you a child, a royal heir, so that you would not have to worry about finding your son; an heir who would better bind the North to all of Acara rather than the threat of war and your Dark power."

"I would love that, too," Mora admitted as she slid into Gregor's embrace. "But my journey has taken that gift from me," she sighed as a tear formed in her eye.

Gregor reached out and stroked her tears tenderly. He loved this woman more than he could say. He would have defied anyone and anything to make her happy.

"Let us not dwell on such things," he said as he quickly changed the subject.

"As you say," Mora agreed. "You are here now. Let's forget about crowns and enjoy each other as only we can."

"I agree," Gregor said as he drew her into his arms.

The sound of their feverish lovemaking resonated out into the corridors of the High Queen's chambers. And for a time, they forgot about anything else except each other.

## Chapter 15

Ben Lee pulled the church van into the parking lot of a small hotel in Fort Lee, New Jersey. He had pushed the speed limit to get himself and his companions to New York as quickly as possible in order to retrieve the Gateway crystals. After successfully battling the Marauder at the church, they had not wasted anytime in seeking out their prize. It was late evening by the time they reached the small hotel. They had all decided to bed down for the night before going to retrieve the crystals. They were tired and worn out from the attack by the Marauder and desperately needed some time to think and regroup.

Simon got out of the van first. He stretched his long legs after the almost five hour journey. He was tall and lean and hated car rides. He looked across the parking lot toward New York. He was amazed by its majesty and its size. He could see the lights of the George Washington Bridge from where he was standing and the top of the Freedom Tower glowing in the distance. He had seen these things on television but nothing compared to the way they looked in person. The sight of these monuments took his breath away.

Reverend Monroe and Purcell got out of the van next. While Simon was lost in the view, the two of them carefully surveyed their terrain. Satisfied that there were no signs of the Marauder, they both cautiously began to relax. Purcell reached back into the van and removed a duffle bag full of weapons that he had taken from his house. As a police officer, he hated to travel with such armaments. He respected guns. However, facing a creature like the Marauder and its hounds, there was no other choice. He reached into his jacket and gave Reverend Monroe the money that his grandmother had given him.

"Why don't you go inside and get us some rooms?" Purcell suggested.

"I got it," Reverend Monroe said as he accepted the envelope and went into the hotel office to book their lodgings.

"I never imagined that it would be this beautiful," Simon mused as he looked at New York over the distant Hudson river.

"It is truly a sight," Ben agreed as he locked the van. "You should have seen it before 911. The towers were really something."

"I can not imagine," Simon said again. There was a child-like quality to his voice.

"Okay," Purcell began. "I need both of you to not get lost in the view and to remember what we're here for. There is a lot riding on our success," he reminded them.

"Purcell is right," Simon said as he turned from the view and looked at the motel. "A rest will do us good. I do not believe that we have seen the last of the Marauder and its hounds."

"I thought you guys defeated that damned thing," Ben said nervously as he looked around at the empty parking lot.

"The Marauder is a creature of pure dark energy. It is not so easily defeated by simple steel. We are lacking in terms of energy weapons that we can use against it. We would be so much better equipped to deal with it if Lethia was with us," Simon sighed.

"But surely we have put enough distance between us and that thing!," Ben cried.

"It has our scent, Mr. Lee," Simon said grimly. "I do not believe that mere miles will prevent it from tracking us."

"Then we better establish a watch while we sleep," Purcell suggested.

"I agree," Simon said wearily.

Just then, Reverend Monroe returned with two keys. He handed the envelope of money back to Purcell. Purcell looked at the envelope oddly. He did not know where his grandmother had gotten the money from but it was definitely coming in handy. Silently, Purcell said a prayer of thanksgiving for his grandmother. She was always ready with what he needed.

"I figured that I will bunk with Mr. Lee and you two can bunk together," Reverend Monroe suggested. "There is a door adjoining our rooms so if anything happens, we are simply a knock away."

"That will work," Simon said. "I guess Purcell and I will take turns taking watch so you two can be refreshed for tomorrow."

Thinking of his lost son and the frightening sight of the Marauder, Ben Lee grabbed his head and shook it vigorously.

"When will this all be over?" Ben wondered out loud.

Reverend Monroe looked at the elder Lee with compassion and empathy. He knew what the man was feeling. He, too, felt the distance and loss of a son. It was a feeling that they shared in common. Silently, Reverend Monroe said a prayer to the Avatar that he would be rejoined with Royal and the others soon. Though he knew that Royal was still angry with him for the deceptions of the past, he was sure their love for one another would eventually heal that wound. Reverend Monroe placed a reassuring hand on Ben's shoulder and squeezed it.

"Take heart, my friend," Reverend Monroe said as he looked off toward New York, "we are in the home stretch now."

"I hope so," Ben mused. "I hope so."

The four men turned from their place in the parking lot and headed for their rooms. In their own ways, they were all weary from the battle with the Marauder and its hounds. Purcell agreed to take the first watch. He took a chair from the room and sat outside of the door of the two adjoining rooms. He sat his bag of weapons down beside him and opened the bag so they would be at quick grab. As Purcell stared out at the empty parking lot, he found himself wondering about his brother, Wisdom, Tisha, and Hue. He swallowed hard as their collective faces went through his mind. As a policeman, it was his job to be in harm's way each and every day. Though you never got used to it, it was a reality of the badge and the weight of the gun. It was simply not in their natures to face the kind of dangers they were all in now. Purcell said a silent prayer to himself that he would be able to get to them before he lost any of them the way he had lost his mother years ago to heroin. Though he was not able to save his mother from the overdose that eventually took her life, he still felt that he had a chance to save those he loved even though they were a world away.

Unseen by Purcell's eyes, or perceived by any of the others, the Marauder and its hounds appeared in the shadows across the street from the hotel. The hulking beast clung to the shadows and stayed clear of the headlights of passing cars. Its empty eyes spied the motel across the street and caught sight of Purcell standing guard outside of their rooms. They had been easy to track for the dark creature. The smell of Acarian blood was very distinct on Earth. The creature looked up at the Earth's moon. It hung high in the sky. It was still early evening. It would wait until the moon vanished and the night was thick around it before it attacked. The Marauder knew its mission: subdue Keyton and kill the others by any means necessary. It had been stopped on its first attempt. It was confident it would not fail on its next try.

Captain Sarison lowered the silken sails and the *Lucky Lady* floated down to the water. Captain Sarison gave the direction and the oarsmen began to row the huge ship slowly through the sea. Lethia came up from below deck and went up to the Captain. She turned and looked at the position of the suns in the sky before turning to him.

"We are nearing the Eastern Regon," Lethia said. "Where do you propose to land?"

"There is only one place on that continent I would dare lay anchor, my ship, and this precious cargo," Captain Sarison said as he spun the wheel of the ship. "We will go to Lampour. I believe the High Queen probably has sent out word across the world about our ship. Lampour is the only state I believe we will be able to glide into without the good High Queen knowing immediately. It will also allow you and your friends to get to the CODA and the Red Desert through the thick," he said.

Lethia thought for a second and frowned at the mention of Eastern most city-state.

"Lampour is an outpost for pirates, slavers, and pleasure seekers," Lethia began as she took out a cigar and began to smoke. "While it will work perfectly as a place for us to reach the CODA plains and the Red Desert beyond, it may pose a host of dangers that we do not foresee."

"I agree with you that Lampour is not an ideal territory, but we are not on an ideal mission. I am hopeful that we will be able to dock and slide into the Eastern Continent undisturbed."

"I hope you are right," Lethia said as she puffed her cigar.

"How is Tildon?" Captain Sarison asked gravely.

"He is the same: stable with little change," Lethia said as she blew smoke out of her mouth and looked up at it sailing overhead. "He would have been dead without the juice from Peku. That Opion is full of little surprises."

Captain Sarison nodded his head. As he steered the ship, he thought about Tildon's grandmother, Anna-Beth, and all the times she had gotten him out of trouble over the years. He would have truly died without her interventions. Other than a few coins, she had never asked him for anything. Now she had entrusted her most prized possessions, her grandchildren, to his care. Though Captain Sarison loved his ship more than anything else, he knew that he must honor his word to his long-time friend more. He could not see leaving them in the care of these strangers, especially with Tildon hurt. In his travels, he had dealt with CODA women over the years. He had familiarity with their distaste of men. He had no idea how these newcomers were going to get them to help them. But, Captain Sarison was a gambling man. He hoped this was going to be the biggest gamble of his life with the biggest payoff.

"I will be going with you when you leave Lampour," Captain Sarison said as he continued to study the wind and the waves. "I will leave my ship in port and come with you."

"You do not have to!" Lethia snapped.

"I promised their grandmother I would see them safely to the end of this journey. No disrespect, but I do not know you. So I do not plan to leave Etera and Tildon in your care. I am a man of my word if nothing else," the captain swore.

"You seem to be a good man." Lethia said frankly. "I do not feel that I would be in a situation where I would have to break your neck. I would appreciate your sword with ours on the next leg of this journey."

"That you have, Lethia, that you have," Captain Sarison said as he nodded his head.

"Go below and get our guests ready. We should be seeing land soon," the captain said as he looked up at the suns in the sky. "I know of a cove we can go into that not normally used by most ships going to Lampour with complicated business."

"Well done, Captain," Lethia said as she put out her cigar and turned to leave. "Well done."

Below deck, Etera sat with her brother, Tildon. She continued to put the secretion from Peku's glands on the wound. From Tildon's moans, she could tell that the gooey yellow liquid was helping him. Etera wet a cloth with cold water and put it on his head. He was still warm to the touch. Etera sighed out loud as she looked at him. She was having a hard time not blaming herself for his condition. If she had not come back to her ancestral home, Tildon would have never been put into harm's way. Etera sighed out loud as tears formed in her eyes. She could not believe that for all the power she had and all the power that the others in her company had, that they could not help her brother. As Etera wiped her eyes, there was a knock at the door. She got up from where she was sitting and opened the door. It was Royal. Etera stepped aside as he came in the room. Royal slowly came into the room and closed and latched the door behind him.

"I suppose you have come to check on my brother," Etera said as she turned to the small cot where Tildon laid.

"No," Royal said. "I came to tell you that we are approaching the Eastern Continent. We will be at the CODA really soon. I promise that we will do everything that we can to make sure he survives."

"I can ask no more," Etera said with tears in her eyes as she sat down next to her twin. Royal sat down beside her and put his arms around her. Etera melted in his arms for just a moment. She could not remember the last time she had been held. It felt good to have someone so close. She looked up into Royal's eyes and smiled. For a moment, nothing else seemed to matter and they felt alone in the world. In that instant, their lips touched and they found comfort in one another.

Unseen by the two, Hue was standing in the doorway. He was stunned by what he saw. As he watched the two of them kiss, he did not know what to do. He had allowed himself to trust Royal and fully let him into his heart. Not since the loss of his mother to breast cancer, had he felt this close to someone. He felt horribly betrayed. Carefully, he closed the door and backed away from Royal. As he crossed the corridor back to his room, he stumbled straight into Wisdom.

"Are you okay?" Wisdom asked as he stopped Hue from falling.

"I'm fine," Hue said as he pulled away hiding his face. "I'm just fine," he reiterated as he vanished into the room he shared with Royal.

Confused, Wisdom went up to the door where Hue had just come from. He twisted the knob and peeked inside, just as Royal and Etera were releasing one another from their kiss. Wisdom shut the door, sucked his teeth and backed away. He looked in the direction that Hue had vanished and shook his head.

"Now, this is all the fuck I need," he mumbled as he took out a cigarette and began to smoke. "Some adolescent love affair bullshit," he grunted. "This shit ain't the 'Real World'."

"That is not all you have to worry about, my friend," Malik said as he appeared out of the shadows.

"What do you mean?" Wisdom questioned.

"This place that you are going to, Lampour?" Malik asked. "I don't know what it is, but I don't have a good feeling about it."

"Can you be any more specific?" Wisdom asked as he crushed out his cigarette and checked the gun at his side.

"I don't know," Malik said as he shook his head. "It's just a feeling of danger that I can't describe. You better make sure you keep Royal close," he said as his image faded.

"Shit," Wisdom cursed as he headed for the deck of the ship. As he moved through the darkened corridor, he found himself regretting that he had ever agreed to any of this. He would rather have been home on Earth with his son, his brother, his grandmother, and the rest of his family. Hell, he would rather have been slinging drugs to this bullshit. Getting on deck, he wanted to find Lethia and Captain Sarison to question them about exactly what kind of place they were all heading.

*Gateway and the Last Priest of the Avatar*

The High Queen Mora slowly climbed the steps to the highest point of the Grand Citadel. She emerged on the roof of the palace. High above Acara City, the wind caught her black and purple robes and they billowed in the wind. She was dressed in the formal attire of her station and wore a beautiful old circlet around her head., She knew that downstairs, in the grand hall, the royalty or their emissaries from all over Acara, were beginning to gather for the convening of another High Court. She sighed to herself as she thought about the tedious business of the days ahead. She would rather be doing anything else than dealing with the petty business of the different Acarian city-states. She would rather sacrifice the lot of them to the Dark God than deal with their collective business. Silently, she said a prayer to the Dark God that he would give her enough patience to get through another convention of the High Court.

At the center of the roof was a large object covered by a darkened sheet. The High Queen went up to it, removed the bindings that held the sheet down and removed the cloth to reveal a huge, jagged, amethyst lodestone. The lodestone was a tool of the High Monarchs of Acara. It allowed them to telepathically communicate with all the royalty of Acara. Once it was activated, anyone wearing a crown on Acara was immediately tied in to her thoughts. In the past, the lodestone was used in times of crisis or war. However, this time the High Queen Mora was going to use it to alert all the royalty on Acara about the presence of the renegade ship, the *Lucky Lady,* and her passengers.

Once activated, she would leave the giant crystal on. The members of the royalty of Acara would only have to concentrate on her and she would be immediately alerted to the presence of her son and his protectors. There would be no place on Acara that would be safe for Von to hide from her. Unlike the past where she relied on others to retrieve her son, this time, once it was determined where he was, she would go to fetch him herself. It was time to put an end to this chasing game. It was time for Von to be by his mother's side and that those who would support him in turning against her would be stopped once and for all. Their heads would be made into trophies and their blood sacrificed on her dark altar.

The High Queen Mora was just about to approach the lodestone when Quan appeared in the doorway behind her. He waited until she recognized him before he spoke. She paused and turned to face her loyal Royal Guard.

"Sorry to disturb you, your Highness," Quan began as he bowed, "I just wanted to let you know that the Royals are beginning to arrive for the opening feast of the High Court."

"Thank you, Quan," the High Queen said as she returned her attention to the lodestone.

The High Queen approached the lodestone and placed her hands on either side of the huge, jagged crystal. She began to concentrate on the new information she had about her son and the vessel that carried him. After a few seconds, the lodestone began to glow and it launched a huge pillar of light into the sky. Once the light reached the clouds, it splintered into countless streams of light that shot out all over Acara. Below, in the High Court, the arriving royals paused as they all received the information about the High Prince from their High Queen. They were astonished. The rumors were officially confirmed. The chamber broke out in a clamor as the royals began to talk about the High Prince.

"Now, my dear Quan, it is just a matter of time," the High Queen said as she stepped away from the purple brick. "Von will be at my side in just a matter of suns. There is no place they will be able to hide on Acara that is safe from my gaze."

"I am sure you are right, my High Queen," Quan said as he stepped aside to let the High Queen pass by him. Quan looked back at the glowing lodestone and smirked. He would not say it to the High Queen, but having faced the young High Prince and his protectors he was not so sure that capturing him would be that easy.

From her room, Tisha looked out the window at the long line of people making their way into the Grand Temple. She could tell they were important, because in front of each of the personages someone was baring a flag with a different symbol on it. The procession reminded Tisha of something out of the Middle Ages, or something that she might have seen on television about the royalty of old England. She had no idea why all of these important people were coming to the Grand Citadel butshe hoped that they were not coming to see Royal or her Simon.

Tisha returned to her bed and laid down. She grasped the arrowhead that Simon had given her in her hands. She meditated on Simon. Her mind and heart were instantly filled with feelings of Simon. Though she was not able to perceive anything about Royal, she could tell that Simon was still on Earth and she could tell that he was horribly troubled by something. It scared her.

Tisha got to her feet and began to pace her room. Though she knew it was probably not wise, she decided to try and contact Malik.

"Malik?" she called out to the emptiness of her room. "Malik!"

She waited, but nothing happened. She was about to call out to him again when the air on the other side of the room began to shift in front of her. She smiled and rushed toward it. However, she stopped short and looked on in horror as the image began to clarify. Instead of Malik appearing, it was Agar. Tisha's head dropped in dismay.

"I am sorry, my lady," Agar began. "But your spy will not be appearing here again. I have made it impossible for any shade other than myself to patrol these halls."

Tisha's eyes began to tear over. She did not know what to say. Malik had been her only lifeline on the outside of the Grand Citadel. Now without him, she did not know what she was going to do. Tisha tried to remain hopeful, but she found her faith suddenly fading. She wanted to believe more than anything else that Simon was going to come for her but, with what she felt from him and her inability to speak with Malik, this hope was suddenly beginning to fade.

"Do not look so forlorn, Little Flower," Ela said as she appeared in the doorway of Tisha's chamber. "I am sure that Keyton will be back at your side soon."

Tisha looked up at Ela and rolled her eyes. She wanted to say something smart, but she found that her tongue could not form the words. She was starting to really dislike this tall, alabaster bitch.

"The High Queen has requested your presence this afternoon at the dinner for the royalty of Acara that have gathered for the meeting of the High Court." Ela explained. "Your handmaidens have vestments for you to wear to the occasion. The fact that the High Queen has invited you to such an occasion is indeed an honor," she added.

"It truly is," Agar chimed in.

Thinking about the invitation Tisha said, "It is hard to feel that anything is special when you are a prisoner."

Ela laughed as she sat down on the bed next to Tisha.

"You will not be a fowl in a cage for much longer, Little Flower. Both Keyton and Von will be here at the Grand Citadel sooner than you think. Once they are here, you will be able to take your rightful place at his side."

"You sound so sure," Tisha said as tears blurred her eyes. She turned away from Ela.

"That I am, Little Flower," Elsa said as she rose. "That I am."

Tisha said nothing in response. She simply watched Ela leave and Agar vanish. She sat for a long time without moving, unsure of what to do next. Then she rose and went back to the window. The procession had stopped and the courtyard below was oddly quiet. Tisha put her hands on her stomach and patted it gently. Though she was only a few weeks pregnant, Tisha felt the baby inside of her move. It shocked her. She had had a baby before with Wisdom, so she knew that at this stage of pregnancy there should be no way that she should be able to feel movement. She was not even out of her first trimester. Instead of it scaring Tisha, she took solace in the miracle of life growing inside of her, and she found hope.

High above the thriving seaside city-state and port of Lampour was the fortress of Its royal family. The family of Rialto had ruled over Lampour since it's establishment at the time of the beginning of the High Monarchy generations ago. King Brill was the rightful ruler of the city-state. In his absence, the rule of the city-state fell to his first child and heir, Prince Janis. With his father away at the meeting of the High Court, Prince Janis sat upon the throne of Lampour as its absolute ruler.

By most standards, Prince Janis was a handsome young man. He stood tall, well over the average height of the average Lampourian. He was dark-skinned with haunting features and riveting, sea-green eyes. His hair was thick and woolly. He wore it long and it fell fluidly down his back in long braids. Like all members of the royal family of Lampour, Prince Janis wore garbs of the finest white cloth. Around his head, he wore a circlet of pure gold that was embedded with the finest jewels. Through his crown, Prince Janis had received the communication from the High Queen about her lost heir and the ship that was carrying him. Though he had no reason to believe that the *Lucky Lady* would wind up in the ports of Lampour, he had decided to check it out nonetheless. Quietly, he sent his personal emissaries to check all the air ships that were anchored in Lampour's trading harbor.

Prince Janis waited patiently on the wall of his fortress until his emissaries returned. He looked up in the sky. A dot overhead got bigger and bigger, until it became clear. It was Prince Janis' personal pet, Altion. Altion was a huge, green, winged serpent. It circled the fortress before landing on Prince Janis' arm. Altion wrapped itself around his master's arm, flapped his wings, and screeched. Prince Janis reached down and fed his trusty companion a hndful of vermin from a bucket. After his feeding, Altion took off from his master's arm and vanished behind him into the fortress.

Seconds later, a dark-garbed, armored guard appeared on the wall. He bowed to his master and waited to speak.

"What have you discovered Greson?" Prince Janis asked.

"There are no unidentified ships in port," Greson began. "But there is an air ship that has lowered its sails coming into port. From the look of it sir, they have something to hide."

"Thank you, Greson," Prince Janis smiled. "I want you and my personal guard to watch the people on that ship carefully until you hear from me," he ordered.

"As you command," Greson said as he turned and left his master on the wall.

Prince Janis smiled to himself. As it was turning out, the refugees were trying to enter Lampour. This was going to work out better than he could ever have imagined. It would fit well into dreams that Prince Janis had been harboring for a long time. He reached into his pants and removed a small, round, silver container. He opened it to reveal a grainy green powder. Prince Janis reached into the container, used his pinky nail, scooped up some of the powder, and put it up his nose. He inhaled deeply as the rush of the drug overtook him. He began to sway on the wall under the rush of the elixir. The power of the drug was so strong, Prince Janis almost forgot about the High Prince and his comrades. As his head cleared, he remembered his long-term plans and retreated into his fortress until it was time for the next step.

# Eastern Continent
# &
# The High Court

# Chapter 16

Ben Lee and Reverend Monroe retired to their room in Fort Lee, in the shadows of the George Washington Bridge. Reverend Monroe placed the crystals that he had used against the Marauder near the door, so that either he or Ben could grab them in case of emergency. Each of the men settled into their beds and tried to find distraction by watching mindless television. They each stared at the screen, trying not to think about the one thing they had in common: the fact that neither of them had their teenage sons to tuck in for the night. It was something they each knew in their own way that, as Black men, they could not take for granted. Finally, as the night wore on, the two fathers finally settled in for the night.

"I cannot imagine what this must be like for you," Ben said as he got into bed. "I mean, being without your son."

"Everything has been happening so fast. If I am honest, I have really have not had time to miss him," Reverend Monroe admitted. "But I do miss him, more than I can say. Even though I know Royal and I have a lot of things to work out, I still feel like his father."

"You are his father," Ben affirmed. "You wiped his butt when he was a baby and wiped his eyes when he cried. Don't let anything make you doubt that. I guess the same way drinking got in the way of me being a good father, the secrets you kept got in the way of you being a good father. Yet here we are, two Black men going after our sons."

Reverend Monroe smiled, "I guess you are right. Neither one of us will allow anything to get in the way of us getting to our boys back."

"You got that right," Ben said as he closed his eyes. "'cause no offence meant, but if you would have told me a week ago that I would be sharing a room with an alien, I would have thought you were crazy and told you to kiss my happy, black butt."

"No offence taken, Ben," Reverend Monroe laughed. "And if you don't mind me saying it, Hue is a very special young man. He has been a great friend to Royal."

"He takes after his mother in that regard," Ben said as he closed his eyes, trying to sleep and not think about his son's smile.

Remembering the way that Ben had charged into the burning church to pull him and the others out, Reverend Monroe said, "I think there is a lot of both of you in him."

Ben said nothing in response. He turned over and drifted off to sleep instead. Reverend Monroe stayed up a while longer, but finally found falling asleep as well. In the other room, Simon sat on the edge of his bed staring mindlessly at the television screen. He found his mind drifting to Tisha. He took out the mateto the arrowhead that he had given Tisha and held it in his hands. He was immediately filled with images of her. He could tell that she was okay, but her spirits were down. He found that she was losing hope that he would indeed come for her. Simon dropped the arrowhead and sighed. He knew that he needed to get to Acara for Royal's sake, but he needed to get there for the mother of his child as well.

As Simon was thinking of Tisha, Purcell came in the room. Looking at the large Royal Guard, Purcell could tell that he was distracted. Purcell sat down on the edge of the bed across from Simon and waited to get his attention.

"I will take over now," Simon said as he stood.

"Are you okay?" Purcell asked as he spread out on the bed, stretching his tired limbs.

"Yeah, I am," Simon began. "I guess I am just worried about Tisha and my son. I just checked on her and she seems to be worried that I will not be able to come for her."

Surprised by his words, Purcell said, "And what do you think about that?"

Simon paused as he considered his roommate's words. Then, he seemed to rise taller than his ever-growing seven feet. He picked up his sword from next to the bed and looked Purcell squarely in the face.

"I am Simon Monroe. I am the Royal Guard of the High Prince of Acara, Royal. Tisha is my chosen mate and she carries my child. Nothing will stop me from getting to either of them." he swore.

"That's my boy," Purcell said as he stuck out his hand. "That is my boy."

Simon took his hand and shook it. Purcell was surprised at the strength and certainty of the grip. It encouraged him as well. Purcell smiled widely.

"You get some sleep," Simon directed.

"I will," Purcell said as he stretched out on the bed and closed his eyes. However, sleep did not come easy to Baltimore's finest. Like Simon, he was worried about his brother, Wisdom, and the situation he had gotten himself into. Unlike him, Wisdom was not prone to making the right decisions. He prayed that his brother would use this experience to grow up. Purcell yawned as he thought about Wisdom's silly grin. Then he found himself hoping his brother would make them all proud.

Simon took the chair that Purcell was using and went outside. He sat down and stared up at the moon. Silently, Simon remembered the last time he had looked up at the sky. It was with Tisha. It was the same day he had told Royal who he really was. Similar to that night, this night was clear and no one was moving in the parking lot around the motel. Simon sighed to himself and settled back in the chair he was sitting in. After some time, he was about to drift off to sleep when in the distance he saw something move out of the corner of his eye.

At first he did not take note of it, then he heard growling coming from the shadows. Then a thick black fog began to cover the entire parking lot. Simon immediately leaped to his feet and grabbed his sword. He turned around and banged on the door to his room and the room that Reverend Monroe and Ben Lee shared. Both doors burst open. Purcell stood in the doorway, his eyes were still red with new sleep, but he had a double-barrelled shot gun locked and loaded. Reverend Monroe stood stark eyed. He held the gems he had used against the Marauder the first time, crossed and glowing in his hands. Ben Lee struggled to get his shoes on as he came out of the room next. He stood behind Reverend Monroe trying to see what was happening. Reverend Monroe pushed him back into the room and closed the door.

"The Marauder is here," Simon announced as he pointed off across the fog-laden parking lot. The words barely escaped his lips when the Marauder and its hounds appeared from across the parking lot. It was barely discernible through the thick black fog. It shoved two vehicles out of the way as it made its way toward Simon and the others. Simon did not hesitate. He leaped from the second tier of the motel and landed on his feet ready for battle, like a wild, predatory cat. Purcell took the stairs with Reverend Monroe on his heels. The three of them met the Marauder and its hounds in the center of the parking lot. Seeing them ready for battle, the Marauder released its hounds. The huge, black, wolf-like creatures charged Purcell and Reverend Monroe. Before they reached them, Purcell leveled a volley of gunfire. The sound of the\discharge brought prying eyes from all the rooms of the motel. However, ther esidents of the motel could barely make out who was in the parking lot because of the dense, black fog that had descended around it. Reverend Monroe crossed the two crystals that he was carrying and a burst of light lit up the night and cleared a pathway through the fog. The bullets and the light from Reverend Monroe's crystals made the beasts scatter.

While the others dealt with the nine hounds, Simon stood off against the Marauder alone. Though Simon stood well over seven feet tall, he looked small compared to the bulk of the hulking, dark behemoth. Simon raised his sword defensively. Seeing Simon standing with his sword, the Marauder could feel his readiness for battle. The energy was in the sweat on Simon's face and the tension in his muscles. The Marauder wanted to take his claws, rip open Simon's chest, take out his beating heart, and feed it to its hounds. Killing was the Marauder's true nature. However, he had been commanded by the High Queen to capture Simon and kill the others. In dealing with Simon, the Marauder reluctantly knew he would have to show restraint. With this thought in mind, he retracted his claws and charged Simon.

In the dense fog the battle raged. As quickly as Purcell was able to shoot one of the hounds, they would turn into smoke and reappear. Purcell struggled to reload his shotgun as two of the hounds charged him. He screamed as he felt their teeth and claws cut into his skin. Purcell went down under the combined weight of two of the creatures. Purcell felt the pressure of the creatures tearing past his protective vest. For a moment, he was sure he was gone. Then he heard the sound of a gun's rapid fire. Purcell recognized the sound of the gun immediately. It was one of his magnums.

The hounds that were on top of Purcell vanished in dark plumes as the bullet hit them. Wounded, Purcell struggled to his feet. Ben Lee was standing over him defensively with the magnum in his shaking hands. Purcell did not hesitate. In spite of his wounds, he found his shotgun at his feet. He and Ben stood back to back firing at anything that moved in their direction. As Ben struggled to reload his gun he tried to control his fear. He grew up on a farm in the South, so he was used to firing guns, but he had never faced anything as carnivorous or as vicious as the hounds of the Marauder. Ben met their glowing, red eyes in the fog and continued to fire along with Purcell.

Reverend Monroe's light attack was faring better than Ben's and Purcell's bullets. The hounds evaporated once they were hit with the light that Reverend Monroe's crystals generated. .The light from the Reverend's crystals also cut a path through the dark fog that the

Marauder was generating. Though the hounds that attacked Reverend Monroe were slower to recover than those that attacked Ben and Purcell, Reverend Monroe knew that the key to winning the battle rested in Simon's hands. The Reverend knew that the key to dispelling the attack by the hounds rested on Simon dispatching the Marauder. He would have to do the impossible.

The Marauder sought to overpower Simon by using its larger size. It pushed past Simon's sword and pinned him against the ground. Surprised by the attack, Simon dropped his sword in the melee. The two rolled around together in the blackened fog on the cold pavement. For a moment, Simon forgot himself. Being this close to the Marauder, Simon felt smothered by the evil that was at the core of the Marauder's essence. He began to shake uncontrollably, locked in the tight embrace of the creature. Like a serpent, the Marauder began to constrict as it wrapped its body around Simon.

Confused by this attack, Simon struggled to break the Marauder's vise-like grip. However, the more he struggled the tighter the Marauder's grip got and the fog seemed to get denser. Simon could hear Reverend Monroe, Purcell, and Ben calling out his name in the distance. He could even see the three of them, now standing side-by-side trying to tame the Marauder's undying hoard. Just when Simon thought that there was no way out of this situation, he found himself reflecting on the lessons about land magic that Lethia had tried to teach him. It hsd worked for him earlier.

"Every world has Logos," she had said on more than one occasion. "You have to find the will within yourself to tap into their power. It might save your life one day," she had chuckled.

At the time, he never quite understood the totality of these lessons. However, now, being so lost and vulnerable in the Marauder's seductive embrace, Lethia's lessons became clear. Simon reached out with his mind, past the Marauder's dark embrace and past its confusing fog. Reverently, Simon tapped into the essence of the land around him and it responded to him instantly, like an old friend. Simon felt a surge of raw energy fill every cell of his limp body. Suddenly, Simon felt stronger than he had ever felt before. The Marauder tried to squeeze harder and renew its embrace, but it was blocked by the energy that Simon was channeling. Renewed by this current, Simon found himself hugging the Marauder back. The dark beast let out a howl of confusion as it began to feel itself being erased by Simon's sudden surge of pure energy. The flow of power was coming from every cell in Simon's body. Likr his merntor before him he was becoming a custodian of the land.

"My God!" Reverend Monroe gasped as he watched Simon emerge from the Marauder's fog glowing in pure, white light.

The Marauder's hounds began to whimper like lost puppies as their energy began to fade. The hounds got smaller and smaller and began to disappear. The dark cloud that the Marauder had cast to hide its assault began to recede. The Marauder struggled to be free from Simon's embrace but he would not let go. Then the Marauder felt the energy of the Gateway crystals that he carried begin to fade. Knowing that without these crystals it may never get back to Acara, the Marauder used all of its strength to break free of Simon's grip. Once it was clear of Simon, the Marauder scowled at Simon and the others before it faded from sight, vanishing into the thick of the night.

Simon came to his feet slowly. He picked up his sword and looked at it oddly. He smiled to himself as he felt the weight of it in his hand. Simon now knew that steel would no longer be his sole weapon against the Dark God and the High Queen. Simon knew that he would be better able to protect and defend Royal, Tisha, and his unborn son. Silently, Simon gave a prayer to the very Earth that he stood upon and the energy within it. Somewhere in the back of his mind, the Logos of the land responded to his fervent prayer.

--We have been here all the time, a voice said to him.

The other three men stared at Simon oddly, not knowing what to make of this new display of power. Before they could interrogate Simon about his newfound energy, they heard police sirens closing in on them from all directions.

"Now how are we going to explain this ?" Ben said nervously as he stared at the guns in his and Purcell's hands.

"We may not have to," Reverend Monroe assured.

"What do you mean?" Purcell asked hurriedly as he looked over to the approaching police cruiser.

"No time to explain," The pastor said. "Just hold hands."

The members of the small group all joined hands just as the first police car turned into the parking lot. Reverend Monroe stood in the center of the group. He crossed the two crystals he had been using against the Marauder and proceeded to overload them. A small Gateway opened around the group and they quickly stepped through it. The remaining light from the crystal wiped the memories clean of all those who had witnessed the battle with the Marauder and its hounds. Further, the spectacle of pure light made the police forget why they were called in the first place. The erasure was so complete that the video cameras around the motel only showed static where the battle once was.

From Reverend Monroe's and Ben's room, the group peeked out through the blinds to make sure they were safe. The motel staff, its patrons and the police ambled around like zombies or drunks, befuddled by the power of the crystals. There was a lot of confusion among those who were in the parking lot, but no one approached their rooms. They were safe for now. They all exhaled and sat down around the mini-bar.

"What happened out there?" Ben stuttered as he pushed the smoking gun he had used in the battle across the bed as if he hated it and he did.

"I sacrificed the one weapon I had to create a localized Gateway for us to make a hasty retreat," Reverend Monroe explained. "When I overloaded it, it wiped out the memories of all those who had seen the battle," he added as he placed the shattered, inert crystals on the bureau.

"Was that dangerous?" Purcell asked as he opened up the refrigerator and got a beer. He popped it open and began to drink. The acidic taste of the beer eased the pain of the bites and scars on his body. Ben watched Purcell drink and his mouth began to water. After the battle, he was craving a drink. Unconsciously, Ben looked away from Purcell's open bottle of beer and the rest of the alcohol in the refrigerator. Since Hue had vanished to Acara, Ben had promised that he would not drink any alcohol. Thus far, he had kept his word. Besides his promise to himself about Hue, Ben was also dealing with creatures like the Marauder and its hounds. He needed to have all of his faculties about him. Instead of thinking about drinking, Ben stuck his shaking hands in his pockets.

"Now that we no longer have the crystals," Reverend Monroe began, "it appears that Simon's new ability is our best weapon if the Marauder and its a hounds return before we get to Acara."

"Do you think they will come back before we get the crystals and return to Baltimore?" Ben asked fearfully.

"Yes, I do," Simon chimed in gravely.

"Where did this new power come from?" Purcell asked. "It would have been helpful in our fight against the Assassin cube."

"I know," Simonsaid dropping his head as he remembered the feeling of raw power that he had tapped into to defeat the Marauder. He found himself wondering if he would have been able to defeat his father, Quan, when he came to Earth and attacked them as the assassin cube. It was a sobering thought. "Lethia began to teach me the secrets of land magic before she left for Acara. That was what I used against the Marauder. I was not sure it would even work here on Earth. It worked better than I even imagined," Simon chuckled nervously, remembering the voice in his head.

"Land magic?" Ben chirped as he shook his head. "Now I have heard it all." He was cranky.

"We better get some rest," Reverend Monroe suggested. "We have to get to the church tomorrow and back to Baltimore before the Marauder re-charges and comes for us."

"How would something like the Marauder re-charge?" Ben asked wide-eyed.

Simon and Reverend Monroe looked at each other knowingly, then they in unison said,

"You don't want to know."

Royal stood on the deck of the *Lucky Lady*. With its signature sails lowered, the huge air ship relied on its oarsmen to make it move across the sea. In addition to the oarsmen's fluid motion, the ship was propelled by the gallantry of the unseenSylphs and so moved across the waves fasterthan usual. For the first time, Royal laid eyes on one of Acara's fabled city-statesin the distance. Standing against the ocean breeze, the white towers of Lampour rose majestically in the distance. It was breathtaking. The city-state of Lampour looked different from the way Acara Citrt looked in his dreams.

Unlike Acara City, Lampour was not surrounded by high walls. The countless buildings of Lampour were built into the side of a mountain that overlooked the bay and port. As the *Lucky Lady* got closer to the port, Royal could tell that it was filled with numerous ships of all different types and sizes. There were people dressed in all different types of fashions moving around the port, buying things from various vendors. The houses of Acara City that Royal saw in his dreams were small and made out of mud. The houses of Lampour were tall and made out of smooth, white stone. These houses were speckled with dark windows that had colored glass which reflected the rays of the suns. Royal looked above the city. High above Lampour was a huge, white marble fortress which overlooked the entire city. Royal surmised that to be the home of the rulers of Lampour. The grandeur of the fortress was unique as were its battlements.

Captain Sarison steered the ship past the port and the bay alongside of the mountain. Royal almost missed it, but he saw a hidden cove nearby. Captain Sarison guided the *Lucky Lady*into the cove and into a hidden port. Wisdom came up from below and walked over to Royal. Royal smiled when he saw his replacement Royal Guard. Wisdom sneered and punched Royal squarely in the chest.

"Hey!" Royal squealed." What did you do that for?"

"I know you are supposed to be this all powerful High Prince," Wisdom began with anger rising in his voice," but I want to know what the fuck are you thinking?" he snapped.

"What do you mean?" Royal said confused.

"I am talking about Hue and Etera," Wisdom continued as he got up in Royal's face.

"Hue saw you kissing her. Look, I don't understand this boy/boy or girl/girl bullshit. But I know that Hue is your fucking friend. And I could tell that you hurt him."

Royal grabbed his head. He wasn't thinking when he kissed Etera. He was going more on instinct than anything else. He didn't think what it might do to Hue if he found out. Royal shook his head. He really wasn't thinking. However, he knew that he had to make it right with Hue. Hue had been his constant companion since he had found out about his powers and had been with him since he had gotten to Acara. If there was one person he needed to have on his side it was Hue. He knew that he had to pick out the perfect time to talk to him when he was away from the others and he would be able to explain himself. This was new terrain he was venturing upon. As a fledgling minister of Gateway Baptist Church, he had counseled others about their relationships but no bur niw he found himself stumbling across with confusion as to how to situation of his own creatiom

Maximus came up behind the young High Prince and placed a heavy paw on his shoulder. He licked at Royal's cheek and nuzzled up close to him. He could smell Royal's concern and confusion from his scent. He tried to smile at his master and provide him comfort. Royal stroked Maximus' head and the familiarity eased his tensions.

"Do not worry about Hue and Etera," Maximus mused. "It will work itself out. You just have to be honest with the both of them. As I told you before, you are still too young to figure out your true joy. When the time comes you will know what is right for you," he reassured him.

"I just don't want to hurt anyone in the process of me figuring all this out," Royal said with tears in his eyes.

Maximus made a buzzing sound and rubbed up against him.

"Do not worry, my High Prince. I have known you all of your life. You will do the right thing. You always do," Maximus said with certainty.

"I am not sure I know what the right thing is anymore," Royal said as he began to cry.

Maximus reached up and licked his tears and tried to smile.

"It will come to you, Royal. Continue to have faith and, most of all, follow your heart," he said as he went below deck leaving Royal alone with the wind in his face to dry his flowing tears.

By midday, Lethia had the entire group gathered together. Royal, Wisdom, Etera, Hue, Peku, Captain Sarison, Tori and Maximus had assembled in the captain's quarters for a planning meeting. They had at last reached the Eastern Continent but they still had a long way to go to get to the CODA plains and the Red Desert beyond. On top of that, they still had to get Tildon, whowas invalid and hovered close to death, to the CODA. As Lethia looked around the tight, candle-lit chamber, she could not believe that they had come so far and still had so far to go. She knew thateven though they had made it to the Eastern Continent that the menace of the High Queen lurked around any corner. Before becoming Grace Monroe, Lethia had been in many battles in her life and broken even more necks, but she had never gone to war with such an odd band as this. She shook her head as she looked at them. The Avatar had jokes.

"We are at a crossroads," Lethia began as she took out a cigar and began to smoke. "However, we have to see this as an opportunity to advance our cause. Lampour is an unpredictable place. I would prefer that we slip through her streets like a serpent in the night and make our way towards the CODA plains. This will not be easy with Tildon in his current condition, but I believe if we leave at the height of night, we will be able to pass through Lampour without incident," she proposed.

"I agree with Lethia," Captain Sarison said, nodding his head. "I will send some of my men into Lampour and get mounts and supplies for our journey. I will also arrange for a wagon for Tildon. My scalawags will be the least likely to stand out as different moving among Lampour's vendors. I will make sure they get cloaks for all of us so we can move under cover."

"I like the way that sounds," Wisdom chimed in. "I like that cloak and dagger bullshit."

"How is Tildon?" Lethia asked as she turned her attention to Etera. The young sea witch felt small and powerless under her gaze.

"His condition remains the same," Etera said. "Thanks to Peku's juices, he has remained stable."

"It is a secret of the Opion that no one else knows," Peku explained as he smiled, looking around the chamber for something to eat to stop the growling in his stomach.

"You are our hero," Tori said as he reached out and rubbed at the top of the Opion's head. Peku began to purr. He rubbed up against Tori and curled his tail along side of him. Tori laughed at the familiar comfort of his companion.

"Let's all go rest for now," Lethia suggested as she puffed smoke. "Who knows when we will have time to rest again once we are on the road?"

The group rose to leave but Royal cleared his voice and got everyone's attention.

"I just wanted to take a moment to thank all of you for what you have done and are doing for me," Royal said. "I do not know what rewards this adventure will bring, but I assure you that if they come, I will share them with you," he promised.

Wisdom nodded at Royal's words. At the mention of rewards, Captain Sarison immediately perked up. His investment in this venture suddenly began to grow beyond his word to the twin's grandmother. Hue looked at Royal blankly. He was mad. He was still hurt beyond belief having witnessed the kiss between Royal and Etera. He looked at Etera and rolled his eyes at her. He knew that he was not a sea witch or special in anyway like other members of the group. However, he had been there since the beginning and put his life on the life as well. More than a reward, right now all he wanted was to go home. Hue dropped his head, trying not to remember Royal's tender lips or his taste.

As the members of the group rose to leave, Royal followed quickly behind Hue. He followed him into the cabin that they shared since they had been on the *Lucky Lady*. Hue tried to close the door behind him, but Royal caught the door with his hand. Hue sucked his teeth, stepped aside, and let Royal into the room with him. Royal went over to the small bed and smoothed out the covers nervously. For a moment, Royal was not sure what he wanted to say to his friend. Then he remembered something. He quickly rifled through his pack and found the comic book that Hue had given him after he landed in the yard of his Shirley Ave. home. Royal cradled the relic in his hand with the same reverence he would his bible.

"You remember what you told me when you gave this to me?" Royal asked.

Hue was standing across the room from his friend trying not to look at him. Instead, he stared down at his sneakered laden feet.

"I said you have to be a hero," Hue paraphrased.

"Yes, you did," Royal reminded as he dropped his head. "And I feel like I have let you down."

"You didn't let me down!" Hue snapped. "You disappointed me and hurt my feelings very badly."

"I am very sorry, my friend," Royal said as he walked up to his friend and put his arms around him. "You have been my closest ally through all of this craziness. I cannot bear the idea that I hurt you. I apologize. I am just trying to figure out who I am," Royal said earnestly.

The sincerity of these last words caught Hue off guard. They quelled any resistance and anger that Hue had at his intimate friend. He reached up and touched Royal's chestnut colored cheek. His fingers lingered there for a long time. Royal found an instant comfort in his friend's touch. He sighed. Locked in each other's embrace, the two retired under the covers of their small bed, waiting for the late hours and what came next.

By the evening hours, Tisha removed her fine armor and put on the garments that were left for her. They were of the finest material that Tisha had ever seen. She was used to wearing jeans and t-shirts, but nothing as fine as this. After she was dressed, Dilga came into the room with a makeup pallet full of colors. The happy handmaiden carefully sculpted out Tisha's features in the purest hues.

"What should I expect from the meeting of this High Court?" Tisha asked as Dilga painted her face.

"You can expect many things," Dilga said. "Of course, there is much business that must be handled, but that happens behind the scenes. Tonight will be a lavish banquet to open the Court. More than anything else, you will see the different monarchs and beings that make up Acara."

"I guess that is not a little thing," Tisha said matter-a-factly as she admired Dilga's handiwork on her face in the mirror.

"No one besides the royals, the Royal Guards, or the priests of the Dark God were ever allowed into the banquet. The fact that you have been invited as a guest of the High Queen is not a little thing. You should be honored," Dilga said simply.

"Honored", the word rolled around in Tisha's mind as she looked at the tattoo that was now engraved on her face. Since she had come to Acara, she had felt many things but honored was the least of those things. She had no idea how she was going to get through a fancy banquet with the High Queen and the rest of the aristocracy of Acara when all she wanted to do was run away and find a place to hide. Unconsciously, Tisha reached up and touched the arrowhead that Simon had given her. He needed to come for her soon. She had no idea how long she was going to be able to hold it together. Besides, being on another planet and having to adjust to that, Ela had put her through all of these strange rituals. At first, Tisha had gone through them just to keep the peace. However, she felt that they had changed her in ways she still could not identify. Tisha shook her head. This was all too much for a girl who was not even out of her teens and was from the urban streets of Baltimore City.

"Now you are done," Dilga pronounced as she slid back from the dressing table.

Tisha rose and looked at herself in the mirror. She was dressed in a wine colored dress with a long train. Though they had removed her hair extensions and left her nearly bald, Dilga had done an incredible job of painting her face. Tisha felt tense but she could never remember looking so good. It was like a prom night she had never had. in Baltimore, thet ime for her high school prom came around, she was pregnant with Little Wisdom. Though Wisdom had said he would take her to the prom in spite of her protruding eight-month belly, she did not feel right dancing under a sparkly glass orb. Instead of dancing till the sun came up, her prom night was spent at home with her cat and her mother, rubbing ointment on her stretch marks. As Tisha looked in the mirror, she wished that tonight would be a do over for her. The main thing missing was the man she loved, Simon. Unconsciously, Tisha rubbed t her stomach. Though Simon was not with her, she figured that she had a piece of him with her.

"It is time, Little Flower," Ela said as she appeared in the doorway of Tisha's chambers. Tisha turned around to face the mother of the man she loved. She was astonished at how Ela looked. Ela was dressed in sparkling silver armor from head to toe that was polished so bright, it almost hurt to look at her in the candle light. Woven through her armor was an earth-green tunic that framed her miraculously painted features. At Ela's side was a long sword that was holstered in a gem-encrusted scabbard. Tisha had to admit that the huge woman was a wonder to behold.

Dilga bowed to Ela and faded from view, as the mother of the Royal Guard came fully into the room. She stuck out her arm for Tisha to take. Tisha looked at her arm with distrust.

"All is well," Ela said. "You look wonderful. Keyton would be proud."

"His name is Simon," Tisha snapped.

Ela simply smiled at Tisha's bravado in that moment, she thought about all that the young woman had gone through over the past few days and she really began to feel for her.

As a token of this growing affection, Ela dropped her head and said for the first time, "Simon would be pround of you."

Hearing the name of her lover for the first time on his mother's lips, a tear formed in her eyes and she reached out delicately and took Ela's arm. The two women smiled at each other for the first time and Ela led Tisha from her small chambers. They walked tentatively through the Grand Citadel, arm in arm, without speaking. They then turned down a corridor and came upon two large, ornate, golden doors. Outside of the doors were two huge Royal Guards who were dressed similarly to Ela. The guards bowed to Ela as the two women approached.

"Are you ready?" Ela whispered to Tisha as they stood before the doors.

Tisha took a deep breath and exhaled, before she said, "I am."

"Then go on, Little Flower," Ela said reassuringly as she motioned for the two guards to open the doors. With great effort, the two huge Royal Guards opened the doors to the Grand Hall of the High Queen Mora. Tentatively, Tisha walked through the doors and met the assemblage of the High Court of Acara. As Tisha passed through the doors, she was astonished by what she saw. The chamber had been transformed from what it was like when she first saw it. The first time she had seen the great Hall, it had been huge and dark. Now, it was well lit with huge candles. Flowers of every possible color were strewn throughout the chamber. The odor of the blooms was so sweet that it was intoxicating to her. From the ceiling, large banners hung down the full length of the hall. Each banner was a different color and contained a different symbol. In the middle of the room before the High Throne, a long table had been erected which was surrounded by high-backed chairs which were filled with the oddest beings that Tisha had ever seen. The beings were of all sizes, shapes, and colors. Some of them had huge wings, others more than two arms, still others were a mix between man and beast. No matter how different they appeared from each other, they all wore crowns indicating their station. The table was filled with all manner of food: cooked, raw, and alive. Though Tisha did not recognize any of the food, the scent of the dishes naturally made her mouth water.

Eat up, Aspion admonished quickly, You are eating for two. And he is a very special child. His chuckle echoed in her ear.

Thisha laughed to herself, Aspion sounded like her mother when she was carryinł

LittleWisdom. Tisha smiled sadly at the recollection

The sound of music caught Tisha's attention next. It took her mind off of her lost son. She looked up. High above the assemblage, an orchestra was playing the softest and most beautiful music she had ever heard. There were four singers in total that were making sounds she did not understand though she still wore the translation crystal. Shecould tell there was something about the music that was magical because as she listened to it, all of what she was feeling earlier vanished and for the first time Acara felt like home to her. If she could, she would have stood there listening to that beautiful music all night. However, there was a pause in the music and one of the musicians stood up and blew through an instrument that sounded to her like a trumpet or a French horn. Later on, she would find out that the instrument was called an Acaba. As he blew through the instrument, everyone at the table turned and looked toward her.

Then someone from above said, "Her Most Royal Lady Tisha, the Mate of the Royal Guard of the High Prince Von, heir of all of Acara."

Tisha's gasp/d as everyone in the room stood and looked at her. She was scared shitless as she tried to recall everything the crier had just said about her. The music began again and the confusion she was feeling was immediately wept away/ Tisha turned toward the head of the table. There were two chairs that remained open: one huge one at the head of the table beneath the High Throne and one off to the right of that. The High Prince Burton and the High Prince Holi were sitting near the head of the table near the empty seats. They rose from their seats and walked up to Tisha. She had not met either of the older High Princes before. Looking at them dressed in their finery intimidated Tisha. She stepped back unconsciously before their splendor. As she looked at them, she could not believe they were both the spitting image of Royal in different ways. Strangely, seeing the familiarity of Royal in both of their faces comforted her. Tisha smiled at them hesitantly.

"Welcome to Acara, my lady," Holi said as he stuck out his arm with wide eyes.

"Thank you," Tisha said quietly as she took Holi's arm.

Holi led Tisha over to the table and helped her sit down in the empty chair that was near the larger one. He poured Tisha a glass of wine before returning to his seat. Tisha quickly began to drink her wine. She was nervous. Then she spit it back into the cup. With the hypnotic sound of the universe, how could she forget she was pregnant,

"Is the wine not to your liking?" Holi asked as he drained his goblet.

"No, it is not that," Tisha said casually. "I am just drinking for two," she announced to Holi's surprise.

"Then we have some fine nectar for you," Holi said as he motioned for a servant. "Bullbus juice would be perfect for you. It is known to help small one's grow," he explained as a servant brought out a large carafe of the orange nectar.

"You are too kind," Tisha said, blushing.

Burton watched his brother with surprise. He was used to Holi coming to these affairs and barely saying a word. It was clear to him that his younger brother was taken with this off-worlder.

"You will have to come and spend time with us," Burton interjected quickly. "Unlike my late brother, I never got to see other worlds. It is a curiosity of mine," he said.

Tisha simply nodded at Burton's word. There was something about the elder Prince that Tisha did not a like at all. He reminded her of Malik when he was alive. Tisha had dated and grown up with criminals, and she could definitely see/that he was one. She could tell that he was not genuine. There was something in his eyes she simply did not like.

She did not make eye contact with anyone at the table. Instead, she sipped her nectar and let herself be lost in the tempo of the music. After a few minutes, one of the musicians hit a gong and everyone stopped and leapt to their feet. Tisha was slow in following the others. She almost spilled her nectar as she rose and she looked around.

"All assembled pay homage to the most royal High Queen of Acara and High Priestess of the Dark God, supreme monarch of us all."

Tisha turned and the huge doors that she had come through stood open. At first, the doorway was empty, then the High Queen Mora suddenly appeared. Tisha's mouth dropped open as she looked at her. She had never before seen anyone look so regal and beautiful. The High Queen was dressed in flowing black and purple robes. Her face was painted flawlessly to match her garb. And she was resplendent in jewels that matched the huge, gold crown that teetered on her head like a halo. The crown was crafted to look like Acara's two suns. In her arm, she cradled a long scepter that seemed to be glowing with power. Tisha could tell there was something special about it from the way everyone was looking at it. The High Queen Mora glided into the room followed by Quan who was dressed similarly to his wife, except he wore a jeweled sash over his shoulder. He pulled out the chair at the head of the table for the High Queen before vanishing through the doors.

The High Queen looked around the table without speaking to all those assembled with their heads bowed. The High Queen raised the Scepter of the Monarchs high over her head and it electrified the very air of the room. It made Tisha cringe and the others jump.

"Royalty and leaders of Acara," The High Queen began in a clear voice. "I welcome you all to Acara City, the Capital of our beloved world. And by my divine right, I open this High Court of the royalty and its representatives of Acara. Like no other time before, we come together to take care of our business and governance. I do not have to tell you that there are those who believe that since my son's return my reign is in jeopardy." She paused and smiled slyly. "But do not be so deluded. I hold the Scepter of Monarchs and the Royal Guard of Acara are at my behest. And by the will of the Dark God we will overcome all, and my son will either join me or meet his maker," she declared as she looked squarely at Tisha and cracked an odd grin. Tisha shrank away from the High Queen's glare. "But enough of that," she paused as she placed the scepter down beside her. "Let us feast on the very best that Acara has to offer tonight, because tomorrow we begin our work," she said as she sat.

Everyone began to go after the different dishes that were placed on the table. Tisha looked at them and the food. She did not recognize any of it. It was all foreign to her. Besides, after what the High Queen had said, she had lost her appetite.

The Marauder still clung to the shadows around the motel in Fort Lee, New Jersey. After Simon's attack, it was barely a trace of its previous glory. It could not even make its hounds manifest. If not for the power of the Gateway crystals that it clung to, it would have been destroyed in Simon's attack. The Marauder knew that it could not cling to the power of the Gateway crystals for long if it hoped to ever get back to Acara. The Marauder looked around at the shadows and it knew instantly what it was going to have to do survive; especially if it was going to be any good at taking on Keyton again now that he was fueled by the power of the Logos.

The Marauder shrank from the shadows around the motel. It moved out through the city as a dark haze of smoke. It passed by the light of more dwellings than it could count. Then it came upon the scent of several humans. From their scent, it could tell that they were disconnected from the city around them.

The Marauder entered the encampment of homeless people around the railroad yard. It reached the first of the men who was lying next to a small fire. The Marauder went up the nose of the man. He began to shake as the Marauder began to absorb his life force from the inside out. The other homeless people ran over to their shaking friend. They looked at him as his body shook and convulsed. Blood began to pour from every orifice. They began to step away as his body imploded and shriveled up into a husk.

"Oh my God!" one of the homeless people yelled.

The words were barely out of her mouth before the Marauder poured out of the mouth of the fallen man. It enveloped the small group of homeless men and women. And just like their fallen comrade, the

Marauder sucked the life out of the members of the group. They all fell down dead, spent of life. The Marauder came out of their bodies and coalesced in its true form. Once again it was back to its right size. It stared at the bodies of the fallen people indifferently. The Marauder stepped over the bodies with no regrets. It looked up at the night sky and let out a blood-curdling scream. It was ready to face Simon and his allies again. This time it knew it would be successful, no matter how many people it had to consume.

Purcell was the first to awake. He stood on the balcony of the motel drinking bad motel coffee. He looked over the side at the parking lot. Cars were still strewn all over and riddled with bullet holes from the night's previous fight. Purcell shook his head. If the pastor had not created that short Gateway by turning his blasting crystals in on themselves, they would have all had a lot to explain. Purcell shook his head as he drank his coffee. He found himself wondering how it would go if they ran into the Marauder and its hounds again now that they did not have Reverend Monroe's crystals to rely on. It meant that only he and Simon would be able to take the battle to them. While his cold steel slowed them down, his bullets didn't stop them. This meant that defeating the Marauder fell completely to Simon. Purcell looked over his shoulder at the slumbering giant. Though he seemed to have an apt new power, from the way he passed out last night, he could tell that having it took its toll. Purcell sighed and bit his lip. This quess had suddenly become even more dangerous.

Purcell was so lost in thoughtthat he did not see Reverend Monroe and Ben Lee approaching. Their arms were filled with bags of clothes and boxes of shoes. The two men were chattering quickly as they came up to Purcell. As Reverend Monroe passed Purcell, he slid him the envelope that his grandmother had given him. The funds were once again coming in handy. Reverend Monroe passed two suit bags to Purcell, a bag, and two shoeboxes.

"Get Simon up and dressed," the Reverend directed. "We'll eat in the van. The faster we get to the church and get the crystals, the faster we can get home. I am dressing you all like ministers so I'll have less to explain."

"I always wanted to wear a collar," Purcell joked.

"I always saw myself as an usher," Ben wise cracked.

"I am happy that you can laugh about this, but we have to keep ourselves focused," Reverend Monroe insisted with a wrinkled brow as he turned toward his room. "We are so close," he mumbled as he went inside, leaving the two Earth men looking at one another.

"What is wrong with him?" Purcell asked.

"He is tense. He doesn't want to admit it but burning out his last crystals last night made him feel vulnerable. He is a crystal keeper, but he finds himself without any crystals. He is out of his comfort zone," Ben said.

"Hell, we all are!" Purcell snapped as he laid the parcels down.

"Yeah, but you can shoot. Hell, I can drive anything. Simon does the heavy lifting. But the Pastor, well he had his crystals and now that they are gone, He is feeling a little useless."

"He said this to you?" Purcell quizzed.

Ben shook his head, "no"

"I am a people person and this wasn't that hard to figure out," Ben concluded.

"Let's just get dressed and get on the road," Purcell said as he finished his coffee.

The two men went into their respective rooms and began to dress. Purcell hit Simon in the head with a pillow to get the big man up. Simon jumped up in a battle stance. He saw Purcell and smiled.

"'Are you okay?" Purcell asked as he began to put on the black suit, white shirt and clerical collar.

Simon thought about it for a minute. He was still woozy from his use of Land magic. He didn't want anyone to know how it had cost him, so he simply said, "I am alright. What is this?" Simon asked as he pointed at the clothing.

"The Pastor bought all of us clerical clothes to wear to the church. I think he got a cassock for you so you would be able to hide your swords," Purcell explained

"Cool," Simon said as he picked up his warping crystal from his bedside and placed it on his wrist.

The two finished dressing and stepped out onto the balcony just as Reverend Monroe and Ben Lee came out of their room. The four men walked side by side to the church van. Purcell went over to the motel office and checked them out before boarding the bus.

"Gentlemen, here we go," Ben said as he swung the bus toward the George Washington Bridge. As they drove across the upper level, all eyes in the van glanced toward the Freedom Tower in the distance. It seemed to have become a de facto symbol of what they were fighting for. Ben put up his GPS and typed in the name and address of the church from memory. The GPS quickly plotted the fastest way to Sacred Heart of Jesus Christ Catholic Church. Reverend Monroe took out his cell phone and dialed the church hone number. Someone picked up after the second ring.

"We are on our way," he began as he looked at his watch. "We will be there in less than half of an hour. Esta bien," he said before he hung up.

After coming down the Westside highway, the van swung across 125th Street through the heart of Harlem and headed toward Spanish Harlem. After a few minutes, the gentrified streets of Harlem shifted from dark brown and white faces to yellow and white faces.

"Man, I remember when Harlem was as black as the ace of spades," Ben said, shaking his head in disgust. "White folk got to take everything from us."

"My mother is white," Simon said shortly.

"I meant no offence," Ben stammered, trying to clean up his statement.

Simon laughed, "None taken. Lethia always taught me that skin color meant different things on our world. Lethis used to teach me it was like Brazil here, everyone is something."

"Well if I had to the choice to be anything, I would stay Black," Ben said, recalling the struggle of his wife against breast cancer until the bitter end.

Purcell did not say anything during this conversation. Silently, he always found his decision to be a police officer a complicated one. His grandmother had raised him to be a good brother and after his mother's overdose, it seemed that everything led him to the police academy. However, from the time he hit the streets, his values had been tested. He got to see how things weren't so white and black. And working the streets, he got to see how he easily could have turned into his brother. Under his badge, he had the same heart.

Reverend Monroe could not engage in any conversation about "race" politics. It was one of those things about being here on Earth that he never really understood. This planet had so much to offer. In a lot of ways, it had more to offer than Acara did. It made no sense to him that its populace was squandering its resources over issues of difference. As he thought about seeing the Freedom Tower for the first time, he tried to hide his tears. It reminded him of the horrors of the High Queen Mora and her worship of the Dark God. He could not imagine how many people she had sacrificed to it, in the name of something holy.

After making several quick turns, the bus of Gateway Baptist Church pulled up in front of the Sacred Heart of Jesus Christ Catholic

Church. As the gentlemen stepped out of the van, they looked up in awe at the size and shape of the traditional gothic Catholic cathedral in the heart of El Barrio, Spanish Harlem.

"Now I can see why King Roman was so fascinated by this edifice," Reverend Monroe said with wide eyes. "It is truly a beautiful building."

"It is," Ben agreed. Silently, he felt like the building was beautiful but with the loss of his wife and the displacement of his son, his temper was short for organized religion.

"Let's just stay focused on what we are here for," Simon reminded them as he strapped his swords to eachleg beneath his black cassock.

The four men walked up the stairs to the church. They entered the cavernous sanctuary space reverently. There was a single priest standing at the high altar before an image of the Sacred Heart of Jesus Christ. As the four men walked down the aisle, the priest crossed himself and turned to face them. He was a young handsome Latino man with Caribbean features and neatly styled dark hair. His smile lit up the sanctuary more than the candles that surrounded it. Reverend Monroe stepped forward and shook the cheery man's hand.

"You must be Father Benedito," Reverend Monroe began.

"Si, Senor, I am," he said. "And you must be Reverend Monroe."

"I am," he said, introducing himself. "I am honored that you took time to meet me."

"It is good to meet you. I hope you had a good drive up from Baltimore," Father Benedito said.

The four men looked at each other and tried notto betray the trials of their journey.

"We were in God's hands," Reverend Monroe managed. "These are my clerical team: Reverend Simon, Reverend Ben, and Reverend Purcell," he said.

The others stepped forward and shook the father's hand.

"Esta bien," he smiled cheerfully. "It is good to meet you all," he said as he turned to Reverend Monroe. "I am surprised that so many of you came to retrieve this relic."

"It is something we have been looking for for a long time," Reverend Monroe said quickly. "It is very valuable to us," he added as he wrung his hands together unconsciously.

"Then let us not wait any longer in returning it to you," Father Benedito smiled as he turned to leave the others in the sanctuary.

"I can't believe we are finally going to be able to get to Acara," Simon said, smiling nervously as he thought about Royal, Tisha and the others.

"We aren't home yet," Purcell warned as he looked around the candle-li tCatholic church.

"But we are closer than we were," Ben interjected as he sat down in a pew.

After a few minutes, Father Benedito returned to the sanctuary with an older Latina woman. The woman carried a small package in her hand wrapped in leather. Reverend Monroe's eyes fell upon the package instantly. He could feel the energy of the crystals reaching out to him. He was surprised at the amount of energy the Gateway crystals still had after all this time. He knew instantly that he would have no problem opening a Gateway with them.

"This is Isabel Lopez gentlemen," Father Benedito said. "She has been at the church for more years than I have been alive. It is her you should thank for keeping your package safe after all this time."

"Que honor!," Isabel blushed as she handed the package to Reverend Monroe's awaiting hands.

Reverend Monroe took the package gladly and looked at the others out of the corner of his eye. They all seemed to exhale at the same time. It had been a long journey for them all to get to this point.

"Would you all like to join us for lunch?Almuerzo?" Father Benedito asked.

The group looked at each other and they all smiled in unison. They had been eating out of brown bags since they took to the road. A home-cooked meal would be a nice way to celebrate their find.

"We would not want to put you out," Reverend Monroe demurred.

"Nonsense!" Father Benedito admonished. "Isabel cooks enough for a small army. I am sure she could put something together for us all."

"Si, padre. Nosotros tenemous arroz con pollo por todos," she smiled. "Y un poco de mi flan."

"Flan!" Reverend Monroe chuckled. "You have to give me the recipe. I would love to cook it for my son," he volunteered.

"Sir, this recipe was given to me by mi Abuela," Ms. Lopez winked. "If I gave it to you, she would haunt me in my sleep!" she laughed

"Isabel," the priest interjected. "You know how I feel about such things. We don't want to frighten our guests. Verdad?"

"Trust me," Reverend Monroe smiled at the group as they looked at one another, "it would take a lot to scare us!" They shared a nervous laugh.

"There you have it," Father Benedito smiled. "Rice and chicken for everyone," he laughed as he rubbed his stomach.

"And don't forget the dessert," Ben smiled. "I would love me some flan."

The group was about to adjourn to the recesses of the church when Simon caught a glimpse of something out of the corner of his eye. He immediately put himself between the growing billow of black smoke and the rest of the group. He tossed off his cassock to reveal his armor, to the astonishment of Father Benedito and Isabel. He drew both of his swords. Following Simon's actions, Purcell reached into his jacket and took out two guns. Reverend Monroe reached for the crystals he had used against the Marauder before he realized that he used them to create a Gateway at the motel. Their power was gone. Ben turned to Father Benedito and Isabel. He quickly tried to get them to move toward the front of the church away from where the Marauder and the hounds were appearing.

"Diosmio!" Father Benedito cried out as he tried to look over Ben's shoulder. "What in the name of God is that?" he asked as he crossed himself.

"No time for explanations," Ben said hurriedly as he used his arms to push the Father and Isabel down the aisle. "We will protect you!" he insisted.

"Come, Padre," Isabel cried as she tugged at his arm. She turned around just as the Marauder and its hounds appeared in the doorway of the church. Her mouth dropped open as she watched the dark creature rise to almost nine feet tall. She shrank back as she stared into the red eyes of the snarling hounds.

"It is a lot bigger than it was," Purcell mumbled to Simon.

"I suppose he spent last night recharging his battery," Simon surmised.

"How did it do that?" Purcell asked.

"You don't want to know," Simon said not taking his eyes off of his enemy.

"Can you do what you did last night?" Purcell asked.

"I will try," Simon exhaled.

The Marauder looked out at the group, holding its hounds at bay. Then its eyes squarely fell on Simon.

"I do not want to hurt anyone else, Keyton," the Marauder's voice boomed throughout the candle-lit church. "All you have to do is come with me and I will leave the others alone if they surrender their Gateway crystals to me."

Simon looked around at the members of his small party. For a second, he truly thought about the Marauder's offer. At the very least, if he surrendered, he would reunite with Royal and he could be with Tisha again as well. Then he turned and looked at the hulking figure of the Marauder and he frowned. How could he ever believe anything a Marauder would say to him. He was an emissary of the High Queen and a being of pure darkness. The very essence of the being was built on lies. The moment he let his guard down, he was sure it would dispatch all the others and drag him back to Acara over their dead bodies. Simon raised his swords and held his ground. He would go down fighting with his comrades before he bowed to the will of this entity.

"I would die where I stand before I go anywhere with you," Simon snapped.

"So be it!" the Marauder's voice boomed. "Then I will take you back in pieces if I have to," it said as it released its hounds."

"Adios!" Isabel yelled as she grabbed Father Benedito by the arm and pulled him back toward the high altar of the church. Reverend Monroe and Ben quickly picked up two iron candleholders and stood in defense of their new friends. Purcell did not hesitate. He began to fire at the hounds as they charged down the aisle of the church. As quickly as he hit them, they burst into fine grey mist before re-forming. Several of the hounds charged at Ben, Reverend Monroe, Father Benedito and Isabel. Ben and Reverend Monroe beat the hounds back with iron candleholders. Surprisingly, the cold iron of the candleholders beat back the hounds. They rolled away yelping at the impact. However, one got past them and headed straight for Father Benedito and Isabel. He pushed Isabel out of the way and took the brunt of the beast's attack. The hound landed on top of him and sank its teeth deeply into the priest's shoulder and scratched at his robes. The father's blood covered the floor of the church, just under the Sacred Heart.

"No!" Isabel screamed as she reached into her bra. She removed a small pouch of yellow powder and threw it into the face of the hound. The hound shrieked as it breathed in the powder, tumbled back and fell still. Ben and Reverend Monroe looked at the old woman in awe as they fought back the other hounds. Isabel winked at them and charged forward using the remainder of the powder to scatter the hounds near her and the others.

"What is that powder?" Reverend Monroe asked as he beat back one of the hounds with the blunt end of the candleholder.

"It is an old trick of Santeria," Isabel said quickly. "Se llama *Asaphededa*."

"I thought you were Catholic?" Reverend Monroe quizzed quickly, clearly confused.

"Soy muchas cosas. I am many things," Isabel said as she positioned herself between the hounds and her fallen priest.

Seeing the priest fall, Simon went berserk. He turned to face the Marauder that was standing waiting for him. Instead of charging him, Simon remembered Lethia's teachings. He reached out with his mind and connected with the energy of the land around him. The Logos. It instantly responded to him. He felt himself filled with the ambient flow of the Earth around him. It filled every cell of his body. Though the Marauder was larger than him and looked more vicious than ever, Simon held his ground. Their eyes met and they charged one another, with the Marauder's waving its claws and Simon brandishing his glowing swords.

The two met in the center of the church with a thud and a burst of white and dark lights. Though the Marauder was bigger and freshly fed, he was surprised by the force of Simon's blow and his wanton aggressiveness. It staggered him. He immediately called his hounds back to him. They withdrew their attack on the others and pounced on Simon. For a moment, Simon was not visible under the weight of the remaining hounds. Purcell charged the scene. However, he was afraid to fire his gun in case he might hit Simon. Instead, he turned his sight squarely on the Marauder and began to unload a volley of bullets.

"Shit!" Purcell cursed as he watched his bullets vanish into the huge beast with little or no effect.

"Purcell, get back!" Reverend Monroe yelled as he lumbered forward with the remains of the candleholder in his hand.

"No!" Ben yelled as he grabbed the elder Reverend by the shoulders and pulled him back.

Purcell stood his ground. He reloaded both of his guns and continued to fire at the Marauder as it got closer to him. He concentrated his fire at the entity's head but it still did not have any effect. It continued to lumber toward him. Purcell closed his eyes as the Marauder was within arm's length. He expected to feel its claws against his throat, when he felt a single sword pass in front of his face. He opened his eyes just as Simon stepped in front of him. Purcell was surprised by the sight he saw. Simon was literally glowing white hot with power.

"Ay, Dios!" Isabel said as she shielded her eyes from the sight of Simon. She pulled the fallen priest protectively to her arms and cradled him.

"No more," Simon said as he dropped his swords and charged the Marauder head first.

The Marauder did not expect such an attack. It was stunned at first by Simon's bravado. Then it screamed as it felt the energy erupt out of Simon. Simon held on to the Marauder with all of his might and sent the ambient energy he had collected from the Earth around him directly into it. The Marauder strained to be free of Simon's grip, but he would not let go. Simon felt the souls the dark entity had acquired the day before. He was sickened by the agony of these trapped beings. Simon swore they would be free. As he felt the energy of the Marauder wane, he reached into the very center of the being and tore its essence apart. The Marauder exploded in a burst of dark light. The hounds that it once commanded faded instantly without its master to power them. Simon fell to his knees exhausted among the ashes of the Marauder. He was about to pass out when he felt Purcell's strong hand lift him to his feet.

"You did it!" Purcell said as he hugged him and held him up.

"No, we did it," Simon panted as he tried to get his bearings. "Now let's get these crystals and create this Gateway and find those we love."

Purcell and Simon turned to the others. Ben and Reverend Monroe were standing over Isabel and Father Benedito. They rushed to their sides. Isabel was cradling the fallen priest in her arms. He was scared and bleeding from a bite from the hounds. He was barely conscious.

"Can you do anything for him?" Ben asked Reverend Monroe.

"I can," Reverend Monroe said as he examined his poisoned wounds. "But we have to get him back to Baltimore where I have my healing crystals. I do not know if we have enough time to drive back and save his life."

"Por favor," Isabel began as she stroked the Father's hair. "I am an old woman, no? I do not understand all that has happened here today or who you are or what you are. But I know Father Benedito is a good man. Unhombre bueno! If you can do anything to save him, please do it. Por Favor!" she cried out with tears in her eyes.

The men looked at each other, unsure of what to do. Then Reverend Monroe stared over the shoulders of the members of the group. He felt a familiar pull from the ashes of the Marauder. He rushed past them, fell to his knees and began to sift through the ashes. The others looked at him as if he had lost his mind until he lifted two long crystals from the ashes. At the touch of the crystal keeper, they began to glow obediently. Reverend Monroe took the glowing crystals back to the group hurriedly. He moved past the others and bent down next to Isabel and Father Benedito.

"I know that you do not know us and there is much we need to explain to you," He began. "But the most important thing for us to do now is heal Father Benedito. For that to happen, I am going to need for you to trust us."

Isabel looked at the group of Black men through her tears and then at Father Benedito. Though she did not know them, she felt that she could trust them. They had destroyed the creature that had come into the church. They had put their lives on the line protecting her and Father Benedito. She would put the care of her beloved Father in their hands, but she would not let him out of her sight.

"Esta bien," Isabel said. "I will trust you, but where the Father goes, so do I. Entiendes?"

"I can understand that," Reverend Monroe smiled. "But we have to hurry."

"Just let me get mi bosillo," Isabel said as she passed the Father's care over to Ben, who was cradling the dazed priest's head. She vanished into the recesses of the church.

"What do you plan to do?" Ben asked.

"We have the Gatewayc rystals that will get us back to Acara, but fortunately we now have an even more powerful set of crystals that we can use without an archway. I am going to use them to get us back to Baltimore."

"Are they strong enough to transport all of us?" Simon asked.

"The Marauder's crystals are even stronger than the ones we retrieved from the church. They were meant to carry it back to Acara from anywhere. I am sure I can open a Gateway for all six of us to get back to Gateway Baptist. Then we can heal Father Benedito and make our way back to Acara."

"Sounds like a plan," Purcell agreed as he sank down in a pew and wiped his brow.

A few seconds later, Isabel returned to the sanctuary with a huge, colorful purse. She ignored the others and bent down next to the Father.

"Que Error," she laughed as she began to rummage through her bag. "I always told him I left my Santeria behind when I joined the church, but I couldn't. I needed my Santos and herbs." She was not getting any argument from the group. It was as much a part of her as her worship as were the saints. "Tell me, do the bites of those things have poisons?"

"I believe they do," Reverend Monroe said frankly.

Upon hearing that, Isabel removed three different bags out of herbs from her bag, chew them up and applied them to his wounds. "These herbs are very strong. They should slow down the poison. Verdad."

"Thank God," Ben exhaled. "Now, it's your turn, Reverend."

"Everyone ge ttogether," Reverend Monroe said as he raised the two long, black crystals over his head. "And focus all of your thoughts on Baltimore and Gateway Baptist," he said as he removed his tuning fork.

"Is this going to hurt?" Isabel whispered to Ben with a wrinkled brow.

"Sweetheart," Ben whispered with a grin, "I really don't know." He reached out and took her shaking hand. "I hope not."

Reverend Monroe stood in the center of the group and crossed the crystals over his head. The air around the group electrified and the space around them began to shift as the Gateway opened around them. A vacuum engulfed them all and they were sucked through the Gateway. Seconds later, the group appeared in the center of what remained of the sanctuary of Gateway Baptist Church. They were all slightly disoriented by the dislocation caused by the Gateway, but they were no worse for the wear. They were about to move when they realized they were not alone. They looked around the rubble that once was the sanctuary of Gateway Baptist church and saw Ms. Loretta Simms standing in the distance with her hands on her hips and her mouth open wide. She had seen the Gateway open and close. She was trembling and her hands covered her mouth. Her bible fell from her hands into the dust of the church.

"Sweet Jesus!" she cried out, not believing her eyes.

Purcell walked slowly up to his grandmother and took her in his arms trying to steady her.

"There is a lot we have to explain to you," he whispered in her ear.

"Yes, you do," she responded as she looked at her grandson. "How is any of this possible?

"There is more going on than you can possibly imagine," Purcell began as he wiped tears from her eyes. "And I promise I will explain everything to you. But first we have a gentleman with us who is hurt. Let us take care of him and I will answer all of your questions. Okay?"

"Okay, Purcell," she said as she wiped her eyes and looked over his shoulder at the others. "I have seen many things in my almost seventy years, but I have to tell you, Purcell, I ain't seen nothing like this before," she remarked.

"I understand, Grandma," Purcell said sympathetically. "I really do."

"Let's get Father Benedito to my study," Reverend Monroe said. "I have healing crystals there. I can take care of him there."

Simon lifted the wounded priest into his arms and led the way toward the study. Ben followed him with Reverend Monroe on his heels. Purcell led his grandmother toward the door and she passed Isabel. The two elderly women looked at each other pensively and paused.

"Hola, Senora," Isabel said, glad to see another elder among the group. "I am Isabel Lopez."

Loretta smiled and stuck out her hand. "I am Loretta Simss."

# Chapter 17

It was evening. Prince Janis sat in his throne room upon the throne of Lampour. He watched the suns set through the windows of his Great Hall. Casually, he fed Altion from a bucket of salted vermin that sat behind his throne. The great winged serpent ate from the pail gladly and was wrapped around a golden perch that sat near the throne. Prince Janis wiped his hands and took out his snuffbox. He looked around the throne room, making sure he was alone. Then he quickly took a pinch of the grainy, green powder from the box and deposited it up his nose. The thrill of the drug enveloped him as he sat upon his throne. The drug, a Lampourian delicacy called Morose, was said to have the feeling of ten massive ejaculations. Though it was legal throughout Acara, Prince Janis still did not want anyone to know he partook of such a delicious diversion. Though his family had become rulers of Lampour, and one of the richest Monarchies because of their cultivation of the aphrodisiac substance, Prince Janis still felt odd about anyone knowing he was dependent on the delicacy.

Filled with sexual bravado, Prince Janis fell back upon the comfort of his throne. For a second, he forgot about how much he disliked Lampour and he longed for a life outside of its salty limits. The feel of the drug was about to subside and he was going to take another dose when his trusted spy, Greson, entered the royal chamber. Greason was a tall, lanky, dark-skinned man, who wore the badges of the royal family of Lampour. Prince Janis quickly tucked his snuff box back into his milk white robes and wiped his nose when he was Greson. He sat up prominently on his throne and waved his man servant forward. Greson quickly came down the aisle to his monarch and bowed.

"My Lord," Greson began. "I have the information that you requested about the rebels and the lost High Prince."

"You have done well, Greson," Prince Janis smiled, stifling a sneeze. "Now let me know what you have find out."

"They have docked secretly in the coves. They have sent emissaries into the city to purchase mounts, supplies, and a wagon. I believe that they will wait for nightfall and try to move through the City. Once they leave Lampour, I have no idea where they intend to go, but I do believe that they seek to go further East."

Prince Janis smiled to himself as he thought about what Greson had presented to him. It gave him an instant idea about how he was going to confront them. Prince Janis reached down and fed Altion once again. He knew that there was only one way for them to get out of the city if they were truly proceeding East. He would post Altion there and his most trusted servant would let him know when they were coming and he would be there to meet them, in one form or another. He smiled widely.

After the dinner opening the High Court was over, the royals quickly retreated to the comfort of their beds for the night. There was very little milling around after the sweets were served. They knew the next day would begin early and would be filled with business. However, as the royals retired they all were secretly reflecting upon the words of their High Queen. Never before has a High Monarch opened a High Court with such a strong statement and presumption of authority. It was almost vulgar. On top of that, she bore the Scepter of Monarchs to punctuate her words. It was a relic that was whispered about but rarely seen. The fact that the High Queen had it in her hands in front of the other royals would be a tale talked about for along time to come.

The High Queen retired to her quarters. She let her handmaidens dispense with her clothing. However, she took the Scepter of Monarchs into her inner quarters with her. She laid it down upon a dresser near her bed and laid down across her bed. The dinner had been brief, but she was exhausted. During the dinner, she felt the full weight of her station and her power. It was like everything she did was under scrutiny by the other royals. As she thought about it, she sucked her teeth in disgust. They were all scavengers looking for a flaw in her armor, an angle they could manipulate for their own desires. She sighed to herself. She was happy this first day of the High Court was over. Mora was about to fall asleep when she heard a familiar tap from the far wall. The High Queen went over to the wall and responded with a rap. Then the wall slid aside and Prince Gregor appeared in the shadows. The High Queen stepped aside and let her blue-skinned lover from the North into her chambers.

The High Queen quickly went over to her door and sealed her chamber. Prince Gregor came into the room and removed his cloak. Once they were sure they were alone, they fell into each other's arms and had along kiss. They fell back on the bed and lost their clothing in the covers. Mora found a unique comfort in Gregory's arms. Like all those of his kind, Gregor released an intoxicating aphrodisiac from his skin when he made love. The smell of his hormones filled Mora's room with a fine mist. Prince Gregor looked deep into Mora's eyes as he entered her. Using his penetrating vision, he looked past her fine brown flesh and joined with the endless energy of her soul. Though she veiled herself in the power of the Dark God, her soul still remained pure. This was the side of her that Gregor loved, not her crown or her power. After their lovemaking was complete, they lay in each other's arms, awaiting sleep.

"How do you feel, my High Queen?" Gregor asked as he ran his fingers through her hair.

"Better now that you are here," Mora yawned as she pressed her face into Gregor's hairless chest. "I wish that moments like this could last always. If life could only be this simple."

"It could be," Gregor protested. "Leave your crown here; you have never had a love for it, and come North with me. I have a castle and lands so far North that no one would ever find us."

"If only it were that simple, my love," Mora smiled. "But I have promised this world to the Dark God. It is an oath I can not break. I am bound to this course by more than my word, I am bound by blood."

"I have no allegiance to either the Dark God or the Avatar, I have an allegiance to you. You can count on me and the resources of the North in your endeavors," Gregor said as he kissed the top of her head.

The High Queen said nothing in response. She cuddled with her lover instead. Her vision drifted from him to the windows of her bedroom. Outside, the suns of Acara were beginning to rise. It had been a day since she had used the loadstone to alert the royals of Acara of the presence of her son. She had not heard anything yet. Though she did not want to admit it, this was troubling her. It could mean anything, but it was troubling her nonetheless. She knew that the time was approaching when she was going to have to deal with her son, for better or for worse.

Reverend Monroe rushed to his bookshelf. He removed several books to locate the place where he hid his crystals. He removed the square, brown healing crystals from the satchel of crystals just as Simon walked through the door with Father Benedito in his arms. True to her word, Isabel was a few steps behind Simon holding her bag. Reverend Monroe looked at the bag ominously. He wondered what kind of secrets the bag held. Like his satchel of crystals, he guessed Isabel's simple bag massed a great deal of power.

"Lay him on the floor," Reverend Monroe directed.

Father Benedito was still dressed in his clerical clothing. It was ripped and torn where the hounds of the Marauder had attacked him. The Father was still unconscious after the attack. Reverend Monroe bent down next to him and examined the wound. It was remarkable. In spite of the poison, the wound was already healing. Reverend Monroe looked at Isabel and smiled. He had no idea what was in those herbs she used but they had definitely stopped the poison in its tracks. It was going to make the Reverend's job much easier. Reverend Monroe bent down next to the Father and looked up at Isabel.

"Senora Isabel, come over here please," Reverend Monroe called.

Isabel placed her bag in a chair and bent down next to the Father with Reverend Monroe. He smiled at her. Then he placed the healing crystal in her hand and held it over the Father's wound. It immediately began to glow.

"Ay, Dios," Isabel smiled as she watched the Father's skin begin to mend.

"Where I come from, this how we take care of wounds like this," Reverend Monroe explained.

"And where is that?" Isabel asked, not taking her eyes off the healing gem.

"I am from the stars," Reverend Monroe said flatly. "I come from a place called Acara." He explained looking for a reaction in Isabel. However, she seemed oddly unmoved by his words.

"I do not know what you expect me to say, Reverend Monroe," Isabel said. "You don't know but after Father Frances died, it was I who cared for your crystals. I was a chica then," she laughed. "He told me before he died that one day someone would come for them. I did not know what that meant. However, I did know that those crystals were a powerful thing, not of this world."

Reverend Monroe looked at the Latina woman and laughed. She was indeed full of surprises. Reverend Monroe turned to Simon.

"It is time for us to prepare to go," Reverend Monroe exhaled.

"I have longed to hear those words," Simon said as he reached into his shirt and grabbed the arrow head that connected him to Tisha." It is indeed time."

"Go to the sanctuary and use your great strength to make a way to the archway that the others used to get to Acara. I will see to our supplies and I will make sure the others are okay before we go."

"I will see to it immediately," Simon smiled as he left the room.

Father Benedito stirred on the floor. Isabel smiled with tears in her eyes. Father Benedito sat up and looked around. He was confused. He got to his feet and stumbled. Isabel caught him. He smiled at her and walked to the window and looked out at Baltimore City.

"How did I get here?" he asked as he rubbed at his head, clearly confused and disoriented. The last thing the Catholic priest remembered was being attacked by the hounds of the Marauderr in the sanctuary of his church in Spanish Harlem.

"I think we have a lot to discuss," Reverend Monroe smiled as he walked over to Father Benedito and placed a hand on his shoulder.

After the banquet was over, all the royals and Acarain dignitaries drifted from the Grand Citadel back to their temporary lodgings. The last people to leave were the two priests of the Dark God who were at the dinner. Fildis and Danthor left the Grand Citadel together and walked through the streets of Acara City back toward the Grand Temple of the Dark God. They climbed the stairs in silence and entered the evil sanctuary. Fildis secured the doors behind them, while Danthor lit the torches around the altar. Once the two made sure they were alone, they met in the middle of the room. The two took off their dark hoods before they began to speak.

"Another High Court begins." Danthor sighed.

"But not just another High Court, my friend," Fildis smiled. "There are more new players on the table than ever before," he said as he rubbed his long fingers together.

"You mean the girl, Tisha, and the missing High Prince," Danthor surmised.

"More than them," Fildis whispered. "The unborn child. It represents a new powe r of untold potentialon this world."

"But how do we get at him?" Danthor questioned. "He is the son of the High Prince's Royal Guard and he is not even born yet. And though that off-world girl appears young, I do not believe that she will just give us her child," he said.

"Oh, Danthor," Fildis laughed. "You have been on this dark path for so long, but you see so little. There is nothing that is happening that has not been forseen. Before this is over, it will be his mother who seeks us out for the sake of her child."

"What do you know, old man?" Dan thor asked.

"Many things," Fildis smiled. "Many things," he repeated as he patted him on the back.

"Alive!" Ms. Loretta screamed. "Alive."

Ms. Loretta began to pace back and forth in front of the remains of the doorway to Gateway Baptist Church. Out of all the things that her grandson, Purcell, had revealed to her since he and the others stepped through the Gateway the thing that had shocked her the most was finding out that her other grandson, Wisdom, was still alive. This fact was harder for her to believe than that her Pastor and his family were from another world.

"How could you keep something like this from me, Purcell?" Ms. Loretta said as she grabbed her head in her hands. "Boy, I raised you and your brother like you were my own. How could you not tell me that he is alive?"

"Ma," Purcell swallowed. "I didn't know how to tell you. I mean, how could I tell you that my brother was really alive and on another planet?" He felt like a little boy in front of his grandmother's disapproval.

"You just do!" she snapped. "I accepted the reality of you boys just as you are. I had to accept the fact that you wanted to be a policeman the same way that I had to accept that your brother was something else. No secrets in this family. I know I taught you that much."

Purcell lowered his head in front of his grandmother's ire. He did not know what to say. He had no idea that she would respond to the truth like this. Ms. Loretta stopped pacing back and forth and slowed down. She closed her eyes and said a silent prayer. Then she turned her attention back to her grandson.

"Can use use this thing to go and get Wisdom and the others?" she asked.

"Yes, we can," Purcell assured her.

"Then come on, boy, let's go get your brother," she said as she passed Purcell and went back into the church. Purcell followed her into the rubble of the sanctuary. Ben and Simon were at the pulpit lifting rubble. Looking at them, Ms. Loretta stopped at one of the burned out pews and kicked off her shoes. She paused for a moment then reached up and took off her wig.

"Ain't no reason to mess up some good hair with heavy lifting," Ms. Loretta said as she winked at Purcell.

"I will never understand you," Purcell laughed.

"I am a lot to understand," she said. "So, what'sthe plan?"

Purcell turned to Simon and Ben.

"We have to get to a natural archway that is buried beneath all of this rubble so we can build the Gateway to Acara," Simon explained.

"Okay," Ms. Loretta said as she bent down, dug in, and started lifting the rubble. The other three men turned and looked at one another. They did not know what to say to one another. "What you waiting for?" she paused." We got work to do!"

The men followed Ms. Loretta's lead and took over the heavy lifting. Ms. Loretta stopped working for a second and looked at Simon. He stopped working and turned to face her.

"An alien, huh?"

"Yes ma'am," Simon said awkwardly.

"I guess they need Jesus on your planet, too," Ms. Loretta said as she returned to work.

"They sho' nuf do," Simon said as he lifted a huge piece of charred wood. "They sho' nuf do."

# Chapter 18

Etera stood on the dock next to the wagon where Tildon lay, moaning slightly. She stared up at the night sky and let the breeze from the water run through her fingers. She found herself wondering where her grandmother, Anna-Beth, was and if she was safe. The last time she had seen her, the Overlord Grimhold and the High Queen's men were closing in on their family farm. Like her, her grandmother was a sea witch. This led Etera to believe that her grandmother could handle any situation. Even when she was enslaved and working in the mines, it was her belief in her grandmother and their ancestral power that gave her the courage to find away to escape. As she looked at the wagon, she only hoped she could pull on similar strength to help get her brother healed.

"How is he?' Royal asked as he came down the walkway from the *Lucky Lady*. Royal was already dressed in a heavy, dark, hooded traveling cloak. He handed a similar one to Etera.

"He is resting," Etera said as she struggled to put on the cloak.

"Here let me help you," Royal said as he helped Etera into the garment. "Etera, may I say something to you?" Royal asked carefully.

Etera finished straightening her cloak then she put a finger up to Royal's lips.

"You don't have to, my High Prince," Etera said. "I know about you and Hue."

"It's partly that," Royal said awkwardly as he looked up at the moons in the sky. "I am not sure about a lot of things right now. I just don't want to hurt anyone while I figure it all out."

Etera smiled as she watched Royal fumble with his words. He looked so attractive to her. She began to blush.

"I don't think you have to worry about that," Etera assured him.

"Why do you say so?" Royal asked with a wrinkled brow.

"Royal, you have already shown your compassionate side," Etera said.

"I have?" He was astonished by her words

"Yes, you have," she laughed. "You are the High Prince of an entire planet. You are fighting your birth mother for control. With all that going on, you are willing to take time out to make sure that my brother gets the care he needs; someone you barely know."

"But he got hurt defending me," Royal protested.

"And a lot more people will be hurt before this is all over. Any one of us might die," Etera said frankly. "The fact that you value everyone of our lives is not a little thing. I think you are going to make a fine High King."

"I believe that one life can make a difference," Royal said earnestly. "In the religion that I practice, one person changed the world with his sacrifices." Royal meant every word. He said them with fervor.

"I would love to hear more about this person," Etera smiled.

"I would love to tell you about him. With all that has happened, I barely have had a chance to contemplate my spirituality," Royal sighed.

"Hopefully, we will have time for such discussions in the future," Etera said as she reached out and touched Royal's face.

The two kept staring at each other for a long time in the light of the Acarian moons. Then Lethia came down the walkway. Like Etera and Royal, she too was covered in a long, dark traveling cloak. She ignored the intamcy of the moment she was interrupting and stood between the two youngest members of their company.

"Royal," She said as she cleared her throat. "It is time for us to go."

"Can we do one thing before we leave?" Royal asked.

"And what is that?" Lethia wrinkled her brow.

"Pray," Royal said flatly.

"I think that is an excellent idea," Lethia nodded.

Moments later Royal, Etera, Hue, Captain Sarison, Tori, Peku, Maximus, Lethia, and Wisdom were all gathered on the dock near the wagon. Though theywere all differed in many ways, they were joined together in a singular purpose and focus. Their cloaks billowed in the cool night air of Lampour. Royal had them all join hands or paws and they stood in a circle. They lowered their heads and waited for Royal to speak. He lowered his head and thought before he spoke.

"God of our unique understanding," he began, "as we come onto land, I ask you to protect our steps as we go forward. We are not sure where we are going, but we know if we put you before us you will keep us safe. And I ask you to especially look out over Tildon who placed himself in harm's way to protect us all. Remember, Tisha, Simon, my father—Reverend Monroe—and all our families who may not be with us, but who are with us in spirit. In the name of my savior, Jesus Christ, I pray. In the name of the Avatar of Acara I close this prayer. Amen." Royal prayed as tears formed in his eyes. It had been a long time since he had raised his voice to any higher power. It instantly made him feel better. He felt that he could face whatever was to come. His faith began to slowly renew.

"Well said," Lethia said as she smacked Royal on the back.

"I have to agree," Tori said as Peku guided him over to the wagon. The two climbed on the back of it and settled down next to Tildon. They carefully wrapped a blanket around him and snuggled up close to him to keep his chilled flesh warm.

"Are you okay?" Hue asked as he came up to Royal hesitantly.

"I am," Royal whispered as he pulled Hue close. Hue was surprised by Royal's actions but he did not resist him. Though he was not one for public displays of affection, he hugged Royal back. As they embraced, Wisdom's eyes went to Etera. Her expression was unreadable. She turned from the group and mounted the wagon.

"You do not have to worry," Maximus said as he came up behind Wisdom. "I am sure they will work it all out," he panted before joining Tori and Peku in the wagon.

"I hope so," Wisdom said as he got on the mount at the head of the group.

Hue stared at Etera at the reins of the wagon. He was about to get in the back of the wagon with the others, but thought better of it. As if reading his thoughts, Lethia nudged him forward toward the front of the wagon.

"Do you mind if I ride up front with you?" Hue asked warily.

Etera was surprised by Hue's question. She stared at him awkwardly for a moment. Then she smiled at him sadly. She had never wished she was anyone else, but the young sea witch found herself wishing she was the young off-worlder; if only for Royal's sake.

"I would like that," Etera said earnestly as she sat back.

Carefully, Hue climbed up front in the wagon next to Etera. They sat silently next to one another.

"Can I ask you something?" Etera asked without turning to look art Hue.

"Sure. I think so," Hue said carefully.

"Do you love him?" she asked flatly.

Hue was surprised by her question but he did not shy away from it. He looked at her squarely and answered.

"I think I do," Hue answered. "Yes, I do."

"That is something we have in common," Etera admitted." I hope it never comes between us."

Captain Sarison was slow to move. He waited until all the others were either mounted or in the wagon. He stood alone on the dock for a second, looking at his great sea ship the *Lucky Lady*. Silently, he admitted to himself how much he hated being on land. His father had always said he was born for the open seas. And once he was man enough, he left his small village and took to the open seas. He had been there ever since. He hated leaving his ship behind, but he had made a promise to Anna-Beth. He was going to keep her grandchildren safe. He turned from his ship, mounted his steed and trotted to the head of the group alongside Wisdom.

"Let's ride," Lethia said as she raised her hand.

With Captain Sarison in the lead, the group began to make their way through the torch-lit streets of Lampour. They had decided on their formation before leaving the ship. Captain Sarison and Lethia took the lead, since they were the most familiar with Lampour and the Eastern Continent. Royal followed them. Then the wagon came, under the protection of Etera and Maximus. Wisdom brought up the rear protecting their steps as they went. They were all tightly hidden under their cloaks as they traveled.

Royal was surprised by what he saw as they traveled. Lampour was the first Acarian city-state he had seen since he arrived on Acara. He knew that all the city-states were supposed to be different but he still did not know what to expect from one. Though it was late in the evening, the polished sandstone streets of Lampour were still quite alive with people. To Royal, most of the people looked like Arabs. They were brown-skinned and dressed in flowing, colorful robes with different kinds of headdresses. Several times the group had to stop to let groups of children who were playing in the street spass in front of them. What surprised Royal the most about the people as he passed them was how much wine and intoxicants they were doing in the streets. He could not imagine such a scene in Baltimore. The police would be everywhere carting people away to central booking; but not in Lampour. Royal watched in astonishment as groups of men and women openly inhaled a dark green powder on the streets and seemed to drift off into a stupor. Royal had no idea what the drug was but the effect was clear. The people who took it seemed to shake, caught up in an inhuman pleasure. Even children on the streets seemed free to indulge in this substance. As they rode, it became clear to Royal that whoever controlled this substance controlled Lampour.

After a few hours of travel between the tight buildings of Lampour, the group climbed a winding path that led out of the city-state. Royal looked up at a huge fortress that was built into the mountain which overlooked all of Lampour. As Royal looked at the castle, a chill went up his spine. Though he could not see any guards, he could tell they were being watched. As they moved past the torch-lit streets, they headed down a winding path lined by trees in full bloom. Moving down the tree-lined path, it was hard to see what was on the other side of them. However, as they moved further and further out of the city proper and climbed the side of the mountain, Royal was sure the number of eyes on them was increasing though he could not see anyone. Finally, Royal caught up to Captian Sarison and Lethia. Both of them had their hands on their swords as they rode. It was clear they felt them, too.

"We have been being watched for some time," Lethia said flatly as she rode hard.

"I think I can stop that," Royal said carefully.

"How?" Captain Sarison asked as he bounced in his saddle.

"I have the ability to control others," Royal explained. "I do not know if I can do it if I can not see them but I can try,"

"Do it!" Lethia commanded.

Royal paused for a moment, then he let his heartbeat join with the energy of the forest around him, the Rigos. He was instantly able to see the countless Lampourian soldiers hiding in the shadows. They were crouching in the shadows dressed in all black hides; they looked liked something out of a movie. To Royal they looked liked ninjas, something from a television show he might have seen. Without thinking, Royal reached out with his mind and attacked them. They tried to struggle at first; then Royal made the suggestion to the group that they were blind. They instantly lost their sight and began sacrambling around in the shrubs bumping into one another and tripping over their twisted feet.

"Forward!" Lethia commanded.

She and Captain Sarison went first down the darkened path, followed by Royal. Hue held onto the side of the wagon as it hurtleddown the pathway. Etera struggled to hold on to the reins. Tori and Peku held onto Tildon in the back of the wagon, while Maximus drew his claws protectively. As the wagon ambled down the path, Maximus stood up in the back and howled at the Acarian moons.

"Muthafucka," Wisdom cursed as he bounced up and down in the saddle of his mount. He had never ridden anything like a horse before and preferred his jeep to the way this hirsute animal ran beneath him. He barely managed to sit firmly in the saddle. He kept his eyes on the darkened road and the back of the wagon in front of him.

Royal looked over his shoulder to make sure the others were keeping pace. Once he was sure that they were, he shifted his concentration to the road behind them. As the soldiers fell from the bushes onto the moonlit road, they screamed as the pavement beneath their feet burst into flames. Royal covered their tracks with his command of the fire. This time, the energy of the Etos responded. Feeling the strain of the use of his powers, Royal began to rock back and forth on his mount. He had never used his gifts like this before and he was feeling the strain of working with the Elementals. He began to buckle in the saddle.

"Royal!" Hue screamed as he stood up in the wagon. Royal was a few steps in front of the wagon and he was barely holding onto his mount. He was about to fall off when Wisdom came up from behind. He matched speed with Royal's mount and pushed him back up into the saddle.

"I gotacha, boy," Wisdom said as he pushed Royal upright. "It ain't nothin' but a rollercoaster ride, son," he told him.

"I am alright," Royal said as he tried to clear his head. He was sweating profusely under the weight of his cloak.

The group did not stop. They pressed their horses on through the trees and down the path. Once Royal had regained his composure, Wisdom fell to the back of the group again. After some time, Lethia slowed the group to a trot. The eyes that had followed them were long gone and she was sure they were dealing with the fire that Royal had started on the road behind them.

After they turned a bend in the road, they came to a sudden stop. There was a huge rock archway in the middle of the road. It was lit up with two huge fires. Standing in the middle of the archway was a single figure. It was a tall, beautiful, dark-skinned woman wrapped in white cloth. She was delicately painted and looked like a Lampourian regal. Behind her was a long cloak made up of feathers that caught the light from the torches and seemed to glow. She wore a huge metal helmet that outlined her carefully painted face.

Lethia removed the hood of her cloak carefully. She dismounted and withdrew her sword.

"Hold, CODA woman," the woman said. "As you can see, I carry no arms," she said coyly.

"Then move fast and be out of our way," Lethia said flatly.

"Before you move forward down this road, I would ask that you allow your oracle to make it so that all of you understand my words," the newcomer said sheepishly. "Who knows? I might have information you may need on your journey."

Lethia looked squarely at the woman. She could not read her. Her thoughts and intentions were closed to the CODA Queen. Lethia did not like that fact at all. Part of her wanted to run the woman through and have them be on their way. However, she was learning that information was an important currency on this journey. Having overheard the conversation, Captain Sarison joined Lethia on the path.

"What do you think?" he whispered in her ear.

"I do not know. Her mind is closed to me. She says that she has information that we might need. She does not appear to be a threat and there is no one else around. I am sure of that. She wants us to allow Tori to use his gift so she may share with us," Lethia explained.

"I do not see any harm," Captain Sarison advised, never taking his eyes off of the beautiful woman. He smiled at her and she smiled in return, but never took her eyes off of Royal. Royal stared at the woman in disbelief. She was by far one of the most beautiful women he had ever seen. If they were on Earth, she could have easily been a supermodel without trying. Royal found himself blushing under her gaze.

"Easy, tiger," Wisdom said as he came up to Royal's mount. He looked over his shoulder at Hue and Etera. "Brother man, don't you have enough going on?" he said snapping Royal back to reality. Wisdom had learned in his life to be wary of beautiful faces. He didn't like this little detour at all. It seemed way too easy. While the others were watching the woman, Wisdom decided to keep his gaze clearly on the road ahead and behind.

"...Except in time," Lethia snapped at Captain Sarison. "Bring Tori forward and let's be done with this. Perhaps the old man can see into her mind where I could not," she whispered. "If she tries anything, I'll snap her neck before she can count to ten."

Captain Sarison walked past Royal and Wisdom to the wagon. He helped Tori down and brought him forward. He told the old man what he wanted him to do. Tori did not hesitate as he used his walking stick to guide him. He went up to the stranger and put a long, whithered finger in the middle of her head. She bowed gracefully to meet his hand.

"Who is she?" Hue whispered to Etera as he looked past Royal at the stranger.

"I do not know but a beauty such as hers can only mean danger in a land like Lampour," Etera said wisely.

Sensing an odd feeling from his friend, Peku jumped down from the wagon and ran up to him. The Opion reached up and severed the connection between Tori and the woman. Tori reached down and patted Peku's head. He let himself be led back toward the others.

"She can speak English now," Tori said as he passed Lethia and Captain Sarison.

"What else did you feel?" Lethia asked suspiciously.

"I am not sure, but she is definitely not what she seems to be," Tori whispered in Lethia's ear. "She is much more," he added as he passed.

"Now that that is done," the stranger smiled feeling oddly victorious. She removed her helmet and released a torrent of long, dark hair. "We can talk like old friends. All of you come close to the fire so I might better see your face and you can see me. Come close so we can talk," she invited as she sat down daintily on the arid ground, letting her hair fall over her shoulder.

The members of the group looked at each other awkwardly. However, they all began to slowly approach the woman. They sat around her in a semi-circle on the ground.

"Aren't you coming?" Maximus asked Etera as he went to join the others.

"I would rather stay here and tend to my brother," she said as she turned her back to the stranger.

"Suit yourself," Maximus said as he galloped to the fire. He was not sure what the two-legs were making such a fuss about. All of his senses were telling him that they had nothing to fear from the pretty lady. The only energy she was exuding was sex and he liked the way it made the fur stand on his back.

Once they were all around the archway and the fire, the stranger rose and stepped to the side of the arch. She removed a blanket and a basket. Carefully, she spread the blanket out in front of the group and placed the basket in the middle. She began to hum a beautiful tune as she began to unpack small covered dishes of finely cured meats.

"Make sure you take one to your distant friend on the wagon," she said to Peku.

Peku picked up the small container and ran it over to Etera. At first, Etera just looked at the food. However, being on the ship for so long she could not remember the last time she had something other than dried foods. She picked up the container suspisiously and opened it. The smell of the food was absolutely intoxicating. Etera was taking a bite before she knew it andwas sharing it with her brother, Tildon.

"While we have this powwow I will watch the road," Wisdom volunteered.

"You do not have to worry, those warriors will not be coming back," she said as she offered Wisdom a container of food.

"And how do you know that?" Wisdom snapped as he looked down at the food suspiciously. It looked good, but it wasn't no McDonalds. He was dying for a Big Mac, not carefully prepared cured meats.

"Because I sent them," she said flatly as she began to eat her food.

Wisdom froze. He did not know what to say. He simply looked at the others and rolled his eyes. He snatched the meal from the stranger's hand and stomped off into the night. Wisdom leaned up against a tree, he sat the food down, and lit a cigarette. He did not like this little detour at all. He liked this woman even less. She seemed too good to be true. Though he was standing on the edge of their makeshift camp, he was keeping an eye on her. He especially didn't like the way she was looking at Royal. She was looking at him like he was fresh meat for the slaughter. He would hate to have to pluck one of those pretty little eyes out.

"Now what is this information you have for us?" Lethia said quickly as she stared at her meal.

"I am Princess Jane," she announched to the group. "The High Queen has used the royal lodestone to contact all of the royals to be on the lookout for you," she announced as she began to pour wine. "We are all commanded by the crowns we share to tell her if we run into you. It is a capital crime for us not to," she explained with a smile. "Fruit anyone?" she offered.

"Is that why you had your men follow us on the road?" Lethia said as she took her first bite of the food.

"No, not at all," Princess Jane said. "They were there to make sure you made it safely out of Lampour. These roads are filled with bandits and all kind of creatures. I just wanted to make sure you made it to your destination safely."

"How kind of you," Captain Sarison said as he tore into the food he had been given. It was some of the best food he had ever had in his life. It made his mouth water. He finished his portion off quickly and was eyeing the rest.

Peku looked at the food oddly. He put a piece of meat up to his nose and sniffed. He took a bite and was overcome by the taste. He looked up at Princess Jane and then grabbed a handful of food and ran to the wagon. He climbed up and gave some to Etera, Tori, and Maximus.

"What did you see Tori?" Etera asked as she took a bite of a small morsel. "I mean when you looked in her mind."

"I am not sure," Tori said as he ate. "She definitely is what she appears to be, but there is something more about her. She is not hiding anything, yet it is not obvious to the eye or the spirit," he said.

"I have not smelled one like her before," Maximus said as he held up a large fruit and tore into it. It was sweet but he wrinkled his nose. "I would prefer meat," he growled.

"I bet she does smell," Hue quipped as he took a small cake from Peku and ate it. "But she can pack a hellulava picnic," he joked.

Wisdom did not join the group. He stood on the outskirts of the small circle near the edge of the wagon. He kept glancing over his shoulder at them talking. He looked squarely at Princess Jane. She seemed to be looking at everyone at the same time and not. She was definitely a seductress. The question he had was why was she trying to seduce them and why had she waited to get them all the way out here to do it. If she had an entire palace to greet them in, why would she meet them on a dirt road by herself. He sucked his teeth, he didn't like this at all. The woman reeked of treachery. He put a hand on his gun protectively.

"Here have some?" Peku said as he went to hand him a piece of fruit.

Wisdom accepted it without looking at it. He kept looking down the road for a raiding party or some other trap. He looked up at the night sky. Other than the moons, it was clear. They were definitely out here by themselves. He wondered if he was being too paranoid. He raised the fruit up to his lips, looked at it, and went to bite in it.

"Do not eat the food," Malik whispered in his ear.

Wisdom froze. He carefully withdrew his lips from the fruit and circled back around the wagon toward the others.

"Why would you commit treason against my mother?" Royal asked before beginning to eat.

"To have the pleasure of meeting you, my High Prince," she said flatly as she handed him the most beautiful piece of fruit he had ever seen and smiled. It literally seemed to glow in the moonlight. It was was as big as Royal's hand, green, and succulent.

Royal began to blush under her gaze. He went to accept the fruit from her hand, but she held on to it.

"Let me, my High Prince," Princess Jane said as she lifted the fruit to Royal's mouth.

Out of the corner of his eye, Royal soon realized that the others seemed oddly distracted. He turned back to Princess Jane and looked at her closely. It was like he was seeing her for the first time. There seemed something transparent about her beauty and her intentions. He immeditaly went to pull away. However, before he did, Royal realized she was bringing up her free hand from behind her. He went to grab it, but she managed to open her hand and blow a handful of Morose in his face.

Royal fell back immediately caught in the pleasure that the drug provided. In his life, he had masturbated. Reverend Monroe had told him that was normal for a boy his age, but he had never felt anything like this before. Ripples of pleasure went through his manhood again and again. It was like his entire body was having an organism over and over.

Princess Jane looked at the others. They were ignoring her, caught up in laughter. They were all caught in the glaze she had placed on the meal. It was an almost imperceptible pollen that she had used on the food. It was impossible to detect if you did not know what you were looking for. Princess Jane took the fruit that had fallen from her hand and crawled over to Royal. She straddled him and held the fruit over his lips and smiled.

"You and I could be such a great team, my High Prince," she said as she held the fruit over his lips. "We could have all of Acara at our beck and call," she declared as she bent down close to Royal. "One night with me and I could make all your dreams come true. Do you prefer me like this?" she asked" as she ran her fingers over his face.

"Yes, I do," Royal said as he found himself getting hard beneath her.

"Or do you prefer me like this?" she asked as she reached between her legs and began to transform on top of him.

Royal felt Princess Jane grow hard against him and he looked up into an equally handsome face. It was Prince Janis.

"Oh my God!" Royal laughed as he reached up to touch Janis' face.

Prince Janis went to bend down and kiss Royal, when he felt the barrel of a gun next to his head for the first time.

"Bitch, if you move, ya dead," Wisdom swore as he cocked the gun.

"Was it something I said?" Prince Janis joked.

"Ya think." Wisdom said as he turned the gun around and knocked Janis out.

It was raining in Baltimore City. Father Benedito stood in Reverend Monroe's study looking at the rain through the window. He was freshly awake from his healing nap, fully recovered after his attack by the Marauder's hounds. He had asked the Reverend to leave him alone for a moment so that he could gather his thoughts after they had spoken.

He was a young priest, but he thought he was seasoned enough before he took over the parish of Sacred Heart. However, nothing in his training at the seminary or in the streets of Spanish Harlem had prepared him for this. Aliens! He shook his head as he ran his fingers over the wet glass. It was cold to the touch.

"Padre?" Isabel said as she stuck her head into the pastor's office, dragging her bag of mysteries behind her. "It is good to see that you are okay," she smiled. "Yo estoy allegre."

"Isabel!" Father Benedito rushed over to the senior woman and hugged her. She let herself be held. She was not used to this level of closeness from the priest. "I am happy to see that you're okay, too," he said as the two settled down in a set of chairs across from the desk. They looked at each other, laughing for a moment, not sure of what to say next.

"I guess they have spoken with you, too," Father Benedito said.

"Si, Padre. They have," Isabel said as she shook her head.

"Do you believe any of this?" he asked her. "I mean, other worlds, Gateways, evil High Queens. It is better than a telenovela, no?"

Isabel laughed. "You know how I love my telenovelas!" she said. "I don't know about a telenovela, but I do know that these are good people."

"How can you be so sure?" Father Benedito asked, frowning.

"Because they took care of you, mi hijito," Isabel said as she leaned in and touched his face tenderly.

"Not just them," Father Benedito laughed as he eyed her bag. "What have I told you about the Santeria?"

"I am an old woman," she said as she hunched her shoulders and winked. "What do I know?"

"I think you know many things," Father Benedito smiled.

"Si, Padre," Isabel said as she rose to leave the room. "I think we should help them. The Reverend and the rest of them are only trying to help their families. There is no greater sin than not to help when there is a need, verdad?"

Father Benedito looked after Isabel as she left. He thought about her words. Then he removed a rosary from his pocket, fell to his knees, and prayed for guidance.

In the remnants of the sanctuary, a radio that they found in the rubble was playing. There were boxes of pizza on one of the shattered pews. Ben, Reverend Monroe, Purcell, Simon, Ms. Loretta, and Isabel were busying themselves with the debris on the pulpit. Simon and Purcell were lifting the heavy pieces and the others were doing what they could to help clear the smaller pieces. Father Benedito carefully crept into the sanctuary from the rectory. The others stopped for a moment as he came into the room. Reverend Monroe went up to him and smiled.

"You okay?" he asked as he touched the man's shoulder.

"I'm okay," he said as he looked around.

"Good," Reverend Monroe smiled.

"The place you have to get to is under there?" Father Benedito asked.

"The archway," Reverend Monroe said. "Yes."

"Yes, the archway," Father Benedito said measuring his words.

The two men laughed. Reverend Monroe sat down on the burned pew and took a slice of pizza. Father Benedito sat next to him and took a slice.

"This must have been a beautiful church," Father Benedito commented as he took a bite of pizza.

"It was," Reverend Monroe said, choking back tears. "I built it for my son, even though he was not really my son, to protect him."

Father Benedito stopped eating. He placed his slice of pizza back in the box and took Reverend Monroe's hand gently.

"Only Jesus can spill blood for mankind. This boy may not have been your birth son, but your love and your tears make him your own." Father Benedito reached up and wiped Reverend Monroe's tears. "Now look, now you are sharing the love you have for your son with me,"

"Yes," Reverend Monroe cried as the others worked.

"What is his name?" Father Benedito asked.

"His name is Royal. He was a Reverend here at the church, too," he confided.

"Good," Father Benedito said. "Then he knows the truth of Jesus. It will protect him no matter where he is. You have to believe that."

"I do," Reverend Monroe said as he stuffed another piece of pizza in his mouth.

"Well, Reverend Monroe, we had better get to work," Father Benedito said as he stood.

"What!?"

"I called my Bishop. Got his smart phone. I told him I was on a holy mission for a few days and would be away." Father Benedito said. "I have faith in you." he added

Reverend Monroe stood up slowly and looked at Father Benedito in awe.

"You would do that for us?" Reverend Monroe gasped.

"Yes," Father Benedito assured. "Besides, he was trying to get me to take a vacation anyway. No me gusta las playas. The sand gets in the collar," he said with a wink.

"Bishops!" They both laughed.

"Well, let's get to work." Reverend Monroe said.

"Let's"

The two holy men stood and joined the others at the pupit.

"I got it," Simon swore.

"It's too heavy," Purcell protested.

"I got it," Simon said as he rose carrying the load of lumber that rose almost eight feet in the air.

Father Benedito stepped back when he got a look at Simon's true size without his warping crystal.

"He is a big boy and still growing." Reverend Monroe said.

"By the Holy Mother," Father Benedeto said as he bent down to pick up a piece of lumber" Yo lo veo. I see."

Tisha was lying in bed. She was still in her fancy gowns from the banquet of the night before. The sun was streaming through the window of her chambers making shadows dance on the floor. Tisha got up from her covers and went over to the window. She looked out at Acara City and the two suns hanging in the sky. As she looked at the city-state, she thought about the night before. Even though she was a virtual prisoner here on Acara, she had to admit to herself that the evening before had been magical. The only thing missing from the evening was Simon at herside and Royal presiding over the festivities. If Simon had been at her side, the evening would have been perfect.

Tisha reached up and touched the arrowhead that Simon had given her. She closed her eyes and thought of him. For a second, she was filled with a rush of emotion. It was Simon and, for the first time since their separation, she felt his hope. She did not know how, but she knew that he had found a way to get to Acara. Tears filled her eyes. He was coming for her! In fact, he was not just coming for her, he was coming for her and their unborn child. Tisha tried to catch her breath as she paced the room. It seemed too good to be true. She had lost track of how long she had been gone from Earth, time seemed to flow so differently her. She need a charge for her iPhone to tell time, she had lost the count of hours. Granted, her handmaidens had explained to her (she didn't know how many times!) the whole idea of counting notches in the candle wax for what she assumed was an hour. She shook her head as she watched the candle wax drip. She never imagined that her memories could be counted in the drippings of a candle. But, it didn't matter now. Simon was coming, and she knew that he would not let anything stop him from getting to her.

Tisha quickly changed her clothing. She laid out the fine gown she had been given on the bed. She changed into the light armor that she was getting used to wearing. She looked at herself in the mirror and grinned. For the first time, she did no tmind the odd tattoo on her face or the loss of her hair extensions. She felt relieved. She only wished that she had away to communicate her good news to Wisdom and the others. However, with Agar patrolling the halls of the Citadel, she knew that was not possible. She turned to leave her chamber.

Tisha made her way down through the Citadel to the pen where the gorda were kept and went to Aspion's stall. Seeing him made Tisha grin immediately. Seeing Tisha, Aspion rose from his bedding. The horned gorda looked up at his master and ambled over to her. Tisha was surprised at the connection she felt to the odd beast. She stuck out her hand and touched his horn. He rubbed casually against her. In the back of her mind, Tisha felt Aspion's voice begin to echo.

--Hold your good feeling close, he advised. All are listening and watching your every move, Little Flower.

Tisha was stunned by Aspion's simple statement. However, it was a reminder that she should not let her guard down. She had to stay clear-headed. That no matter how good the night before was, she was still a prisoner here. And there were forces constantly at work trying to change her into something she was not. As these thoughts ran through her mind, Tisha found herself thinking about the banquet from the night before. In particular, she found herself focusing on Mora's two uncles, Burton and Holi. She found herself wondering why she had not met either of them before last night and why the first meeting was in such a public forum.

"Hmph!" Tisha said as she reached out and fed Aspion grain. Thinking about the two High Princes, it was Holi who had left her with an uneasy feeling. She did not like the way he looked at her. It was like the odd little man was trying to undress her with his eyes. She would have to watch him. And if she got the chance, she would try to meet up with Elric and see what he had to say about the two mysterious High Princes. At the very least, it would be information that could help Royal. Anything that she felt she could do to help Royal could only support Simon's role as his Royal Guard. She was feeling more and more that she had to support Simon in this regard the more she found out about Acara. When they were all together, she would have a full treatise to tell about her time on Acara.

--Now you sound like the wife of the next King of the Royal Guard, Aspion whispered in her mind. And you wonder why I was born to serve you! he laughed.

"I hope you don't think I'm vain," Tisha said as she rubbed at his scales, "When I say that thing about. . ."

--Stop, Aspion screamed out inside her head making her ears ring. —I am sorry if that was too loud. But you still have to learn not to speak out loud when we speak. In the silence of our minds, none may enter.

It is the Moritan way. And though you were not born one, you are becoming one."

--Gotcha, Tisha whispered inside of her head.

--And by the way, Aspion laughged. –You were quite correct about the High Prince Holi. He was more taken by you than may know."

--Why me? Tisha asked rhetorically.

-- The youngest son of the High Prince Roman has always been a collector of sorts; in parituclar, rare things. Are you not the rarest of things his self has ever seen? Aspion asked clearly and pointedly?

--I am going to watch that one, Tisha said, rubbing at her head.

--We both will, Aspion assured her as he found a cool place in the rough to lay in the shade.

Tisha made sure his buckets were filled with water and fresh grain before turning on the heels of her boots. She looked over her shoulder and smiled at the odd-looking gorda. She made a mental note to herself that Simon would not only have to rescue her but the large, lizard-like creature, too. She could not imagine leaving him behind. Though she had only been joined with him a short time, she felt as tied to him as she did to her long-time pet, Mittens, back on Earth. However, unlike Mitten's who's affection she enjoyed, there was a depth to her connection with Aspion that she never knew before and that she was truly enjoying.

After spending some time with Aspion, Tisha went over to the workout area that Ela had taken her to. She bowed her head to the other Royal Guards as she passed them. She went over the workout area where Ela had first introduced her to the throwing weapons. She looked at the metal weapons on the table carefully. Then she turned her attention to the target that lay a few feet away. Carefully, Tisha picked up the throwing tools and began to throw them at the target. After a few misses, she began to hit it point blank. She smiled to herself. It was turning into a good day after all.

"You seem happy," a voice said from behind Tisha. It came out of nowhere and made her jump. She almost knocked over the table of throwing weapons.

Tisha turned just in time to see Agar appear out of thin air. She sucked her teeth. All the glow of her day began to vanish with his appearance. She hated this ghost more than she disliked Ela or even being on Acara. The fact that he could be watching her without her knowing and appear at any moment was unnerving.

"Don't you have anything better to do," Tisha snapped as as she rolled her eyes. "Go find a cemetary to haunt and shit."

Ignorning her outburst and truly not understanding the fullness of her rancor, Agar reiterated, "You seem extra happy today?"

"Just another day in Zumunda," Tisha said as she turned back to what she was doing, trying her best to ignore Agar's irksome presence. Then she touched her stomach. She smiled. She remembered that, for some reason, neither Agar nor the Dark High Queen could see into her thoughts. Her secrets were her own. She turned back to Agar and looked at him squarely. For the first time, she was not afraid of him and it was all do to her unborn child. "Maybe I am happy," she said snidely as she breezed past him.

Agar watched her as she went. He hated the fact that he could not see inside of her mind. However, he hated the fact that he existed in this form between life and death more. Yet, at the very least he could still serve his High Queen. And he felt that he could serve her best by keeping an eye on the Little Flower, Tisha.

# Chapter 19

Royal opened his eyes. For a second, he forgot where he was. Then he remembered the feel of Princess Jane / Prince Janis over him and the effect of the powerful drug that had been used on him. Royal sat up slowly in the dust of the road and shook his head. He had never had a hangover before, but he guessed this was what it had to feel like. His head was pounding, his throat was dry, and he felt off balance. Royal looked around for the other members of his party. They were laid out around a small fire just off the road side. In the distance, Royal caught sight of a man tied to a tree. As Royal looked at him, he remembered the way Princess Jane had transformed when she was on top of him. He had never felt anything like it before.

"You alright?" Wisdom asked as he approached him carrying a mug of hot coffee, a cigarette dangling from his lips. The smoke rolled around the edges of his fade haircut which was quickly growing in.

"I'm good, thanks to you," Royal said, managing a slight smiled as he took the cup of hot java.

"No problem, dude," Wisdom said as he helped Royal to his feet.

"Is everybody okay?" he asked Wisdom as the two walked toward the fire.

"Yeah, it seems so. I think folk feel a little bit stupid," Wisdom chuckled. "But that's not the first time I seen folk taken in by a pretty face."

"True enough," Royal said as they reached the others. The only person who was awake other than Wisdom was Lethia. She sat close to the fire picking it with a stick. Wisdom could tell that she was deep in thought.

"So what's the plan?" he asked as he sat down next to her.

"We continue East and find the CODA," Lethia said as she took out a cigar and began to smoke. "I say we snap the good prince's neck and be on our way.".

Royal cringed at the former queen of the CODA's words. Though he felt violated by what this person had done, he hated the idea of taking a life unnecessarily. Besides, if this person had wanted to see them dead he had more than ample opportunity. As Royal thought about it, he remembered the words Jane/Janis had said while hovering over him. It seemed that this monarch of Lampour wanted to get out of his kingdom more than anything else. Royal thought that perhaps those longings could be used to form an allegiance with the Prince, instead of creating yet another enemy.

"Before we do that, let me talk to him, or her, and figure out if we're dealing with an enemy," Royal said thoughtfully.

"What?" Lethia snapped. "He tried to poison us. And he clearly wanted to violate you. I say let's spill his blood and be on our way," Lethia said as she rose and drew her sword.

Royal stood up immediately blocking Lethia's path. Both she and Wisdom were surprised by his actions. For a second, no one moved. They stood there staring each other down, no one wanting to give ground. Finally, Lethia recanted. She put her sword away and sat back down by the fire. She turned her back to Royal and gave her cigar more attention.

"Fine," Lethia pouted as she bit the tip of her cigar.

Wisdom winked at Royal and sat across from Lethia next to the fire. He positioned himself so that he could watch Royal as he approached the interloper. Though he was sure he had bound him well, he was not taking any chances with the High Prince's safety. As Wisdom watched Royal approach the stranger, he found it odd how easily he was falling into this new role as his Royal Guard. It was unlike anything he had ever done previously. Though this experience had taken him completely out of his element, it was making him feel good about himself in a way he didn't recognize. He smiled to himself. He imagined that the way he felt protecting Royal was similar to the way his brother must feel as a police officer in Baltimore everyday of his life. Wisdom suddenly had a renewed respect for his older brother. After going through all of this, Wisdom did not know how he would ever be able to go back to his life as a drug dealer. For the first time, he found efficacy in the plan Tisha had laid out for him when they were together. Perhaps it was not too late for him to get his GED and change his life. It would be funny that coming to another planet would help him change his life. At the very least, it would give his grandmother, his brother, Tisha, and his son something to be proud of.

Royal approached the prince of Lampour slowly. Janis was looking off toward the Acarian sky and the growing light of a new day. He was not struggling against his bonds at all. He was simply sitting still and calm. When he caught site of Royal, he nodded his head and tried to smile.

"Your Highness," Prince Janis said evenly," I would bow, but considering my current situation, I guess I should be happy I still have my life."

"If you don't mind, I have some questions for you," Royal said simply as he sat on the ground a few feet away from his captive.

"Ask what you will," Prince Janis said glibly. "I don't think I will be going anywhere anytime soon. That off-worlder of yours can truly tie a knot. I am sure he might be fun in many ways," he said matter-a-factly.

Royal simply nodded.

"How is it that you can be both a male and a female?" Royal asked carefully.

Prince Janis looked up in the sky once again as if he was considering his words carefully before answering. Then he looked at Royal squarely.

"It is a feature of the royal family of Lampour," Prince Janis began. "For as long as we have existed, my ancestors have been able to live as both male and female. Shifting between the two. It is something we tend to do more when we are younger. Once we mate, we tend to assume one form or the other most of the time. However, it is something that is sometimes beyond our will to control," he explained.

"Why is it that you came on to me as both a male and a female?" Royal asked gingerly.

Prince Janis smiled widely at him before answering. "My High Prince, I had my eye on you ever since you came into Lampour. As it became clear to me that you were-- how do I say—open to either gender, I thought my kind might pose a tantalizing delight for you. I meant you and your party no harm," he assured im. "I just wanted to offer you yet another option."

"How can we be sure of that?" Royal asked.

"The High Queen sent out an edict to all of the Royals of Acara to be on the look out for you. It would have been simple for me to let her know you were in Lampour. I would have surely gained her trust and everlasting favor," he sasid candidly. "And though my father cowers at her throne, I find her darkness at the very least distasteful, no disrespect. And particularly unlady like; again, no disrespect."

"None taken; but why this focus on seducing me?"

Prince Janis looked at Royal with surprise. He wrinkled his brow in disbelief. He could not believe his ears. He was finding this surpringly simple young man to be very complicated indeed. It made him even more charming. Prince Janis found him to be a true breath of fresh air from the other self-righteous royals he was used to being around.

"You are to be the next High King of Acara. You lived on another world," Prince Janis said. "For all the riches and privileges that I have, I have only known Lampour. And regardless of the many delicacies that it provides, I yearn for more. Please forgive my methods, if not my intent."

"Is that why no one was able to perceive you as a threat?" Royal asked.

"It is. To you, I am truly harmless, but selfish," Prince Janis laughed as the first bits of light began to dance across the morning sky.

Royal thought about everything he had heard. He looked at this beautiful, black man who sat before him. Though he disliked the methods that Prince Janis had used, he found that there was something about him that he actually liked. He guessed it was his brashness and the deliberateness of his honesty. Royal looked back over his shoulder; the others were coming out of the stupor Prince Janis had left them in.

"Do not worry about your party," Prince Janis assured. "I only gave them a dab of Jucca pollen, enough to put them to make them happy and put them to sleep."

"And that green dust you sprayed in my face?" Royal asked.

"Morose," Prince Janis smiled. "Did you like it?" he teased.

Royal did not know what to say. All he could remember was the overwhelming sexual potency of the powder and the way it affected him. He had never experienced anything like it It was like his entire body was having an orgasm over and over again. For as intensely pleasurable as it was, it felt horribly unnatural. It was something he did not want to experience again.

"Morose is an acquired taste," Prince Janis said bluntly. "The secret of my family's ability to make it is what our fortune is built upon.

Though we have mounds of it in a cache known only to a few, it is sold in small quantities across the planet. Your uncle, the High Prince Burton, buys his weight's worth every year that I have known him."

"It seems you know a lot about mixing things," Royal said thoughtfully.

"I do. All of the royals of Lampour are taught from birth the intricacies of chemical compounds and their effects," Prince Janis explained.

"My friend, the one in the wagon, he has been poisoned. If we untie, will you look at him and tell us how he is doing?" Royal asked.

Prince Janis batted his eyes and bowed his head. "For you, my High Prince, I can do that.

"I'll see what I can do," Royal said as he rose.

He walked quickly back over to the others for a candid conference.

"Are you satisfied Royal?" Lethia said as she rose from the fire. "Can I snap his neck now?" she asked impatiently.

"No," Royal said firmly. "I think we have need for him."

"Where is the woman from last night?" Hue asked as he scratched his head "And where did he come from?" he asked looking at Prince Janis, clearly confused.

"I think he is she," Captain Sarison said to Hue as he scratched his head. "I should have thought about something like that! Oh, Lampour!" he laughed, "you have always been full of mysteries."

Looking at Prince Janis from a distance, Etera sneered.

"I think I prefer him as a female," she said honestly.

Turning his attention from the group to Royal, Wisdom asked, "What do you mean we need him?"

To answer the question, Royal explained all that Prince Janis had revealed to him in their conversation. He left out none of the details. Though he was embrarrassed about the intentions of Prince Janis' affection, he did not hide it from the group. If these people were willing to risk their lives for him, he would not keep secrets from them. As he told the tale of his interrogation of Prince Janis, he paid particular attention to both Hue and Etera. He could tell that they were startled but he could not read their expressions beyond that. However, he could tell that they were thinking deeply about the details of the conversation.

"I think it would be good to have someone who knows poisons to look at Tildon," Tori interjected. "We need to know how he is doing."

"Bah!" Peku snapped. "My secrets have been keeping him well. I have plenty of spit left for him. Watch me!" he shouted as he pursed his lips and created a huge ball of white phlegm.

"I know you do, Peku, but we still should check on his condition," Tori said as he scratched at the Opion's head. "Save what you have for later, we may be in need of it."

"Are we sure we want to let him loose?" Hue asked. "I mean, who knows what else he is capable of? I mean, my God!"

"Do not worry, little friend," Maximus growled as he licked his paws. "If he steps out of line or gets to close to Royal, I will swat him," he assured him.

Hue looked at the big beast and hunched his shoulders. He knew that Maximus was a capable fighter. However, he felt very nervous about this new person. If he could morph from one gender into another and was a master of poisons, who knew what he was capable of? Hue looked to Lethia for support in his doubts. He could tell that the queen of the CODA was getting tired of all this conversation.

"Etera, Tildon is your brother," Lethia said. "I say it is up to you. Either way, a decision must be made. We need to get to the CODA and the Red Desert beyond. Time is not on our side. The High Queen is already on our tail."

Etera felt on the spot. However, she did not doubt Lethia's logic. She had gotten her brother into this situation. He was like the silent member of their party. He could not make decisions for himself, so she had to make decisions for him. Her grandmother would have it no other way if she was there.

"Release him," Etera said as she went over to the wagon. "Release him and let's be done with this."

Captain Sarison reached into his belt and handed Royal a knife. Royal walked over to Prince Janis. The Prince looked up and his eyes fell upon the blade that Royal was carrying. He swallowed hard and closed his eyes. He expected Royal to slit his throat or to run him through. Instead, Royal cut the ropes that were holding him. Prince Janis was surprised. He got to his feet slowly. He looked around, confused.

"Will you see to our friend, Tildon?" Royal asked.

"You are asking me, your High Prince?" Prince Janis asked.

"I guess I could take control of you," Royal began. "But I don't know if you would be able to really tell us anything then. I would rather simply ask."

Prince Janis looked at Royal with renewed respect and attraction. He had been around royals all of his life and was not used to being treated the way that Royal was treating him. Silently, Prince Janis wished he had taken a different approach in terms of meeting the High Prince. He felt horribly embarrassed. Perhaps then things would have been different between them. As he looked at Royal, he wondered if he would ever have a chance with someone like him. Despite all that he possessed, Prince Janis would love to have someone that he could love without having to use morose or some other concoction. It felt odd to have so much and, at the same time, feel like you truly had nothing.

"For you, my High Prince, I will take a look at him," Prince Janis said as he bowed before the son of the High Queen.

Prince Janis gathered his robes and walked over to the group. He paused before them. Royal introduced the Prince of Lampour to all the members of his party. They were unsure of how to react to Janis considering that several hours earlier he had drugged them. Janis could tell that Lethia and Maximus were the most on guard. He could tell that if he made the slightest odd movement, they would be ready to take his life.

"Let me see your friend," Prince Janis said humbly as he gathered his flowing white robes around him.

Royal led Prince Janis over to the wagon. Etera stared at the Prince of Lampour with suspicion and caution. Prince Janis smiled at Tildon's twin before he climbed onto the wagon. He carefully un-wrapped him from the bedding they had placed around him to travel. He got all the way down to his clothing before Tildon opened his eyes. Tildon caught the Prince's hand before he got to his wound. Not recognizing the Prince, he found a knife that was tucked into his belt. Tildon found the strength to raise the blade to the Prince's throat. Surprised, Prince Janis fell back in the wagon. Etera climbed in the wagon and calmed her brother.

"It is alright," Etera said soothingly. "He is here to help."

Tildon looked from his sister to Janis. He slowly put down his knife, relaxed, and closed his eyes. Etera turned to Prince Janis and nodded. He carefully approached Tildon and un-wrapped his wound. The skin was cracked and grey. It was still oozing a fine, green discharge. Prince Janis bent down and smelled the wound. He pulled back at the pungent odor. Though the wound had the unmistable odor of the Opion's secretions, the poison was still present and active. Prince Janis wrinkled his nose. He climbed down from the wagon with Etera and returned to the group.

"Well?" Etera said hurriedly.

"First of all, it is a miracle that he is still alive," Prince Janis said honestly. "Aldam is a poison that is not even of this world. It is said that it fell from the sky and we accidentally discovered it. It causes a quick and painful death. There is no known cure. The Opion's secretions have slowed it down and eased the pain, but it is still actively causing his organs to shut down. How did he come by this?"

"He was infected protecting me," Royal said grimly as he looked past Janis to the wagon where Tildon lay. He lowered his head with silent regret. Wisdom came up behind him and placed a reassuring hand on his shoulder.

"How much time?" Lethia asked flatly.

"Even with the help of the Opion, I would say no more than five or six Suns," Prince Janis predicted "I am truly sorry."

Hearing these words, Etera burst into tears. She did not know where to turn in her grief. However, Hue found her. As he held her, Hue remembered what it was like to watch his mother, Sylvia, waste away from breast cancer. He knew intimately that seeing someone you love die like that made you feel powerless. He escorted Etera from the group towards the wagon. As Etera cried in Hue's arms, she remembered her journey from the slave mines back home. She wished she had never brought this fight to her grandmother and her twin. She would have preferred to remain in the hopeless pits mining ore than to see her brother die like this.

"We must get to the CODA immediately," Lethia said. "The eternal spring is his only hope."

"The eternal spring?" Prince Janis gasped. "I thought that was only a myth."

"No, it is not Prince of Lampour," Lethia declared. "It is very real. Not even I, as the Queen of the CODA, fully understand its secrets. But, it appears that not even the power of the Avatar or a chemist like you can save young Tildon. It is his only hope. We just have to find the CODA in time."

"Are they that hard to find?" Royal asked hurriedly.

"The Eternal Spring is kept by the elders of the CODA, the oldest women in the tribe. Even when I was Queen of the CODA, I was not sure where the elders were or what secrets they kept. That is the CODA way. We must find the tribe first and get the elder with them to take us to the elders and convince them to take us to the Eternal Spring."

"Do we have enough time?" Captain Sarison asked grimly.

"We will have to make it," Lethia snapped. "It is time for us to get back on the road."

The group began to stir as Prince Janis raised his hand.

"I may be able to help you find the CODA," he said evenly.

"How, man? Speak." Lethia commanded. "I am a master of Land magic, a former CODA Queen and not even I can guarantee finding them quickly."

"As Prince of Lampour, I trade with the CODA often. And like you said, they are almost impossible to find. So we have made a pact, when I have something I think they want. I send my companion to them," he explained.

"Your companion?" Wisdom questioned.

"Yes, my companion," Prince Janis said as he stepped back from the group. He raised his arm and let out a high-pitched cry. The members of the group grabbed their ears. Seconds later, Altion appeared in the sky overhead. It circled the group for a moment, before landing on its master's arm. Prince Janis reached into his robe and gave his pet a treat.

"The CODA will see Altion for leagues and think I have something to trade. They will meet you on the road," Prince Janis said with confidence.

"Then let us be on our way," Lethia said as she directed the group to the wagon and their mounts. As she turned, she paused and went up to Prince Janis until they were standing eye to eye. "You have redeemed yourself, young prince. Now I expect that you will tell no one that we met."

"No problem, CODA queen," Prince Janis said as he stepped back in fear. "Your secret is safe with me. In fact, if you ever have need of the troops of Lampour, get me a message and I will meet you wherever I have to."

"What about your father?" Lethia asked.

"He leaves the guard of the city-state to me. My father is a good man, but he prefers countting his coin to acts of war. The troops are loyal to me to a fault, well trained, and always ready for battle," Prince Janis said.

"I knew I liked your smell, no matter if you are a male or a female," Maximus growled as he patted Janis on the back before retreating to the wagon.

As the others went to their mounts, Royal went up to Prince Janis. They stared at each other awkwardly for a moment. Then Prince Janis reached out and took Royal's arm. He carefully transferred Altion from his arm to Royal. He reached into his robes and took out his bag of treats and gave them to Royal. He petted the flying serpent on the head fondly.

"Altion has been my constant companion for most of my life. After you find the CODA, please be sure to send him home," Prince Janis asked humbly.

Thinking about his connection to Maximus, he knew the importance of having a familiar. He shook his head. He would make sure Altion got back to his master. Prince Janis gave Royal his bag of treats. Royal gratefully took the bag. He reached inside and gave Altion one of the dried treats. Altion left his master's arm and wrapped himself around Royal's arm.

"Good," Prince Janis smiled. "He likes you."

"Well, I like him, too," Royal said playfully.

"You will have time to enjoy him later," Prince Janis said. "But right now he has work to do" Prince Janis said as he accepted him back. "Seek the CODA," he directed as the winged serpent lifted off from his arm. Altion screeched as he circled the group over head.

As Prince Janis thought he snapped his fingers.

"What is it?" Royal asked.

"I have one more thing for you," Prince Janis said as he ran back over to the rock archway. He lifted his feathered cloak from the dirt and went over to the wagon. He carefully climbed on board with the great cape. Maximus caught his arm protectively as he began to cover Tildon with the cloak.

"It is okay," Royal said as he went up to the wagon.

"What is that for?" Etera asked.

"My cloak is made of the finest feathers you will find in Lampour. The feathers transform the light of the suns to heat. I think it will keep your brother comfortable on the road," Prince Janis explained. "It was also blessed by the priests of the Avatar many years ago before they fell. It will give your brother strength."

"Thank you," Etera nodded her head with tears in her eyes.

"It is the least I can do after poisoning you," Prince Janis smiled as he climbed down from the wagon.

"Ya think," Hue said snidely.

Ignoring Hue, Prince Janis returned to the road where Royal was still standing. The two looked at each other and smiled awkwardly.

"We have to go," Lethia commanded.

"I wish we could have met under different circumstances," Royal said. "I think we would have been friends."

"I think so also," Prince Janis said as he reached out and touched Royal's face tenderly. "Good journey, High Prince."

"Good journey, Prince of Lampour," Royal said as he walked over to his mount.

"Are you okay to get back?" Wisdom asked as he went to his mount.

"I know these roadways well. I am fine. Keep the High Prince, he is one of a kind," Prince Janis said to Wisdom as he proceeded down the path.

"I will," Wisdom assured under his breath.

Lethia took the lead and the others fell into formation. They proceeded down the roadway through the large archway and headed out of Lampour. Prince Janis stood alone in the middle of the road watching the small party continue down the path. He looked up in the sky. His trusted companion, Altion, led the way for them out of Lampour into the barreness of the plains. He was sure that if anyone could guide them to the CODA in time to help their friend, Altion could. As Prince Janis thought about the group, oddly it was the image of Tildon that stuck out in his mind more than anything else. Though the fallen warrior had not said a word to him, there was something about him that drew Prince Janis. It was for that reason he had been so quick to give up his cherished cloak for Tildon's protection. It had taken years to make it out of the fallen feathers of rare birds.

As Prince Janis turned back up the road toward Lampour, he straightened his tunic and sank back into his hood. With dawn appearing over his shoulder, Prince Janis effortlessly transformed into Jane. She smiled as she glanced over her shoulder at the High Prince and his party. She was sure that when they met again they would not meet as enemies, but as allies.

Simon lifted the last piece of wreckage from the pulpit with a huge grunt. For the first time, the group was able to see the passageway under the pulpit. Reverend Monroe got up from where he was sitting and looked down the passageway. He was excited about the possibility of what lay beneath.

"We have done it, Simon," Reverend Monroe smiled. "It is time to go home."

Simon looked at the Reverend. He did not know what to say. All he wanted to do was run down that passageway, open the Gateway, and be off to Acara but he resisted the urge. There was still a lot for them to do before they left.

"It is time to get ready to go," Simon said with tears in his eyes. All he was thinking about was getting to Tisha and back at Royal's side. He felt that he had a lot to make up for.

"We could not have done this without all of you," Reverend Monroe said as he turned to the others. "I can't thank you enough. At the very least, I assure you that we will do everything we can to get your loved ones back to you."

Ben, Purcell, Ms. Loretta, Isabel, and Father Benedito were all sitting on the pew in front of the pulpit. They were exhausted. They were covered in soot from the rubble they had been moving. Though

Simon had done most of the heavy lifting, the others had assisted where they could They were all happy with the outcome. Ben was particularily happy with what he was hearing. In addition to the strain from all of the physical work, he was silently having withdrawal symptoms from his cold turkey approach to ending his alcohol abuse. Staying busy gave him something to focus on instead of the nagging desire to have another drink. He wanted his son home as soon as possible. He was even thinking about going into rehab once he was sure Hue was safe. After all that was happening, some rest would do him good.

"Are you alright?" Ms. Loretta said as she turned to Ben.

"I'm okay," he smiled. "I'm just ready to see my son."

"You ain't never lied," Ms. Loretta smiled. "I want my boy back, too. I know he wasn't that good when he was here, but maybe going to another world will change him for the better. I hope so."

"We have to pray for the best all the way around," Ben said. He was having trouble believing that he was saying what he was saying. Perhaps hanging around all of these holy men and women was having an impact on him after all.

"I will make room for the Father and Senora Lopez in the rectory. Then I will set the crystals in the Gateway. We should be ready to go by tomorrow," Reverend Monroe said.

Simon and Reverend Monroe led Isabel and Father Benedito back into the rectory. The rest of the group left slowly from the sanctuary after turning the lights out on all the work they had accomplished.

After dropping Purcell off at home, Ben made his way to his Shirley Ave. home. It was early evening when he got to his house. He could see the lights were on in his living room as he made his way up the walkway. He entered the house to find his daughter sitting on the livingroom sofa. She was dressed in an oversized Morgan sweatshirt and a pair of leggings. She was curled up with Chinese take-out, watching television. Ben came into the livingroon and sat down next to his daughter.

"How was your trip?" she asked.

Before her father could answer, Sapphire curled up in his lap like she did shen she was a little girl. Ben was taken with her show of affection. He placed his hand on her cornrowed head and stroked it delicately. It was at rare moments like this that she reminded him of her long lost mother, Sylvia. Ben looked up at the television screen. He could not remember what was on. All that he could think about was that it was good to be home. The only thing that was missing was his son, Hue. It was time to bring him home.

Lying in her father's lap, Sapphire was lulled to sleep.

"Sapphire," Ben said as he tapped her on the shoulder.

"Huhmp?" Sapphire said as she stirred in his lap.

"What if I told you I could bring your brother back?" Ben said cautiously.

Sapphire's eye's popped open. She looked at him like he was crazy. They had buried her brother, Hue, along side his mother, Sylvia. Granted they had not been able to retrieve his body because of the fire, but she knew there was no bringing him back. Sapphire continued to look at her father like he was crazy.

"Daddy, don't toy with me," she snapped. "You can't bring back the dead," she said as she stood and began to pace the room.

Ben looked at his daughter with sympathy. He could not imagine going away the next day and not telling her what he was facing. He was a realist. While he had heard Reverend Monroe's promise, he knew there was a real possibility that neither he nor Hue might come back. It would mean that Sapphire would be all alone in the world. Facing that stark possibility, he had to tell her the truth.

"There is so much I need to tell you, little girl," Ben said as he got to his feet and went over to her with a tender expression of concern.

"What do you mean Daddy?" Sapphire questioned.

He led Sapphire back over to the couch. Slowly, he began to talk to her about monsters, off-worlders, and Gateways. Sapphire's eyes stayed wide open as they talked into the early morning hours.

Father Benedito tried to sleep, but he could not. He tossed and turned before he finally got up. He went over to the window and looked out. He was a young man and he had not seen much of the world. He had grown up in Spanish Harlem. And like many Puerto Rican urban boys from his era, he had made a lot of the wrong choices when he was younger. It had been Father Francis who had guided him out of the storm and onto the right path. The old priest had taken aliking to him and had been a second father to him as well. He was an altar boy at the Sacred Heart when he first imagined himself being the custodian of the Holy Host. This image had led him to college, seminary, and his eventual ordination as a Catholic priest.

Years later when Father Francis died, Father Benedito was honored that the Bishop had tapped him to take over the parish of the largely Spanish-speaking immigrant congregation of the Sacred Heart. For the last few years, he had fulfilled his duties with humility and honor. He thought that, like his mentor, he would grow old and die under the mantle of his Savior. However, over the last day or so, he had been introduced to possibilities he had never imaged. Now, for the first time, he was doubtful of the idea of returning to his daily activities. He could return to Spanish Harlem, save souls, and act like none of the past day or so had happened, or he could join the cause of a righteous few and liberate an entire planet from evil.

Father Benedito laughed to himself. He could not believe that he was even considering such a thing. Ever since he was a boy he had a fascination for the stars. Now, he was faced with the possibility of not only seeing them, but actually going to one. How could he turn down such an opportunity? Father Benedito fell to his knees. He took out his rosary and began to pray. He prayed long and hard for guidance from his Savior and his saints. When he rose to his feet, he had made up his mind. He did not know what the journey would entail but if they would have him, he would go to Acara. His mind was made up.

Father Benedito put on his clothes and left his room. He tiptoed across the floor and knocked on the door of the room where Isabel was.

"Venga! Come in," the elderly Latina woman said.

Father Benedito opened the door. Isabel was sitting on the edge of her bed. She was sitting with a tray of tea and two cups. Her ever-present bag was tossed across the bed. Father Benedito moved slowly into the room. He smiled as he looked at his secretary. He shook his head. She had that look on her face like she was expecting him. He sat down at a small desk across from her.

"You want some tea?" she asked.

"Si," Father Benedito said. "That would be nice."

Isabel poured him a cup of tea. For a moment, the two sat with each other, enjoying the familiarity of their company as they drank their tea. Father Benedito looked at Isabel. She had been watching him for most of his life. She had been there when the hit-and-run took both of his parents and left the brilliant, bright-eyed boy alone in the world. She shook her head, without Father France, she didn't know what would have happened to him. Somewhere under the visage of the old Sacred Heart, they had all become family. She was as close to her church family as she was to her own.

"There is much on your mind," Isabel said matter-a-factly as she sipped some tea. When she thought no one was looking, she sweetened the dark drink with some spiked libation. She smiled glibly and sat back and drank. "Too bad that los perros did not survive the last battle. We could have learned so much more from them."

Father Benedito laughed. "You are truly an evil woman!" he scolded her with familiarity.

"Incredible!." she smiled. "You know me so well. I know that look in your eye, and as we were working today, I could see you were wondering," she laughed.

"Si, es la verdad. I have been thinking about many things," Father Benedito admitted. "I love the church, Isabel. I do. And I loved Father Francis and I love you. I take the vows that I took seriously, but I have the chance to see another world," he marveled. "It is a dream come true for me, a young man from El Barrio walking across sand that our feet have never touched and doing the Lord's work at the same time."

Isabel listened to Father Benedito. She sipped her tea. She looked up at him and smiled.

"Mi hijo," she sighed. "I can not tell you to go or not to go." She paused. "You are a young man, but I know you. If you do go, you go as a priest and never forget your vows." Entiende?"

Father Benedito smiled, "I will always be a priest."

"And who knows?" Isabel said as she shrugged her shoulders. "Perhaps being a priest will help these people on their journey."

The two Puerto Ricans visiting Balitomore for the first time sipped tea and shared a laugh into the early morning hour. Neither one of them knew what tomorrow held, but they both knew that tonight could be the last time they ever laid eyes on one another.

Purcell crossed the threshold of his Federal Hill home. His muscles were sore and he was tired. It would be good to spend a night in the comfort of his own bed. It was good to be home. There were no assassin cubes or Marauders here. There were only the shadows of the memories of his life. Purcell passed by the picture of his mother, Purcilla, Wisdom, and himself on the wall. It seemed like so long ago since he had been with either of them. Now it was time for him to go get his brother back. He knew that Wisdom was not a saint and that he might not even be a goodperson, but he was his brother and he needed to go get him. More than for himself, he owed it to his mother, his grandmother, and Little Wisdom.

And there was Hue to think of. He felt oddly responsible for him as well. It had been his idea for Hue to get involved with the church in the first place. He thought he was saving Hue from himself when he got him involved in the youth group at Gateway Baptist Church. Little did he know that he was getting Hue involved with off-worlders. It didn't matter to Purcell that he was gay, Hue was like a little brother to him. He was as much family to him as Wisdom and his grandmother were. He had to go get him, too.

Purcell kicked off his shoes and went over to the refrigerator. The naked light of the refrigerator filled the darkened room. There was nothing in the icebox but half-filled cartons of Chinese food and half-finished bottles of beer. Purcell got himself a beer and went into the bedroom. He turned on the television. The news was on. It felt odd after having experienced so much to be home and simply watching television. He had no idea what going to Acara would be like, but he felt that it would ultimately bring his family back together. He guessed he was learning to have faith after all.

Purcell finished his beer and climbed into the familiar comfort of his bed, without taking off his clothes, and hugged his pillow. He wrapped his arms around it the way he used to hold onto his brother when he was a child. Purcell had dated many women in his life, but as of late, he had left much of that behavior behind. He did not know when and how, but he felt like love was right around the corner for him. Purcell drifted off to sleep thinking of the promise love and the love of family.

Reverend Monroe began to get things in order. He sat at his desk in the half-light of his study. He unrolled the satchel of crystals and gems that he had brought with him from Acara. He took out a small stone. It was a memory stone on Acara, but on Earth it was a perfect diamond. He would leave it for Ms. Loretta with instructions on how to liquidate it. On the outside chance that he never came back to Earth, he wanted Gateway Baptist Church to continue. More than any of the trustees and deacons, he found that he trusted Ms. Loretta most of all with keeping the legacy of the church alive. Though he had created it to hide Royal here on Earth and used its fantastic power to fuel his sermons, the Church was more to him than that. It was part of the fabric of Baltimore and the life blood of the community. No matter what happened, it had to live on.

Reverend Monroe got up from the desk and turned the light of fin his office. He walked down the hallway to the ruined sanctuary. He looked around at the remains of the sanctuary and smiled sadly. He would miss this place. He hoped that somehow he would see it again. However, more important than getting back to this place, he had to go and get his son. Reverend Monroe climbed up to the whole where the pulpit had been and climbed down into the catacombs beneath the altar. Reverend Monroe took a small crystal out of his pocket. He blew on it and it burst into light. He used it to guide him down the tunnel. After a few minutes, he reached a natural archway. He carefully removed the Gateway crystals the others had used to get to Acara from the archway. They were fragemented and their energy spent. He looked at them grimly. They had truly been drained in the effort to get the others to Acara. He replaced them with the ones they had retrieved from the catherdral in Spanish Harlem. They began to glow immediately. Once they began to glow, Reverend Monroe took the crystals the Marauder had and held them up to the Gateway crystals. He pointed at the Gateway crystals and transferred the energy from the Marauder's crystals to the others. The Gateway began to glow instantly. It was fully charged and ready to go. Reverend Monroe smiled. It was time to go home.

It had been a long day of business with the royals and the members of the High Court. The High Queen retired to her chambers. She was tired of dealing with the petty business of these royals. However, the duty came with the crown. The High Queen was about to have her handmaidens take off her clothes when she saw a shimmer in the far corner. She knew it was Agar. She shook her head. She had almost forgotten about the shade she had commissioned to patrol the hallways of the Grand Citadel. She sat down on the edge of the bed and waited for him to appear. Though her day had been long, she knew that if he was coming to her in her private quarters, it was important.

Agar appeared in a distant corner. He bowed to his High Queen. She waved him over to a small table where she had assembled a late night dinner for herself.

"You don't mind if I eat while we talk," the High Queen said as she pulled a large piece of meat from the platter.

"I was speaking with Tisha today and she seemed awfully happy," Agar began.

"The girl is pregnant, living in the Grand Cathedral, she wants for nothing. What does she have to be unhappy about?" the High Queen said idly.

"Though I could not use my dark powers to read her, there seemed to be more to it than that. Then I remembered she wears the promise crystal that connects her with Keyton," Agar continued.

"So?" the High Queen said as she contuined to eat.

"So, your Highness, I took the liberty of going to the Dark Temple to check in on the other Marauder you summoned, to find out whether it felt anything from its twin.

"And?" the High Queen asked as she looked up from her plate.

"It is no more," Agar dropped his head.

The High Queen got up from where she was sitting. Agar took a step back. Her face was unreadable.

"Tell me the rest,"

"Before it was destroyed, it communicated with its twin that those on Earth had found means to return to Acara on their on. Then, nothing." Agar explained.

The High Queen listened to his words with no expression.

"You have done well, Agar, by bringing this to me," she complimented. "Now leave me to my thoughts."

Agar bowed again and vanished with a shimmer.

Alone once again, the High Queen removed her crown. All of a sudden, she was feeling the weight of it. Then she turned around and angrily flipped over the table full of food. As quickly as she lost her temper she caught herself. She was tired of failure. It seemed that no matter whoever or whatever she sent to do her bidding against her son and his emissaries, they failed her. She shook her head. All of her life she had had a hard time relying on others. She supposed that this was yet another situation that she was going to have to manage herself. Once she was sure where they were, she would go herself to retrieve her son. Once he was in her hands, Keyton would come to her. It was as simple as that.

Once again, there was a familiar tap on her far wall. She rushed to it and let her lover into her chambers. Prince Gregor stepped in from the shadows. He looked at the wreckage in the room and then back at the High Queen.

"Are you alright, my love?" he asked carefully as he drifted over to her.

"Nothing I can't handle," she assured him as she drew him near and kissed him.

# Chapter 20

The paved roads of Lampour soon gave away to open plains. Altion hovered just over their heads as they proceeded into the open wilderness of the Eastern Continent. While the mounts had no problem traversing the trails, the wagon shook vigorously with the others on board. Etera fought to hold onto the reins as they pushed forward. From behind, she could hear her brother moaning. The sound of his moans kept her focused on the roads they were traveling. As they moved inland, Etera could feel the energy in her shifting. She was a sea witch. She gained her power from the water. The farther away they got from the sea, the more she began to feel her powers wane. She was feeling horribly normal.

As they rode, Hue kept an eye on Etera. He could tell that the journey inland was taking a lot out of her. Several times he offered her food or water, but she refused. She was of singular purpose: saving her brother. Hue understood the level of commitment she was expressing. He and his family had done the same thing for his mother, Sylvia, before she succumbed to breast cancer many years ago. Hue looked down at Etera's hands. They were white-knuckled from the holding the reins so tightly to keep the wagon on course. Without breaking rhythm, Hue reached over and took the reins from her hands. He had never steered a wagon before but he had been watching Etera all day. He just kept his eyes focused on the landscape ahead and a tight grip on the reins.

By midday, they were well onto the open plains. The suns of Acara were beating down hard upon them. They discarded the robes they were wearing and lightened their armarment as they rode. As they made their way across the plains, they found a huge, lone tree. Its branches were spread out and cast a shadow across a patch of grass. As they reached this tree, Lethia slowed her mount.

"Let's take a rest here, eat, and water the mounts," Lethia said.

"Good idea," Captain Sarison said as he slowed his mount. He was a man of the seas. Though he had survived more storms on the seas than he could remember, he hated traveling by land animal. It was unnatural for him. He would have much preferred to take his air ship. However, the huge ship was powered by the mystical sea salt waters of Acara. It would fall like a rock this far inland. He could not remember the last time he was away from his vessel. Though he was not there, he trusted his men and he knew they would take care of the *Lucky Lady*.

Maximus leaped out of the back of the wagon. He put his nose up in the air and took in a whiff of the land around them. He sensed numerous small animals around but he could tell that, for the most part, they were alone out there. Maximus stretched his legs and rolled around in the grass. He was unsure exactly how long he had been back, but he found himself missing his pride. He had been barely weened from his mother's breast when Lethia took him to Earth. He really wanted to see his people, the Manda, but most of all, he wanted to see his father, King Puton. He had been especially close to his father before he was taken away. Though he felt a strong bond to Royal, it was nothing like the connection he had to his father and his people. He sorely missed them over his time away.

"How is he?" Etera asked as she stretched and turned around to check in on her brother.

"He is stable," Tori said as he felt across the feathery cape that Janis had left for him. "It is good that Janis left us this cape. It keeps him cool under the sun and warm at night."

"At least, he was good for something other than drugging us and trying to rape Royal," Hue said sarcastically. He meant it.

"You are just a ray of sunshine," Peku said as he began to ramble around in the back of the wagon. The Opion found a piece of fruit, sat back, and began to eat. Peku lay back and looked up at the suns in the sky. He had seen little of Lampour but he much preffered the shaggy woods of his Lost Islands. He missed the sweet water of the veins and laying in the arms of the trees. While he was happy to be of assistance to his old and new friends, he hoped that one day he would be able to return to the Lost Islands, the veins, and the simple life he had left behind. Who knows? By the time he got back, he might have his mating stripes, the dark lines that would appear on his back signaling that he was ready to be a father. He laughed at the thought as he squeezed the enzyme from his gland. Imagine, him the father of wide-eyed Opions!

Wisdom got off of his mount near the tree. Royal followed him. The two stood near their mounts watching the others unpack a lunch. Altion swooped down out of the sky and wrapped itself around a nearby branch. Royal raised his arm and the flying serpent flew over to him. He reached into his pocket and fed their guide. Once he was full, Altion leapt from Royal's arm back to the shade of the tree's branches.

"Royal, can I ask you something?" Wisdom said.

"Sure," Royal smiled. "You are my Royal Guard, after all."

"I don't know about all of that. But seriously, what did Janis give you?" he asked. Wisdom did not miss much.

Royal was surprised by the question. Then he reached into his pocket and gave the silver container to Wisdom. Wisdom took it from his hand and opened it to reveal the grainy, green powder. Wisdom looked at it suspiciously.

"It is called morose," Royal told him. Then he explained to Wisdom what Janis had revealed to him about the drug and the power of its effect. He also told Wisdom that it was the thing that had made Janis' family the fortune they currently had.

"How do you feel about this?" Wisdom asked.

Royal hunched his shoulders.

"I don't know," Royal said honestly. "I already have the power to control people and I really don't like the idea of doing that. I don't know how I feel about drugging folks, too."

"You should have concerns about that," Wisdom said honestly. "I never thought that I would say this, but being around you and the others, I have truly begun to re-think my life in Baltimore. I mean, I was all about the money. It didn't matter who I hurt or what I did to get it. Now I see there can be another way," Wisdom said, surprised by his words.

Royal smiled and tears formed in his eyes. Life was filled with small mircales.

"There is always another way, Wisdom, even when we may not see it or believe it. I know a little bit about some of the stories of your life from you and your grandmother. And it hasn't been fair. I have to admit, I was slightly scared of you when we first met."

"I was scared of me, too." Wisdom interjected. The two shared a laugh.

"But now I see a whole new you," Royal said. "I have come to rely on you as my protector, but more than that, I have come to respect your advice. You have pulled me up when I needed to be pulled up. Your mother would be proud of you," Royal said honestly.

"I know my grandmother would be proud of me," Wisdom smiled.

"No, not your grandmother, Wisdom," Royal interjected. "Your mother."

The word hung in the air like lead. Wisdom was stunned. He bent over and grabbed his knees. He did not like to think about his mother, Purcilla. However, it was clear to him that his pain about his mother's drug use, and her eventual overdose in front of him, had shaped so many decisions in his life. Tears formed in his eyes and fell to wet the grassy knoll upon which he was standing. Royal placed a reassuring hand on his shoulder and let him release.

Hue walked up to the two of them slowly.

"Is everything alright?" he asked out of concern.

"It is," Royal assured him. "Just give us a minute."

Hue nodded his head and faded back around the tree. He sat with the others. After a few minutes, Wisdom composed himself and wiped his eyes. He took several deep breaths and stood up.

"You okay?" Royal asked tenderly.

"I am," he said.

"Good," Royal said. "Lets go get something to eat and see where the others are."

"Hey, Royal?" Wisdom stopped him.

"Yes?" Royal turned.

"Let me hold on to the Morose." Wisdom said. "You are a minister as well as a High Prince and holding drugs is not who you are. I been holding drugs for most of my life. I got it for you."

"And if we need to use it?" Royal asked carefully.

"From what you said, they gonna be some happy muthfuckas," Wisdom winked as he stuck out his hand.

Royal smiled as he handed the container to Wisdom. While he appreciated the jesture that Janis had made in giving it to him, he really did not want the responsibility of having to take possesion of it. It would take him along time to forget the unnatural feeling that it gave him and the after-effect. He had no desire to take it again but he did not want to have it with him as a constant reminder of the experience.

Under the hot mid-afternoon suns of Acara, the group settled down to eat. There was not much talking as they ate the dried rations. They had been riding since the early morning hours and they were tired from being in the saddle for so long. Only Lethia seemed to be oblivious to the experience. In fact, the further they rode out on the plains, the more energized she seemed to become.

As Lethia ate, she looked at the land that had given birth to her and from which she first drew power. Looking around, she had a slight resentment for the presence of all these men in the land that had given birth to her. As a member of the CODA, except for mating, they had no contact with male-dominated society. On Acara, it was thought that the CODA hated men. However, it was against the CODA belief system to hate. They did not hate men; they disliked the ways that male-dominated society oppressed others and created nothing. On the plains, the women of the CODA were free to exist, develop and create. Lethia had forgotten how much she missed being with the CODA. Though the spirit of the Avatar was sacred to the CODA, It usually respected their right to live without men. By acquiescing to the Avatar asking her to take care of Simon, Royal, and Maximus, she had made the ultimate sacrifice for a CODA. She had earned the position to be their Queen through trial by combat but she did not know if she deserved to take on that mantle again. She had been living with men for almost twenty Earth years. She knew the rules of the CODA, but in her heart she did not know if she could truly embrace all of their ways again. Being Grace Monroe was as much apart of her now as being Lethia of the CODA.

Lethia got up from where the others were eating. She went to her mount and got her swords. She walked off into the distance and began to perform a sacred form. It caused her to stretch every muscle and joint in her body, while it opened up her energy center to the land around her. Lethia felt a rush of energy fill her body. She knew that it was not the CODA way to help men. To get the CODA to at least listen to them, she was going to have to regain her place as their Queen. Althea had always been her rival, but there had been no other person strong enough for her to leave in charge. Althea would not return the mantle of power to her without a fight. In fact, she might even have to kill her to get her station back. Lethia sighed as she raised her swords over her head. If that was what was required, she would give her a quick death by snapping her neck. It was the CODA way.

Back by the tree, Royal was sitting with Hue eating sandwiches. Royal looked at Hue and smiled. Though Hue was covered in a fine spray of dirt from the ride, Royal had to admit how truly handsome he was. He had never thought of another male like this before. However, the more time he spent with Hue, the more he felt things he had never felt before. Hue smiled when he realized that Royal was looking at him. Royal blushed and turned back to Lethia. She was making her way back to the group.

"Is that critter of yours ready?" Lethia asked gruffly. "We should get back on the road while we have plenty of light."

Royal looked up in the tree. Altion was resting his head. He raised his arm and the flying serpent immediately came to life. He leaped down from the tree and wrapped himself around Royal's arm. In the Bible, Lucifer had caused the downfall of men. For this reason, Royal had always disliked snakes. He was having a hard time believing that he was now relying on one for guidance. Altion looked at him and licked its fork-like tongue. Then it leaped into the sky and began to circle. The others got on their mounts in formation. On the wagon, Etera was about to pick up the reins, when Hue slapped her hands.

"Why don't you sit with your brother for a while?" Hue suggested. "I'll take the wagon."

Etera was about to protest when she thought better of it. Instead of protesting, she smiled.

"Thank you," she said simply as she climbed into the back of the wagon. She got under Janis' cloak with Tildon and wrapped her arms around him. His skin was clammy. He opened his eyes and smiled at Etera.

"Not much longer, brother," she said as the wagon began to move, "not much longer."

Reverend Monroe opened his eyes to what could be his last day on Earth. He lay among his covers for along time, just enjoying the comfort of their feel. After sometime, he got up from his bed and stretched. He went over to the window and looked out at Baltimore City. It was a beautiful summer day. Reverend Monroe could not believe that he was about to leave this all behind. He had spent almost twenty years of his life on Earth. He had grown to love this planet. He hated the idea of leaving it all behind but he knew it was time. He had to go get his son. Even if Royal was still angry with him, it did not matter; seeing him was more important than any issues they had between them.

Remembering his houseguests, Reverend Monroe showered and dressed quickly. He went down to the kitchen and started cooking. By the time he had the coffee boiling Father Benedito and Isabel were coming to the kitchen. Isabel was stunned to see the reverend at the stove. Father Benedito laughed at her response.

"Ai, Dios!," Isabel said as she sat down at the table, happy with surprise. "You cook ?"

Reverend Monroe laughed as he went over to the cabinet and took out plates and cups.

"The woman that came with me to Earth was many things, but she was not a cook. She was good at breaking necks, though. Like snap! If I waited for Lethia to cook, we would have all starved to death", he laughed as he poured cups of coffee for his guests.

"You see, Father?" Isabel said as she slapped the young priest on his back. "This man cooks! Por que usted no cocina?"

"La verdad?" Father Benedito smiled as he sipped his coffee. "It is not that I can't cook, it's that you just do it so much better than I do. Who would want to eat my huevos rancheros?"

Isabel wrinkled her nose, shook her head, and slapped her bag.

"You are full of excuses," she scoffed.

"I think I will miss your cooking most of all," Father Benedito said earnestly.

Reverend Monroe was caught off guard by their conversation. He was unsure what to make of it. Instead of being intrusive, he filled their plates with scrambled eggs, grits, and bacon. He made an extra large helping for Simon who had not come down yet. There was enough food on Simon's plate for four grown men. He put his plate in the microwave to cool. Reverend Monroe poured himself a cup of coffee and joined his guests at the table.

"Muy bien," Father Benedito smiled as he ate. "For someone not from Earth, you have surely learned how to cook! The taste reminds me of home in Harlem."

Reverend Monroe laughed.

"I had to learn to cook," he explained as he wiped his mouth. "I had two growing boys in the house."

As he said that, Simon came into the room. Unlike the others, Simon was already dressed for their trip. He wore light leather armor. He greeted everyone at the table, got his food from the microwave and sat down. For a moment, no one spoke. The only sound in the room was the sound of the forks hitting the porcelain plates. Then Isabel cleared her throat loudly and looked at the priest. He caught her eye, sat back, and wiped his mouth.

"There is a matter I would like to speak with you all about," he began slowly.

Simon looked at Reverend Monroe oddly and they both stopped eating, giving Father Benedito their full attention.

"What is it?" Reverend Monroe asked.

"Like you, I am a man of the cloth, a different cloth, but a cloth nonetheless" he said. "And I know it is an issue of vanity, but I have always dreamed, since I was a nino, of seeing the stars. I never thought such a thing was possible, but then you came into my church. I believe this is was a sign from God. I am aware that you are going to go fight a great evil and get your son back and rescue the others, and with your permission, I volunteer to go with you."

Reverend Monroe and Simon were shocked by the request. Neither of them knew what to say. However, Simon was the first to break the silence.

"Father," Simon began, "you saw the Marauder and the hounds. You see what kind of dangers we will be walking into. I mean, come on now."

Father Benedito shook his head and smiled.

"I saw that creature. A devil is a devil in any form. I was not always a priest and a person of faith. I grew up in the streets of Spanish Harlem. I was even in a gang in my younger years. I am not scared of danger or dying. I might be a little rusty, but I doubt I will be a liability in battle," he said earnestly. "Como mis hermanos en Sud America, sometimes you have to wrap a rosary around your gun and fight for what you believe in."

Reverend Monroe and Simon looked at each other again. They could both feel the sincerity in the priest's words.

"What do you think, Senora Isabel?" Reverend Monroe asked.

"No se," she shook her head. "I know the Father now and I knew him before he became a priest. He was, how do you say, a beast, and if he believes that he can help you on your journey, I would trust him."

"Okay then, Father," Reverend Monroe said. "You can come."

"You won't regret it," Father Benedito declared as he smiled and began to gobble down the last of his breakfast.

Simon finished his breakfast in a brooding silence. He was not as convinced as Reverend Monroe about Father Benedito coming with them to Acara. He had left Acara when he was a small child but Lethia had told him stories about the planet and its dangers. He was aware of the perils that they would face once they arrived. The last thing he needed was another person to have to worry about. He did not care how "wild" the good Father was supposed to have been in his former life, there was no guarantee that he was able to look after himself now. However, Reverend Monroe had already given his consent and he did not feel that he could contradict him. All he could do was hope that they would not eventually regret his decision with one of their lives.

By mid day, most of the group had gathered at the church in the remnants of the sanctuary. Reverend Monroe, Simon, Isabel, Ms. Loretta, Ben, Sapphire, Purcell and Father Benedito were all gathered near the pulpit area. They were surrounded by several bags of food, weapons, and supplies they had all gathered for the journey. Reverend Monroe and Simon were surprised that Ben had told Sapphire about them butwhen he told them why he had disclosed to his eldest child, they understood. They were all surprised that Reverend Monroe had agreed to let Father Benedito go with them. They really did not understand his rationale, and no one thought that they should challenge his decision.

As Reverend Monoroe looked at Father Beneditio, there was something about him he trusted immediately. He had faith in the young priest. And he liked him.

"Do you think Father Benedito going with them is a good idea?" Ms. Loretta asked Isabel candidly as she checked the food she had prepared for the group for their journey. It was stacked neatly in color-coded Tupperware®.

"I understand your concern." Isabel said. "Before he became a priest, Father Benedito was a hellion. I do not want him to go, but I understand that he is young and this is a chance of alifetime, being young. So I say, let the young be so."

"This is all crazy," Sapphire said as she sat down. She could not take her eyes off of Simon. She was not used to seeing him without his warping crystal and in full body armor. "I am having a hard time believing all of this. I think I am going to be sick. I mean, aliens in the church. Who would have ever believed it?"

Isabel and Ms. Loretta laughed.

"I have seen many things in my years, but nothing like this," Ms. Loretta said.

"Si," Isabel agreed. "I have practiced Santeria as well as Catholicism, but this is even outside of things that I have seen."

"I really don't want my father to go," Sapphire said as she watched him check a bag of guns with Purcell. The vison sent chills up her spine. She had never seen her father carry firearms before. "I know he thinks he can drive and do anything, but we have lost so much over the years, I really don't want to lose anyone else," she said with tears in her eyes.

Ms. Loretta stopped what she was doing and wrapped her arms around Sapphire. Holding Sapphire made her feel like she was holding one of her own children. Seeing her in tears, Purcell came up to her and sat down. He reached out and took her hand. He had not seen Sapphire in years, since she was a little girl. He was surprised at how attractive she had become. Silently, he was blown away by her beauty. The little girl with pigtails who he used to chase around had grown into a beautiful, young woman.

"Are you okay?" Purcell asked.

"She is worried about her father," Ms. Loretta said. "I can't say I'm happy about you goin' either. But someone's gotta go get our family back together."

"Hey, little girl," Purcell said as he took her hand. "I'm not going to let anything happen to your father. I swear."

"But who gonna look out over you?' Ms. Loretta asked.

"Me," Simon said as he stepped forward, standing at his full size.

They all looked at him. He was an imposing figure, standing well over seven feet tall in his armor.

"I lost the others," Simon said frankly. "That was partly because I was facing my own father in battle. I am over that now. I plan to help Royal free our world and get the others back to Earth, I promise you that," he pledged.

"Little girl," Ben said as he came over to the others, "I'm gonna be alright. I know this is going to be dangerous, but I have to go and get your brother. I would do the same thing for you. I owe that to your mother."

"I have an idea," Purcell began. "While we're away, why doesn't Sapphire stay with my grandmother. Grandma, you wouldn't mind?"

"No not at all," Ms. Loretta said "I would love to have her there. If she could stand being around the twins."

"That would be really nice. Staying in the house by myself, I don't know what I would do," Sapphire said as she wiped her eyes.

Father Benedito smiled as he watched the others. He went over to the bag of weapons that Purcell had bought. He reached inside and took out a magnum. He had not held a gun since he had taken his vows. He had done many homilies against violence in the community. He could not believe that he was going against so much he had ministered about.

Yet he knew from what had been described to him that he might have to use violence in this journey. He liked to believe this was going to be a holy crusade. As he held the gun, he remembered his study of the Knights Templar in seminary. He never thought he would do anything akin to their crusade. And now he felt like that was exactly what he was going to have to do.

Isabel watched Father Benedito with the gun and shook her head. She could not believe that this was the man she took the Eucharist from every Sunday. She knew about his past as a bad ass, but seeing it first hand was another thing. Isabel unconsciously reached down and felt for her bag. The bottle she kept was still there. She was going to have to have a drink after all of this. She was not looking forward to the long ride home without Father Benedito at her side. She also was not looking forward to the talk with the bishop she was going to have to have once she got there. While she enjoyed a good relationship with the priests atSacred Heart, she was not a fan of the presiding Bishop. He knew of her Santeria roots and did not approve. Besides he was a white man, who really did not understand what was required to do ministry work in a Latino, urban Barrio. It was something Father Francis understood in the years before Father Benedito, and something he passed on to him.

Reverend Monroe went up to the others and caught Ms. Loretta's eye. She passed Sapphire off to her father and Purcell and went over to her pastor.

"I want to give you something," Reverend Monroe said as he handed her a small satchel.

"What is this?" Ms. Loretta said as she looked inside. In the half-light of the ruined sanctuary, she caught sight of the diamond. She almost dropped the satchel as her hand began to shake.

"I am turning all of the accounts of the church over to your care and leaving that diamond with you. There are instructions in a file in my office about who to call to liquidate it. There should be enough there to rebuild the church and the youth center across the street," Reverend Monroe explained. "I don't know if I will ever be coming back, but this church was as much a part of me as Royal or Grace was. I need to know it will be rebuilt and will be in good hands."

"But I ain't no reverend or even a trustee," Ms. Loretta said, shaking her head in confusion.

"But you are the heart and soul of these old bricks. You have been here since I first opened

"But I ain't no reverend or even a trustee," Ms. Loretta said, shaking her head in confusion.

"But you are the heart and soul of these old bricks. You have been here since I first opened the doors. You are about the only person I would ever trust with its rebuilding," he smiled.

"I don't know what to say, Pastor," she said as tears welled up in her eyes.

Hearing the word 'pastor' from her lips hit Reverend Monroe in the center of his stomach. He knew that where he was going, he would not be hearing that word again. It was good to hear it one last time, especially from a woman like Ms. Loretta.

"Just say you will do it," he pushed.

"Okay," she said. "If you do one thing for me."

"Anything," he promised.

"Get my children home," Ms. Loretta said evenly.

"I will do my best," Reverend Monroe promised. "I will do my best."

"'Nuff said," Ms. Loretta smiled sadly.

Seeing the exchange between Ms. Loretta and Reverend Monroe, Simon carried the bags down into the tunnel beneath the pulpit. Purcell met him at the top and handed him the remaining bags. Once they were done, they gathered with the others around the burned pew.

"It is time," Reverend Monroe announced finally.

There were handshakes, kisses, and hugs all the way around.

"Reverend," Father Benedito turned. "Can we all pray before we go?"

"I think we should," Reverend Monroe agreed.

The group stood in a circle and held hands. They all closed their eyes. Looking around the sanctuary, Reverend Monroe was too choked up to speak. He turned to Father Benedito to give a final prayer.

"Father, would you give a word?" he asked.

Father Benedito was surprised and honored at the same time. He could tell from Reverend Monroe's face what it meant for him to leave this church behind.

"Dear Lord, we ask you to bless this endeavor as we go forward. Continue to keep those who we seek and may we meet on our journey, and keep those we are leaving behind behind safe. We seal this prayer with the prayer your son taught us," he prayed before the group said the 'Our Father' prayer in unison.

Before the circle broke, Simon said, "And as we go forward, we ask for the help and guidance of the Avatar, the living spirit of Acara."

"Amen," they all said before they broke circle.

"I am going to have to get used to that," Father Benedito said to Simon with a smile.

"There is a lot for all of us to get used to, Father," Simon responded candidly.

Finally, the group said their goodbyes to Isabel, Ms. Loretta, and Sapphire. They left them alone as they climbed down into the tunnel beneath the pulpit. They picked up the bags that lay between them and the Gateway and proceeded to the archway. It was glowing with an unnatural power.

"Adios," Father Benedito said as he crossed himself.

"Are you ready Father?" Purcell asked.

"Si, mi hermano," Father Benedito smiled as he picked up a bag. "I think I was destined for this," he smiled.

"I hope so," Purcell said.

"Gentlemen, are you ready?" Reverend Monroe asked as he removed the tuning fork from his pocket.

The men looked at one another and nodded.

"Do you know where on Acara we will wind up?" Ben asked nervously.

"Of that, my friend, I am not sure," Reverend Monroe said honestly. "But I believe that the Avatar will keep us safe from the High Queen."

"I hope you are right," Simon said evenly silently recalling the fight with his father as the assassin cube. He was not ready to face anything like that again yet.

With that, Reverend Monroe stepped forward and tapped the Gateway with the tuning fork. The energy from the archway immediately began to expand and it engulfed the members of the group. They were sucked through the Gateway and vanished on their way to Acara.

Burton sat with Holi in the catacombs beneath the Grand Citadel. The two High Princes sat drinking wine. They were alone. Their Royal

Guards were posted outside of Holi's workroom. Though they trusted their Royal Guards more than anyone else, certain conversations were not even for their ears; especially when they were speaking of treason against the High Queen, their niece.

"I can not believe that she went to get the Scepter of the Monarchs," Burton said as he put up his feet on a stool. "She was already more powerful than the both of us, but now with the scepter, she is nearly indestructible."

"You worry too much, my brother," Holi shook his head. "Her getting the scepter is not a sign of power, but desperation. She is showing that she is afraid. She is afraid of her son taking her throne. This is a good thing."

"What do you mean?" Burton said as he sat up.

"My brother, don't you see," Holi smiled. "She is so worried about her son, that she is not worried about you. All you have to do is be patient and wait for the right moment. If you are lucky, they will destroy each other and leave the High Throne to you."

Burton laughed with glee.

"I never thought about such a thing," he smiled.

"What you need to do now is to push her to confront this young upstart and when the two meet, you must be there and make sure they destroy one another," Holi said as he sipped his wine. "The plan is simple but effective."

"That is what I love about you, brother," Burton laughed. "I love the way you think. I just wish that when I assume the throne there was something I could do for you."

Holi sat back as if he were thinking for a minute. Then he sat up and looked at his brother candidly.

"There is something that I want," Holi admitted.

"For you, anything," Burton said sincerely.

"I want that off-worlder woman to be mine," Holi said bluntly.

"But she has been claimed by the Royal Guard and is promised to Keyton," Burton shook his head with surprise.

"If we are getting rid of the young High Prince, then there is no reason to keep his Royal Guard around," Holi surmised.

Burton laughed at his brother's guile.

"If that is what you want," Burton sighed. "You know I can refuse you anything," he said as he rose to leave. "I have hidden from the business of the High Court long enough. Let me go see what these royals are up to," he said as he turned, leaving Holi alone with his thoughts.

Holi sat back on the couch sipping his wine. As he sat there, he remembered the way Tisha looked from the night before. Though she was preganat for another man, her sexiness and her radiance were shining through. Holi had had his fair share of affairs over the course of his life, but no one had struck him the way that Tisha had in a lifetime. She had warmed him in places that only his chemicals had in a long time. His brother may aspire to be the High King, but he aspired to finally find a bride worthy of him that would make him happy.

Deep within the catacombs of the Crystal Hive, Lancer tended to the maintenance of the archways of the catacombs. As the senior crystal keeper, it was his job to make sure that they all stayed clean, debris-free, and ready for use. He went one by one with his tuning fork and checked on the certainty of their efficacy. Every thing appeared to be in order as he went about his daily work. However, as he went deeper into the catacombs and to the more obscure archways, he began to be overcome by a strange feeling. The energy hit him in the gut and the elderly man grabbed for the wall. It was a feeling that was familiar and new at the same time. Someone had activated crystals that he had personally grown. However, the energy of these crystals was slightly different. They had been altered somehow. The only crystals that he had grown had been the ones he gave to the Marauder that was sent to Earth. There was no way that their use should affect him this way unless they had been tampered with.

He stopped to catch his breath. As quickly as the feeling had appeared it passed. Though it was painful, he had to smile to himself. The only person on Earth who could have possibly altered the energy of the crystals that he sent was Arkon. He laughed to himself as he remembered his young apprentice. As he recalled, Arkon was good at manipulating crystals but not particularily good at growing them. It was one of his shortcomings that Lancer had thought would keep him from becoming a master crystal keeper, like himself. The fact that he was able to strip energy from crystals that he had made meant he had grown considerably in his power. Lancer laughed out loud. He was proud of his surrogate son after all this time. Now, after so many cycles, he could feel that his son was coming home.

Lancer sighed to himself at the thought. He knew that his duty to the High Queen was to tell her what he felt. In fact, with the entire guild of the crystal keepers at his disposal, he supposed that he could discover where the Gateway had opened on Acara. He shook his head, 'No', at the thought. He had been the master of the Crystal Hive when the High King Roman sat on the throne. He even called the High royal friend. Though the guild of crystal keepers remained neutral in the battle between the Dark God and the Avatar, he had been raised as a devotee of the Avatar. He did not like the way the High Queen had swayed the entire planet away from worship of the Avatar. It was not just a religion to her but an obsession. He was afraid of what she and those other dark-robed zealots had planned for his beautiful world if their power went unchecked.

"Good Journey, Arkon," Lancer whispered as he gathered his robes and turned to leave the catacombs. "Good Journey, old friend," he repeated as he laughed out loud and his voice echoed though out the vacant catacombs.

# Chapter 21

Altion continued to soar overhead and guide the group across the barren plains. There was a hot, crisp wind that followed them as they rode. The plains were flat and covered with thick grass. The suns of Acara rained heat down upon the travelers as they traveled. By the time evening came, they were well into the uncharted region of the Eastern Continent. Mountains loomed in the distance as they approached. Etera with Tildon at in the back of the wagon under the cloak that Janis had provided. The feathered cloak cooled them under the suns' heat and protected them from the wind of the early evening.

"Etera," Tildon said weakly.

"Yes, dear brother," she tried to smile.

"Let me go," he said simply. "This is as good a place as any. I am not worth all of this effort," he pleaded.

"Hush, Tildon," Etera cut him off as she wiped a tear from her eye. "You have to realize that your life matters."

"But I am only one man," Tildon coughed. "The High Prince has a whole world to worry about."

"You would be surprised, brother," Etera said as she stared at the back of Royal's mount.

"This royal seems to understand that on a planet of many, one life can make the difference."

"If you say so, sister. I will hold on," he said with a shiver.

Just then, Altion screeched in the sky over head. Though they were far from the trees and mountains, the flying serpent seemed to be signaling them. Lethia raised her hand and the group haulted. Lethia scanned the distant trees with her avian eyes and smiled. Royal rode up next of her.

"Is that them?" Royal asked hurriedly.

"Unsure," Lethia said. "But there is a scouting party among the trees."

"How many do you think there are?" Captain Sarison asked as he tapped his sword protectively.

"Probably three or four," Lethia said with a smile on her face. "Wait here," Lethia said as she kicked her mount and rode off toward the trees.

Wisdom came up beside Royal, got off his mount and stretched his legs. He took out a cigarette and began to smoke. He looked at the pack and sighed. He was down to his last pack. He did not know what he was going to do when he finished them. Cigarette smoking was one of the few vices he allowed himself. He had tried to stop many times, but had always been unsuccessful. He guessed that unless he found an Acarian package store somewhere, he was going to have to go cold turkey. Wisdom laughed to himself. Yes he missed his son and his family, but he would have never thought something as simple as a cigarette would make him feverish and homesick for Baltimore City.

"Where did Lethia go?" Wisdom asked.

"She went to greet a scouting party of the CODA," Royal explained.

Tori got out of back of the wagon, supporting himself on his walking stick. With the help of Peku, he joined the others.

"We have found them, Tori," Royal smiled.

"Now the real battle begins, my High Prince," Tori said glumly.

Royal did not know what to say to this. He simply turned and looked at the trees. Lethia and her mount had vanished into the thicket. Lethia got off her mount once she was in the trees. She did not see the scouts, but she could feel them looking at her. She did not draw her sword. It would have been seen as an act of aggression. She would be filled with spears and arrows before she even got a chance to see who she was fighting. Instead of raising her weapon, she let out a guttural call. It was the CODA cry. She waited to see if there was a response from the trees, but nothing moved. Then she let out the call again. After a few seconds, there was movement from ahead among the trees. Then three figures appeared from among the foliage. They were women covered in tree bark, dirt, and leaves. They each carried a spear and had a long bow on their backs. Lethia smiled as she looked at them, they were young women and were probably children when she left the CODA.

"Ho, good women of the forest and the plains!" Lethia said as she nodded her head.

One of the three women stepped forward. She was an attractive young thing under the dirt and leaves. Lethia smiled at her. She was probably no older than Royal.

"I am Cree of the CODA," she introduced herself. "Who are you woman? You travel with men but you know our most sacred call," she said suspiciously.

"I am Lethia, the seventeenth queen of the CODA," Lethia said firmly as she met the young woman's gaze.

The three young women looked at one another for a second then burst into laughter.

"Queen Lethia is a myth that is talked about by the fires by the elder ones," another of the young women said.

The word myth stung Lethia and she squinted. It was hard to believe that she had been gone from the tribe so long that her exploits as Queen were now considered only a myth. She shook her head. In caring for Royal and Simon over the last several Earth years, she had given up so much of herself. In asking her to be Grace Monroe, caring for these boys, and going to Earth, the Avatar had required a true sacrifice of her.

Ignoring their rebuff, Lethia said "I have business with the acring Queen Althea and the Elders. I do not have time for this," she snapped, beginning to lose her patience.

"If you are indeed Lethia, then prove yourself," the third young woman challenged.

"That would not be a problem," Lethia said quickly. "I could kill you all where you stand, but if I did, I doubt I would find the rest of the tribe in time to take care of my business. So if you know the legends of Lethia, then you know I am a master of the land."

"True," Cree said. "You are one with the Logos."

"Then behold!" Lethia cried as she drew her blade and slammed it into the ground. The ground rippled under the feet of the three young women and they were tossed aside. They came to their feet slowly and looked at each other in disbelief. Then Cree came forward and fell to one knee. The other two women followed. Lethia smiled to herself as she replaced her sword at her side. She exhaled. It felt good to finally be home.

"I will have the men with me, set up camp on the edge of the woods," Lethia said. "Then I will take the other young woman with me and we will go see Queen Althea."

"I will wait for you here, Queen Lethia," Cree said, bowing her head. "I will send the others on so they will know you are coming."

"Agreed," Lethia nodded as she turned and went back toward the edge of the thicket. She got on her mount and rode out to the others.

They all looked at the Queen of the CODA expectantly. She smiled at them as she reached into her pack, took out a cigar and began to smoke.

"We have found the CODA," Lethia announced, "at least, a scouting party. They will take me and Etera to the CODA and we will make our case. The rest of you will make camp at the edge of the woods here and wait to hear from us."

"Why can't we all come?" Royal asked nervously.

"No man may know and see where and how many CODA there are," Lethia explained. "I am taking Etera with me in case I fail. She can come back and let you know."

"I don't want to leave my brother," Etera protested.

"We are doing this to save your brother," Lethia snapped.

Hue came up to Etera and put a reassuring arm around her.

"Don't worry, Etera," Hue said. "I will look after Tildon. You go with Lethia.

"Okay," Etera nodded.

Lethia got on her mount and pulled Etera up behind her. The men watched as the two women of their party crossed the plains and vanished into the woods. Then, they slowly made their way toward the edge of the woods. While the others began to unpack their gear; and set up a makeshift camp. Hue got into the back of the wagon and tended to Tildon. He opened a canister of water and wiped his forehead. Tildon was hot to the touch.

"Where is my sister?" Tildon asked as he reached up and took Hue's hand.

"She went to get you help," Hue smiled.

"All of this for me?" Tildon shook head. "I don't matter that much."

"Everyone matters," Hue assured him. Then Hue remembered that he had some pain medication.-He reached inside his pocket and took out a packet of asprin. He tore it open and fed the pills to Tildon. Tildon looked at the small, white tablets oddly but did not protest. He swallowed them with a gulp of water.

"You are truly kind," Tildon smiled as he pulled the cloak Janis had given him up to his neck.

"I guess I am," Hue said with a wink.

Maximus stood outside of the wagon. He had fully transformed into his canine form. He went over to the edge of the woods and sniffed the ground. While he could not pick up the sent of the CODA women or Lethia and Etera, he immediately caught the scent of Lethia's cigar. He got the general direction they were going in. He peered deep into the woodland and watched the birds scatter at the smoke trail Lethia left behind.

"You know which way they went don't you Maximus?" Royal asked as he came up behind his familiar and rubbed at the fur behind his ears.

"I do," Maximus said. "Lethia left a trail for us to follow if we need to."

"Good," Royal said as he walked back over to the others. They were sitting on rocks and trying to start a fire. Royal placed his hand over the wood and twigs they had gathered and it immediately burst into flames. The Etos responded happily to their master.

"Good man!" Captain Sarison said. "At least we will have hot food tonight."

While the others settled down near the fire, Wisdom went to the back of the wagon and took out his bag of guns. He carefully took an inventory of what he had left. It was enough to defend them for a period of time, but it wasn't enough to fight a war. He did not know what he was going to do when he ran out of ammunition. Lethia had told him to learn how to use a sword, now he found himself seriously considering her offer.

"I am going to send Altion back now," Royal said to Wisdom. "We may need Janis' help before all this over. I want to make sure we stay on his good side."

"Good idea," Wisdom said as he cleaned one of his guns.

Royal walked to the edge of the encampment. He looked up in the sky for Altion. Altion appeared out of the clouds. Royal raised his arm and the flying serpent swooped down and wrapped itself around his arm. Royal smiled at their guide and fed him some treats.

"Thank you, Altion. Now go home to Janis," Royal commanded as he cast him into the sky. He watched the serpent linger overhead for a moment before it turned back toward Lampour.

"Didn't Janis say he would send his men to help us if we needed him?" Tori asked as he approached Royal. Peku was leading him.

"Yes, he did," Royal said.

"How will he find us without Altion?" Tori asked.

"Prince Janis is crafty," Royal smiled. "I am sure he will find a way if we need him to reach us."

"Too bad he did not have a potion for that," Peku laughed as he jumped around.

Royal went over to the fire. The suns were setting in the sky and a cool breeze was coming across the plains. Hue wen tover to Royal and sat down next to him. The two smiled at each other and curled up close together. Royal smiled at the familiarity of their contact. He reached into one of his packs and removed his travel-sized Bible. It had been a long time since he had taken time out to read his Bible. Before coming to Acara, he studied his scriptures everyday. It was time for him to get back on that routine; with all that was happening, he needed to nourish his soul. But now, the routine seemed foreign to him as he cracked the binding and started to read.

Cree led Lethia and Etera deep into the forest. The further they got into the woods, the thicker the trees and foliage appeared to grow. The light from the suns soon became obscured by the branches of the huge trees overhead. As day passed into evening, Cree unearthed a torch that had been hidden beside a tree and lit it. They traveled on through the woods in no particular direction. As they went along, Etera tried to make sense of the direction they were going. As they got deeper into the forest, she quickly realized that it was impossible to make sense out of where they were going. There were no landmarks or trails that were easy for her to follow. Etera began to get nervous the further they went. It reminded her of the time that she spent on the road running from the henchmen of the High Queen. As they rode on, Etera found herself wishing she was near water. She was a sea witch and she drew the majority of her power from water. Without it, she had a few tricks she could do, yet she still felt powerless.

Feeling Etera's grip tighten around her waist, Lethia patted Etera's hand.

"Do not worry, Etera," Lethia reassured her. "I will not let anything happen to you."

"Okay," Etera replied.

As they approached a particularly dense part of the forest, Cree raised her hand and Lethia stopped her mount.

"Leave your mount here," Cree said. "We go on by foot from here."

Lethia got off her mount and helped Etera down. The two women followed Cree into the thickest part of the woods. As they moved on down the path, Lethia could feel eyes on them from behind every tree and boulder. Like the members of the scouting party, there were countless CODA women concealed in the brush. They weren't hiding as much as they were watching. As they moved through the trees, they began to hear huge drums being played in the distance. Lethia smiled. They were the sacred drums of the CODA. It had been years since she had heard them. The sound of the drums energized her and she picked up her step.

They were soon greeted by the glowing light of torches in the distance. They came upon an enormous, well-lit pit in the middle of the forest. There were three huge drums in the pit. Each drum was being played by two women with batons. A lone woman stood in the circle. She was dark-skinned and she was wearing the hides of several animals. Her hair was matted and covered with leaves. At her side was the scared sword of the CODA. Lethia had left it with Althea when she went on this mission for the Avatar. It was time for her get it back. Lethia knew that even though she had given up the leadership of the CODA to Althea willingly, getting it back was not going to be that simple. The two women had been rivals all of their lives, and had never liked one another despite having fought together side by side on many occasions. More than anything else, the CODA was a sisterhood and they had both been counseled by the elders on their dislike for one another. But, it did not seem to help. Lethia was prepared to kill Althea if she had to, to get to the elders.

"Wait here," Lethia said to Etera as she began to climb down a knotted rope into the pit.

"Be careful!" Etera said as she felt countless people emerge from the darkened jungle around her.

"Just another neck to break," Lethia winked at her as she descended into the pit.

Once she was on the floor of the pit, Lethia walked up to Althea. The two rivals looked at one another and smiled. It was not a meeting of old friends, but of bitter rivals.

"It has been along time, sister," Althea said.

"Yes, it has," Lethia replied. "But I have returned and it is time you step aside and let me resume my rightful rulership of the CODA."

Althea laughed.

"You must have lost your mind in your time away," Althea said, shaking her head. "You come here with men and you expect me to step aside and let you take over. You stink of them! You do not deserve to be CODA queen- or even to be among us," she snapped.

"If that were so, the Avatar would not have choosen me to tend to the High Prince," Lethia countered. "The High Queen would see this world ruined. I can not stand for that to happen."

"So, instead of a woman, you would support a man being on the throne of our world?" Althea asked sharply. "You have truly been away from the tribe too long! Why don't you abandon those who you have come here with and take your place with us among the trees and fertile land?"

"You know I cannot do that," Lethia said grimly.

"I will only make that invitation to you once, sister." Althea said bluntly.

"Then we have nothing else to say," Lethia said as she drew her blade.

"So be it," Althea said as she drew the sacred blade of the CODA to the cheers of the crowd of women staring down from above.

By the sound of the drums, the two women circled one another, neither one of them giving ground. Then they charged each other. The sound of their swords rang out through the pit. Lethia summoned the energy of the ground around her. It knocked Althea off of her feet. Lethia charged her to the cheers of the audience above. Before she could land a blow, Althea called upon the energy of the fire, the Etos, and ignited the torches around the pit. The flames leaped from their torches and surrounded Lethia. Lethia fell back, stunned by the attack. In her time away, Althea had mastered the energy of fire. This made her even more deadly than she was before.

Angry and stunned, Lethia shook off the flames that sought to envelop her. She was slightly burned but she still held her sword high. Once again, Lethia called upon the energy of the land around her. The ground under Althea's feet transformed into quicksand and began to suck her into the ground. Althea struggled to get free and Lethia charged her. Once again, she called upon her control of fire. From the torches, several small, horned creatures of pure fire appeared. Lethia recognized them immediately. They were the Etos, the dark spirits that lived in fire. They normally lived in the center of the planet but, somehow, Althea had willed them up from the very depths of Acara. Lethia did her best to use her sword to keep them at bay but as she cut into them, they simply reconstituted themselves. Althea looked on with pride as she sought to free her feet from the ground. She knew she had her.

Etera watched on in horror as the Etos surround Lethia. She knew she was in trouble. Etera also knew that even though she was surrounded by many CODA they were not paying any attention to her. Etera turned her attention to the night sky above. She could make out the clouds through the trees. With all of her will, she called out to the dark, billowing masses. She concentrated on rain. Just as Lethia began to give way to the Etos, the sky opened up and the pit was filled with a downpour. The Etos shrieked and vanished from view. Freed of the fire beings, Lethia charged Althea. She was still stuck in the groundup to her knees. Lethia raised her sword. She saw herself taking Althea's head off. It was the way of the CODA. But after all that Lethia had gone through as Grace Monroe and being around Reverend Monroe, it was not her way anymore. Instead of killing her, she hit her with the hilt of her sword and knocked her out cold.

Lethia stood over her nemesis, victorious. She bent down and picked up the sacred sword of the CODA from the dirt. She tossed her blade aside. She raised the sword over her head to the cheers of the countless women who encircled the pit. She was back. She was home now. She was Queen again. As she looked down at Althea, she wondered if defeating her was the easy part. Now it was time to confront the elders. While the CODA were ruled by a Queen, there was a counsel of elders that kept the secrets and rituals of the CODA. They were the oldest women in the tribe. They rarely showed themselves. They lived separate, even from the rest of the CODA. They were the keepers of the eternal spring. It was used when a CODA warrior was mortally wounded in battle and deemed fit for rebirth. No man had ever been allowed to access its waters. Not even as Queen could she make the elders do something they did not want to. All she could do was to ask. Lethia hoped that because of the evil of the High Queen, and her relationship with the Avatar, she could sway them.

"As your Queen, I seek a conference with the elders," Lethia shouted to those assembled.

Cree came down the rope that Lethia had used to enter the pit. She fell to one knee and bowed her head.

"It is time for us to celebrate the return of our true Queen. Can't it wait?" she asked. "Seeing the elders, I mean."

"No, my business is urgent," she assured Cree.

Cree nodded her head. Then she let out a particular call that Lethia had never heard before. Once Cree let out the call, it was carried through the women hovering above them. It went on through the crowd and out into the darkened jungle.

"Now what?" Lethia asked.

"We feast, we celebrate your return, and we wait!" Cree cried jubilantly.

With that, ropes dropped to the pit and the audience of women descended. They represented all the races and beings of Acara. Some were blue-skinned from the North, while others had wings and were from the South. Others were from the west and had yellow skin. However, they were all dressed the same way in the colors of the woods. As the women descended, the torches were relit, tables were erected, and drums began to be beat. The women came from all corners and greeted the return of their queen by falling to one knee in salute. Lethia lost track of Althea in the crowd. She found herself wondering if letting her live was a mistake.

As the merriment went on, the pit filled with a huge throng of women. Lethia allowed herself to enjoy a portion of the celebration. It had been years since she had been in the presence of the CODA. She had forgotten how much she missed it. As she danced, she found herself reflecting on all she had lost going to Earth. Etera stood back in the shadows of the merriment. She ate sparingly and waited for the elders to appear. After some time, Lethia came over and pulled her aside.

"I owe you, sea witch," Lethia whispered in her ear.

"What do you mean?" Etera said as she wrinkled her brow.

"It does not rain here often," Lethia reflected

"I do what I can," Etera smiled as she sipped her wine.

"Now let's hope it was not for naught," Lethia swore.

She was about to get pulled back into the merriment when she noticed a shadow appear from above. She turned around immediately. Standing in the shadows over the pit of dancing women was a lone woman. Even from a distance, Lethia could tell that she was older than all of them. She wore a dark brown cloak that was covered with grass and leaves. She removed her cloak to reveal a time-weathered face and flowing white hair. Lethia recognized the woman immediately. It was Patel. She was one of the oldest of the elders. She had been old when Lethia was born.

Patel made her way down one of the knotted ropes. It should have been hard for a woman her age, but she did it with ease. She ignored Etera and went up to Lethia. The two women hugged and fell to one knee in salute of each other.

"It is good to see you, old friend," Patel said.

"It is good to be seen," Lethia smiled.

"The Avatar has kept you well on your journey," Patel commented. "I see much wisdom in your eyes. You wear it well."

"I do not know about that, but I survive," Lethia told her.

"Now, what is it that you need that you would summon one of us?" Patel asked frankly.

"The pool of eternal life," Lethia said evenly. "One of the warriors on this great quest was poisoned by Aldam. There is no cure, except the promise of the pool. He sacrificed himself to save the High Prince. The High Prince has taken time away from usurping the High Queen in order to save this young man."

Patel listened to Lethia. Her face was unreadable.

"What you ask has never been done before," Patel said flatly. "The eternal pool is a gift from the stars to the CODA. A man has never bathed in its divine waters."

"As Queen of the CODA I thought that I would never raise men, but when the Avatar came to us, I did it's bidding at great personal cost to me," Lethia countered.

"You believe that doing this is worth breaking a fundamental law of the CODA?" Patel asked.

"I do," Lethia said firmly.

"You know this is not a decision I can make by myself," Patel stated. "But what I will do is grant this young High Prince and the afflicted an audience before the elders. I promise you nothing," she said flatly.

"As always, you are fair and wise Patel," Lethia said humbly. "When will it be done?"

"Tonight," Patel said. "There is no reason to delay. I will arrange an escort for them."

"Will I accompany them?" Lethia asked.

Patel shook her head, "No. If this High Monarch wishes for the CODA to break one of its most fundamental laws, he and he alone may travel with the afflicted," Patel said with finality as she walked away.

"I thought you were Queen?" Etera whispered as she watched Patel summon several of the other dancing women to her.

"I am." Lethia said. "But the CODA respect age more than title and the elders may override even the Queen if it is deemed in the best interest of the tribe. At least Patel is willing to let Royal plead his case. Now it is up to him. Tildon's life is in his hands now."

Etera exhaled. At first, she was not happy that she had gone with Lethia but as it turned out, she was glad to have been there. She had been able to help. But regardless how much she wanted to save her brother, she was happy not to be Royal. She would not have wanted to have to face this council of elder women.

In the early hours of the morning, Lethia and Etera returned to the small camp. The men were sleeping near the remnants of the fire. Royal and Hue were hugged up close to one another. Royal had fallen asleep reading his Bible. Maximus was the first to move when he heard the rustle in the bushes. He transformed instantly into his full canine form and began to growl, immediately waking the others. Captain Sarison and Wisdom scrambled to their feet, weapons in hand. Royal rolled over and raised his hands protectively over Hue. Tori and Peku hid down in the wagon, covering Tildon.

"Hold!" Lethia shouted as she and Etera emerged from the forest on her mount.

The men were relieved to see them and ran up to them. Lethia was slightly burnt and scarred from her battle with Althea, but she looked sturdy in the saddle. Etera got down off the horse and hugged the members of the group. Lethia quickly waved them over to the fire. Etera went over to the wagon to check on Tildon while the others talked. Royal sat down next to Lethia and snapped his fingers. The fire erupted immediately. The other members of the party waited for the newly enshrined Queen of the CODA to speak.

"I have my title back," Lethia began. "It was not easily won. I may not have gotten it back without a little help from our sea witch," she said as she took out a piece of cigar, lit it, and began to smoke.

"That is a good thing," Hue sighed. "Now we can help Tildon."

"It is not that simple," Lethia said. "Even being Queen, I cannot make the CODA elders change their laws or ways. I made our case to one of the elders and she agreed to hear our plea for Tildon."

"That is a good thing," Wisdom said. "Right?"

"They will only hear from Royal. There is a group of scouts in the thicket to escort you to them. They will take Tildon with you, as well." Lethia explained.

"He will go alone?" Maximus growled. "I do not like it."

"Me, neither," Wisdom said shaking his head as he put his shotgun across his lap. "I mean, I'm supposed to be your Royal Guard. You ain't supposed to be out of my sight."

"It is the only way," Lethia said. "Remember, the elders were the ones who allowed me to go to Earth and tend to Royal and Simon. I can assure his safety."

Royal got up from where he was sitting. He looked at the wagon. He watched Etera tending to her brother. He knew what he had to do. He handed his Bible to Hue. Royal went over to his pack and put on his cloak.

"I will go," Royal said.

"I don't like this," Maximus growled as he began to pace back and forth.

"I will be alright," Royal assured his friend as he went up to him and rubbed at the fur behind his ears.

"Are you ready?" Lethia asked.

"I am." Royal nodded.

"Then, be off," Lethia directed.

Lethia went over to the wagon. She helped Etera with Tildon. They wrapped him in Janis' cloak and helped him down from the wagon. Royal got up on his mount and they carefully put Tildon on the back of the horse behind him. Tildon hunched over and laid heavily on Royal's shoulder. Royal smiled at his comrades as Lethia led his horse into the trees. Once he was discreetly among the trees, several women appeared. They were older than the original scouting party that Lethia and Etera had encountered but they were similarly camouflaged. Each carried a longbow and a spear. They bowed to their new queen and took the reins from her hands. One of the women reached up and blindfolded Royal and Tildon. Then they began to lead them through the trees.

"Do you think they have a chance?" Etera asked.

"Only the Avatar knows now," Lethia said as she watched them vanish in the rising morning light.

Royal let himself be led through the forest. He did not resist or try to figure out which way he was going. All he did was hold onto Tildon's hands around his waist and try to stay upright in the saddle. Tildon laid on Royal's back. Royal could hear that his breath was shallow and labored. As they went over rocky terrain and uphill, Tildon would groan in pain slightly. With every groan, Royal would tighten his grip around Tildon's hand reassuringly. As they moved, all he could think about was how this young man had risked his life to save him. Tildon did not know him and had never seen him before, but on the word of his sister alone, he had placed himself in harm's way for him. Royal did not care about being a High Prince or vanquishing a mother he did not know. All he cared about was returning the debt he felt that he owed this young man. Thinking of the Aldam flowing through his veins, Royal knew that it could easily have been him that had been poinsoned. He was sure that the lethal concoction was meant not for Tildon, but for him. The stark realization sent a shiver up his spine.

After along time riding his mount came to a sudden stop. One of the scouts reached up and removed the hood that had been covering Royal's head. It took a moment for his eyes to adjust to the shift in light. Then he was astonished by what he saw. He was in a small grove that was surrounded by the biggest trees he had ever seen. The bark of the trees appeared to be lined with silver and gold. The trees sparkled in the suns' light. All of the foliage in the small grove was close to the ground and dripping with dew. Small animals and birds ran around in abundance. They seemed to look at Royal with curiosity. Ahead of him was a huge rock formation jutting out of the ground. There were five figures standing all around it. Each of them wore a different, natural-colored cloak that was dripping with leaves. All of the women were older and different hues of Black and yellow with dirt coloring their skin.

Looking around at the women and feeling the sacredness of the grove, Royal felt like he was in a holy place. The feeling reminded him of being at home on Earth in the sanctuary of the church right before service began. The scouts that had escorted them to the grove helped Tildon down from the mount. They wrapped him in Prince Janis' cloak and laid him against a tree. One of the scouts opened a gourd and let Tildon drink from it. Royal did not know what was in the gourd, but Tildon seemed to perk up immediately.

Royal got down from his mount as the other scouts vanished into the woods behind him. Before approaching the women Royal sat down on the ground, removed his sneakers, and rolled up his pants legs. He got up and approached the women reverently.

"That is far enough, High Prince," Patel said as she raised her hand.

Royal stopped immediately. As he looked at the women, he found that he had broken out in a cold sweat. He made eye contact with each of the women and tried to smile. They did not smile in return. He did not know what he was going to say to any of them to get their assistance. Royal said a silent prayer to both God and the Avatar, asking for guidance.

"We are the elders of the CODA. I am Patel. This is Elisa, Morta, Backa, and Nia," Patel said, introducing the others. As she said each name, the corresponding woman simply nodded her head in response.

"I am Royal Monroe," Royal said. "First of all, I want to thank you for allowing me to speak with you. Queen Lethia and Tori made it clear to me that this is not your way. I am honored to be in your presence," Royal said sincerely.

The women seemed unmoved by Royal's sincerity. For a moment, no one spoke. They all stood there, looking at one another.

"Why are you here?" Elisa asked finally.

"I need your help for my friend," Royal replied as he glanced back at Tildon. "He was poisoned trying to save my life. There is no cure for the poison. It is called Aldam. I was told that his only hope is the eternal spring that you have access to."

"Have we not done enough?" Nia cut him off. "We followed the will of the Avatar and sent our Queen away to protect you. Though we hold the Avatar sacred, we hold our ways equally so. The CODA do not help men. Now you want us to give you access to one of our most sacred possessions." Nia paused. "Why are we even listening to this?" she asked her sisters.

"Where I come from," Royal interjected, "I was trained as a holy man. One of the things my Earthly father always told me was not to be inflexible. He told me that my faith must always be malleable to make room for God's miracles. I am asking you to have that kind of malleability."

"Surely you know that you are at war with your mother," Morta interjected. "In war, there is death. It sounds to me like this young man has earned an honorable death."

"There is no honor in dying prematurely," Royal countered. "I was taught to believe in a savior who was crucified for what he believed, then he was resurrected. And like my savior, you have the power to bring this young man back to life. Don't let traditions and rules stop you from making that miracle happen," Royal pleaded.

"You are a passionate young man," Morta observed. "The CODA live and die by our belief in the power of the feminine. We may not agree with everything that your mother does as High Queen, but she is a woman nonetheless. She should be allowed to make her mistakes; men are allowed to make mistakes all the time, without consequence. If we help you any more than we have already, then we are choosing you over your mother. How do we know you will not make worse mistakes than she?"

"I can't promise you that I won't make mistakes if I ever become the High King," Royal said earnestly, "but I do know that I won't sacrifice this planet to a devil. . .or Dark God or whatever," he assured them.

"The CODA only really interact with men we discover during our mating times," Patel explained "Did Queen Lethia ever tell you what happens if a CODA woman gives birth to a male child?"

"No, she did not," Royal said carefully as he swallowed. He was unsure if he wanted to know.

"They are given back to the land," Backa said coldly. "That is how much we believe in a female-only society. If we are willing to give male babies back to the land, why should we help a grown man like this one?"

Royal was horrified by what he had heard. He could not believe that the woman he knew as his Aunt Grace would take part in any tradition like this. His view of Lethia was shattered. He bit down hard on his lip. Again, he found himself wondering what kind of world this was. Royal was overcome with the image of these babies being left alone in the woods. He burst into tears to the surprise of the elders.

"Why do you cry?" Nia asked. She was surprised by his response.

"I can't understand how you could let your babies die," Royal shook his head and wiped at his eyes. "I mean, give them away, but not leave them to die."

"You are an off-worlder," Elisa said. "You do not know of the history of the royals of Acara. Their hands are tarnished with the blood of countless women."

"We do not need to justify our ways to this off-world High Prince," Nia said shortly.

"But we allowed ourselves to be pulled into this power struggle when we sanctioned Lethia's involvement," Patel reminded them.

"The Avatar is our divinity," Backa said. "It would have been a sin to refuse it."

"Then don't refuse it now," Royal interjected.

"What do you mean?" Morta asked.

"The Avatar is a part of me. It is as much a parent of mine as Jul and the High Queen Mora." Royal explained.

"Impossible," Morta said.

"Not impossible" Royal said firmly. Then he explained to the elders what Tori had told him about the facts of his unusal birth. The elders looked at him suspiciously. Then Patel walked up to Royal and looked deeply into his eyes. As if she did not believe what she saw, she placed her palm on Royal's head. Royal closed his eyes and opened himself to her. Deep inside, Patel felt it – the essence of the Avatar.

"It is true!" Patel declared with tears in her eyes as she backed away from Royal. "He is the Avatar in coporeal form."

Royal was totally surprised by what happened next. The five elders of the CODA all fell in unison to one knee before him. He was overcome by this gesture from these proud, powerful women but he could not let himself get caught up in the reverence. He heard Tildon moan from behind him. From the sound of his voice, he could tell that he was getting weaker.

"Will you help him?" Royal asked humbly, fighting back tears.

"We will," Patel said for the others.

The elders of the CODA rushed forward in unison. They all walked up to Tildon and removed the cloak that Janis had left him. With Royal by their side, they helped carry Tildon to the huge rock where they had been standing. They went to oneside of the structure. There was a groove in the side. It was just big enough for a person to pass through. The women squeezed though one at a time and passed Tildon through. Royal followed them.

They were in a small, hidden alcove. Like the trees outside, the walls of the alcove were coated with the same silver and gold film. It gave the alcove a supernatural glow. In the center of the alcove was a deep pool of still water. The water was clear and at the bottom of it, you could see a large rock that was made of the same silver material that coated the walls of the alcove. Looking at the pool, Royal could feel a pulse emanating from the spring.

"This is the eternal spring," Patel said. "This rock fell from the stars generations ago when the CODA were young."

"We soon discovered that it had the power to renew the life of anyone bathed in the waters that came from it," Nia explained. "We have been the keeper of it ever since. It is one of the CODA's greatest secrets."

"It is a gift from the Avatar," Elisa said reverently. "It is a gift that we gladly share with the walking embodiment of that spirit. You may discover, young man, that you are neither male nor female. Somehow, you may be something else that will unite all our peoples."

Royal did not say anything to this last statement. All he was focusing on was Tildon. He simply nodded. He did not want to say anything that would upset the trust he had been able to garner with the elders. They slowly stripped Tildon down to his undergarments. His skin was ashen from where the poison had begun to take over his organs. The five elders began to chant in rhythym as they lowered Tildon into the water. His body sank like a stone the moment it entered the water. He was submerged up to his head so that only his face was visible. He floated motionless with his eyes closed in the shimmering water. Once he was in the water, he began to convulse violently. The pulse that Royal felt began to intensify with Tildon in the pool. Then, Tildon's eyes popped open and he began to rise out of the water.

"Tildon," Royal smiled as he bent down next to the pool.

Tildon looked up from the pool and smiled. His face was flush, healthy and full of color.

"Yes, High Prince," Tildon said. "Yes."

High above the sands of the Red Desert the sky opened up. Then out of a swirl of light, several figures appeared. Simon, Reverend Monroe, Ben, Purcell and Father Benedito materialized out of the dislocation in space. They landed in the sands of the Red Desert and rolled against a rock formation with all of their bags. Oddly enough, Father Benedito was the first to his feet. He was slightly disoriented from the leap between Earth and Acara but he was slightly paranoid that he would not be able to breathe the air on Acara. He took several deep breaths to make sure that he could breathe. It took him a few minutes to adjust his breathing back to normal. He looked up at the sky and was shocked to see Idris and Itor shining brightly down upon him.

"Ay, Dios mio," he whispered as he fell down in the red sand and let the heat and light of the suns touch his face for the first time. He sat there for a long time, bathed in the light of this new world. If he had any doubts about making this trip to Acara, in this moment they all faded away.

"You can't be serious?" Ben said as he got to his feet and looked around at the emptiness of the desert. He immediately sat down under the half-shade of the rock formation and rolled up his pants legs. He had never liked taking his kids to the beach when they were younger because he hated the sand. Now, as he looked around, all he could see was miles and miles of it. He sighed out loud. There had to be a better way. "Shit," he cursed.

Purcell got to his feet slowly. He put on his sunglasses immediately. Instead of being wowed or annoyed with the terrain, he began to gather their bags to make sure everything had made it through. He was sure to secure their food and the little bit of water they did bring with them in the shade. Under the kind of heat they were experiencing, it would be easy for it to spoil. Purcell stretched and began to walk the perimeter to make sure they were alone. Purcell was being a police officer to the core.

Simon got up next. He did not know what he expected Acara to be like, but not like this. There was only red sand and rocks for as far as the eye could see. Simon stripped down out of his armor and wrapped his hands around the arrow head hanging from his neck. He immediately concentrated on Tisha. He wanted her to know that he was indeed close and that he was coming for her. He had no idea where on Acara he was, but the fact that he was at least on the same planet as Tisha meant there was hope now. In addition, he was prepared to assume his divine role as Royal's Royal Guard. Lethia had trained him in hand-to-hand combat as well as most weapons. Now he could summon the energy of the land around him. This would make him a better protector for Royal. Not to mention that if he ran into to father, Quan he would be more than ready.

"By the Avatar," Reverend Monroe sighed. "Why did you bring us here?" he wondered out loud as he looked around. Prior to coming to Earth, he had studied most of the geography of Acara. He recalled it like he knew the back of his hand. This was the Red Desert on the Eastern land mass of Acara. It was one of the most isolated areas on Acara, similar to the Lost Islands. When the red-robed priests of the Avatar were alive, this was the land they held most sacred. For them, all life on Acara originated from these lands and when the High Queen went about her extermination of them, this was where they supposedly returned to.

Reverend Monroe guessed that there was no reason to doubt the wisdom of the Avatar. It was about making the best out of a bad situation. He got to his feet and rallied the others around him. He quickly explained to them where they were. He also made it clear that if they were there, there had to be a reason for it.

"We just have to have faith," Reverend Monroe concluded.

"Faith?" Ben said as he looked around trying to find some shade. This was why he never liked Black church or churchgoers. They had a way about them of making everything bad that happened to you about faith. He shook his head and kicked at the sand. For him, sometimes in life, somethings were simple bad luck. Popping out of a hole in the sky in the middle of a sand lot was the epitome of bad luck for him. At the very least, he was sober. In this heat, a drink would have killed him; probably stopped his heart altogether.

"Everything is going to be alright," Reverend Monroe said calmly.

"How can you be so sure?" Ben said sarcastically.

"Because we are not alone," Simon said as he pointed to a rock formation a few feet away.

Purcell reached into one of his bags and put his hand on his gun. Father Benedito fought to make out the shape of the person framed by the rays of Acara's two suns. All he could see was the person's long, red robe. He could not imagine how the person could survive in all this heat in such a garment. He looked like a monk from one of the Franscian orders.

"You know this man?" Purcell asked suspiciously.

"I do not know him, but I know his dress," Reverend Monroe said. "He is a priest of the Avatar."

"I thought they had all been destroyed?" Simon questioned.

"I guess not," Reverend Monroe said as he began to walk toward the man. The priest climbed down from the rock formation and made his way over to Reverend Monroe. For a long time, the two men talked in whispers that the group could not hear. Then together they walked back to the group. The priest's face was obscured by his hood and he was looking down. Reverend Monroe was smiling oddly.

"Gentlemen," Reverend Monroe said as he cleared his throat, "I want you to meet Jul Acnarian. He is the last priest of the Avatar."

"You say that to say…?" Ben questioned. He was getting hot. "How does that help us?"

"Calm down, Ben," Purcell advised.

"Don't tell me to calm down. I am only here to get my son back and that is all," he remindedhim.

"Ben," Reverend Monroe said, grabbing his arm. "Jul is Royal's birth father."

"Dios mio," Father Benedito said as he crossed himself. "Dios mio,"

Tisha was outside of the Grand Citadel in the pens of the gorda. She was feeding Aspion and humming to herself. It felt good to be outside and doing something other than sitting in her chambers. As she rubbed at Aspion's horn, a feeling overtook her. She dropped the feed that she was giving Aspion and gripped the arrowhead around her neck. Tears burst into the corners of her eyes and she fell back on the ground. It was Simon. Somehow, someway, he was on Acara and he was planning to come for her. Tisha could not believe what she was feeling, but she was sure of it. Considering the way that Acara City was built, it would take an army to get to her through the City's defenses. Not to mention all the soliders and Royal Guards around the Grand Citadel, it wasn't like Simon was going to be able to walk right in and get her. Tisha dismissed her doubts. If Simon had found a away to get to Acara, he would also find a way to rescue her. She had to have faith. Faith. The sound of the word felt funny coming from her mind. It made her giggle.

And if Simon was on Acara, he would be able to help Royal challenge his mother for leadership of the planet. With all that Tisha had seen of Acara, Tisha could only hope for a change in leadership. The people of Acara did not seem to be that different from the people she had grown up with in Baltimore City. They seemed to live simple lives and want a better life for their families. However, the High Queen's obsession with the Dark God and the way she ruled appeared to be surpressing them. From what she had seen at the banquet of the High Court, none of the rest of the royals appeared to be in a position to challenge Mora. In fact, they seemed to be bending over backwards to cater to her. Perhaps having Royal grow up away from Acara was the Avatar's way of assuring that he would have a value system that would be strong enough to challenge his mother. Tisha could only hope so.

--Now you are thinking like a true Acarain, Aspion said in the back of her mind --The Avatar is truly wise.

--I hope it is wise enough to get us out of all of this, Tishsa answered.

--Faith, Little Flower, Aspion counseled. --Faith,

Silently, she wished she could speak with Malik again. However, she knew that was impossible with Agar patrolling the corridors of the Grand Citadel. Tisha shook her head. She never thought she would be in a position where she had to rely on a ghost to get news or send messages; especially, someone like Malk Jones. Everything that Wisdom had told her about him led her to believe that he was something other than a benevolent spirit. However, here on Acara he was turning into exactly that. Tisha guessed that traveling to another world and fighting an evil High Queen was enough to give anyone a second chance. Tisha only wished she had sent Malik to check on her son when she had the chance. Being away from little Wisdom was turning out to be the worst part of this experience. Since being away, Tisha went to sleep every night trying to picture little Wisdom's face. It was one of the few things keeping her sane.

Tisha's hand fell casually to her stomach. Though she was in the early part of her first trimester, this pregnancy was nothing like her first. Ofcourse, she guessed that it had something to do with the fact that Simon was not human and something to do with the rituals that Ela had put her through; and just being on Acara, in general. All the prenatal things that Tisha had done with little Wisdom and taken for granted, she had not been able to do with this baby at all. On top of that, there were all of these strange energies that she was dealing with. It seemed as if every time she turned around, someone was trying to get in her mind or body. Somehow, her unborn son protected her from this invasion, but it left her wondering what kind of life it was that her child would have. And even though she was far from thinking of a name for him, a name kept popping up in her mind. It was Dewa. Tisha tried to dismiss it several times but it would not leave her.

--Sometimes powerful beings are born with a name, Aspion said in her mind –If he has named himself, he is surely destined for greatness.

Tisha put her hands on her stomach absently and shook her head. This was all becoming too much!

"You seem deep in thought, Little Flower," Holi said as he came around the corner into Altion's pen. He was smiling widely as he looked at her. He was holding a single moon bud in his hand. Unlike the other moonbuds that Tisha had seen, this one appeared to be frozen. It was sparkling with dew. "I made this for you," he said as he offered her the delicate flower.

Tisha was surprised at the gesture. For a moment, she did not know what to do. Then she accepted it slowly and smelled it. She was surprised at the scent. It was many times stronger than it was naturally. Tisha was surprised and she smiled in spite of herself. She turned away so Holi could not see her blush.

"How did you do this?" Tisha asked.

"I made it in my lab," Holi explained. "I thought that since you like moon buds, it would be a way for you to keep one with you permanently. They can be so fragile and their scent fleeting," he explained.

"Thank you," Tisha smiled as she looked at Holi suspiciously and took the flower from his shaking hand. Holi held onto the precious bud for a moment too long, then let he it go. He winked at Tisha slightly and bowed his head to her.

Tisha was stunned as she looked at him. She could not believe that Holi was flirting with her. She could not tell how old he was but she guessed he looked just a few years younger than her mother or father. At the banquet, she had assumed that he was being kind and welcoming to her. Now, he was acting like a dirty old man. His leer made Tisha step back and cross her legs. And he knew that she was promised to Simon. Tisha shook her head. How dare he come on to her! She was lonely, but she was not that lonely.

"I think I should get back to Aspion," Tisha said as she backed away from him and cracked a half smile.

"Surely, my lady," Holi said cheerfully as she began to back out of the pen. "I will see you later," he said as he walked away with an arrogant assurance.

Tisha watched him leave. She waited until she was sure he was out of sight before she moved again. She went over to Aspion and touched his horn. As she stroked it, she found that she was overcome by emotion. Sensing her distress, Aspion began to lick at her with his thick tongue.

--Do noy worry about him, Little Flower, -- I will send signs to his gorda to keep him away from you. I am sure he would not like my horns.

Tisha reached out and hugged her gorda. For the first time since she had been on Acara, Tisha let herself cry. She did not know how, but she needed Simon to come for her soon or she was going to lose her mind. She wrapped her arms around Aspion protectively.

--I am here Little Flower, Aspion assured.—And I will let nothing happen to you," he roared somewhere in the back of her mind. It gave comfort to Tisha's tears.

The High Queen sat in her chambers looking out of the window. She had just finished eating het breakfast and was waiting for her handmaidens to bring in the clothes she would wear for the day. Thinking about the day that lay ahead, she sighed. It was going to be a long day of meetings about land disputes and trade agreements. She was not looking forward to dealing with all of these diputes, but she knew it was important as a means to keep peace among the city-states. The High Queen could not wait until she fulfilled her convenant to the Dark God and would be done with all of this. She looked over at the Scepter of Monarchs near the bed. She was happy to have it at her disposal. It would amplify and direct her enegies if she needed it. Besides, it would make it clearer and easier for her to capture Von.

"Your Highness," Quan called as he stuck his head in the room. "They are waiting for you in the main drawing room."

"Tell them I will be there shortly," the High Queen said without taking her eyes off the window.

Quan turned to leave, but thought better of it. He turned around and walked up to his High Queen. He placed his one good hand on her shoulder.

"What is it?" Quan said gently.

"I am tired of all of this," the High Queen said wearily. "I am tired of carrying the weight of this crown. I am tired of trying to get my son back at my side," she said as she dropped her head. "All I have is my faith in the Dark God. It keeps me going, Quan. If not for that, I do not know what I would do," she said earnestly.

"I am here for you, too, Mora," Quan said softly. "And no matter what, I will be by your side until all is made right," he swore.

"And we will make it all right, Quan," the High Queen said as she turned to her Royal Guard. "We will make it all right."

# Chapter 22

It was evening. The suns of Acara were beginning to fade into the horizon. Wisdom sat with the others around the fire waiting for Royal and Tildon to return. Through the course of the day, Lethia had come and gone. She had quickly settled into her role as Queen of the CODA. The others were surprised at how easily she had stepped into her role. It had almost been two Earth decades since she had led the tribe. They watched as her natural-born leadership skills kicked into action. Seeing the concern on both Etera's and Hue's face, she had vanished into the forest to check in on Royal and Tildon's status.

"They have been gone so long," Hue sighed as he looked up at the sky and the suns' fading light.

"I don't like this at all," Maximus growled as he came to his feet and stuck his nose in the wind trying to pick up Royal's or Tildon's scent. Even hi sstrong senses were not able to pick upeither of their scents in the trees. He had lost their scents soon after they disappeared into the brush.

"The elders of the CODA are rumored not to be easy," Tori commented as he rubbed at Peku's fur. "Nonetheless, I have watched the young minister. If anyone can get through to them, he can."

"Regardless," Wisdom began as he lit a cigarette, "I should a went with him. I mean, I am supposed to be his Royal Guard. Royal's safety is my primary responsibility," he said as he shook his head and began to sulk.

Captain Sarison listened to the conversation without commenting. He kept his eyes on Etera instead. He could tell that the conversation was making her even more uncomfortable. She was sitting by the fire wrapped in her cloak, rocking gently. Captain Sarison could not imagine what was going through her mind. He had known the twins since they were bablings bouncing on their grandmother's knees. Though he was a spiritual client of their grandmother's, he had watched them grow up from afar. He was there when the twins first arrived after the sudden death of their parents. His ship had been in port when Etera had been taken away by the High Queen Mora. He remembered when Tildon had first picked up his blade. Oddly enough, he had been there for most of the major changes in their lives. Besides his oath to their grand mother, he guessed he felt like a father to them. He got up from where he was sitting and went over to Etera. He sat down next to her. He was not sure what he was going to say, but he felt that he should say something. Instead of speaking to her, he reached into his tunic and produced a flask.

"Drink," he said as he handed the flask to her.

Etera looked at the flask. She thought about it for a second, then she took it. She screwed off the top and took a deep swig. The taste of the strong whiskey stung the back of her throat. She began to cough then handed it back to him.

"Thank you," Etera said as she wiped her mouth. "This waiting is really hard for me. I promised my grandmother that I would take care of my brother. I never imagined anything like this."

"I have been a captain for a long time and I have lost many men under my command," Captain Sarison reflected. "You are too young to have gone through half of what you have."

"My grandmother always told me it was the nature of being gifted," Etera said with tears in her eyes. "She said it went with the power."

"Bah!" Captain Sarison said wrinkling his face. "You are a young woman. Your life should be filled with joy and simple things."

"Someday," Etera said. "Someday," she repeated as she warmed her hands by the fire, thinking of Royal with a smile. "Someday."

As the group sat waiting in silence, watching the fire, they heard a rustling in the trees. Maximus was the first to get up. Wisdom dropped his last cigarette and turned around. Hue put his bowl of food down and smiled. Captain Sarison and Etera stood up in unison. Peku helped Tori get to his feet. They all turned toward the trees just as Royal emerged from the brush. There was a moment of silence from the group until they realized that Royal was leading his mount. Seated in the saddle was Tildon and he was smiling. To their surprise, he looked heathy and vital. There was a new, rosy color in his once flushed cheeks. Tildon jumped down off of the mount and jogged up to the others. The group embraced him immediately. Etera covered her brother with kisses and hugged him tightly.

"It is good to see you, brother!" Etera cried out.

"It is good to be seen," Tildon sighed in agreement.

"I really did not think the elders of the CODA would help us," Tori admitted.

"Now you say so," Peku quipped. "You are a botton boo!"

"Nor, I," Tildon agreed. "But you should have heard the High Prince," he paused and turned toward Royal. "He was masterful in dealing with them. I owe him my life."

Royal was overcome by Tildon's words. He did not know what to say. He simply stood on the outskirts of the group smiling. Tildon walked up to Royal, fell to one knee, and bowed his head reverently.

"You saved my life, my High Prince. Where you go, I will follow. Where you go, my sword will be yours to command," Tildon said sincerely.

Royal reached down and helped Tildon to his feet.

"You risked your life for me first, Tildon. I could do no less for you," Royal smiled. The two young men embraced under the weight of the setting suns. "Go get something to eat and spend time with your sister."

"Thank you again," Tildon smiled as he turned back toward the others who invited him into their midst, slapping him on the shoulder.

"You did a good thing," Wisdom said as he slapped Royal on the back. "It had to be good. It made me drop my last cigarette," He laughed."

"You needed to stop anyway," Royal kidded.

"I know. I know. But not like this," Wisdom whined'

The two shared a laugh as Royal came into the camp. He sat down next to the fire and Hue busied himself with making something for Royal to eat. Normally, Royal would have protested but he decided against it. He was tired after his interaction with the CODA elders. Yes, he was happy that he was able to get them to heal Tildon. He was still haunted by the vision of all the male babies of the CODA being sacrificed. Royal grabbed his head as he thought about it. While he understood it was their custom and where it came from, he still felt horribly responsible for these lost lives. For the first time, Royal was feeling the gravity of being a High Prince and possibly the next High King.

"Are you okay?" Hue asked as he handed Royal some food.

Royal smiled, "It was along day. I learned a lot about Acara from being with these senior women. I also learned a lot about the customs of the CODA that I find troubling."

"What did you learn?" Hue asked.

Royal took a deep breath and described the customs of purging the male children from the CODA that was told to him. He also made it clear to Hue why the women of the CODA felt like they needed to do it that way. He could tell by Hue's face that he was horrified.

"My God," Hue shook his head. "This place is crazy!"

"I know it may seem that way Hue, but I have learned as a minister not to judge," Royal said. His voice was labored and his soul heavy.

"I know," Hue cut him off. "But somethings are just crazy. . ." his voice trailed off.

"I don't know enough of these women's history or the reality of this planet to judge them," Royal reiteratered. "I just hope as we go forward that they can find another way."

"Let's hope so," Hue sighed as he kicked off his shoes and lay down next to Royal.

As the two of them were sitting there around the fire, Etera walked over and sat down. She was smiling widely.

"I can not thank you enough for bringing my brother back to me," she said.

"He saved my life," Royal reminded her. "It was the least that I could do," he said as he blushed.

"I will always be there. Both my brother and I will be there for you, Royal, I swear," she said as she leaned overand kissed Royal's face before retreating to her bed.

"What happens now?" Hue yawned.

"Now we will go to the Red Desert and find my father. I think many of the answers that I want are waiting for me there," Royal explained.

"Then the Red Deser tit is," Hue said and yawned. "I am overdue for a tan."

"You are so crazy," Royal said as he lay against Hue. "I just want to get there."

"We will, Royal," Hue said reassuringly as he stroked his hair, "Who would have thought that we woud have gotten this far?"

"You're right," Royal sighed as he drifted off to sleep. He was tired from his bartering with the elders of the CODA. As he slept, he found himself dreaming of the defenseless babies the CODA cast away. He could hear them crying in his dreams.

As the others slept, Lethia found herself inundated with the business of the CODA. It was Cree and Patel who spent the evening filling Lethia in on almost twenty Earth years of events that had happened to the CODA. Lethia was surprised that in her time away, Althea had managed the business of the tribe seamlessly. In fact, under her lead, the number of women in the tribe had increased substantially. They had had several conflicts with pirates and land raiders that had sought to take land sacred to the CODA. They had been victorious every battle and buried their enemies. Lethia was surprised that the CODA were trading so much with Lampour.

Traditionally, the CODA preferred to be self-sufficient and nomadic. However, under Althea's rule, they had created a considerable trading relationship with Lampour. Lethia was surprised to find that a Gateway had even been created on CODA land. Patel had been trained as a crystal keeper and was the guardian of the Gateway. It was used on rare occasions. Under Althea's lead, they had used the Gateway more as a tool in battle. They would teleport a batallion behind their adversaries, while they attacked from the front. It made their battles swift and easy.

Though they possessed a Gateway, no one from the CODA had been to the capital since Lethia left. With the High Queen slaughtering the priests and priestesses of the Avatar, and with Lethia kidnapping her son, the CODA were not welcome at the High Court. In fact for the first few cycles after Lethia's departure, it was the tacit policy of the High Queen to kill any CODA woman on sight. Only as a result of time, and their nomadic status, did they fade from the High Queen's area of concern.

Hearing about how well the tribe was doing, Lethia found herself wondering if she had done the right thing in taking her crown back. While she was on Earth living as Grace Monroe, she could think about nothing else other than the CODA. But, she had not considered how much being around Simon, Royal, Reverend Monroe, and being a member of Gateway Baptist Church had changed her. She still felt like a CODA at heart, but she had not been living that way for almost twenty Earth years. Not to mention that in the fight with Althea, Lethia had accepted assistance from Etera. The woman that she was before she left would never have done such a thing. It was not the CODA way and not how they choose their leader. Feeling the weight of the crown on her head, Lethia knew she had a lot to consider. Yet she knew that would have to wait for now. She still had to get Royal to the Red Desert and help him defeat the High Queen.

"Is there anything else you desire right now, my Queen?" Cree asked.

"No, you may go," Lethia said, waving her away.

Cree bowed her head and vanished into the brush, leaving Patel and Lethia alone in the woods. Lethia removed her crown and sat down with the elder. The two women broke open a large, brown fruit and began to drink its nectar. It was a rare delicacy that Lethia had not tasted in a long time. It was definitely better than Arkon's cooking.

"You have done a good job with that young man," Patel said as she drank.

"It was unexpected," Lethia said frankly. "This experience has changed me more than I thought."

"Keeping one's oath to the Avatar usually does," Patel said wisely. "It usually has more going on than is obvious. And when you keep your word to the spirit, it will change you in ways you can't imagine. It has the power to even to change a CODA, though we try to be status quo in our ways."

"I am changed, Patel," Lethia admitted. "I fear that it may have changed me in ways that disqualify me to lead the CODA long term."

Patel laughed as she broke open another fruit and began to drink.

"Perhaps it is not that you are no longer qualified to lead the CODA, perhaps it is that you are meant to do more," Patel said frankly.

"Through all of this, I have never seen myself as doing more than returning here," Lethia said as she gestured at the woods around her.

"Lethia, I have known you for a lifetime," Patel laughed. "You are a fine warrior. Maybe one of the best warriors the CODA has ever known. I do not believe that you are any less worthy to be CODA Queen because of your experience. Maybe it is your destiny to take the value system of the CODA all over Acara. The goal of the CODA was to insure the safety and development of women. Maybe now, the dream of the CODA will go beyond these woods and trees."

"I never thought about it that way," Lethia said as she looked up at the night sky, charting the path of the Acarian moons.

"Royal is a man or he will be. For that reason, the CODA will always keep our distance, but he is also the living embodiment of the Avatar. For that reason, we will do whatever we must to help him. First and foremost, we are sworn to uphold our allegiance to the Avatar. The Avatar first brought us to the safety of these plains and helped us to develop our code. Maybe it is time for that to expand further," Patel explained.

Thinking about what Patel said, Lethia's eyes widened. She smiled to herself as she took out a cigar. Patel looked at the rolled up tobacco oddly. Lethia took out a match, lit the cigar, and began to smoke it. Then she handed it to Patel. Patel looked at the glowing stub suspiciously. Then she took it from Lethia's hand and began to puff. As she did, her eyes widened and she smiled.

"What do you call this?" Patel asked.

"A cigar," Lethia laughed as she took it from Patel and began to smoke.

"You must tell me more about this Earth and its wonders," Patel said with wide eyes. "I think I like this tobacco."

"I will," Lethia laughed. "But it will have to wait. I have to get Royal and the others to the Red Desert."

"Why do you want to go there?" Patel asked as she reached for the cigar hungrily.

"Royal's father is there. We think that he will have some more information we need before we face the High Queen," Lethia explained.

"That is a long way from here," Patel thought out loud.

"Not if we use the Gateway," Lethia suggested carefully.

Patel did not show any expression. Lethia could tell that she was thinking. She got up from where she was standing and began to pace back and forth. Then she reached down and took the cigar.

"Because Royal is part of the Avatar, I can not see refusing you," Patel said finally. "Come at dawn and I will send you there."

Lethia got up from where she was sitting. She reached into her armor and removed two cigars and handed them to Patel. Then the two women embraced. It felt like old times.

"While I am away, I would like you and Cree to stand in my place as Queen, Lethia directed. She seems young, but there is something about her I like."

"Good choice," Patel agreed. "She is good CODA and will be loyal to her Queen. I will come for you at first light."

"Until then," Lethia said as she picked up her crown and headed back through the trees toward the others.

Patel stood silently and watched Lethia leave. She smiled to herself. She had raised Lethia from infancy and was proud of her. Deep within her spirit, she felt the Avatar was not through with her yet. Over her shoulder, Patel heard a slight rustle in the trees that did not seem natural. She turned instinctively and began to scan the foliage. After a long time of watching, this elder of the CODA turned back to her seat among the trees. She sat down and began to drink from the large fruit she had shared with Lethia. Then she lit one of the cigars that Lethia had given her and began to smoke.

In the distance, Althea was lying in the dirt. She had overheard the entire conversation between Patel and Lethia. She stayed down wind from them so they would not get her scent while they talked. Althea was a trained assassin. Probably, the best the CODA ever had. She knew how to hide her whereabouts from others better than anyone else. She never thought she would have to use her skills to spy on other CODA, but she never thought she would see the day when she was no longer CODA Queen.

Unlike the elders, she did not agree with them helping the young High Prince. Yes, he might be the living embodiment of the Avatar but he was still a man. It went against everything the CODA stood for to help a man; most especially in his quest to unseat a fellow woman. Althea shook her head. To her, it was blasphemy. As Althea shrank away, she made up her mind what she would do. She would use the Gateway and go to Acara City. Like the other royals, she knew that the High Queen wanted to know where the High Prince was. She had worn the crown and receieved the message like the others. Now she could deliver this information in person. She would not just deliver the information. She would volunteer her services to the High Queen to assist her in capturing the renegade High Prince. In doing so, she would gain favor with the High Queen, get rid of Lethia and, at the same time, regain her crown.

Father Benedito opened his collar. He and Simon unrolled a huge, silken tarp. They hung it in between two of the rock formations. While they held the tarp, Ben and Purcell secured the corners with hammer and nails. Once the tarp was secured, they pulled it tightly. Immediately, the tarp cast a large shadow over the area. It also cooled the wind as it passed through it. Reverend Monroe and Jul moved the packs the group brought from Earth under the tarp. Jul dug a large hole in the ground near one of the rocks. He placed his hands over the hole and it immediately began to fill with water. While Jul summoned water from the arid ground, Reverend Monroe gathered a few twigs. He reached into his bag and withdrew his satchel of crystals. He picked out two of them and crossed them over the wood. The crystals began to glow and they sent a spark into the wood, igniting a fire.

The group of men huddled under the tarp and arranged their bags. They were all surprised at the way the tarp cooled the hot air of the desert. The men sat in a semicircle around the fire. Jul smiled as he looked at them. Then he closed his eyes and began to pray. As he felt the power of the Avatar move through him, he reached out and touched each of their heads. Purcell, Ben, and Father Benedito felt an odd tingle in their brain.

"There we go," Jul said. "Now we will all be able to communicate," he said, smiling, "in both English and Acarian."

Ben, Purcell, and Father Benedito looked around in surprise. They could not believe that they understood Jul's Acarian tongue.

"A miracle!" Father Benedito smiled. "This is truly a world of wonders," he said as he looked up again at the twin Acarian suns.

"I see you like Idris and Itor," Jul commented as he followed the priest's gaze. "Are the suns where you come from not as spectacular?"

"The Earth only has one sun," Ben said. "And to my knowledge it does not have a name."

Jul laughed at this revelation. "One sun? I can not imagine. You will soon tell me that your world only has one moon."

"Si, amigo. It does." Father Benedito chimed into the conversation.

"Our worlds are truly different, but when I look at you I can see they are the same in some truly remarkable ways. My son was lucky to find a place to grow up where he could so easily fit in. I am happy for that."

"You will also be happy to know that I raised Royal to be a holy man," Reverend Monroe said. "The religions on Earth are very different from those on Acara, but I believe they gave Royal a strong moral core."

"I could ask for nothing more than that; especially being a priest of the Avatar," Jul said, sighing. "The only thing I could have asked more would have been to be there and raise him myself, but that was not to be," he said sadly.

"Do you live here alone?" Purcell asked as he looked around at the rolling sand dunes.

"For the most part," Jul said. "There is a group of beings that live in the rift between the desert and the Eastern plains called the Arcana. They are an insular, peaceful folk. I sometimes spend time with them. They are the weavers of this tarp we are under. And there is Bly, of course."

"Bly?" Purcell and Simon asked in unison.

"Bly," Jul repeated as he got to his feet and stepped out from under the tarp. Standing in the hot, open air, Jul let out a cry and held up his arm. After a few minutes, the huge fire Roc appeared on the horizon. It circled the small encampment before it landed on his master's arm. Jul walked back over to the group holding Bly. Bly was bigger than any bird the group had ever seen. It was larger than an eagle and had fire red feathers and a huge beak.

"This is my dearest friend, Bly," Jul smiled proudly. "He is a Fire Roc, one of the few things indigenous to this bleak bit of terrain. More than a friend, he keeps me fed by hunting for me."

Father Benedito's eyes widened as he looked at Bly. He got to his feet and walked up to the priest and his pet tentatively. The priest was amazed by the bird's size and its fire red feathers. The other men got to their feet and went over to the priest and his pet. As they were looking at Jul and Bly, Ben pulled Reverend Monroe aside.

"Arkon?" Ben began, "I know this is all amazing to you guys, and I can't believe I am on another planet either, but I am here to get my son back and take him home."

"You're right," Reverend Monroe said as he dropped his head. "I am here to see my son, as well."

Overhearing this conversation, Jul cast Bly back up into the sky and waved the other men back under the tarp. They sat down around the fire.

"I know that some of you are here for your own reasons," Jul said. "But I want you to know that Royal and his cohort are on their way here."

"How do you know this?" Ben asked quickly.

"I see things," Jul said frankly. "I felt you coming and I know Royal is on the way. Being here in the Red Desert the gifts that I have have been given are amplified. There is no place more sacred to the Avatar than these sands. As his last priest, I am heir to those gifts."

"So all we can do is wait?" Ben sighed as he kicked at the sand.

"I have been waiting for much longer than that," Jul said as he looked off in the distance at the setting suns and the moons rising on the horizon.

In the catacombs of the Grand Citadel, Holi sat in his laboratory with his Royal Guard, Bilk. The two were enjoying another of their long moments together alone. Holi had grown up here among his potions and chemicals with only Bilk as his constant companion. In fact, days would go by and Bilk would be the only person that Holi would see. As the third son to the High King, he was almost forgotten by everyone. He had grown up in the shadows of his niece, the High Queen, though he was barely older than she was.

Like many High Royals, he had had his fair share of lovers over the years from all over Acara. He had thought to marry many times, if only for the company and to see his children grow. Now that he was slightly older, he preferred ~~his~~ experiments with his potions to experiments of the flesh. However, all that had changed when he saw the off-worlder, Tisha. There was something about her that made him feel young and vital again. Perhaps it was because she was like an experiment that was not so easily solved. He did not know why, but he had to have her.

"You seem deep in thought, my High Prince," Bilk observed as he poured Holi a fresh drink. "I have not seen that look in your eye in a long time."

"A new fire has been lit inside of me, old friend," Holi said candidly. "I have eyes for

that young off-worlder. And in these things that will transpire in the suns to come, my reward shall be her."

"Love is a fickle prize, my High Prince," Bilk said honestly. "Be careful where you place your desire, lest you be disappointed."

"You think that I have not thought of this?" Holi laughed as he drank. "Would it not be funny, after all of this, if I was the last High Royal standing? They leave me alone with my potions and chemicals. I sit on the throne when my niece and High Prince go off to fight their battles. I am my brother's confidant. No one would expect quiet Holi to have a plan."

"I would expect nothing less," Bilk said as he sipped his wine and sharpened his sword.

# Chapter 23

A cool wind blew dew from the forest onto Hue's face. The spray of dew made Hue open his eyes. He smiled as he looked over at Royal. Royal was still asleep. He was lying close to Hue with his arm around him. Hue smiled to himself as he lay back enjoying the comfort of their closeness. As Hue lay there, a rustling in the trees drew his attention. He turned his head just as Maximus emerged from the trees. He had a small animal between his teeth. Maximus went over to the fire and began to gnaw at his breakfast. Looking at him, Hue almost forgot that for as human as Maximus was, he was partly a wild animal. As he watched Maximus tear into the flesh of the animal, he hoped he would never be on the other end of those jaws.

As Hue was watching Maximus, Lethia emerged from the brush. She clapped her hands several times to wake everyone up. The members of Royal's group slowly uncurled from their bedding and sat up. Now that she had their attention, she waved them all over to the fire. They sat down near the flame and waited for the Queen of the CODA to speak.

"First things first," she began. "How are you Tildon?" she asked.

"I have never felt better," Tildon smiled. "I feel strong. . . and hungry!" he laughed.

"Let me get you something to eat," Etera volunteered as she got to her feet, went to the wagon, and gathered their supplies.

"Sweet things," Peku mused as he stuck his nose up in the air. "I want sweet things," he cried out as he ran toward the wagon. "All this dry makes me want to die. Now that Tildon is well, you don't need my special spit anymore," he whined.

"We will always need you, Peku," Tori reassured him.

The others turned to watch Etera and Peku go through their food. Peku immediately began to struggle with Etera over some fruit. The basket she was holding fell from her hands. Peku immediately grabbed a piece of rare fruit and ran under the wagon to Etera's great consternation.

"Peku!" Etera called after him to the laughter of the other members of the group.

"I will go and help her," Royal volunteered as he got to his feet.

"No, wait Royal," Lethia protested. "I have more news that I need to share."

"What is it?" Tori asked as he leaned in and warmed his hands over the fire.

"A Gateway," Lethia said. "The CODA have a Gateway and a crystal keeper. I spoke with her last night and she said we could use it to get to the Red Desert."

"Wonderful," Captain Sarison smiled. "That will take a litany of suns off of journey Eastward," he sighed.

"Then what are we waiting for," Wisdom said as he rose. "Let's go!"

The others got to their feet immediately and began to pack up their bedrolls. Tildon ran to the wagon where Etera was fighting with Peku over the fallen food and found himself something to eat. Maximus finished eating the meat from his morning hunt and licked at his claws. Hue kicked dirt onto the fire and went into the woods to change his clothes. Using his walking stick, Tori made his way back to the wagon and helped the others tame Peku. Captain Sarison tended to the mounts and fed them for the journey. While the others worked at striking the camp, Royal found himself hanging back. Noticing this, Wisdom went up to check in with his charge.

"Are you alright, man?" Wisdom asked as he reached for a cigarette in his pocket before remembering he did not have anymore. He sighed to himself and bit his lip instead. He could taste the nicotine.

"Yes, I am okay," Royal began as he dropped his head. "I was excited by the idea of meeting him – I mean, my birth father – at first. More than just helping me figure out away to deal with my mother, I wanted to know about my past."

"Is that a bad thing?" Wisdom asked.

"I don't know. Arkon. . .I mean Reverend Monroe has always been my father. Sure he lied to me, but he had his reasons. I don't want to feel like I am betraying him," Royal explained.

"Brother man, I feel what you're sayin', but at least you got two fathers that you know love you and a powerful spirit in the mix. Don't get me wrong, I love my grandmother and I loved my moms when she was straight, but I would have given anything to have had a dad. Who knows? Maybe I would have made different decisions with my life. You aren't betraying Rev. by meeting your dad, you are just filling out your story, that's all."

"I never though about it like that," Royal admitted with tears in his eyes.

"It is going to be alright," Wisdom said as he wrapped an arm around Royal. "Come on, let's hit the road."

"Yes, you are right," Royal said as he swiped at his eyes and got to his feet.

The members of the group unhitched their mounts from the wagon and packed their supplies on their backs. They tied their mounts to the trees for the CODA scouts to pick up later. Lethia led the members of the party into the woods. They walked for a long time with Lethia to guide them by the light coming through the tall trees. After some time, Patel stepped out from among the trees. She was dressed in a cloak of leaves that was the same color as the ground. She was covered in dirt and had twigs in her hair. She bowed her head to the Queen of the CODA and Royal and waved to the others.

"Quickly now," she said as she led the group along the trails. She led them down a tight trail through the forest to a natural archway between two trees. Crystals dangled from the edges of the archway. They glowed as they caught the light from the Acarian suns. Patel went up to the Gateway and took out a tuning fork. She surveyed the crystals carefully. Then she used the tuning fork to activate one of the crystals. It began to glow and the portal opened.

"Thank you, elder mother," Lethia smiled as she hugged her.

"I will see you soon, Queen of the CODA," Patel smiled.

"We owe you, Patel," Royal said as he bowed his head to her and fell to one knee as he had seen the others do.

"Just do right by women, young High Prince, and that will be payment enough," Patel said honestly.

"I have no chicel," Royal declared. "Lethia raised me as my Aunt Grace for all of my life. I also served as a minister over a congregation – aspiritual house of worship – of women for most of my life. I could never knowingly do anything to hurt women."

Patel looked at Royal, measuring the truth of his words. She bowed her head to him and stepped aside.

"Let's do this," Lethia said as she turned to the others.

"Before you go, Queen Mother," Cree said to Lethia. "I am the Horn Carrier of the CODA," she said as she produced a long animal horn from under her cloak. "If you need us, sound the horn at the Gateway and we will come to your aid."

"Thank you, Cree," Lethia smiled as she took the horn. "You are showing me that you are a true asset to the CODA and a rightful Queen to hold my sword in myabsence."

Cree blushed and bowed to her Queen.

"There is no higher compliment than that," Cree said as she stepped aside.

With that, Lethia and the others stepped through the Gateway. The space within the Gateway swallowed them whole and it instantly closed.

"I never thought I would see a time when the CODA would help men," Cree said honestly to Patel.

"We are entering into uncharted times, Cree," Patel said frankly. "And before this is over, I am sure we will be faced with the same choice again."

Levan was teaching a class of young crystal keepers in the crystal hive. He was in the middle of his lecture when he felt an activation of a Gateway from within the catacombs. He immediately dismissed the class of yellow-robed students and went to the gilded doors that led to the catacombs. He rang a bell near the door and a battalion of guards assembled by his side. He withdrew the key from his robes and opened door. He was surprised to see a face that he had not seen in many years. Though she was dressed in land-colored clothing and wore a hood, he recognized the former Queen of the CODA immediately.

"Queen Althea," Levan bowed as he stepped aside. "The High Court has already begun. I would have expected you suns ago."

Looking at the men, Althea shrank back at their smell. It was a funk she immediately found distasteful. She hated being in the city more than anything else. However, she got over her disdain of the city and the foul smell of the men. She stepped out of the shadows of the catacombs and removed her hood.

"No longer Queen, Levan. I am just Althea of the CODA now," she said bluntly.

"What happened?" Levan asked.

"I have no time for that right now, crystal keeper," Althea snapped. "I need to have an audience with the High Queenimmediately. It it of the highest Acarian business. I bring news of treason."

"I do not know if that is possible," Levan protested. "Especially since you are no longer Queen of the CODA."

"I know where her son is," Althea said flatly.

Levan was stunned by her words. He turned to the head of the battalion.

"Take her to the Grand Citadel!" Levan commanded. "Speak with the Royal Guards and no one else."

As the guards led Althea out of the crystal hive, Levan watched them leave. He thought about what she had said. The words rang in his ears. He shook his head. He knew that no good would come of this. Acara was indeed at war.

On the edge of the Red Desert stood a natural archway made of stone. It overlooked the gap called, The Grind, that separated the plains from the Red Desert. An array of silk lines was strung across the canyon, connecting the two sides. Along the silken lines were countless small huts made out of the same silk. These huts were the home of the

Arcana. The Arcana were a peaceful tribe of multi-limbed beings that lived here in the wastelands between the plains and the Red Desert. Like the CODA, they were nomadic and rarely seen. However, the silk they spun was valued all over Acara for its strength and the beautiful garments that were made from them.

As Lethia and the others stepped outside of the natural archway they were disoriented from the space dislocation. Captain Sarison fell to his knees and threw up. He hated going through Gateways. At moments like this, he missed the open sea and his air ship. Looking around at the rolling sand dunes and hot sky, he was at a loss to say just how much he missed them. Captain Sarison said a silent prayer to the Avatar that he would be back on the high seas soon. Hopefully, with a ship filled with treasure or ast least Arcana silk that would make up for his current discomfort.

"Oh shit," Hue said. He could not believe how hot it was. He looked up at the way the suns were lined up in the sky and immediately began to peel off his layers of clothes. He reached down and touched the sand. It was too hot for him to take his shoes off. As he looked around, and he thought about what of Acara he had seen, he disliked this place most of all.

"Dear Avatar," Etera cried out at the arid land. She looked up at the sky— there was not a cloud to be seen. More than the heat, she would be helpless here separated from water. Seeing the look on his sister's face, Tildon went up to her and withdrew two swords.

"Do not worry, sister, I will protect you," he swore as he unrolled Janis' fine feathered cloak and put it over himself and Etera. The cloak immediately cooled them down from the heat of the desert.

"Is she going to be alright?" Royal asked out of concern.

"Yes," Tildon said. "It is this place. It is so devoid of water that it frieghtens her. I will keep her safe."

"You are a good brother," Royal complimented him.

Tildon blushed and bowed his head.

"She did the same for me to get me to this point. I can do no less for her," Tildon said earnestly.

Lethia and Wisdom began to look around the desert. They noticed a shadowed rock formation near by. They directed the group over to the formation and set up a small camp in its shade.

"We are going to have to conserve water," Tori advised as he shrank back in his robes for comfort from the scorching heat.

"I don't *like this* sand," Peku said as he picked up a hand full, put it to his lips and spit it out. "It tastes like minced meat," he lamented.

Maximus was miserable in the thick, red sand. His paws sank deep into the sand. He began to growl uncomfortably. He found nothing about being here that felt comfortable. He had only been a babe when he was taken from his pride but he still remembered the cool air and adundant water of the rain forest he called home. Royal was his family now, too. They had grown up together. He would never leave him.

Lethia motioned to Wisdom to come close.

"Let's go down into the Arcana village," she said. "They will know how to reach Jul."

"Okay," Wisdom said immediately.

Lethia turned her attention to the group.

"Wait here for us," she said. "We are going down into the village to see if we can find Jul. Tildon, Maximus, and Captain Sarison, stand guard."

Tildon was on his feet immediately with both swords in his hands. Captain Sarison simply nodded.

"Be safe," Royal said as he put a hand on Wisdom's shoulder.

"I will," he assured him. "I didn't survive the streets of Baltimore City to be taken out here." He added a wink.

The two shared a laugh as Lethia and Wisdom turned to the edge of the cliff. They walked for a ways through the sand before they found a long line of knotted silk that led down to a rope bridge. They looked at each other and began to descend. After a few minutes, they landed on the rope bridge. They steadied themselves and walked into the heart of the Arcana village. It was made out of several crude huts with fire holes in the center that were connected by strings of strong silk. They stood in a makeshift village square that was made out of tightly woven silk. As they looked around, there were signs of life but no visible inhabitants.

Lethia drew her sword and Wisdom pulled out a gun. They stood there for what felt like forever, until a small boy appeared in the doorway of one of the huts. He was dressed in a tan tunic and had a pleasant, brown face. The thing that shook Wisdom the most about the young man was the fact that he had four sets of tentacled arms. The boy looked at Wisdom and Lethia and smiled. Then with his upper set of arms he began to spin a line of silk. He attached it to the doorway of the hut he was in and climbed down the strand into the village square.

On bare feet, he stood little more than a child, he walked up to Lethia and Wisdom. As he came up to them he smiled. Once again Wisdom was shocked by what he saw. The boy had a mouthful of the most jagged teeth he had ever seen. His teeth were covered with the strands of the silk that the village seemed to be made of. Looking at him, Wisdom couldn't stop staring at him thinking he had bitten off more than he could chew.

"Welcome," the boy said as he bowed his head in an archaic form of Acara.

"Welcome to you," Lethia said as she put her sword away and motioned for Wisdom to lower his gun.

"I am Ikin," he said by way of introduction. "I am the leader of this village of Arcana."

"I am Lethia, Queen of the CODA, and this is my friend, Wisdom. We come in peace." She said frankly. "Our weapons aside," she added.

Ikin looked at her skeptically yet continued to smile.

"We know of the CODA," Ikin said. "And some of our villages have even traded with you. Only our women folk, ofcourse. What can I do for you and your tall friends?"

"We seek a red-robed priest by the name of Jul," Lethia told him.

Ikin folded all eight of his arms and began to back away slowly. It was as if Lethia had said a bad word or insulted him.

"There are no red robes left," he said quickly. "Please leave us as you found us."

"We mean you no harm or the one called Jul," Wisdom interjected. "There is someone in our company who Jul has been waiting for a very long time," he explained

Ikin stopped and smiled once again, slyly.

"Is this person who seeks Jul a little bit older than me?" he asked hurriedly.

"Yes," Wisdom nodded. "The person is Jul's son," he said prematurely to Lethia's chagrin.

Ikin's eyes immediately widened. He walked up to Wisdom until they were almost face to face. Then he proceeded to smell him. Wisdom was stunned by the young man's action but did not move. The Arcana ran his beak-like nose all over Wisdom, until he was sure his scent was true.

"I see that you are telling the truth," Ikin said happily. "Bring your friends to Vishnu for shelter immediately. The desert can be hot and beyond unforgiving. I will see what we can do about finding Jul for you," he offered.

"Go and get the others," Lethia directed Wisdom.

Wisdom did not hesitate. He turned to leave the same way he and Lethia had come. As he left the small village, he turned as countless other Arcana emerged from the silk huts and surrounded Lethia. He went across the rope bridge and climbed up the side of the cliff. He carefully retraced his footsteps back to where he had left the others. He quickly told them about meeting Ikin and the village of Vishnu. He also told them about Ikin's promise to find Jul. everyone quickly gathered their things and made their way through the sand. They tripped as they went. Each step felt like three as they made their way to the rope and down the cliff. .

"I don't like this!" Peku said as he peeked over the side of the cliff. "Opions were not made for climbing. That is a long way down and that rope is real thin."

"Do not worry, Peku," Tildon said smiling. "You kept me alive. I am not going to let anything happen to you."

"Yeah, but that was my spit juice," he pointed out. "This is a long fall."

Tildon laughed as he grabed the Opnion by his tail.

"You promise?" Peku whined as he jumped into Tildon's arms.

"I got you," he assured.

Peku held onto Tildon's neck as he began to descend down the rope. The others followed him down the line and onto the rope bridge. Lethia turned and smiled as the others met her in the middle of the small village. Once they were all assembled eyes began to appear in all of the huts. Then slowly lines of webbing fell from the doorways and a host of Arcanians descended the lines. They tentatively joined Lethia and the others in the middle of the courtyard.

"Oh, my God!" Hue mused as he looked at all of the eight-limbed figures gathering around them. They looked like something out of a Spiderman movie.

"Don't stare," Wisdom whispered as he nudged him. "Be cool."

"I'm trying," Hue said. "But they look like cartoon characters."

Royal nudged his companion.

"You are the red-robed's son!" Ikin said as he walked up to Royal and sniffed him.

"I guess I am," Royal nodded.

"I can smell your father on you. Your father has been a friend to Arcana for many years. He knew my father before he was killed," Ikin explained as he lowered his head.

Seeing the grief on the young man, Royal bent down next to him.

"What happened to your father?" Royal asked.

"He was killed by pirates. They come to our villages from time to time trying to either capture one of us, so we will spin our web for them, or to take our webbing," Ikin explained.

"Ah!" Captain Sarison chimed in as he looked around at the village. "Arcanian webbing is very valuable. It is light, but stronger than metal," he thought out loud as he looked around, calculating the bounty before him. The captain of the *Lucky Lady* could not stop himself. It was his nature.

Seeing this quality in her protector, Etera elbowed him severely. He immediately stopped and began to whistle away the fortune he saw.

"I will send a note on a fire roc to find your father," Ikin offered.

"A fire roc?" Royal questioned.

Ikin smiled and put one of his upper hands in his mouth and whistled. Then, from behind the largest hut, a huge bird appeared. It circled overhead before landing on one of Ikin's arms.

"Good meat," Maximus growled as he eyed the giant fire roc.

"Easy, Maximus," Royal cautioned him as he stroked his fur.

Ikin looked at Maximus suspiciously and raised his arms defensively.

"He is okay," Royal assured him. "Aren't you big boy?"

"Ofcourse," Maximus agreed. He was licking his lips inspite of himself. He could taste the bird's rich meat.

"This is Nano," Ikin said, introducing the bird. "He belonged to my father. One of his sons, Bly, has been the constant companion of your father since he came to the Red Desert many cycles ago. Nano will bring him to us," Ikin said confidently as he cast Nano into the sky.

Everyone watched the giant fire roc vanish into the light of the suns. Lethia put a heavy hand on Royal's shoulder.

"Now, all we can do is wait," Lethia said to him.

"I know," Royal agreed.

"Are you okay?" Hue asked.

"I will be," Royal said. "I have waited this long to meet my birth father. I can wait a little bit longer."

"Until he comes, you would honor us by being our guests," Ikin declared as he clapped all of his hands. Several of the Arcana assembled took the packs from the members of the group and led them toward a vacant hut. As they moved, Royal looked over his shoulder toward the place in the sky where Nano had vanished. He found himself wondering about this man called Jul and what it would be like to meet his birth father a man who had given him away to Arkon and Lethia.

The High Queen rested in her quarters, lying on her bed. The High Court had only just begun, but she was already tired of all the affairs of governing the concerns of the planet. She would have much preferred to be spending time in the Grand Temple worshiping the Dark God. It was the only solace she seemed to have these days, besides her time with Gregor. Mora was stunned at how much she was beginning to look forward to their moments together. Not since Jul had she felt that she had a mate who really understood her and would do anything for her. Part of her wanted to run away with him to the Northern Region and vanish into the mountains. However, she had made an oath to deliver all of Acara to the Dark God and she knew there was no way of breaking that promise or what the promise actually meant for them all.

On top of that, she had not heard anything from the other royals about Von. She would have expected to hear from one of them by now. None of them had the power or resources to challaenge her, but she did feel they had the will to scheme against her. She shook her head. There seemed to be enemies coming out of every corner. However, for all of her power she could not see them. It was like the very elementals had turned against her. And she had the sneaking suspicion that they were closer to her than she imagined. The High Queen made herself a promise that she would trust no one besides the Dark God, Gregor, and her Royal Guard. Outside of that loyal group of confidantes, the High Queen knew that she was alone in her pursuits.

The High Queen got up from her bed and lifted the Scepter of Monarchs from her bedside. She went to the mirror and straightened her robes. She looked herself in the eye and put all of her doubts away before she faced the next session of the High Court. She was about to leave her quarters when she felt a familiar presence enter her outer chamber; it was Quan, her Royal Guard. She did not say a word until Quan entered the room.

"I know I am running late, Quan," the High Queen said as she adjusted her crown.

Quan walked up to her and took her gently by the arm. She turned and looked at him oddly. This was an unusual gesture, even for him. Before she pulled away, she could tell that he was smiling wildly.

"What is it Quan?" the High Queen asked, slightly annoyed.

"You have a visitor," Quan said excitedly. "They say they have information on the young High Prince and they will only give it to you."

The High Queen's mouth dropped open. She could not believe her ears.

"Where is this person?" she asked hurriedly.

"She is waiting in the throne room," Quan said.

"Let's go!" the High Queen cried as she brushed past him and hurried through her chambers, almost tripping over her feet. Quan was on her heels immediately. The two rushed past countless people in the corridors on the way to the throne room. Two Royal Guards opened the huge doors to the throne room and let the High Queen and Quan pass. The High Queen immediately ascended the risers to her throne and sat down. She motioned to Quan. He went to the front of the throne room and brought a cloaked figure forward. The High Queen looked down on Althea expectantly without moving. Althea bowed before the High Queen and waited to be acknowledged.

"Arise," the High Queen said. There was no emotion in her voice.

"I bring you greetings, my High Queen, from the CODA of the Eastern Continent," Althea began. "I am Althea," she reminded the High Queen.

"I know who you are, Queen of the CODA", the High Queen snapped, cutting her off.

"Your highness," Althea began as she cleared her throat. "I no longer bear that title. I am simply Althea of the CODA now. I have been replaced in my role by the interloper, Lethia," she explained.

At the utterance of Lethia's name, the High Queen squinted with rage but did not speak. Ignoring this truth, the High Queen continued her interrogation.

"I hear that you have information for me," she said matter-of-factly.

"Before I lost the crown, I did receive your edict about your lost son," she continued. "Before leaving the CODA to come here, I overheard Lethia say that she was taking the young High Prince to the Red Desert to see his father."

"His father!" the High Queen bellowed. She stood up, beside herself with fury.

"Yes," Althea replied. "He lives in the sands of the Red Desert. He is the last priest of the Avatar."

The High Queen was winded. She fell back on her throne, deep in thought. More than hearing about her son, she could not believe that Jul was still alive. She was never sure if he was killed in the puge of all the priests of the Avatar, but she had hoped so. She could not imagine after all this time that he was still alive. The idea that he was making contact with their son infuriated her. The High Queen had placed this dilemma of recapturing her son in the hands of others for the last time. It was time she took matters into her own hands. And perhaps this time, she would do more than recapture her son, but rid their world of the man who had seduced her into bearing Von the first place with his amythist eyes. It was time to act.

"You have done well, Althea, for that I will be ever in your debt," the High Queen declared. "Whatever you need, you may ask."

"All I require is the return of my rightful place as Queen of the CODA— and the head of Lethia," she said bluntly.

"You will have that and more, I assure you," the High Queen promised. "Quan, see to quarters for our honored guest and cancel all business of the High Court today. Gather to me my most trusted advisors for a private luncheon and we will see to our plans."

"As you wish my High Queen," Quan bowed as he led Althea out of the throne room, leaving the High Queen alone with her thoughts of conquest and victory. It was time for Von to come home.

There was sand everywhere. It was impossible to get away from it. Sand covered everything, even under the tarp that Jul had put over their small encampment. Purcell spent most of his time getting the sand out of the guns and ammunition that he had packed for the journey. Ben spent most of his time to himself, sulking about not seeing his son. Father Benedito was filled with wonder about anything he could discover about the desert. He was inundating Jul with questions about Acara. Finally, Reverend Monroe, Arkon, were spending time telling Jul stories about Royal.

"Come close, gentlemen," Jul called as he waved them over to the fire. "I will cook lunch for us."

The men gathered around the fire. They watched as Jul cleaned the carcass of several small animals that Bly had provided for them.

Purcell looked at the meat with quiet disgust.

"Ah," he began," I think I'll stick to the Tupperware meals that my grandmother provided for us."

"I have learned to be a good cook," Jul assured him as he began to cook the meat over the fire.

"I think I prefer my grandmother's macaroni and cheese to road kill," he mumbled as he settled back under the tarp and began to eat.

"Gimme some of that!" Ben said as he licked his lips. "I was trying not to eat too much, 'cause I don't see a bathroom around here, but I can't pass up some home-cooking from Baltimore."

"I think she may even have some ribs in here for you," Purcell said as he rifled through a refrigerated bag.

"Bring it on," Ben smiled.

Looking at the choice in food, Father Benedito did not know which to choose. None of it looked like anything that Senora Isabel would cook for him. He decided to try a little of each. He was surprised to find that they were tasty but none rivaled Senora Isabel's cuisine. As the men ate under the silken tarp, they were disturbed by the sound of flapping wings overhead. Jul got up immediately.

"Is that Bly?" Reverend Monroe asked, wiping rib sauce from his lips.

"No," Jul smiled. "It is Nano, Bly's father."

Jul went out into the desert and stuck out his arm. He untied the note on the fire roc's leg and tossed him back up into the sky. He read the note feverishly with wide eyes.

"What is it?' Purcell asked.

"I do not know," Reverend Monroe responded with concern as he walked up to Jul and placed a hand on the man's shoulder. There were tears in his amethyst colored eyes. "What is it?" he asked.

"Von is here," he said simply.

# Chapter 24

Evening fell over the Arcana village. The light of the moons shined down on the rift between the cliffs and lit up the silk of the huts, making them glow. The Arcana were all sitting around a fire in the center of the village enjoying their evening meal. They preferred to eat small rodents, while the others snacked on dried rations. The sound of their laughter drifted up to the hut that they had given to Royal, Hue, Tori, Tildon, Maximus, Captain Sarison, Wisdom, and Peku. The men of the group were splayed out on mats on the floor. Hue stood looking out of the door of the hut at the Arcana. He could not take his eyes off the multi-limbed people, fascinated by how they moved. Out of everything he had seen since coming to Acara, these people were the strangest. They even trumped Maximus with their oddity.

"Stop staring!" Wisdom admonished Hue as he rummagedthrough his bag for a cigarette that he knew was not there. His sudden lack of nicotine was making him profoundly irritable, even more than being on Acara.

"I'm sorry," Hue said, "but have you seen these people?"

"There are a lot of things about being here that we are simply going to have to get used to," Royal said as he led Hue away from the doorway.

"You have not seen anything if you think the Arcana strange," Tildon added.

"Acara is made up of many beings," Tori said wisely. "I cannot imagine a world with only one kind of being."

"I mean look at me, Hue!" Maximus said as he rose up to his full stature.

Hue shrank back into the shadow of Maximus' mass. As he looked around, again he found himself wondering why he was here. He guessed that after all they had been through, he was lucky to still be alive and in one piece. Wisdom got up from where he was sitting and went outside. Wisdom watched the Arcana bask in the glow of their evening meal. He kicked at the webbing of the ground nervously. He would have loved to have a cigarette. He sighed out loud and stretched as he looked at the moon. At that moment, he found himself wondering how his son and grandmother were and he wished he was home with him.

In the other hut, Lethia and Etera sat together. Since they startedon this trip, they had had few opportunities to be on their own without the men. Lethia sat back and lit acigar, while Etera covered herself and cleaned off the flow from her cycle. Since fleeing from the slave mines and finding her family again, just having the space to take care of herself was a soothing comfort. Once she was done, she changed her clothes and sat back. Growing up, her grandmother had told her about the mysteries of the Red Desert. Now, being here, she could feel the power of the spirit in the sand under the Arcarian moons. Etera closed her eyes and let herself be rocked by the power of the spirit. She had felt the essence of the Avatar before, but nothing like this. It was everytwhere.

"What do you feel?" Lethia asked as she smoked her cigar.

"It is hard to describe," Etera mused. "Though it appears that there is nothing alive here, it is probably the most alive place I have ever felt."

"Ah, I agree. As you know, I am connected to the land," Lethia reminded her. "I feel more powerful here than I have ever felt before."

"I hope we will not need it," Etera said gravely.

"I am not sure, my dear," Lethia said as she smoked.

Just then, there was a screech from outside. It was the unmistakable sound of Nano returning. However from the sound of its wings, Lethia could tell that he was not alone. She rose with Etera on her heels and looked outside. They looked out at the night sky, just as two large fire rocs descended into the Arcana village. Royal and the others came out of their huts as they heard the sound of the fire rocs. They did not have time to marvel at the big birds, seeing several shadows appear in the distance on the web bridge leading to the village.

The first face that Royal could make out was that of Reverend Monroe leading the small group of men. Royal was overcome with emotion. He leaped down from the doorway of the hut and rushed into his surrogate father's arms. The two held onto each other for along time. They could not believe their eyes. It was too good to be true.

"Dad!" Royal cried. "I can't believe that you're here!"

Reverend Monroe smiled as he ran his hand over Royal's face.

"I told you that nothing would keep me from you," Reverend Monroe swore as he pulled Royal close again. "And I didn't come alone."

"What do you mean?" Royal questioned as he looked over Reverend Monroe's shoulder. Father Benedito, Ben, Purcell, Simon, and Jul made their way into the village square.

"I know that you know Mr. Lee and Officer Purcell," Reverend Monroe began. "But this is Father Benedito. The Gateway crystals we used to get here were hidden in his church by your grandfather a generation ago."

"It is good to meet you, mi hijito." Father Benedito smiled, sticking out his hand to grasp Royal's. "I have heard a lot about you young man," he said.

"I don't know what they told you, but don't believe it," Royal said candidly.

"I am humbled that your father has allowed me to have this experience with them. They are good men. Muy bien hombres," he assured Royal.

"Yes, they are," Royal said as he put his head on his surrogate father's shoulder.

"Royal!" Simon shouted, tears forming in his eyes as he approached.

"You are here!" Royal bellowed as he jumped into Simon's huge arms.

Easily, Simon lifted Royal up over his head and swung him around. The two hugged and laughed like children in a playground.

"I see that Wisdom kept you safe," Simon smiled.

"He did an excellent job," Royal declared. "He has not left my side since we got to Acara."

Simon exhaled. He could not believe that Wisdom had been able to keep Royal safe considering what they must have faced since coming to Acara. He shook his head as he looked toward Wisdom. He remembered all the times he had overheard his grandmother praying for him and the things she said about his character. Simon guessed that she was right. He was truly turning into a blessing from the Avatar.

"Is my brother, okay?" Purcell asked hurriedly droppoing his packs as he entered the village square.

"See for yourself," Royal said as he motioned to the hut from where he had just come. As Royal lowered his arm, the others were quickly coming down a line of silk from the hut. Wisdom was the first to meet the group. He paused when he saw his brother. For a moment, he did not know what to do. Then to Purcell's surprise, Wisdom rushed him and they hugged. Wisdom was beside himself with emotion. He did not know why but he was crying. It was as if a lifetime of pain was pouring out of him. All Purcell could do was hold his younger brother.

"I'm here," Purcell said as he kissed his brother's head. "I'm here."

"Man, I never thought I would see you again," Wisdom sobbed.

"You are my little brother. I told you I would always be there for you." Purcell explained with glee. "Besides, I had to make sure you weren't fucking things up."

"How could I do that with you as an example," Wisdom winked.

"How is grandma and Little Wisdom?" he asked hurriedly.

"They are both fine. Grandma knows everything and she packed some of your favorite food," Purcell explained.

"You mean I got macaroni and cheese?" Wisdom laughed as he began to tear at his brother's bags.

"I think she may have packed some chit'lins for you, too," Purcell assured him.

"She is the best!" Wisdom said as he sat down, cross-legged, and began to open the plastic containers.

"I think if you look under that one, you may find something that you need." Purcell directed.

Wisdom looked under the containers of food and was stunned to find three cartons of cigarettes. He immediately dropped the food and opened a pack.

"You 'shonuf know your little brother!" Wisdom said, laughing as he lit a cigarette. "I was about to try and smoke a branch. I was having a mega nicotine fit!"

The two shared a nervous laugh.

Ben stood watching the others with wide eyes. He was not impressed by the Arcana and their multiplearms or their village from webs they spun. All he wanted was to lay eyes on his son. He was about to lower his head when he saw a dusty figure emerge from the shadows of the hut that the men occupied. It was Hue! Hue's face lit up when he saw his father. Hue almost fell down the rope getting to him. The two met at the threshold of the hut and embraced.

"Dad!" Hue cried out as he hugged Ben. "I can't believe that you're here! How did you find out everything?" he asked in a rush of words.

"That is a long story," Ben said. "Did you think I would let you run off to another planet and not come and get you?" Ben asked reassuringly.

"I hope you didn't worry too much," Hue said.

"Your sister and I only thought you were dead, that'sall," Ben said as he punched his son's shoulder. "You had me and your sister worried to death!"

Hue was stunned by his father's words. He had not thought about how his actions would affect his family. He lowered his head. Seeing the effect his words had on his Hue, Ben lifted his son's head and smiled at him. There were tears in his eyes.

"Reverend Monroe told me that all you were trying to do was help your friend," Ben said as he put his hands on his son's shoulders. "Your mother would be proud."

Hue was shocked by what his father said. He did not know what to say. Ben pulled his son to him again and kissed his head. After all that he had been through, he could not believe how good it felt to simply hold his son. It satisfied him more than any drink ever could.

"Ah, come on, Dad," Hue said as he pulled away. "How is Sapphire?" he asked quickly.

"She's okay now that she knows what's going on. She's staying with Ms. Simms until we get back home," Ben explained.

"As long as she is alright," Hue exhaled.

"It is good to see you, boy," Ben said. "I thought I had lost you like I lost your mother. I could never live with that", he swore.

"You don't have to worry, Dad," Hue assured him. "They kept me safe."

"I took good care of him," Maximus growled as he rubbed up against Hue. "He is a good young man."

Ben looked at Maximus' canine form and nearly jumped out of his skin.

"This is Maximus," Hue said. "He is, or was, Royal's dog. As you can see, he is much more than that."

"I see!" Ben said, laughing as he shook his head. He had seen a lot of things in his days but nothing had prepared him for eight-limbed people or a talking dog. He found himself wishing he could find something to drink. However, as he looked at his son, he knew that that was the last thing he needed. More so than bourbon, he had what he really needed.

Lethia, Etera, and Tildon stood back watching the reunions with the rest of the Arcana. Peku sat on Tori's shoulder whispering in his ear, telling the blind man everything that was going on. Father Benedito was sitting with the Arcana. He was smiling ear-to-ear, clamping hands with the Arcana children. For him, this was a dream come true. He had actually made contact with an alien life form. Any reservations he had about leaving his parish quickly faded as he looked into the faces of these wide-eyed children.

Simon went up to Lethia. The two stared at each other through the haze of her cigar smoke. Impulsively, Simon reached out and took

Lethia in his arms. Lethia let herself be hugged by her surrogate son. Though she hated to admit it to herself, it was good to see him.

"Okay that is enough," Lethia said gruffly, before introducing Simon to the others. "You have done good, boy," she said, complimenting him.

"I had the best teacher," Simon assured her. "I have a lot to tell you." he began.

"There will be plenty of time for that later," Lethia said as she cut him off. "We have a lot to talkabout so that we can figure out our next steps."

"You are correct," Simon agreed, bowing his head as he turned and walked over to Wisdom who was finishing up a mouthful of chit'lins and another cigarette. Simon sat down next to him. For a moment, the two sat in an odd silence.

"I can not thank you enough," Simon said earnestly. "You kept Royal safe for me."

"No problem, big fella," Wisdom said, chewing a mouthful of food. "He's a good kid."

"Still, I can imagine it must not have been easy," Simon mused.

"Well, it hasn't been a walk in Druid Hill Park," Wisdom admitted.

"And we still have to get Tisha," Simon said.

"I know," Wisdom agreed as he continued to eat. "And your baby," he added.

"So, you know about that too?" Simon asked carefully.

"Yeah, I know," Wisdom said bluntly, not displaying any emotion as he remembered that he had not seen Malik in some time.

"I don't know what to say," Simon said earnestly.

"Look man," Wisdom sighed. "It just means we got more in common. In a funny way, that makes us family, on account of the fact that our kids our brothers. We just gotta go get her."

"But she knows we are here!" Simon said as he gripped the arrow around his neck. "And

We will fetch her."

"Yes, we will." Wisdom agreed as he high-fived Simon's hand.

Reverend Monroe took Royal by the shoulders and led him to the edge of the village square. There, standing in the shadows was his birth father, Jul. Jul had waited on the outskirts of the reunion watching everyone re-acquaint themselves. It had been so long since he had been around so many people, he felt awkward. As he watched Royal hug Reverend Monroe, he felt strange. It was hard to believe he had a son. Prior to his vow to the Avatar to sire the next High Monarch, he had taken a vow of celibacy. Though it was hard to admit, he did love Mora. He had felt the darkness growing inside of her when he was with her. However, there was nothing inherently evil about her, but her pain over her father had opened a portal in her soul for darkness to fester. It was from that dark place that she had pledged herself to the Dark God and massacred all the priests of the Avatar. It was still hard for him to reconcile the portion of her that he loved with the person that she had become. It was hard for him to believe the tender girl he fell in love with was capable of such unspeakable evil.

As Reverend Monroe led Royal up to Jul, their eyes met for the first time.

"Royal," Reverend Monroe's voice cracked nervously, "this is your birth father, Jul, the High Priest of the Avatar."

Royal looked up into Jul's amythest eyes, searching for some sort of connection. Though he could see that the man's eyes were filled with emotion, Royal felt nothing for him. He was a stranger to him; a story that he had heard. Looking back at Reverend Monroe, Royal knew who his father really was. It was the man who had dried his tears when he was a child, taught him about the Bible, and raised him to love the Lord all of his life. Nothing would ever change that. Royal reached out and took Reverend Monroe's hand, then he turned his attention to Jul.

"It is good to finally meet you," Royal said simply.

"I have waited here for you, for what seems like a lifetime," Jul said carefully as he sized up his son. "There is much we have to speak of. There is much we need to get ready for."

"Whatever you have to tell me," Royal began, "you can tell everyone. They have all risked their lives for me to be here. At the very least, I owe them the truth."

"Well said, young High Prince," Jul said as he opened his arms. "Let us gather around the fire and I will tell you my story."

Royal turned on his heels and went to collect the others. He began to gather them around the fire with the rest of the Arcana. Lethia made her way to Reverend Monroe and placed a hand on his shoulder.

"You have done well," Lethia said to Reverend Monroe. "I know this can not be easy for you."

"It isn't. I knew this day would come, but seeing Royal with Jul is difficult for me," he admitted.

"He will always be your son, Arkon," Lethia assured him. "You raised him into a fine young man. I have seen it shine through in every situation we have encountered since coming to Acara. It is a result of your wise parenting. Though there was a time when I would have gladly broken your neck, I am happy I did not," she said sincerely. "It would have been a waste," she concluded.

Reverend Monroe laughed as he thought about Lethia's hands around his neck.

"I'm glad you didn't either," Reverend Monroe agreed as he lowered his head. Lethia reached out and pushed his head up immediately.

"You have nothing to hang your head about," she said, chastising him. "Now, let's go see what this priest has to say," she said as she led Reverend Monroe over to the fire.

Finally, they were all gathered in one place. They all sat cross-legged around the fire with the entire Arcana village. Jul stood up before them and removed the hood of his robe. He looked into each of their eyes before he began to speak.

"What I will now speak of, few actually know," Jul began. "As I look at you, I can see that Tori told you some of how we came to be here. I remember him well from my time in Acara City."

"And I remember you, Jul," Tori said as he stroked Peku. "I still had eyes then," he reminisced sadly.

"That you did, my old friend. But, it was a dark time in Acara. The High Queen was in the process of slaying all the priests of the Avatar. Those who were not killed found a hiding place here in the sands of the Red Desert," Jul explained.

"My father told me about those years when I was young and only had six arms," Ikin said as he sat back against Father Benedito and began to spin a web bowl. Father Benedito carefully placed a hand on Ikin's shoulder and stroked the young man's fine hair. He smiled in response.

"During that time, I was still a young priest of the Avatar and I knew little of the world outside of the Eastern Realm. As I heard about the slaughter of my brothers and sisters by the High Queen, it became my responsibility to ferry many of them to the Red Desert. I did not know all the secrets of these sands then, but I kept my oath to the Avatar by helping those who came. Then one day in my daily prayers, I was approached by the Avatar itself," Jul paused and shook his head. "In truth, I thought I was crazy at the time. I did not believe that I was worthy of such an overture from my beloved diety, but as I communed with the spirit I soon realized it was real. The Avatar made me the offer to join fully with it, so my true personage would be disguised to all. Once joined, it had me to go to Acara City and court the High Queen herself," he continued.

"Ah," Tori interjected. "I was a seer of some ability when I had my eyes and I was blind to your true identity."

"Once I agreed to that joining, no one knew who I was. I barely recognized myself beyond the color of my eyes which are a rarity even among my people." Jul looked off into the night sky as he continued to think about those years gone by. "So I went to Acara City, disguised as a noble from a Lost Island and presented myself at the High Court. I was immediately taken into the bossom of the royals. I was wined and dined by them. I slowly became a fixture at the Hight Court. The further I got involved in the matters of state, the more I caught the eye of the High Queen," Jul reminisced. "This was the hardest time in my life. There I was, shrouded and safe from the death my other brothers and sisters were facing in the company of the person who had ordained their deaths. Over time, I became the secret lover of the High Queen. I soon discovered that for as much as I wanted to hate her, she was more complicated than that," he said earnestly.

"What do you mean?" Royal asked hurriedly with a wrinkled brow.

"I realized that the woman who was to become your mother was a lonely soul being manipulated by her uncles into her devotion to the Dark God. I also realized that she had a deep, abiding pain over a father who was never there for her. As much as I wanted to hate her, I found myself truly falling in love with her," Jul admitted. "And it was from that love, that you, Royal, were conceived. Once Mora told me she was with child, it was truly a bittersweet day. I did not know how to feel. I was following the directions of my creator in delving into a relationship with her, but it was my heart that I was lying to in each moment with her. The days before your birth were some of the sweetest days of my life. I remember spending hours with the High Queen in the garden of moon buds, talking of nothing but spending a lifetime together with her," Jul said with tears in his eyes. "Yet, like all acts of faith, you soon find yourself tested. Right before you were born, the Avatar came to me and directed me to abandon both you and Mora. And though it was the hardest trek I have ever made, I turned my back on the woman I loved and my unborn child and I returned here to the sands from which I was initiated as a High Priest of the Avartar. When I got here, I soon discovered that I was the last priest of the Avatar. Everyone else, who had been chosen to wear the red robes was dead."

"I know that after I was born, Lethia then stole me away to Earth with Simon and Maximus," Royal said, trying to piece it all together. "But I do not understand why my mother did not have anymore children. I mean someone to replace me."

"She could not," Jul said as he sat down. "After you were born and taken away, the High Queen ascended to being a High Priestesss of the Dark God. That is a very rare thing. It gave her access to dark energies never known here on Acara, but it robbed her womb of the power to create life. It is for that reason she yearns so fiercely to have you back at her side. You are the only rightful heir to the High Throne. You are the final link in an unbroken chain of succession that goes back to the founding of Acara. For that reason, your mother desperately wants you with her."

"Wouldn't it be more peaceful just to wait for her to die and I become High King than start a war?" Royal asked.

"That would be true, my son, if we were only talking about succession. However, your mother in her thrist for power and control over all of Acara made a blood oath with the Dark God. In making this oath, she swore that Acara would belong to him forever. More than being an heir, she needs for you to join her in fulfilling that pact with the Dark God," Jul explained as he stared into the fire.

"On Earth, we call the Dark God Satan," Royal said. "I could never worship him or honor any pact with a dark force. I could not," he swore.

With the utterance of these words Lethia, Reverend Monroe, and Father Benedito all looked at one another with silent pride and reassurance.

"It is for that reason we must remove Mora from the throne," Jul said finally.

"For that to happen, wouldn't we have to kill her?" Wisdom asked as he took out a cigarette and began to smoke.

"Not necessarily, my friend," Jul smiled. "There is another way."

"And what would that be?" Simon asked as he leaned in toward the fire.

"When the High Monarchy was founded there was an obscure check placed on its power.-The heir to the throne can assume power, if he or she can convince five of the major royal city-states to challenge the sitting High Monarch in the Grand Citadel. If they stand in their full crowns before Mora, the power of the High Monarchy will pass to you, Royal," Jul explained. "If you can do this the Scepter of Monarchs and the High Crown which hold the power of the High Monarchy would become yours."

"Then that is what we must do," Tildon interjected. "We have to convince five of the major royals to stand with us."

"They may not agree with the High Queen, but convincing a group of the most powerful royals to commit what amounts to treason is not a small thing," Lethia said. "Many of the royals do not agree with the High Queen, but they fear her power and her wrath."

"True," Etera agreed. "I was imprisoned in the mines with many people whose sole crime was saying something against the High Queen. Many of them had nothing to lose and they spoke out against the High Queen, convincing some of these royals to stand up against her might be harder than you think."

After along silence, Captain Sarison said," Yeah, I have to agree. Having sailed the sea and sky, I have seen most of this world. Getting royals to work together will be tricky," he said as he rubbed his chin

"Look at me," Tori said solemnly. "I failed to find Royal when I was in her service and she took my eyes. There are many stories like mine and Etera's. There are also far worse I believe."

"But if she had not taken your eyes, you would have never met me!" Peku said as he danced by the flames.

"True, my little friend," Tori said as he reached out to touch his companion. "You are the best thing about being blind," he said, laughing.

Seeing the weight of the conversation on his friend, Hue got up from where he was sitting and sat down next to Royal and put his arm around him protectively.

"What are you going to do Royal?" Hue asked.

"I don't know," Royal exhaled as he grabed his head. "This is a lot to take in for one night. I think I need to sleep on all of this."

"Makes sense," Captain Sarison agreed.

"Esta bien," Father Benedito said as well as he saw the weight of the information on Royal. "I think some rest would be a good thing. sleep bien, amigos."

"Make some room for our new guests," Ikin said to some of the other Arcana around the fire as he got up, leaving his woven bowl behind beside Father Benedicto.

Father Benedito picked up the finely woven bowl and held it up to the moonlight. It was by far one of the most beautiful pieces of work he had ever seen. As he watched these simple people scramble to make space for their new guests, his heart immediately went out tothem. He found himself wondering in this struggle for power between the High Queen and those supporting Royal, who would speak for the Arcana? Father Benedito picked up his small bowl and made his way into a hut that had been made available to them.

Everyone got up from where they had been sitting and retired for the evening. Only Wisdom sat alone near the fire, eating some of the food that his grandmother had fixed for him. Eating the food reminded him of the sights and smells of Baltimore City. Each bite made him remember all that he had left behind. He was eating more out of loneliness than anything else. It was good to see his brother and the others; however, it reminded him of how much he had left behind. Wisdom liked the idea of being on what he felt like was the right side of things for a change, yet he missed his son more than he could say. Wisdom was about to retire for the evening when the air near him began to shimmer. He knew immediately it was his shade, Malik.

"Hey, boy," Wisdom said as he stopped and looked up.

"You need to warn them, Wisdom," Malik said quickly.

"Warn them about what?" Wisdom asked.

"The High Queen is coming and she is coming in force," Malik warned.

Wisdom sighed to himself. For a moment, he sat silently looking up at the night sky. He did not know what to do with this information. As he climbed the webbing into his hut, he decided it could wait until tomorrow. The group had had enough information for one night. They needed to have one night of peace. The morning would bring another reality.

The High Queen sat alone in the Grand Citadel of the Dark God. She was on her knees praying to her divinity. She had placed the task of getting Von back into the hands of others. They had all failed her.

Now it was time for her to take matters into her own hands. She was not going to allow anyone else to prevent her from securing her son. It was time to take off all the restraints.

As the High Queen knelt, she began to concentrate on the altar in front of her. As she did, it began to vibrate with dark energy. The High Queen raised her arms in front of herself. She summoned forth the remaining Marauder, the twin of the other that she had sent to Earth. The space behind the altar began to bend and shift. The Marauder appeared out of nowhere with its hounds behind the grand altar. The High Queen smiled at the hulking beasts. The Marauder was bigger than when she first conjured it and its hounds were even more ferocious. The High Queen knew that the loss of its twin had increased both its power and its rage. The nine hounds were seething with anger and they were ready for battle. They drooled ruthlessly, ready for attack, and she could tell that they had a taste for blood.

As the High Queen sat before the Marauder and the altar of the Dark God, Quan, Ela, and Tisha walked in behind her. They waited patiently in the shadows until she acknowledged them, then they stepped forward. The High Queen stood up from where she was kneeling and turned to face them. They all bowed to her respectfully. Tisha grimaced as she looked past the High Queen at the Maurader and its hounds. The sight of the Marauder frightened Tisha more than anything she had seen on Acara thus far and made her blood run cold. She covered her stomach protectively as she felt herself begin to get sick.

--Do not worry, I will protect you, she heard a voice say from deep inside of her. At first she thought it was Aspion talking to her, her gorda. Then she realized that it was not him at all, but her unborn son, Dewa. It sent shockwaves through her. She did not know what to think. However, all she knew was that she was indeed safe.

The room was sweltering with dark energies. Tisha had the uncanny fear that this intense dark vibration would have an impact on her unborn baby. Sensing the impact that the Dark Temple was having on Tisha, Ela placed a hand protectively in the middle of Tisha's back and steadied her.

"Quan, come to me," the High Queen motioned for her Royal Guard to join her at the grand altar.

Quan walked up to his monarch and bowed before her. The High Queen reached out to the altar of the Dark God and lifted the Scepter of the Monarchs. The jewel on the end began to glow with a dark light. The High Queen placed the end of the scapter on Quan's forehead. He began to shake as his body shivered in the dark light. Underneath his cloak, his body began to expand with energy. His canine-like arm began to grow and his dagger like arm became sharper. Quan could feel the souls of the men initially joined with him to create the assassin cube stir. Quan screamed out in agony as he was charged by the High Queen's dark energies.

Ela squinted as she saw her mate shudder in pain under the touch of the High Queen. For the first time in her life, Ela—the second in command of the High Queen Mora's Royal Guard--dared to reach for her dagger against her High Queen. Seeing this, Tisha stepped in front of Ela, and caught her hand. She carefully grabbed Ela's hand and stopped her from removing her dagger. Though she despised the High Queen, Tisha knew that Ela, one of the most seasoned of the Royal Guards, did not stand a chance against the powers of the High Queen. Restrained by Tisha's quick thinking, Ela removed her hand from her blade. Looking from her life partner to Tisha, Ela shed a rare tear and bowed her head. Ela took a careful step back to hide her face in the shadows and used all of her training to veil her thoughts.

Somewhere in the back of Ela's mind, she heard her gorda speak to her.

--Mistress, hold your hand, her gorda warned her. --No good can come from this. It is not time yet for dissent.

The word 'dissent' rolled around Ela's mind and calmed her anger in a way that only her gorda could.

"Now you, Tisha," the High Queen called as Quan staggered back into his mate's waiting arms. He had grown so large under the infusion of dark energy from his mistress that Ela could barely hold his huge form.

Looking at Quan, Tisha was terrified. She had no idea what the High Queen was going to do to her and her unborn child; part of her wanted to turn and run. However, she knew there was no place she could run to: the Grand Citadel, the Crystal Hive, the funeral pyre of of the High Monarchs, none of those places. She shook her head. There was nowhere for her to go. Tisha took her breath and stood her ground instead. It was an act of defiance. After a moment, Tisha exhaled, said a prayer, and willed her feet forward. Tisha walked up slowly to the High Queen. She had never been afraid of the High Queen before; however, seeing her using dark energy had left Tisha terrified. She stopped a few feet away from the High Queen and waited for her to speak. She looked down at her shoes and held her breath.

"Ela tells me that the weapon you used to defeat my Royal Guard is actually a wagon of sorts," the High Queen said matter-a-factly.

The comment caught Tisha off-guard. She turned to look at Ela for direction but she was busy tending to Quan's new bulk. Quickly, Tisha turned her attention back to the High Queen.

"Yes, it is," Tisha said as she looked over at the tarp in the far corner of the Dark Temple that covered Wisdom's SUV. Tisha remembered using it to ram into Quan when he came to Earth and tried to capture Royal. She was not trying to be a hero at the time. Her action was more instinct than anything else, but she had managed to trap Quan against the wall of Gateway Baptist Church, forcing him to transport them both back to Acara.

"Come with me," the High Queen said as she walked with Tisha over to the jeep. "Help me," she commanded.

Reluctantly, Tisha helped the High Queen uncover the SUV. Tisha was surprised at the condition the SUV was in. It was burnt and smelled of smoke, but it was still intact. Looking at the jeep, Tisha could not help but remember all the time she had spent in it with Wisdom. They had conceived their child in its leather seats. Now it seemed like a lifetime ago, so much had happened since Little Wisdom's birth.

"Does it still move?" the High Queen asked as she looked in wonder at the charred, black vehicle.

Tisha looked at her oddly as she struggled to open the door to the driver's side. Once she got in, she found the key still hanging from the ignition. She turned the key. To her surprise the engine turned over. It began to hum, but it did not start. Tisha checked the dashboard. She was surprised to find that the gas gauge was on empty. She was about to get out of the vehicle when she noticed a picture of her son on the dashboard. It shocked her and brought tears to her eyes. She could not believe that Wisdom had kept it there. She had not been gone that long, but she had almost forgotten what her son looked like. Seeing him staring back from Wisdom's dashboard renewed her strength. She scooped up the photo and put it in her tunic. She got out of the vehicle, hid her tears, and went up to the High Queen.

"I think it still works," she began. "But it is out of gas, I mean fuel to make it run."

"Gas?" the High Queen questioned with a wrinkled brow.

"It goes into that small doorway in the back," Tisha pointed. "It is the fuel that makes it run."

"Get back inside and try and make it move again," the High Queen directed.

Tisha looked at the High Queen oddly but she did not want to question her. She climbed back into the driver's seat and turned the key. While the engine idled, the High Queen went over to the gas door and put the tip of the Scepter of Monarch's into it. The vehicle began to shake as it was filled with dark energy. Tisha almost threw up as the dark flow enveloped the entire vehicle and came pouring out of the vents. She was about to jump out of the jeep when the engine miraculously turned over. The High Queen smiled as she looked at Tisha's wide eyes over the dashboard.

"Is it running now?" the High Queen asked.

"It is," Tisha called from inside of the jeep.

"Good," the High Queen said, nodding her head, "turn it off."

Tisha complied and got out of the vehicle. She walked back up to the High Queen who was smiling happily. Tisha could tell she was satisfied with herself.

"We will go to the Red Desert and retrieve my son," the High Queen announced. "You will guide me in this contraption into battle. I want to show my son and his allies that I can have mastery not just in my world, but on theirs as well."

Tisha was shocked by the comment. She had not considered the idea of the High Queen coming to Earth. However as she stared at Wisdom's SUV glowing with her dark power, she had to admit the real possibility of it. It scared her more than she could fathom. She could not imagine the Dark God on Earth. Speechless, Tisha shook her head in fear. She turned to Ela and Quan. Ela was struggling to hold her husband up. Ignoring the High Queen, Tisha went up to Ela to help her supportQuan.

"Tomorrow, I am putting together a force and we will go to the Red Desert and finally retrieve my son," the High Queen announced as she turned to the Marauder. "Come with me," she said to it as she turned to leave the Dark Temple. "Ela, take Quan back to the Grand Citadel to rest. He and the Marauder will lead our forces into battle," she directed as she left the with the Marauder behind her.

Tisha helped Ela carry Quan. For the first time, she could see genuine concern in the eyes of the mother of the Royal Guard for the man she loved. Tisha could tell that Ela truly loved Quan and was concerned about what the High Queen was doing to him. Looking at him, he was barely recognizable after another dose of the Dark God.

"You know this shit is crazy?" Tisha dared to say as she struggled to help Ela hold up Quan's increased weight.

"It is not mine to question, Little Flower," Ela said grimly as she put Quan's arm over her shoulder, "but to follow and to protect."

Tisha did not say anything in response to Ela's statement. Though the woman tried to sound certain, her tone was betraying her. Tisha hoped that would be enough to make a difference in the uncertain days ahead.

Royal laid on his mat in the hut for a long time listening to the breathing of the people around him. With all that he had heard and experienced from the previous evening, he could not sleep. At this moment, he would have preferred his crazy dreamtime to the anxiety he was feeling. The group was looking to him to make some kind of decision. They were looking for him to lead. If he never felt the weight of being called the "High Prince" before, he felt it now.

After lying there for a long time, he decided that he needed to stretch his legs. He stepped over Hue and walked to the entrance of the hut. He shimmied down the rope and almost fell over Maximus, who was guarding the entrance. Royal paused and hugged his faithful companion. One of the things he missed with all that had happened was their alone time. Though he had grown accustomed to Maximus' transformation and was glad for his protection, he missed their silent alone times, especially their long walks.

"You alright?" Maximus asked, yawning.

"Just stretching my legs," Royal admitted.

Maximus put up his paw and blocked Royal from advancing. Maximus put his nose up in the air and sniffed. He did not pick up any scents that he did not recognize. The young High Prince was indeed safe.

"Okay," he said reluctantly. "But I am going to keep one eye open, just in case I need to swat someone," he growled.

"Over-protective puppy!" Royal joked.

"Stubborn human!" Maximus shouted back.

The word human rolled around in Royal's mind as he looked around at the Arcana village. He was feeling many things but human was the least of those things. Royal walked carefully to the village square and squat down by the fire. It was still burning. He warmed his hands and let the conversation and comments from earlier play back in his head again and again. As he recalled all that had been said, it just made him feel more confused. Finally, after going over things in his head for what seemed like the hundredth time, he decided to pray. First he did the "Our Father" prayer, then he found himself speaking to the spirit of the Avatar. He did not expect a response from his supposed third parent, he simply needed to unburden himself.

After a few minutes, as Royal was about to rise, he felt a familiar feeling coursing through him. It was the Avatar. The feeling swept him up. It was around him and inside of him at the same time. Royal stared into the fire, he felt hypnotized by the essence of Acara. Finally, it spoke to him inside of his head in a warm familiar tone.

--I am here for you Royal, the Avatar said,--As I have always been.

"I don't know what to do," Royal said as he began to cry softly. "The responsibility is huge and I am just a kid."

--You do not have to bear it alone, the Avatar assured him.-- I have given you all you need. You will make the right decisions, it added as it began to fade.

Royal thought long and hard on what the Avatar had said, but he could not make heads or tails of it. He sighed to himself and turned back toward his hut. He was surprised to run into Father Benedito who was approaching the fire. The priest was still wearing his collar though the desert was hotter than hell.

"Hola amigo," Father Benedito greeted him. "You can't sleep either?" he asked.

"No," Royal replied, shaking his head. "Hearing all of that last night was a lot for me. I want to do the right thing, but I don't know what the right this, "he admitted.

"I can't imagine the stress you are under," Father Benedito said sincerely. "You are a young man and you should not be responsible for the outcome of an entire world. Incredle4 ! It is akin to Christ carrying the blessed cross," he added as he crossed himself.

"None of this has been fair for any of us," Royal agreed.

"As excited as I am about being on another planet and meeting folk like the Arcana, I can't help but sympathize with your situation," he confided.

"What should I do?" Royal asked rhetorically with tears in his eyes.

"Pray and have faith in His son, your father, and the HolySpirit." Father Benedito said sincerely as he placed a reassuring hand on Royal's shoulder. "He will deliver you."

"I will try, Father," Royal said, "I will try."

# Chapter 25

Royal woke up late in the next morning. He stirred from his covers and looked around the hut that the Arcana had provided for him and the rest of his group. He was alone. He sat up and stretched. Oddly, he had slept soundly after his interaction with the Avatar and Father Benedito. He was surprised at how easy it was to talk to him. He knew Father Benedit owas a Catholic priest but Royal was stunned at how open he was. After having thought about their conversation and his interaction with the Avatar, Royal had made some decisions. He hoped he was going to do the right thing.

Royal sighed, got to his feet and put on his clothes. He stuck his head out of the hut. Like the previous evening, everyone was sitting around a small fire in the village center. Royal climbed down the line from the hut and joined them. Hue and Etera immediately handed him a plate of food. Royal thanked them and began to eat. As he ate, he found himself studying Jul who was sitting across the fire from him. Jul was intentionally not meeting Royal's gaze. As much as he wanted to know his son, he did not want to make him feel uncomfortable by assuming too much intimacy too quickly.

"I have something to tell you all," Wisdom said as he put his food aside. "I got a message from Malik last night."

"Malik?" Reverend Monroe questioned.

"Yes, Malik," Lethia interjected. "It appears that Wisdom's stand-in status as a Royal Guard has given him a true shade."

"So, he is your shade?" Simon asked as he remembered his interaction with Malik.

"What is a shade?" Ben asked.

Lethia quickly explained the relationship between an undead spirit and how it is locked to one of the living. She also made it clear to them that it is a rare thing and a way for the spirit to be elevated. She told the group that Malik had been very helpful in the past by giving them warnings and information.

"What did he tell you?" Hue asked.

"He told me that the High Queen knows we are here in the Red Desert and she is building an attack force to come for Royal," Wisdom said bluntly.

Royal got up from where he was sitting and began to pace back and forth. He knew that this moment would occur but he thought he would have more time. Simon got up from where he was sitting and went over to Royal. He put his arms around him and held him. It had been so long since Royal had been in Simon's protective arms. He felt at home in his embrace. Royal began to sob gently. Unconsciously, Wisdom went over to them and stood by just to be available.

"Is he going to be alright?" Tildon asked Etera.

"This is a lot for him," Etera said to her brother. "He will make the right decision. He always does."

Tori hurriedly got up from where he was sitting. He was shaking uncontrollably. Peku went up to him and tugged at his pants leg.

"Are you okay?" Peku asked.

"Remember? I am supposed to be in exile," Tori reminded his companion. "I do not know what the High Queen will do if she finds me here."

"Do not worry," Captain Sarison assured him. "We will protect you."

"How can you protect me, if you can't even protect yourselves?" Tori snapped. "The things I have seen this woman do are beyond lethal. I mean, my God, she took my eyes with a wooden spoon!" he revealed.

Overhearing this, Ben flinched. He had experienced the danger of the Marauder first hand and had seen what it had done. He had had his fill of all of this and putting his son in danger. It was time to go. He stirred uncomfortably by the fire and sat his plate down. He had lost his appetite.

"It's time we get out of here," Ben whispered to Hue.

"What do you mean, Dad?" Hue questioned. "I can't leave Royal. He needs me."

"What he needs is the Seventh Fleet or a nuclear bomb," Ben said flatly. "Boy, you been on quite an adventure here. I don't think anything in your life will ever compare to this, but this is life and death stuff. It's time to go home."

Hue did not want to argue with his father in front of everyone. As he looked around, he found himself wondering what he was doing there in the first place. Yes, he had feelings for Royal, but that was not enough to protect him from the darkpowers of his mother. Hue found himself wondering if his father was right and it was time for them to go home. Nothing back in Baltimore City would ever be this dangerous. There was no bit of heroin or crack this lethal.

As the other's talked, Purcell checked the two large bags he had brought with him through the Gateway. He began to count out rounds of ammunition and the number of grenades he had packed. He had brought enough stuff with him to take out a small militia. He figured that finding his brother would be a task, however, rescuing Tisha would take some real muscle. Then, from the bottom of the bag, he pulled out a set of battery-powered clippers and smiled at his brother.

"You got to be kidding me?" Wisdom laughed. "My line has been fucked up since I got here."

"Hey, if we gonna die," Purcell began as he turned on the clippers, "we might as well look good!"

"Royal, are you okay?" Father Benedito asked as he walked up to him.

"I am okay," Royal said as he separated from Simon and sat back down next to the fire. Maximus immediately came up next to him. Royal rubbed at his neck and smiled. "First of all, I think that I want to ask all of you to be members of my Court," he said to the shock of those assembled.

"Including me?" Ikin asked as he clapped his hands happily.

"Yes, including you, Ikin," Royal smiled. "In one way or another, you have all risked your life for me or advised me. I couldn't have done any of this without you," he professed humbly. "I don't have anything to offer you all but that title for now, but if we are successful, I am sure that I will be able to offer you much more," the promised.

The promise of treasure made Captain Sarison sit up immediately. He found himself smiling happily. Perhaps keeping his oath to the twin's grandmother was going to pay off after all. He rubbed his hands together in spite of himself. It was hard to fight his true nature.

"What are you going to do about the High Throne?" Jul asked.

"Well I do not believe that we could take on the High Queen directly," Royal reasoned. "Therefore, we have to try and find five royals willing to challenge her. Once we do that, we can sneak into the Royal

City and seize control. It is the only thing that seems to make sense," Royal said thoughtfully.

Lethia smiled as she looked around, cherishing Royal's good reasoning. It was a conclusion that she had reached last night when Jul had mentioned it. However, instead of telling Royal what to do, she wanted him to come to his own conclusions. She was glad that he had made the right decision.

"What are we going to do about the High Queen coming here?" Jul asked. "The Arcana are peaceful people. They don't have a way to defend themselves against the High Queen. I am afraid she may try and exterminate them if we just leave."

"No, we can't do that," Royal said quickly as he looked at Ikin. He could not imagine the peaceful Arcana having to face an army of the High Queen's. Remembering Tildon's life threatening wounds, he would not knowingly put others in the line of fire for him.

"I can alert the other villages and we could go into tunnels in the side of the cliff," Ikin said quickly. "Then we would spin the doorways closed. It has protected us before. It will protect us again."

Royal looked around at the wide-eyed Arcana and shook his head, no. He was not willing to take the risk.

"No, it is time we face her and let her know she can't continue to hurt people," Royal said flatly.

"We are strong," Etera said. "But are we enough to stand up to a battalion of the High Queen's best. She will probably bring a legion of Royal Guards. They are more than a match for us. I don't have much power here; we are too far inland, too far from water," Etera said nervously.

"Do not worry, sister, we will find away," Tildon assured her as he put an arm around her shoulder.

Lethia stood up and asked Wisdom for a cigarette. She wrinkled her brow, she was deep in thought. She looked up at the cliff face that hoovered above them, then at those assembled.

"Ikin?" she called. "Can you get others from your other villages to come here?"

"Surely," Ikin said, smiling. "I can have them here in no time."

"Good," Lethia said. "What we will do is dig a ditch along the far cliff side on the side of the desert. If the Arcana are willing, we will have them cover it with their webbing. It is nearly indestructible. We will lay in wait there and be ready for the High Queen's forces."

"Que bueno!" Father Benedito said. "That is a great idea butwhat will we do for bodies to fight?"

"I will summon the CODA," Lethia said. "I will use the Gateway and get as many as I can here. I will summon them using the Horn of the CODA."

"I will go to Janis," Tildon offered. "He promised to help us if we asked him."

"That is right!" Royal smiled. "Between the two, we should be able to protect the Acarana and surprise my mother. She will not be expecting a full force against her."

"Not to mention I packed enough thunder to stop a small army," Purcell said as he patted the bags he was huddled next to "I am sure the High Queen's forces aren't used to grenades and bullets," he laughed.

"We have a plan!" Maximus growled as he jumped around happily. "I can taste the blood of our enemies."

"While we do this," Royal began, "I will confer with Lethia, Jul, and my father to figure out which royals we will focus on to unseat the High Queen."

Everyone began to scramble around to put the plan into effect. Tori sat down by the fire and leaned on his walking stick. All he could think about was the pain of losing his eyes at the hand of the High Queen cycles earlier. Grimly, he remembered how she had two of her Royal Guards hold him down and she personally used a tool to scoop out his eyes. He could not remember how long she had left him wounded and bleeding on the floor of the Grand Citadel before she exiled him to the Lost Islands. Her actions against him were just the pinnacle of evil actions he had seen her perform over the years. While the others seemed so sure about their ability to face her in battle, he was not so sure. He had experienced first hand what she was capable of. The idea of facing her in battle, even with the High Prince at his side, was something he was not looking forward to.

The High Queen sat on the jade throne in the Great Citadel. While Quan recovered from the infusion of dark energy that the High Queen had bestowed upon him, Elric had been activated once again to stand by the High Queen's side. He stood tall and ready in the shadows behind the throne, protecting the High Queen. The High Queen had put off the business of the High Court and called for several of her most truested allies to meet with her.

The High Prince Burton, High Prince Holi, Prince Gregor, Levan, the Dark Priests Danthor and Agar, Althea, as well as Queen Enora were all gathered in the Grand Citadel before the High throne. The High Queen immediately sealed the room. Once the room was sealed, she quickly told the others what she knew about the death of the Marauder and the whereabouts of the High Prince. She also told them about the vehicle that Tisha brought from Earth and her intent to ride it into battle. She made it clear that she was not going to put retrieving her son in anyone's hands other than her own.

"We are here to support you, my High Queen," Burton said as he stepped in front of the others.

"It is time for the High Royals to work together and bring this young upstart home," Holi added. "We stand with you!" he pledged.

The others were surprised to hear Holi be so vocal. It was out of character for the younger of the two High Princes. They were used to him being cloistered away in the catacombs and silent. Even the High Queen was surprised at her uncle's bravado. She looked at his smiling face suspiciously. The High Queen preferred when things remained the same and were predictable. Normally, the High Queen would have left Holi on her throne while she went on this mission. However, this change in attitude had her concerned. She would take him with her to keep an eye on him.

"I want you all to come with me," the High Queen commanded. "I have already upgraded Quan for this battle and I have the Marauder ready to leave. I am only taking the Royal Guard with me this time; only the Acarian best. We will capture Vonl this time or leave a trail of blood."

Royal was surprised at how fast the Acarana worked. Ikin had sent Nano out to to all of the local villlages. The Acarna started arriving with digging tools just moments after Nano's departure. Under the direction of Lethia, they began to dig a trench in the sand that was chest deep. While some dug with their multiple limbs, others spun a shield over it. Since they had no idea when the High Queen was going to appear, the Arcana were working in shifts through the night to make sure the defences would be ready for whenever the High Queen attacked.

Unbeknonwst to Hue, Royal had requested private sleeping quarters for the two of them. Royal did not want anyone to think that he was taking liberties because of his title. However, he wanted a space and privacy for Hue and him to have time to themselves. Since they had arrived on Acara and admitted to each other what they felt about each other, they had not really had any time to themselves. In addition, Royal felt that the impending confrontation with his mother was going to be a pivotal moment in his life. No matter how much he wanted to avoid it, people were going to be hurt, or worse, in his name. It was something he had never thought about and hated to imagine. He had been raised to be a person of peace and love yet circumstances were proving that he was quickly going to have to learn to be otherwise.

No matter how much he wanted to believe differently, this battle was going to change him forever. As such, he wanted to mark the occasion with one good memory. He couldn't think of someone better to spend it with than Hue. After thanking the others again for their work and their sacrifice, he made his way across the compound. He stopped to tickle Maximus who was posted outside of his hut on guard duty. Royal climbed up into the hut, settled back on a mat, and waited for Hue.

After a few minutesof waiting, Father Benedito escorted Hue to the small hut. Hue left the front line of workers at Royal's request. He did not know what his friend wanted with him, but he obeyed nonetheless. Hue hated leaving the others at work on the trench. He had finally found something that he could do. Granted, he did not have four sets of arms like the Arcara but he was coordinated and task-focused. Nevertheless, Hue left the work line and went to the hut he had been assigned with Royal. He passed by Maximus who was snoozing lightly with his head on his paws. Maximus looked up at him and rolled over as he saw Hue. Hue climbed up into the Hut to find Royal sitting on a mat waiting for him.

"Hey," Hue began as he dusted off his clothes and came into the hut. "You wanted to see me?"

"Yeah," Royal said awkwardly. "I thought we could spend some time together before this conflict happens."

Hue was surprised by Royal's words. He did not know what to say. He began to blush. He walked over to Royal slowly and sat down next to him. For a moment, the two sat next to one another. The tension in the air was thick between them without either of them knowing what to say or do next.

"I just wanted to spend some time with you before any of this happens," Royal admitted.

"We have been spending time," Hue said awkwardly.

"I know," Royal agreed as he traced lines on the floor with his bare foot. "Maybe I wanted a little more than that," he managed to say.

Hue was stunned. He found himself looking at Royal differently. He had always liked him and he had definitely enjoyed their kiss; however, he had never dreamed it would get further than that. He knew that he was more experienced in physical relationships than Royal, but he never imagined that he would be this forward. Hue smiled happily.

"I never imagined," Hue stammered.

"Me neither." Royal said as he reached out and touched Hue's hand. "But with all that is happening, and going to happen, I want to be close to someone. I think I need that."

Hue nodded his head. He was reminded of the days before his mother died and how alone he felt. She hadn't been the only one fighting breast cancer —thewhole family had been fighting it with her. It had taken a toll on all of them in different ways. Hue remembered how much he wished he had someone to be with during that period of time. He desperately wished he would have had a Royal to hold onto during his time of need. Suddenly, Hue forgot about the past he had left behind and focused all of his attention on Royal.

"I am here for you," Hue assured him as he leaned in and kissed his lips.

"I need you," Royal admitted as he pulled Hue close to him.

"I know," Hue said as he hugged him back. "More than I can say."

# Chapter 26

Tildon proudly wore the cloak that Janis had left for him. He emerged from a Gateway at the end of the Lampourian City-State limits. He did not delay. He made his way away from the open plains and through the mountain passage that led to Lampour. He thought he was going to have to figure out away to get past Janis' guards. However, he soon realized that he did not have to. Once they saw his cloak, they all bowed and made way for him. Without asking, he soon had a royal escort all the way to the stone white-walled palace of Lampour.

Tildon made his way through the courtyard leading to the castle proper. The guards at the gate looked at him oddly as he approached. They blocked his way with their spears defiantly. Tildon showed them his cloak, but they still did not budge. He was about to plead his case to them, when a man emerged from the shadows. It was Greson, Janis' most trusted servant. Upon seeing Tildon's wide eyes and the cloak he wore, Greson directed the guards to step aside. Tildon walked into the castle from the courtyard and bowed his head to Greson.

"Greetings, Sir," Tildon began. "I bring a message for Prince Janis."

"You can tell me," Greson said suspiciously as he eyed Janis' cloak, "and I will relay it to him."

Tildon shook his head, no.

"I beg you go, Sir," Tildon said, clearing his throat. "What I have to tell the Prince is for his ears only."

Greson studied the young man before him thoroughly. For a moment, he was unsure of what to do. However, because he wore Janis' cloak and the sincerity of his request, Greson decided to relent.

"Leave your sword at the door and I will see if my master will receive you," Greson said.

Tildon took off his sword and left it at the door. He then followed Greson up a set of winding stairs that led to a long hallway. Greson had Tildon sit on a small chair while he vanished behind a set of blood red drapes. Tildon sat looking around absently at the art in the hallway. He patted his leg up and down impatiently. He recalled Janis' promise to Royal when they had met. However, he had been raised to be suspicious of royals and the motives of their promises. He was sure that his support would come with some price. He just hoped he was smart enough to negotiate his support.

Inside the royal hall of Lampour, Janis sat upon the throne. After the inerlopers had left he had returned to his tedious life of looking out over the affairs of the grandest city-state on the Eastern Continent. He had been doing it so long that it was second nature for him. Though his father, King Brill, was the rightful ruler of Lampour, it was Janis who propped up the throne, which included training Lampour's army. Lampour needed a force that had to be feared. It was the Gateway to the East and most trade for the realm came through Lampour. As such, there was a constant threat to Lampour's safety. Lampour was one of the few city-states that had an active fleet of=air warships. From the window of the palace, Janis could watch them soar. He was proud of his fleet.

Janis returned to his throne. He reached into his fine white clothes and removed an octagon-shaped box. Looking at it, Janis found himself missing the silver case he had given to Royal. It was one of the few things he had from his mother. She was from a remote area of the Eastern Realm. It was from her that Janis had inherited the ability to shift genders. His father had not found out about it until after they were married. Since Lampourians marry for life, there was nothing he could do once they were married. So, aside from being Queen, Kita secretly served as the male general of Lampour's army. In her male form, she protected Lampour well for decades until she was killed in battle with pirates who were trying to take over Lampour's trade routes. All Janis had left of his mother were the small containers she cherished and her weapons.

Janis was about to open the container, when Greson came forward. Janis tucked the case back into his robes and waved Greson forward.

"Your Highness, may I speak with you?" Greson asked as he bowed.

"Ofcourse," Janis said.

"You have a visitor," Greason announced.

"Not now," Janis shook his head "I have dealt with enough for today. You handle them."

"Your Highness, this visitor wears your feathered cloak," Greson explained. "I think it is one of the interlopers you had us watch."

Janis stood up immediately. He straightened his robes and took his crown from beside the throne. He unrolled his pants and put on his slippers. Just then, Altion flew in through the window and wrapped itself around its perch. Janis reached down and gave him a snack. He did not know what he was thinking when he allowed Altion to lead Royal and his allies to the CODA. Altion was his constant companion since he was a child. He could not imagine being without him. He was glad he was back.

"Send him in," Janis directed.

Greson turned on his heels and went out into the hallway to fetch Tildon. Tildon walked down the aisle toward Janis. He fell to one knee before him and bowed his head. Seeing his face, Janis jumped to his feet and ran to him. He lifted Tildon to his feet and hugged him.

Tildon was surprised by his sudden show of affection. Tildon smiled and hugged Janis back.

"I did not think I would be seeing you again," Janis said honestly.

"I would not be here if the young High Prince did not need your help," Tildon said honestly.

"I did what I could," Janis said, hunching his shoulders. "Where are the others?" Janis said with concern. "Are they well?"

"Yes, they are fine," Tildon assured him. "They made it to the Red Desert."

"I am glad to hear that," Janis said with relief.

"The High Prince sent me here because he wanted to take up your offer of assistance," Tildon announced.

"What does he need?" Janis asked slowly.

Tildon was about to explain the situation when he turned and looked at Greson.

"You can trust him," Janis said confidently. "Greson is my eyes and ears. Anything you say to me you can say in front of him."

Tildon slowly explained how they had met Jul when they got to the Red Desert. Then he explained to them about the impending attack from the High Queen. He told Janis that he had been sent here to ask for his help, while Lethia had gone to rally the CODA. Tildon also made it clear to him that the reason why they were preparing to meet the High Queen in battle was to protect the peaceful Arcana from her assault.

"Your Highness," Greson interjected. "We should stay out of this. Lampour has no quarrel with the High Queen. You could be bringing war to your father's kingdom," he advised.

Janis walked back to his throne and sat down. He stared out of the window across from the throne, deep in thought. He did not want to drag Lampour into an all out war with the High Queen. However, he had given his word that he would support the young High Prince. Candidly, he was tired of living his pampered life in Lampour. Helping the High Prince would give him a chance to flex his muscles. He really had no faith in the Avatar; however, he did not like what he was hearing the High Queen do in the name of the Dark God.

"Greason," Janis said as he stood up. "Sound the alert. Summon a full regiment of the Lampourian's obsidian guard."

"Are you sure?" Greason questioned carefully.

"Arm them thouroughly and dress them in mercenary blacks without Lampourian insignias." Janis directed. "And get my armor. I will be leading them into combat."

"The High Queen knows you," Greson advised. "She will see your face and an attack on Lampour is soon to follow."

Janis smiled.

"True, Greason," Janis smiled before he began to transform. "But she has not seen Jane."


Lethia came through the Gateway in the CODA forest. She paused for a moment and looked at the sky. Then she took out the Horn of the CODA that Cree had given her and blew through it. After a few minutes, Lethia heard a rustling in the trees. Then several lines dropped down from out of the trees. Numerous CODA women appeared in the branches and descended the ropes. They were all armed with bows and arrows as well as swords. Once they saw Lethia at the Gateway, they recognized the mythical leader of the CODA immediately. They all fell to one knee in salute. Then Cree and Patel emerged from the thicket. Cree walked up to Lethia and bowed, handing her the sword of authority of the CODA.

"She is coming for him isn't she?" Patel said matter-of-factly.

"Ofcourse," Lethia agreed.

"And you are here to ask us for help," Patel conjectured as she took out one of Lethia's cigars, lit it, and began to smoke. "The elders foresaw this."

"I am Queen, but you and the elders advise me," Lethia explained.

"If we do this," Patel began as she took Lethia by the arm and began to walk her through the forest," there is no going back. We will be at war with the High Queen."

"I know," Lethia agreed. "But it is the right thing to do."

Patel laughed.

"The right thing to do is not always with out reverberations," Patel added.

"What do the elders say?" Lethia asked hurriedly.

"You know for us to act, you have to have all the elders in agreement," Patel explained.

"I am aware," Lethia nodded.

"There is a large force with supplies ready to go through the Gateway," Patel announced as she pointed through the trees. "The rest of the CODA are securing our lands in case the High Queens sees fit to retaliate against us."

"It is the right thing to do," Lethia assured her.

"We will see," Patel said. "While the other elders work to ensure the safety and well being of the CODA. I will be joining you in the Red Desert."

"I would be honored to have you," Lethia said earnestly.

"You think there is room on the front lines for an old lady?" Patel asked as she handed Lethia the cigar.

"There is room enough," Lethia smiled as she took a deep drag of the cigar.

In the middle of the night the Arcana continued to sing and dig at the defensive line they were creating at the cliffside of the Red Desert. Under the guidance of Simon and Wisdom, they continued to dig and spin a wall to protect the line. While they dug and spun webbing, Father Benedito and Ben served the ranks of Arcana and gave them water. Purcell and Reverend Monroe buised themselves by checking the weapons they did have. Purcell showed a few of the Arcana how to hold guns as Reverend Monroe, although strictly taboo, made sure their crystal charged weapons were set. Tori and Etera made bandages and set up a space for those who would inevitably be wounded. Finally, Captain Sarison and Peku were on the boundaries of the encampment keeping watch for attack.

Down in the deserted Arcana village, Jul made his way through the village square to the hut where Hue and Royal had retired. Maximus looked up from his post as the red-robed priest approached. He looked at the hooded man suspiciously and raised his claws until he caught Jul's distinctive scent. Once he was sure who he was, he laid back down. Up in the hut, Hue rested on Royal's bare chest. Hue slipped in and out sleep as he stared at Royal. He had a permanent smile on his face. He still could not believe what had transpired between them. He was about to fade back into slumber, when he felt an odd tug at the edge of his consciousness. It was like someone was gently calling his name inside of his head.

Carefully, Hue got up from where he was lying. Hue quickly put on his clothes. He tiptoed to the doorway of the hut and stuck his head out. He was surprised to see Jul standing beneath the doorway a few feet from Maximus. Jul stepped away from the edge of the hut, then turned and motioned for Hue to join him. At first, Hue did not know what to do. He looked over his shoulder. Royal was still fast asleep. He looked back out Jul. Jul was standing still, patiently waiting for him. Hue climbed down the rope from the hut, stepped over Maximus and joined Jul in the center of the village.

"Is everything okay?" Hue asked with a wrinkled brow as he yawned.

"Yes things are fine," Jul assured him as he placed a hand on Hue's shoulder. "Can I ask you something?"

"Anything," Hue responded.

"How much do you care about my son?" Jul asked bluntly.

The question shocked Hue. His mouth dropped open and he blushed. He was unsure of what to say. In addition, he did not know if he felt comfortable talking to Jul about his feelings toward a son he had just met.

"Why do you ask?" Hue demurred.

"It is important that I know," Jul said. "Before I give you something he might need."

"I care about him very much," Hue responded. "I think I love him."

Jul placed a hand on Hue's chest and closed his eyes. As he felt Hue's heart beat, he felt the sincerity of his words. He smiled.

"Good," Jul exhaled. "We don't have much time."

"Much time?" Hue managed to spit out before Jul grabbed him by the arm. Then the wind and sand began to swirl around them.

It turned into a twister and the two of them vanished in a cloud of smoke. Maximus looked up with sleep-filled eyes to an empty village square. He began to sniff around. He was not sure if something had just happened. Then he laid back down and drifted off back to sleep.

It was morning. Holi made his way through the Grand Citadel to Burton's chambers. He was followed by his Royal Guard, Bilk. They were both dressed in shiny armor and had swords at their sides. Ilson stood outside of Burton's chamber at attention. Bilk stood on the otherside of the door next to Ilson. Holi knocked on the chamber door and waited for his brother to acknowledge him.

"Enter," Burton called.

Holi entered the room. His brother was standing in front of his window, putting on his cape. Holi went up to him and helped him gather the cloth around him. They both turned at the same time to look out of the window. The Royal Guards were amassing in formation in front of the Grand Citadel upon their gorda. In front of them were the few dignitaries who the High Queen had gathered in the Grand Citadel when she announced this campaign. The Marauder came through the archway leading to the Grand Citadel. It was followed by Wisdom's SUV which was being dragged in on ropes by slaves.

"I see our niece is pulling out all the best on this mission," Burton commented.

"I know," Holi agreed as he leaned against the window sill. "I can not remember the last time we were all out of the capital city. Who will be sitting on the throne?"

"She is leaving Elric in charge," Burton told his brother. The two shared a laugh at the expense of the young Royal Guard.

"He barely has hair on his manhood." Holi shook his head. "And he is still growing in stature as a Moritan."

"It is her decision," Burton said. "She is High Queen. For now."

"For now," Holi agreed as he followed Burton from his chambers.

Ela looked down at Quan with concern. She took a damp rag and ran it over his forehead. Since the High Queen had touched him with the Scepter of Monarchs, he had been in and out of consciousness. Ela found it hard to tend to him. She was scared for her mate. He was literally seething with power. It was not the role of the Royal Guard to ever question the High Monarchs, but as Ela was looking at her mate and she found herself wondering if the High Queen was going too far.

"You worry unnecessarily, my love," Quan said as he opened his eyes.

Ela was surprised by Quan's sudden words. She sat on the edge of the bed and stroked his face. He was still her husband, but she could sense the change in him. It was deep in his eyes, the unabiding touch of the Dark God's energy. It was coursing through his veins and empowering him in a way that no Royal Guard had ever been empowered before. Turning him into the assassin cube had not been enough for the High Queen, she had to make him more. As Ela stroked his lupine limb, she wondered if any of them were going to survive this.

"We must dress you," Ela said ignoring her concerns. "The Royal Guard is assembled outside ready to march on the Red Desert and capture Von."

"Then I must rise, so I can lead them," Quan said as he rose from his covers. Ela took a step back as she looked at her mate. He was still the same person, but he was much bigger than he was before. He was literally towering over her. Ela was not even sure if his weapons would fit his hands now. In all of the history of the Moritans, Ela could not recall if there was ever one as big as Quan was now. Ela turned away from her mate, shielded her mind from him, and picked up her long bow and quiver. It was time for her to bring Tisha to the gathering.

Gregor handed the High Queen the Scepter of the Monarchs. She accepted it from his hand and looked at herself in the mirror. She was draped in a yellow tunic that covered her light armor. She decided to take her double axe and wore it over her shoulder. She wore a simple jeweled circulet that identified her station. Though she felt sure of herself and the force she had assembled, she still had to admit that she felt nervous. No matter what the outcome was, she was going to see her son for the first time in what felt like a life time.

"Are you alright?" Gregor asked as he put his hands on her shoulders.

"I am fine" she assured him as she kissed his hand. "But do me one favor?" she asked.

"Anything," Gregor smiled as he took her hand.

"I hate to say it, but I need you to watch both my uncles. I first thought that they were loyal, but as of late I am not so sure," she admitted.

"Have they done something?" Gregor's voice trailed away.

"No, they have been nothing but supportive," the High Queen said anxiously. "They have almost been too supportive. As members of the royal family, I cannot read them. They introduced me to the Dark God at first and raised me when my father was not there."

"I know," Gregor recalled.

"Yet, as of late they have both seemed more guarded than usual and have been talking to one another in whispers," the High Queen explained.

Gregor nodded his head and went up behind the High Queen and hugged her. She leaned back against him and smiled. For a moment, she almost allowed herself to be overtaken by the seductive quality of his hormones. However, she quickedly reminded herself of the task she had before her and cleared her head. She pulled away from Gregor.

"Go now," the High Queen directed him to the secret passageway. "I will meet you outside."

"As you wish," Gregor said as he put on his hood and turned toward the passageway. "Do not worry, Mora. We will be victorious."

The High Queen did not say anything. She simply waited for him to leave. Once the secret passage was sealed, the High Queen took the Scepter of Monarchs and hung it off of her side. She turned and walked out of her chamber. She made her way through the Grand Citadel and out into the courtyard. Once she appeared on the steps, musicians sounded trumpets from above her head. Elric appeared on the steps behind the High Queen, safe in her shadow.

"Hold the High Court until I return and guard my throne," the High Queen commanded.

"All will be well until you return," the young Royal Guard promised.

"I trust you, Elric," the High Queen said as she began to march down the steps. Once she reached the last step, two young Royal Guards fell in line behind her carrying her banners. The High Queen walked down through the legion of Royal Guards upon their gordas. They all bowed their heads to their High Monarch as she passed. The High Queen reached the head of the procession. Quan was seated next to Ela on their gorda with Tisha's gorda in between the two of them. As the High Queen looked at the oddly horned creature, she knew that it predicted this moment.

At the head of the procession, the High Queen passed the members of nobility who she had asked to accompany her. They all sat upon their mounts in the shadow of the Marauder and its hounds. The High Queen got to Wisdom's jeep. It had been polished and adorned with the symbol of the High Queen. She stopped at the door and looked at Tisha. Tisha got up out of the driver's seat and went over to the passenger side. She bowed and opened the door for the High Queen. The High Queen got in the vehicle and raised the Scepter of Monarchs through the opened sun roof. All the riders behind her readied their mounts.

Levan stepped from behind the jeep and went up to the archway that separated the Grand Citadel from the rest of Acara City. He looked up at a crystal on top of the archway and took out his tuning fork. He began to imagine the Eastern Realm, then he pictured the Red Desert in his mind. As he did so he plucked his tuning fork and activated the crystal, a Gateway instantly opened

"Forward," the High Queen commanded Tisha.

Tisha put the jeep in gear and led the procession through the Gateway.

# SIEGE

# Chapter 27

The swirling gust of wind and sand re-appeared in a remote area of the Red Desert. As quickly as it appeared, it dissipated, leaving Jul and Hue standing among the dunes. Hue fell out of the vortex and landed on his behind. He began to spit as he tried to clear the sand from his mouth. He slowly got up from his feet and brushed off his clothes. He kicked off his sneakers and poured the sand out of them. He sighed out loud. He had been trying to keep the bulk of the sand out of his shoes since he had gotten to the Red Desert. Now all of his effort was for naught. Jul walked over to Hue and helped him to his feet. The enigmatic priest was standing there looking at Hue with his purple eyes, his expression was blank. "Okay, dude," Hue said angrily. "Are you going to tell me why you have kidnapped me?"

As if ignoring Hue's question, he simply said, "Time is short."

Then Jul began to walk across the sand. Not knowing what else to do, Hue followed him. They walked for a few minutes until they reached four rock formations sticking out of the sand. The rock formations cast an odd glow across the surface of the sand. Jul went into the center of the formation and reached down into the sand. He quickly began to wipe away some sand to reveal a trapdoor in the ground. Jul opened the door and looked over his shoulder to make sure that Hue was still close by.

"You can't expect me to go down there," Hue protested.

"Would you rather stay up here alone?" Jul said over his shoulder.

"When you put it like that. . ." Hue chuckled as he followed Jul down into the tunnel.

Once they were in the tunnel, Jul reached up on the wall and removed a torch. He whispered a word to the torch and it burst into flames. "Come on, we have a long way to walk."

"I don't suppose you'll tell me where we're going," Hue grumbled.

"You will know when we get there," Jul said flatly as he led Hue down the long tunnel. They began to walk on for hours. They eventually reached a set of stone steps. They descended down through the tight rock tunnel lit by the light of the torch. As they descended, Hue noticed that the heat of the desert was fading away and the tunnel was getting cooler. After some time, the tunnel opened up into a large rock cavern.

Hue was amazed by what he saw. There was a shimmering pool of silver liquid in the middle of the cavern. In the middle of the pool was a large white stone altar. There were several stones leading from the shoreline to the guilded altar.

"What is this place?" Hue asked.

"This is the most sacred place for the priests of the Avatar. When the High Queen Mora decided to exterminate the priests of the Avatar, many of the priests escaped here and returned their life force and knowledge to this pool. I have been the custodian of it since that time," Jul explained.

"Why have you brought me here?" Hue asked with confusion.

"If Royal is going to recapture the throne, he is going to need someone with access to the power and wisdom of this pool to guide him and retrain a new generation of priests for the Avatar," Jul declared.

"That makes sense," Hue agreed." I thought you would be that person"

Jul shook his head, no.

"To be honest Hue, after I was joined with the Avatar and Royal was sired, I was never the same. The kind of power that needs to be harnessed to defeat the High Queen I can no longer muster. I am merely a flicker of the flame I once was," he explained. "I must also admit, I am tired. Living here in the Red Desert and keeping alive has drained me. It is time for me to pass the power I still have and the power on this most sacred place on to the next generation."

"We ll let's come up with a short list or get a set of volunteers," Hue's voice cracked as he suddenly realized the significance of being here with Jul.

Jul laughed as he slapped Hue on the shoulder. Hue did not find anything funny about what he was saying. He was serious.

"I think I have found my successor," Jul said flatly.

Hue's mouth dropped.

"Who do you mean? Me?" Hue laughed out loud.

"Yes, you," Jul said. "I have watched you with Royal. I can see that you truly love him and will not betray him. Like his Royal Guard, you will stand with him against the forces of the Dark God. More than standing with the man you love, you will be working to save an entire planet."

Hue was taken aback by what he was hearing. He stared at the rippling waves of the silver pool. Since coming to Acara, he had wondered why he was there. Perhaps this was the true reason that Royal had fallen from the sky on his Baltimore City lawn. Maybe all of this was in the greater scheme of the Avatar, including his attraction for Royal. Though Hue had taken to going to church, he had never felt like he fit in. It wasn't the fact that he was gay. It was the fact that he felt like he never quite knew what was exciting everyone else. It felt foreign to him. It was hard for Hue to believe in a benevolent diety that had something good for him since it had taken away the thing he loved the most, his mother. But now, as he stared at the pool, he was not so sure. Maybe all the roads of his life had been leading here and to making this choice, to become something greater than himself.

"How will this change me?" Hue asked. "Will it hurt?"

Jul laughed at his candor. He sat down next to Hue and began to open his robes. He revealed a silver gem that was in the center of his chest. It looked like it was made out of the same elements as the pool. It reminded Hue of mercury from science class, except that it was solid instead of a liquid. As Hue looked at it with wide eyes, he could tell that it was pulsating as if it was alive. It was like a human heart, except it was on the outside. Hue could not help himself. He felt drawn to it. He reached out and touched it. The crystal was cool to the touch and seemed to touch him back. It was like greeting an old friend. Hue could feel it vibrating with power. He pulled his hand away.

"In this ritual, the heart stone of the priests of the Avatar will be transferred to you with all the power and knowledge it holds," Jul explained.

"What of you?" Hue asked with concern. "If you give up this kind of power to me, what will happen to you?"

Jul exhaled and looked off toward the ceiling of the cave. He removed his hood and smiled sadly.

"I have lived longer than any man should," Jul said honestly. "I have kept my oath to my god and I lived long enough to see the face of my son. I believe that is enough for any man," he said as a tear fell from his eye. He quickly looked away from Hue and wiped the single tear.

"This shit is impossible," Hue said as he grabbed his head.

"It is," Jul agreed. "Yet it is the choices we are left with. What do you choose?

Hue got up from where he was sitting. He walked to the edge of the pool and looked out at the glorious altar that floated in the middle of it. He thought about all he had experienced since he found out that Royal was from another planet. He also thought about all he had experienced since he had decided to assist him. Most of all, he considered his heart and what he felt for the young High Prince. Then he remembered the words of Royal and how Royal had asked him to be part of his High Court. Royal trusted him. He knew that Royal trusted him enough to take him into his heart and into his bed. He would not let him down; especially not now, with his mother coming to subdue him or worse.

"How do we do this?" Hue asked humbly.

Jul walked up behind Hue and placed both hands on his shoulders. Hue felt himself lifted off of his feet.

"It has already begun," Jul said.

Ben woke up early that morning. He looked around the hut he shared with the other males of his group. They were all still sleeping. He crept from the hut and slid down the line and looked around. The small village was deserted. However, the fire still smoldered in the middle of the village square. Before going to sleep, Ben had decided it was time for him to collect his son and leave this adventure behind. He was a bus driver, not a warrior. And his son had aleady gone through enough in his life with the loss of his mother to be caught up in any kind of world war. Though he had grown attached to the others over the course of their journey, he felt like it was time he took his son and got back to Baltimore City, a simple life of riding his route and taking fares. He did not know exactly how he was going to accomplish this, but he felt like he had to try.

Ben knew that Hue had spent the night with Royal the night before. He really did not have an issue with Hue spending the night with Royal or even them being intimate. Ben's brother had been gay and had left home as a result of it, so he was keenly aware of the need to be a support. He also knew that if his wife were still alive, she would not have had a problem with her son's sexual orientation. Sylvia had been one of the most accepting people he ever met and she loved his brother. She was particularly hurt when he left for parts unknown. It was that trait that had made him love her. Yet he knew that if Hue and Royal had been intimate, getting Hue to agree to leave his side was not going to be easy. There was nothing like your first love. However, as a parent, Ben felt like this situation was far from average and he had to protect his son from danger, and this situation was beyond dangerous.

Ben walked over to the edge of the village. Maximus was still asleep outside of the hut that Royal had taken over the night before. He looked up immediately as Ben approached. Upon seeing him, he did not move and drifted off back to sleep. Ben walked up to the prince of the Manda and stood still. Then he cleared his throat to get Maximus' attention. Maximus looked up from where he was sleeping and licked his canines.

"I need to speak with Hue," Ben announced nervously.

"Hue is not in the hut with Royal," Maximus explained.

"Did he leave to go to the bathroom or something?" Ben asked.

"No," Maximus yawned. "He left the hut sometime this morning. I thought he was in the other hut."

Ben began to get concerned and started to tap his foot.

"No, he never came into the other hut last night," Ben said.

With this statement, Maximus came fully awake, the hairs on his neck stood up defensively, and he got to his feet. He stretched and began to sniff the ground.

"Wait here," Maximus said as he charged toward the village square.

Ben took a deep breath and began to pace back and forth. He had not come this far to lose his son now. As he waited for Maximus to return, Royal stuck his head out of the hut. He was still half-dressed from the evening before. Upon seeing the father of the person he was just intimate with, he began to blush. However, as he looked at Mr. Lee he could tell that there was something more on his mind than what had happened between Royal and his son the night before. Royal quickly retreated back into the hut and finished dressing. Then he slid down the line from the hut and came up next to Mr. Lee.

"Is everything okay?" Royal asked carefully.

"It's Hue," Ben said. "We are not sure where he is." he said flatly.

Royal's stomach sank. The night with Hue before had been perfect. He could not have asked for anything more. Now to hear that he might be missing was more than Royal wanted to consider.

"Maximus is looking for him now," Ben explained.

"I am sure he is around," Royal said hopefully as he licked his lips. They still held the taste of Hue's lips, yet he had an odd sense of forboding.

The two waited patiently under the Acarian suns for Maximus to return. After about fifteen minutes, Maximus came galloping back toward them. Royal reached down and got a bottle of water and fed it to Maximus before he spoke.

"Hue is gone," Maximus said as he wiped the water from his lips. "I looked everywhere. He is not in the village or along the trench that the Arcana dug. His scent vanishes in the middle of the village square."

Royal looked at Mr. Lee and neither of them knew what to say. However, they were both thinking the same thing. They both feared that the High Queen Mora, or one of her operatives, had somehow come into the village and kidnapped Hue. It was a horrible thought.

"The funny thing is, when I lost his scent he was definitely with Jul, and Jul is not anywhere to be found either," Maximus explained.

"Do you think the High Queen has them both?" Ben finally said.

"No," Maximus said, shaking his head. "There are no signs of the Royal Guard or any Dark energy in the village or on the trench. Yet in the place where I lost both of their scents, there is a residue of energy of the Avatar."

"What does that mean?" Ben asked with a squint.

"The only other person who has access to Avatar energy other than me is Jul," Royal surmised. For some reason, he took Hue from our camp."

"Oh great," Ben said as he threw his hands up in the air. "This shit was becoming ridiculous."

"I don't think you have to worry, Mr. Lee," Royal said consolingly. "If Hue is with Jul, there has to be a good explanation. I don't think Jul would hurt him."

"How can you be so sure, Royal?" Ben countered . "You just met the man the other day. I know he is your long lost father and all, but shit, come on. . .he has Hue."

Royal did not know what to say to his point. On one level, Mr. Lee was correct. He had just met his birth father a day ago and had barely had a conversation with him. However, everything that Royal had felt about the Avatar made him feel safe and good. And if Jul was the Last Priest of the Avatar and commanded that energy, he couldn't do anything to hurt someone his son cared about. Could he? Would he? As Royal, Ben, and Maximus stood trying to sort all of this out, Ikin came running up to them.

"High Prince!" Ikin called.

"Not now, Ikin," Royal snapped, beside himself with concern. "I'm trying to deal with something."

Ikin lowered his head.

"I just wanted to tell you that CODA women are coming through the Gateway," Ikin mumbled.

Royal caught himself. He placed a tender hand on Ikin's shoulders and tried to smile.

"I am sorry I snapped at you," Royal apologized. "I'm just dealing with a lot this morning."

"I can understand that," Ikin smiled.

"Tell me something, Ikin," Royal began. "It appears that Jul has vanished with my friend, Hue. You know him better than we do. Do we have anything to worry about?"

Ikin reached up and scratched his head with four of his arms.

"I do not think so," Ikin said reassuringly. "I have known Jul all of my life. And before me, my father knew him. I have known him to be nothing but honorable. If he has taken your companion away, he must have a good reason."

"A good reason," Ben threw up his arms again. "That is real helpful right now," he choked out.

"Okay," Royal exhaled. "One thing at a time," he sighed out loud. "I need to go and see about the CODA troops. Maximus, go and wake my father, Arkon. Tell him about Hue and see what he has to say about Jul. I am going up to the trench." Royal turned to leave butt hen stopped and turned back to Mr. Lee. He went up to him and took his hand.

"No matter what happens, we will find Hue. I promise you that," Royal swore to him.

Ben was surprised by the young man's earnest tone and the look of emotion in his eyes. He could tell that he really felt for his son. He exhaled. The look in Royal's eyes eased his conflict.

"I believe you, Royal," he nodded. "Go on up to the trench High Prince."

Royal smiled to himself. He nodded to Mr. Lee again. Then he took Ikin by one of his eight hands and led him away. Royal and Ikin jogged through the village and up to the cliffside. They went up the ladder to the defensive line that the Arcana had dug. It was filling quickly with the women of the CODA. They organized their bows, arrows, spears, swords and supplies in the trench. They took no notice of Royal or Ikin as they passed among them. Then Royal caught sight of Lethia. She was standing with Patel at the end of the trench. They were supervising the CODA warriors in preparing the defense of the trench and the village of the Arcana.

"Place the spears there!" Lethia directed the troops as Royal and Ikin came up to her.

"You are here!" Royal smiled as he went up to the woman he knew as his Aunt Grace. Even though she had not been wearing her warping crystal for some time, Royal was realizing that she was still the same person who had raised him with Reverend Monroe. She was someone that he could count on. By bring the CODA warriors she had proved herself again.

Caught up in emotion, Royal threw his arms around her to the chagrin of Patel and the other CODA. Lethia let herself be hugged, then she pushed him away briskly.

"War of any kind is never an easy thing," Lethia explained. "We have to be ready. I am sure the High Queen will want to make an example of us. I suggest the Arcana leave immediately. They have done a great job. Now it is time for us to do ours."

"Is there a place where the Arcana can hide?" Royal asked as he turned to Ikin.

"There are caves only known to us," Ikin said as he scratched his head. "I will direct my people to leave immediately."

"What about you Ikin?" Royal asked.

"If it is all the same to you, High Prince, I would prefer to stay," he said as he bowed his head.

"This is no place for an Arcana," Lethia said flatly.

Ikin looked at her and laughed.

"You will discover, CODA Queen, that I am not a typical Arcana. Beside, someone will need to send for my people once the danger has passed and none of you can do that," he said bluntly.

"I will make sure he is protected," Royal offered.

"Are you sure you can guarantee that?" Patel interjected.

"If we can't watch each other's back, then what use is all of this?" Royal answered quickly.

Patel simply nodded her head in agreement. Though she had no respect for men, she was growing to like this young High Prince. He always seemed to know the right thing to say. Though they had been faithful to the Avatar in its project to capture the young High Prince, she gave little thought to his character. Perhaps having him grow under the shadow of the CODA Queen was exactly what he needed to make a true man and monarch out of him after all.

"Royal has already started to build his High Court with those of us who are here with him," Lethia explained to Patel.

"They have proven themselves to me," Royal said. "Who else should I trust?"

"Good answer, young High Prince," Patel said as she eyed Lethia with approval.

"And I know that the CODA do not interact with men," Royal said carefully as he slowly fell to one knee in front of Patel. "But I would gladly have that court include an elder like you as well. I want to build a world where we can all be free and equal."

Seeing the young High Prince salute the CODA elder and hearing his words brought the CODA warriors to a stand still. They could not believe their eyes. It was one thing to ask the CODA for help. It was another thing altogether to ask them to be an intergral part in building a new Acara. Not to mention the fact of having enough respect for their ways and traditions to formally salute their elder. It was unheard of for a High Monarch to do so. The CODA women mumbled amongst themselves. They were truly impressed and imboldened by Royal's action. Silently, they swore they would hold the line for this new monarch to the last woman.

"Rise, High Prince," Patel said as she reached out and took Royal's hand. She could not remember the last time she had touched a man. It felt awkward to her. "If you continue to prove yourself as you have been, and the other elders agree, I would be glad to serve this new world," she said as she helped him to his feet.

"An Acara for all people!" Lethia said as she raised her sword to the cheers of the CODA women behind her.

"Okay," Royal exhaled. He felt like he had jumped another hurdle successfully. "Now we just need to figure out where Hue and Jul were."

"What happened to them?" Lethia asked.

Royal quickly filled the Queen of the CODA and Patel in on Ben's and Maximus' discovery. They looked at each other oddly as Royal turned to leave with Ikin.

"What do you think that means?" Lethia asked Patel.

"It is hard to say," Patel admitted. "The priests of the Avatar are good but secretive in their worship of the Avatar. If Jul has taken Hue, I am sure it has something to do with the Avatar."

"I only hope whatever it is, Hue survives it," Lethia said with a scowl.

Ben Lee went back to the hut where the other men were. By the time he climbed inside, they were awake. The men looked up from their conversation as he entered. From the look on his face, they could tell that something was wrong. Reverend Monroe rushed to him and placed a consoling hand on his shoulder.

"What is it?" Reverend Monroe asked carefully.

"It is Hue," Ben announced. Then he explained that Hue was missing and that it appeared to them that Jul had something to do with his disappearance. The men were shocked. They all sat still, frozen in the truth of the information. No one knew exactly what to say or to do.

"I never trusted that red-robed freak," Captain Sarison said as he got to his feet. "Let's organize a search party and find where Hue is!" said the captain, surprised by his words. He had grown to like the young man. He did not care much for his relationship with Royal, but he had seen that many times before in his life. He knew that if Hue was missing, Royal would be distracted. And with the High Queen coming, this was not a time for idle distractions. The captain wrinkled his brow and patted his sword. Hue had to be found and quickly.

"No," Tori raised his hands. "Jul is a good man. I am sure of it. He is the last priest of the Avatar. If he took Hue, he had to have a good reason. We should trust him."

"Trust him?" Ben said. "We don't really know anything about him. Do we even know if he is who he says he is? I mean, my God, what kind of people are you? A guy shows up in a red robe and proclaims he is the second coming of Christ and you all fall in line! I don't even know if he has a last name. What kind of name is Jul away?" he snapped. "Sounds shady to me. And those freaky purple eyes. I mean, do we even know if those are real?"

"Mr. Lee," Simon began, consolingly. He could tell from the man's conversation that he was nearly hysterical. "I know you are concerned, but I believe Jul to be the real thing. There has to be have a good reason for his actions. We just have to figure out what they are."

"Do we even have time for that?" Wisdom cut Simon off "I mean, the High Queen will be here sooner instead of later. We gotta be ready."

"I hear you, baby bro," Purcell interjected. "But they are both important. Remember Hue is not just a young man. He is a special young man, but he is still on another planet. It is our responsibility to protect him."

"I been doin' that," Wisdom assured his brother. "I even gave him a gun and showed him how to shoot."

"What!" Ben snapped. He was livid "You gave my son a gun. Are you crazy?"

"I had to do something," Wisdom explained. "He was almost eaten by a plant! I wanted him to feel like he could take care of himself."

"Oh shit!" Ben said as he grabbed his head. "I think I'm gonna be sick."

"You really aren't helping," Pekua\ mumbled under his breath to Wisdom.

"Here," Reverend Monroe said as he helped Ben to his feet. "Let me take you for a walk."

Reverend Monroe and Ben Lee left the small hut and went into the village square. The others watched in silence as they left. Once they were gone, they quickly picked up the conversation.

"A gun, Wisdom?" Purcell said, shaking his head. "What were you thinking?"

"I was thinking that Hue needed to protect himself," Wisdom countered. "You and all your good intentions weren't here to protect nobody," Wisdom snapped as he pushed past his brother and left the hut.

"You need to take it easy on your brother," Tori said. "He has been protecting Royal and Hue since they arrived. He may not be a Royal Guard, but he surely acts like one. More than protecting them, he has been advising Royal; wisely, by my estimation. Remember he is both plagued and gifted with a shade. Without which, I do not think any of us would have been as successful as we have been."

"Ah, I agree with the sightless one," Captain Sarison said as he walked up to Purcell. "I do not know who your brother was, but I have fought beside him and I find him true," he said as he turned to leave the hut.

"Come, Peku," Tori said as he rose to his feet. "We have work to do."

Peku grabbed Tori's hand and led him out of the hut, leaving Purcell alone with his thoughts. As Purcell stood there thinking about his brother, Father Benedito came back into the hut. He had been out preparing breakfast during the earlier conversation.

"Is everything okay? Todoestabien?" he asked carefully.

"I don't know" Purcell said as he rubbed at his temples. "I just don't know."

Captain Sarison stole a moment away from the others. He was near the Gateway that the CODA had come through hours earlier. He looked out at the village of the Arcana below. He shook his head. If he had his ship and his men, he could make a fortune from the raw webbing that it took to construct this place. He turned away from it and dismissed his thinking. In his years at sea, he had tried to sail under the radar of the High Queen and her forces. Thus far, he had done a good job at staying away from her. Now he was running headfirst into a conflict with her. He found himself wondering if he would sacrifice his life for his own honor.

"Captain Sarison," Peku said as he ran up to the man.

"I would rather be alone," Captain Sarison grunted.

"Even for wine?" Peku said.

"Wine?" Captain Sarison said with a raised eyebrow. "Why did you not say so?" he laughed. "Pull up a rock."

The Opion settled down next to Captain Sarison and dropped a flask from his mouth. He pushed it with his nose up to Captain Sarison. Captain Sarison picked up the flask and examined it suspiciously.

"It seems the Arcana can do more than spin twine," Peku said as he jumped around waving his tail.

Captain Sarison took off the top of the container and took a swig. He was surprised by the flavor and texture of the brew. It was a rare delicacy. It was real good.

"Ikin looked at you and he gave this to me to share with you," Peku said.

"I am starting to like that little Arcanan," Captain Sarison laughed as he put an arm around Peku. "Let us toast, my friend."

"To what?" Peku asked.

"To the good fight and those of us who are about to die," the Captain of the *Lucky Lady* said as he took a deep drink and handed the flask to Peku. Peku looked at the man oddly, then took the flask into his hands and drank. As they sat up on the cliff drinking, they felt the Gateway begin to rumble. It was being activated from the other side.

Captain Sarison rose to his feet, drew his sword, and pushed Peku behind him. However, the first mount to emerge through the Gateway was Tildon's. He was followed quickly by another steed that carried Princess Jane. Behind the two of them, in lines of two dressed in lightweight black fighting gear was the elite guard of Lampour. Though it must have been brutal under the intense suns of the Arcana desert, they were dressed in light black to disguise their true allegiance. After the rows of fighters came through, they were followed by wagonloads of supplies. All Captain Sarison could do was smile. To his surprise, it seemed as if the Prince/Princess of Lampour was being true to his/her word. As he took measure of her force, he found himself wondering if death was indeed a certainty.

The CODA women made room for the troop from Lampour to move into the shade of the gap created by the Arcana. The force from Lampour was largely male, though there were some senior female officers in their ranks. The CODA women looked at each other oddly as the seasoned warriors from Lampour fell into a tight formation with their weapons. Unlike the CODA, the Lampourians ignored their allies and went about the business of setting up for battle. Seeing this break in the CODA troops, Lethia rushed into the gap.

"CODA!" Lethia raised her voice and her swords. "Hold the line!" she commanded.

The wild women of the CODA immediately fell back into formation beside their awkward allies. Princess Jane and Tildon walked up to

Lethia. Tildon was surprised at how good he felt. He never thought that for a moment he would ever believe that a High Royal could do any good; especially after what had happened to his twin, Etera. But, his attitude was beginning to change. As Tildon looked around, he knew that it would take a rare spirit to get the CODA to fight with anyone other than women. He guessed that Royal was turning out to be that rare spirit. In addition, he had an odd feeling about Princess Jane. He knew what she was, though he did not fully understand the secrets of how it worked. At first it had made him feel odd. However, the more he was around her and watched the way she commanded her troops, the better he felt about her. As they traveled at full gallop to the Gateway, he found himself having pride in wearing her cloak. It was a new feeling for him.

Tori and Etera busied themselves by preparing and organizing supplies. They filled gourds with water and wine from the secret supply chamber of the Arcana. They also folded bandages and organized a space for any of their troops that would undoubtedly be wounded inbattle. They were overjoyed when word reached them that Tildon had returned with Princess Jane and that she had brought additional healing remedies and sutures with her.

As the two of them organized their makeshift triage station, they sang old folk songs. They each were surprised that during their mutual times of exile that they both had protected their sanity by singing to themselves. When Etera was in the Flasion mines, it was these songs of her youth that kept her spirits up as she watched countless younglings be abused and dying around her. For Tori, singing had been the initial balm he used to soothe the loss of his eyes and a great deal of his soothsaying abilities. While he still retained reminants of his previous glory, he was nothing like he had been before. His 'sight' was choppy and his other skills were minimal. Prior to losing his eyes, he did not realize how much he had relied on both his sight and his gifts. When the High Queen took his eyes, she not only stripped him of his honor and power, she shattered his identity; something he had spent a lifetime grooming. As he folded bandages and sorted tonics, he found himself missing his past glory. He knew it was vanity, but he missed his abilities anyway.

As the two of them sang childhood lullabies, they were each fighting off their own fears about facing the High Queen. They both knew firsthand the kind of evil and abuse she was capable of. They could only imagine what she would be like on the battlefield when she was fighting for something she really wanted, like Royal and Simon. And they both knew that she wanted Royal more than she wanted anything else. Understanding her thirst for her son and with the previous failures to retrieve him, they each knew that this was not going to be a little skirmish. Blood would inevitably be spilled on both sides. The history of Acara was full of wars by rival city-states and ambitious royals. It was for this reason the High Monarchy was created. However, no one knew of a time when members of the High Royal family got into a skimmish. There was too much power in their ranks to court such disaster.

"Do you think we are going to get through this?" Etera asked Tori.

"I do not know," he said as he shook his head. "I believe in the Avatar and the young High Prince but I know what the High Queen is capable of. I fear that other than Lethia, no one else does," he said as he rubbed nervously at the bandages that covered his eyes.

"I wish there was more water here," Etera said as she touched the ground. "I would have more power to help. There are not even clouds in the sky," Etera observed as she looked up.

"But your sight is still strong," Tori smiled. "I can feel that about you."

"But I am not trained like my grandmother was," Etera sighed as she folded another bandage.

"I can help you with that," Tori offered.

"You can?" Etera smiled.

"I was first and foremost a soothsayer. I was trained since I was a child to be able to have mindsight. I would be honored to help you," Tori explained as he sat his weary bones down. "Besides, I need to pass on what I know to someone before I die."

Etera covered her ears and shook her head.

"Do not say such things," Etera snapped.

"Death is part of life, child. What frees you is being able to face that which is inevitable," Tori explained.

"Maybe I have seen too much death," Etera said as tears formed in her eyes. "My parents, maybe my grandmother, people at the mines..."

"But you have survived," Tori reasoned. "And not only because of your powers, but because of who you are. The Avatar must have a purpose for you."

"I can only pray," Etera smiled as she wiped at her eyes.

Just then, Royal appeared in the area set aside for the wounded. Etera was surprised at how he looked. She was used to a lightness and joviality in his step, but Royal appeared frazzled and out of sorts. Etera dropped what she was doing and went up to him and sat him down. She took his hand in hers and cradled it gently.

"Are you okay?" Etera asked Royal.

"I will be fine," he assured her. "I came here ask you and Tori for help."

"Anything," Tori said as he moved in the direction of the voices.

Royal then told them that Hue and Jul were missing. He wanted to ask them if either of them could use their sight to find out where they were. Etera looked at Tori.

"It is better if we try together," Tori reasoned. "The Red Desert is like no other place on Acara. If Jul has taken Hue into the bowels of the desert, it will take all of our sight to be able to find them, and to break any veil."

"I will follow your lead," Etera said.

"Come, take my hands," Tori offered.

Etera sat down next to Tori and took the old man's hands into her own. He gripped them tightly. Then slowly the two of them began to breathe together. After a few minutes, their hearts and minds were in synch. For a moment, there was nothing but light and sand in their mind's eye. Then after a few minutes they began to get pieces of a vision. They felt that Hue was definitely with Jul. They also could sense that some ceremony was being preformed but that was all they saw before their minds were brought back. They quickly reported what they saw to Royal. Royal did not know what to make of what they said. At the least he could tell Hue's father that he was still alive.

"Thank you," Royal said as he rose to leave. He wanted to say more to them, but he did not know what to say. He simply left the triage area to find Mr. Lee.

"Did you recognize that ceremony?" Etera asked Tori.

"No, I did not," Tori said honestly. "But I felt that it was very ancient. Maybe as old as Acara itself"

"Why would Jul be doing a ritual with Hue?"

"That, my dear, maybe the greatest mystery of all," Tori admitted as he turned back to his bandages.

While the others ate lunch, Wisdom and Purcell unpacked the weapons that Purcell had brought from Earth and the remaining artillery that Wisdom had left. They set up a station for themselves next to a rock formation that was just behind the trench. It was near a glorious tent that the Arcana had woven for the High Prince just before they left. Since the two groups had joined, the Sims brothers had not really had anytime to talk to each other alone. Purcell explained to his younger brother about their journey from Baltimore City to New York to get the Gateway crystals. He also told him how they defeated the Marauder there and eventually made the jump to Acara. Purcell also gave Wisdom updates on his son and grandmother. Wisdom was relieved to know that his son was alright. Hearing about his son and the courage of his grandmother made Wisdom even more strident about rescuing Tisha.

Once Purcell finished, it was Wisdom's turn to give updates. He explained to his brother about their time on the Lost Islands. He told his brother how Lethia had had gone into the ground and healed herself and how he had taken down the huge tree. He demonstrated to Purcell how the sap of the tree had changed him by using a knife against his skin. Purcell was astonished to see that his brother's skin would not break. Then, for the first time, Wisdom admitted something to his brother that he had thought he never would. He told him that he had killed Malik Jones, his former mentor in the drug dealing industry. Purcell was not surprised by this admission. He had assumed it. However, Wisdom went on to tell him how his actions against Malik had bound the two of them together spiritually. Now Malik was his shade and how, such, he had served them. In addition to giving Purcell updates, Wisdom told his brother about how serving Royal had changed his spirit and how he wanted to be more like his big brother; someone his son could be proud of. Hearing this, Purcell pushed the hand grenades he was holding aside and wrapped his arms around his little brother.

"I never wanted anything but that for you," Purcell smiled.

"I guess I had to want it more for myself," Wisdom admitted as he accepted his brother's embrace.

"This is good to see," Malik said as he appeared out of the corner of Wisdom's right eye. "When I was alive I tried to be a father to

Wisdom, but all the time I knew I couldn't. You can't form that kind of relationship when its polluted by sex, drugs and money. I am happy you two have found each other again. It almost makes dying worth it," he joked.

"Thanks for keeping my brother safe," Purcell said sincerely.

"Other than for shooting me, I guess Wisdom wasn't all that bad," Malik said with a wink.

"Fuck you," Wisdom snarled as he reached out to hit Malik on the shoulder, forgetting for a moment that he was a ghost. Wisdom's hand passed through Malik and he almost fell over. Once again, his big brother steadied him. "Do you have anything for us?" he asked as he regained his composure.

"Yeah," Malik said. "I almost forget with all this brotherly love. The High Queen is coming with an army this time. Mostly, Royal Guard, a Marauder, and a host of other muthafuckers. Her forces have already come through a Gateway on the otherside of the grind. She could not get through the Gateway here because of her dark magic. Blah.Blah.Blah," he said as he hunched his shoulders. "Don't ask me how I know that last little bit, I just got a feeling. At the rate they are moving, they will be here by morning."

Wisdom and Purcell shot each other a tense glance.

"And Tisha is with her," Malik added as he began to fade.

"It's on now," Wisdom said as he rubbed his hands together.

"It sho' 'nuf is," Purcell said as he reached into one of his bags and pulled out two bullet-proof vests. They both said "POLICE" across the front. As Purcell helped Wisdom strap his on, he looked down at the word and smiled. He wore it proudly.

"I got to get this information to Royal," Wisdom said as he turned to leave.

"Yeah," Purcell said as he stopped fussing with the straps.

"I am proud of you," Purcell said." I really am"

Hearing this, all Wisdom could do was smile. He turned to leave under the watchful eyes of his brother. As Purcell turned his attention back to their weapons, he felt for the first time that his younger brother was no longer in his shadow and it felt good.

Simon sat near the tent that the Arcana had erected for Royal. He was holding the arrow that he and Tisha both wore. Besides the words brought to him and Royal earlier from Wisdom, he was sure that Tisha was coming. He got up from where he was sitting and went into the tent. Royal was there with his father, Reverend Monroe, and Lethia. The members of the house of Monroe were together once again.

"It seems as if a lifetime has passed since we have all breathed the same air together." Lethia mused.

"The Avatar has brought us back together to save Acara," Reverend Monroe said as he reached out and touched Royal's face. "In front of you all, I want to apologize to my son for not being truthful with him since birth. He is truly a great young man and he deserved at least that from me"

"No," Royal countered, cutting him off. "I see now that you did what you had to do. All roads have led us to this point, the beginning of a new High Court for Acara. With the dawn, we take the first bold steps," Royal said with weariness in his voice.

"And I swear to you, Royal," Simon began as he bowed before him,"I will be the first of your Royal Guards and we will protect a new throne built on the light of truth and the Avatar."

"It begins here," Lethia said with pride as she reached down and picked up a handful of the red sand and let it fall between her fingers, "where life on Acara began."

Royal thought about all that was being said. Then he looked up into the sky. It was twilight. The twin suns of Acara were setting on the horizon. Looking at these life-giving orbs, Royal had an idea.

"Simon, bring Ikin to me," he said quickly.

Simon did not question the directive. He simply slipped from the tent. Lethia and Reverend Monroe looked at each other oddly, but did not say anything. After a few minutes the young man appeared before him. Royal got up from where he was sitting and pulled Ikin aside. For a moment, the two spoke in whispers. Then Ikin bowed his head and ran from the enclosure.

"Are we ready for the morning?" Royal turned to Lethia.

"As ever we will be," Lethia said as she took out a cigar and lit it. "Princess Jane is a welcome addition to the CODA. Our numbers are many. I think we will truly surprise your mother."

"Not to mention the weapons that Purcell brought with him." Reverend Monroe reminded them. "The Royal Guard has never encountered bullets and grenades."

"Good," Royal said finally. "And there is still no word about Hue and Jul ?"

Lethia, Simon and Reverend Monroe looked at one another then shook their heads, no. Royal sighed and lowered his head.

"I think I will retire for the evening. So I am at full strength for tomorrow," Royal announced.

"We must protect you," Simon interjected. "No one expects you to be in battle. We all have trained for this Royal, you have not."

"It does not matter," Royal said. "I am not going to sit on my thumbs in the shadows while others put their lives on the line for me. That is not the kind of High Prince I will be."

"But Royal. . ." Simon protested.

"No," Royal said firmly, shutting him down. "With the powers I have, and with you and Wisdom beside me, I should be fine. No— I will be fine," he said with assurance.

"I think Simon has a point," Lethia argued.

"This is not open to debate. Find me some armor and I will stand ready to defend the grind," Royal said and turned to Reverend Monroe. "Like David before Goliath, the battle will begin with me throwing the first stone."

Reverend Monroe could not say anything in the face of his son's good reason or his Bible reference. Just then, Ikin came back under the tent with a piece of finely wovencloth under his arm. Royal took it from his hand and unrolled it. The cloth bore a likeness of the twin suns of Acara, Idris and Itor.

"Well done, my little friend," Royal complimented.

"I try," he said as he stepped aside.

"The suns of Acara give it life, just like on Earth. Therefore, we will fly this standard over the trench. Though we may be at war, I come to improve life for all Acarians," Royal swore as he ran his fingers over the cloth.

"If you are resolute on fighting tomorrow, then I want to see you to your quarters," Simon said. "This maybe your last night of peace for a very long time."

Royal did not say anything to this. He simply followed Simon out of the tent. He did not want to remind him of all the nightmatres he had had leading up to this point. He also did not want to reveal that he would only be able to rest when Hue was returned to his side. As he walked through the trench, Ikin followed him and hoisted the first banner over the camp. The combined forces of Lampour and CODA cheered with approval. All Royal could do was smile, however, in the back of his mind he found himself wondering how many of these good people would find their blood on the sand.

Reverend Monroe watched Simon, Royal, and Ikin left before turning back to Lethia.

"Well?" Reverend Monroe asked.

"Well? What?" Lethia said simply to be annoying as she smoked her cigar.

"What do you think of our boy?" Reverend Monroe asked honestely.

Lethia thought about all that had happened over the last few suns and all she had seen before answering,

"Honestly, he does not sound like a High Prince anymore," Lethia said. "He sounds like a High King."


Royal looked up from the Arcana village at the line of troops from Lampour and the CODA warriors. They had filled in the trench tightly and were bunked down for the night. Huge torches were lit along the trench illuminating the line. Royal had never been responsible for anything like this before. He was relying heavily on Princess Jane's and Lethia's expertise in terms of waging this battle. If it came down to war with his mother, the High Queen Mora, he would rely on them to lead his troops. He felt comfortable with that.

As Royal went to his hut, he was feeling the enormity of the task in front of him. As he looked up at the darkened doorway, he sighed out loud. He wished that Hue were here with him. No one seemed to understand why his birth father had taken his intimate friend away. And with the High Queen's troops coming, they really did not have time to worry about Hue. It was a luxury he could not entertain right now. All he could do is hope and pray Hue was all right and return to him after this skirmish was over.

"High Prince Royal?" Father Benedito said as he came up to him from behind.

"Yes, father?" Royal smiled weakly. "What can I do for you?" he sighed.

Father Benedito smiled and walked up to Royal and took his hands caringly in his own. He looked into the young High Prince's face with tears in his eyes. He nodded his head up and down.

"I have watched you today," the priest began. "I do not know much about this world, but I do know a little bit about people, verdad. And you, young man, should be very proud of yourself."

Royal was taken aback by the sincerity of the priest's words. He did not know what to say. Then he bent down and put his face in his hands and began to sob softly. Royal was not exactly sure why he was crying. He did not know if it was the unexpected nature of the compliment or just the fatigue of the entire experience. Father Benedito walked up to Royal and placed a hand on his shoulder.

"Do not cry, my young friend," he said softly. "I can not know what it is like to have the weight of a world on your shoulders.,no. But I know that your faith in this thing you call the Avatar and Our Savior must be strong to have carried you this far."

"It is all I have left," Royal said candidly. "Especially without Hue here. I am running on fumes."

"Then maybe I have a reason for being here after all," Father Benedito smiled.

"What do you mean?" Royal asked.

"If you allow me," Father Benedito said as he pointed to Royal's hut. "I put something in there for you."

"For me?" Royal questioned.

"Venga. Come," Father Benedito said.

Royal followed the Catholic priest up the line into his hut. He was surprised to see a small table set with a loaf of bread and a simple glass of wine. Royal went up to the table and sat down immediately. He closed his eyes and began to pray for all those on the line, for himself, for those who advised him, for Hue, and finally, for himself. As he prayed, Father Bnedito washed his hands in a separate basin of water and wiped them.

"Venga," the priest said as he reached out and held Royal's hands. "You are a reverend, too, in your own denomination. Let us consecrate this table together."

Royal reached out and took the priest's hands.

"But we're of different faiths?"

"Ah, but in His house, we are all the same. Lo mismo," the priest reminded him.

Royal bit down hard on his lip and nodded his head in agreement.

"Then let us begin," Royal said as they both lowered their heads in prayer.

# Chapter 28

Reluctantly, Tisha drove the jeep through the trees until they receded, giving way to the open plains. The High Queen sat next to her in the passenger seat, giggling like a child as they moved across the plains. Looking at her, she reminded Tisha of the first time she had taken Little Wisdom on a car ride. There was an abosulte joy she was getting from the motion. However, as Tisha looked at the woman sitting with the Scepter of Monarchs at her side, she reminded herself that she was not a child at all. They soon reached the far side of the cliffside of the grind. Carefully, Tisha stopped several feet from the edge. The view from this side of the grind was breathtaking. Tisha had never seen anything like the Great Rift before. It reminded her of a smaller version of the Grand Canyon. Looking at the natural splendor, Tisha got sad. It was such a shame that a placeof such beauty was about to be the site of a grand battle.

Tisha waited on the edge of the cliff until the rest of the High Queen's forces caught up to them. It amazed Tisha how fast the High Queen's forces moved. It was true, the gordas that carried the Royal Guard and the mounts that pulled their supplies moved like a finely-oiled machine. They were regimented and fast as they traveled in lines of two, carrying the High Queen's banner high overhead. The High Queen's banner was simply a black flag with a gold crown on it. Looking at it, Tisha felt as though it was a symble of doom. She had no idea how Royal and the others were going to face this elite force. Silently, in her mind she found herself praying to the Avatar for assistance and guidance. Though she went to church, Tisha had never been big on prayer. She guessed circumstances made you evolve.

--Now you are thinking like a true Moritan, Aspion laughed in the back of Tisha's mind.

--I don't know about being a Moritan, but I am really scared for the others, Tisha admitted,--This bitch is not playing. She has come to take them out.

--The closed fist may look strong, but it still cannot crush a pebble, Aspion mused—Nothing happens in this game by accident or error. Do not get caught up in what you see, only hold on to what you believe--he said as his voice faded from Tisha's mind.

For a moment, Tisha had the crazy idea of hitting the accelerator and driving the SUV over the side of the grind. It would surely kill her and the High Queen, making way for Royal to become the next High King. Perhaps she would have done it, if she was not carrying Simon's unborn child. She no longer had only herself to think of. She had Little Wisdom to consider as well as Dewa. Not to mention the fact that she knew that her suicide would shatter Simon. Tisha eased her foot back from accelerator. She would bide her time and listen to Aspion. Instead of rash action she would have faith.

"Are you with me Little Flower?" the High Queen asked as she looked at the grind.

"I am here," Tisha said as she snapped to attention.

"Good," Mora said with a smile. "We are almost there. This is not the spot, but we are close."

"What do you want me to do?" Tisha asked.

"Drive along the edge of the grind. I will tell you when to stop," she commanded.

Tisha put the SUV in gear and began to drive carefully along the edge of the grind. The High Queen had Tisha drive along the edge of the cliff until they reached the deserted village of the Arcana that connected the two sides of the canyon. Under the direction of the High Queen, Tisha drove Wisdom's black SUV to the edge of the cliff side with the procession of solidiers behind her.

The High Queen opened the door of the jeep and stepped outside. She looked across the canyon towards the trench that the Arcana had dug. She grimaced as she caught sight of Royal's flag flying high over the enclosure. She could not believe that he had the audacity to raise a banner. Who did he think he was? The High Queen felt as if her lost son was beginning to take himself entirely too seriously. She sighed out loud. It was time to put him and those who dared follow him back into their places. As she stood there grimacing at the flag, the rest of her war party took up position behind her. Quan came lumbering forward, waiting for her command.

Without looking at him, the High Queen said, "Tell the division to set up camp on this side of the divide."

"As you command," Quan bowed as he turned to fulfill her orders. Quan's steps were labored under the weight of dark gifts that his charge had given him. However, no matter how fatigued he was, he would carry out her orders without delay. He had failed her before. He would not fail her again.

"Quan?" The High Queen called to him, stopping his forward motion. He turned to face his monarch.

"Make sure my banner flies high above the camp," she insisted.

"I will raise it myself." Quan bowed as he stepped away.

The members of the Royal Guard and the rest of the High Queen's hand-picked assault force took up position on the far side of the grind. They began to unfurl tents and lay out weapons, preparing for their assault. As the camp began to take form, the High Queen raised a personal enclosure for herself on the back quarter of the camp. While the rest of the Royal Guard prepared for battle, she summoned her uncle, the High Prince Burton to her. Ilson, Burton's Royal Guard, took up position outside of the tent while the High Prince entered his niece's dwelling. He bowed to her and waited to be summoned to her. She looked up from a meal and waved him close.

"Burton, it is still my desire to get the young High Prince by myside more than anything else. That is my goal," she began.

"I understand," he agreed, hiding his true feelings from his niece's prying eyes.

"Though all those whohave aligned with him will pay with their lives, I do not want him to know that," she explained.

"I see," he was non-committal with his comments.

"Go into the village below under the white flag of honor. Tell the interlopers that I seek an audience with my son before this campaign begins," she said to Burton's surprise. He was not used to his niece being diplomatic.

"It is not for me to question you," Burton stumbled on his words. "But do you think this is wise?"

The High Queen raised an eyebrow and rose to her feet. Burton took a step back unconsciously as he saw her reach for the Scepter of Monarchs.

"Uncle," she exhaled, "do not question me. Need I remind you that we are here partly because you failed me before? I have my reasons," she said flatly.

Seeing the look on the High Queen's face, Burton knew not to test her resolve. He simply bowed and stepped back from her.

"As you wish," he assured her as he left the tent.

Once he was gone, the High Queen returned to her meal of fresh fruits and hot meat. Behind her there was a shift in the tent's flaps and Prince Gregor stepped out of the shadows. He crossed the expanse of the tent, bowed to his lover and took up a position at the small table next to her. Mora did not look at him at first. Then she carefully shoved her plate in front of him. For a moment, the two lovers shared a meal in silence enjoying each other's forbidden company. As they finished eating, Prince Gregor sat back in his chair and wiped his mouth. He reached out and took Mora's hand in his to get her attention.

"I hate to say it," he confessed, "but I do not trust your uncle."

Mora looked at her lover's yellow eyes and laughed.

"The reason that both Burton and Holi are here, my dear, is because I, too, have my doubts about their agendas," she said flatly. "My uncle works too hard to hide his thoughts from me. He does not realize that that tells me there is indeed something there I must be leary of. Though I have loved both of them like parents, I would have no problem with dispatching either one of them," she assured Prince Gregor. "They are here only as long as they serve a purpose."

"If you don't mind me asking," he began, "why is it that you want to meet with your son? Would it not be better to simply attack and subdue him?"

"Perhaps if he was in any locale other than the Red Desert, yours would be an easier plan," she explained. "The Red Desert is a realm sacred to the Avatar. My dark gifts and those of the dark priests are strained or useless there." She paused. "Besides, Gregor, I would still try and reason with my offspring. I would like our first meeting to not be at the edge of a sword or lance."

Prince Gregor rose from the table and leaned in and kissed his lover. The High Queen reached up and ran her fingers over his blue skin. She smiled at her lover.

"As ever, you astound me with your wisdom," he said as he vanished out of the back of the tent. The High Queen sat for a moment alone listening to the Royal Guard settle in all around her. She got up from where she was sitting and gathered her robes around her. She went over to the mouth of the tent and opened the flap. She stared across the encampment that had sprung up around her. She looked across the expanse at the trench where she knew her son and his allies had settled in. Though to the naked eye there was little movement, however she could feel the presence of her enemies. She smiled to herself as she caught sight of the huge Marauder and its hounds at the head of encampment. It was just a matter of time now.

"My fucking Jeep!" Wisdom mumbled as he watched his black SUV pull up to the edge of the grind. He could not believe that the High Queen had commandeered his wheels and was using it. Angrily, he trudged back through the trench past the warriors from Lampour and the CODA. He went to the back of the camp where Royal was gathered with the others. They were in conference about the size and scope of the enemy they were facing. Wisdom could tell that they were trying to be positive, but the overall mood was grim.

"Cree has finished scouting the force we are facing," Lethia told them. "And it is an entire legion of Royal Guards, a few Dark Priests, and a Marauder," she explained. "I have to tell you that I knew the High Queen would come in force but I did not expect all of this."

"I know those guys are big and armored and all," Purcell interjected. "But I brought enough ammunition with me to take out a city block. They have never faced that kind of firepower before. It should give us an edge."

"I do not know what that means, Purcell," Princess Jane said as she took a bite of fruit," but I have studied the tactics of the Royal Guard. They move like a heavy mallet. The warriors of Lampour rely on trickery and stealth in battle. We have defended our shores against greater numbers before and lived to tell the tale."

"And we also have a Gateway right here," Reverend Monroe reminded them. "If necessary, we can get everyone through it and avoid this confrontation."

"Just like a man," Patel snapped. "The CODA have committed to this endeavor and though we are outside of our element, we do not run and hide like a bush mite in the forest. If need be, I can send for more CODA to stand with the young High Prince. The elders of the CODA follow the will of the Avatar and if we die in its service, it will be a glorious death."

Hearing these words, the reality of the confrontation weighed in on Royal's shoulders. He sighed to himself as he thought about all the young souls that filled the shaded trench the Arcana had dug. He also thought about what could possibly happen to the peaceful Arcana if he disserted them and they were discovered by his mother. Seeing the weight of the situation on him, Simon went up to Royal and placed a reassuring arm around him. He knew that no matter what he decided to do, he would not leave his side. He had been separated from him once before and he had managed to find his way back to his side. Now that they were together again, he would defend him with his life.

"Do not worry, Royal," Simon said reassuringly. "No matter what, you will make the right decision. I believe in you."

"I really don't want anyone to die unnecessarily," Royal admitted with shaking hands. Sure, he had learned about war growing up being home schooled on Earth, but this was the real thing and any decision he made could cost someone he knew their lives. It was an impossible situation.

"Stand fast, High Prince," Lethia directed with a scowl as she saw him begin to waver in fear. "Life without honor is death. Death fighting for what you believe in is the only true life worth living. Unlike many of the others, I know how you were raised. Find solace in your faith and proceed with honor," she advised him. "Have a backbone or the High Queen will not have to kill you. I will snap your neck. You were raised to have honor. I will accept nothing less from you," she snapped.

Hearing Lethia's words, Royal exhaled. Though she was not wearing her warping crystal, looking at her, Royal could hear echoes of his Aunt Grace in her tone. It comforted him. It reminded him of who he was and what he had come from. Royal sat up straight and took in a long stream of air before he began to speak again.

"Okay," Royal said as he tried to dismiss his anxieties. As he looked around at those who were assembled, he found himself missing the certainty of Hue's innocent smile more than anything else. He could not believe that his father had robbed him of that at the moment when he needed him the most. "Dad, will you get Father Benedito for me and let's pray before we proceed?" he asked.

"Of course," Reverend Monroe said as she left the small tent. The others followed him out into the blistering heat of the Red Desert. Simon, Purcell and Wisdom took up guard outside of the tent that Royal was inside of while the others made their way toward the line.

"Prayer?" Patel whispered to Lethia as they paused before joining the ranks. "If this one was not the progeny of the Avatar, I would not support him in leading our warriors into battle."

"You forget, elder mother," Lethia interjected, cutting her off. "He is not from Acara. He was groomed with values outside of our own. We must believe that the Avatar had a reason for this. I am not a novice to war, but I have seen this boy in battle and though his hand is reluctant, his might is sure."

"I trust you, CODA Queen," Patel said. "And I believe in the Avatar most of all. We shall see what this campaign delivers," she added as he watched the first of the High Queen's banners rise above the grind on the other side.

Simon, Wisdom, and Purcell waited outside of the tent where Royal was. They stood in silence as they watched the High Queen's colors rise over the otherside of the canyon. Simon gripped the blue arrowhead around his neck. He could feel Tisha reaching out to him across the width of the canyon. He sighed in relief. He could tell that she was not in any danger and her spirit was strong. He could also feel the heartbeat of his son beating inside of her. The baby was growing quickly and its odd parentage was somehow protecting it and his mother. Though Simon knew that his primary responsibility was to protect Royal, he knew that given the chance, he would find a way to rescue to Tisha. He did not know how he was going to be able to accomplish this task with her surrounded by a legion of Royal Guard under the command of his father Quan, but he was going to have to try, if he had the opportunity.

Seeing the distant look in Simon's eyes and seeing him holding onto the crystal, Wisdom asked, "What is it, big fella?"

"It's Tisha," Simon began. "She is with the High Queen in the camp across the grind," he announced.

"You shittin' me!" Purcell said with surprise. "Is she okay?"

"Yeah," Simon assured him. "She's fine. I can feel her. She is strong and brave as hell. She is trying to figure out a way to get to us, I can tell."

"That is a hell of a woman you got there," Purcell said, chuckling out loud.

"Yes, she is," Simon agreed. "And she knows that we are all here rooting for her, too."

Wisdom walked over to the rock formation where Purcell had laid out their weapons. He picked up a double-barreled shot gun and checked the chamber. It was loaded and ready. Though he was invulnerable because of the sap of the tree from the Lost Islands, Wisdom still needed a weapon. Looking at Simon, Wisdom knew that the other Royal Guards were as large, if not larger. But he also knew that, all of this Middle Age bullshit aside, he believed that cold steel would be the great equalizer in this battle. He had to be ready. He had killed before. However, this time it was not for money or territory. It was for family and honor. Somehow, getting ready to take someone's life for these reasons weighed heavy on his spirit.

"You don't have to worry about a thing," Wisdom said as he looked across the ravine at where his Jeep was parked. "That is my baby's mother, too. We gonna get her," he assured Simon as Reverend Monroe returned up the path with Father Benedito. The two holy men bowed to the warriors and entered the tent. Royal was sitting patiently waiting for them. Now that he was not in the sight of the others, he felt that he could let down his guard. He quickly hugged his father and then Father Benedito. The priest was surprised by Royal's familiarity, but he accepted the hug and hugged him back. Perhaps there was a reason for him to be here after all.

"I see them, Royal. Yo puedo verlos" Father Benedito said as he shook his head, looking from father to son. "Are you afraid? Tiene miedo?"

"I am," Royal admitted.

"We all are," Reverend Monroe chimed in.

"Then perhaps we have to be like David before Goliath," the priest advised, echoing Royal's words from earlier without knowing it.

"Then let us join hands and pray for our sling shot!" Reverend Monroe said as he reached out and took both men's hands.

Ikin hummed in the shadows of the trench as he busied his hands with a project he had been working on since the night before. Captain Sarison sat watching the Arcana with an odd fascination as the youth knitted together knot after knot of webbing. Though Ikin had warned the seaman to slow down, Captain Sarison was indulging in another jug of the fine wine of the Arcana. He swore to himself that if he made it out of this situation alive he would find a way to make a deal with the Arcana for the sale of their brew. More than their webbing, it was their wine that he was finding more valuable. He fancied himself a drinking man from his early youth, but he had never been as taken by a brew as he was by the Arcana wine. Though it was early in the day,

Ikin had made a rich store of it available to the warriors that had come to stand guard over his land. Though it was intoxicating, the brew did not dull the senses the way other libations did. If anything, it improved the moral of the CODA and Lampourian forces, helping them meld together.

Peku had found a task for himelf besides escorting Tori around. He was the glad shepherd of the brew from the Arcana's secret stores to the rest of the ranks. As they watched the legion of the High Queen entrench itself across the ravine, the spirits of the combined force was oddly high and expectant. The normally surly and nomadic CODA were even finding a rare reprieve in their tense alliance with the mixed gender troops of Lampour. Thankfully, the web-lined trench created by the Arcana cooled the tight space housing the forces. As Captain Sarison watched the heavily armored Royal Guard prepare for battle across the ravine, he found himself realizing that their armor would be an impediment in the heat of the region. Not to mention the large Moritans would constantly need water to cool themselves in battle. Though he stared at the ominous presence of the Marauder and the he spied the dark-robed priests of the Dark God, Captain Sarison found himself oddly optimistic about the outcome of the upcoming battle.

Sitting in the shade of the trench, Captain Sarison leaned back and opened another flask of the Arcana brew. He was about to start to drink when he realized that someone was standing over him. His hand fell to his sword instantly. He opened his eyes and was surprised to see Ben Lee standing there. The elder Lee looked haggard and bewildered. Captain Sarison smiled and waved the man over to his side. Ben sank down in the sand under the tarp knitted by the Arcana. He looked wantonly at the flask of wine in the Captain's hand. He watched as the Captain took a deep drink, then he harmlessly went to hand the bottle to Ben.

Ben stared at the bottle for what seemed like a lifetime. More than anything else, he wanted to drown his sorrows in the bottom of that flask. It didn't matter what it was, whether it was bitter or sweet, as long as it promised to take his mind off of his worries about his absent son. However, as much as he wanted to suppend his sobriety, he resisted temptation. Since all of this had happened, he had put liquor down. His drinking had been the thing he used to forget about the death of his wife from breast cancer, but his sobriety was the thing that was leading him back to his son. It had not only taken him from Baltimore City to New York, but from Earth to Arcara. He wanted to drown his pain in the bottom of the bottle that Captain Sarison was offering, but he had to have faith that his sobriety was going to bring him back his son.

"No, thanks," he finally said as he looked away from the flask. He was shaking slightly and his brown features were flushed.

"Ah, old man, I know that look," Captain Sarison said as he withdrew the flask quickly with an oddly timed burp. "Perhaps you have seen too many nights at the bottom of a tankard of spirits."

Ben laughed and rubbed his hands together as he got up and began to walk away.

"I guess a person can not hide anything around here," he said as he began to move from within the trench. Sullenly, Ben moved from inside the trench to the triage area behind the front line. He guessed he could drown his sorrows in helping to prepare for the inevitable wounded. One thing about having a terminally ill spouse, he had picked up some nursing skills. As he entered the small triage area, he was greeted by Etera, Tori, and Tildon. They were preparing slings for the wounded and medicines for their wounds.

"I would have never thought that we would need grandmother's teachings in this way," Tildon commented.

"Life prepares us for many jouneys we do not expect," Tori said as he rubbed at his sightless eyes. He had intentionally stayed far away from the front line. The memories of the torture at the hands of the High Queen were still fresh within him. He did not want to chance another encounter of her wrath.

The three turned happily and welcomed Ben to join them in their work. However, as he folded bandages, Etera could see the deep hurt and longing upon him. She stopped what she was doing and went over to him and took his hand. He was surprised at her forwardness. He stared into the young girl's face with pain and rememberance. She reminded him very much of his own daughter, Sapphire.

"Do not be of heavy heart," she said as she took his hand. "I see the burden upon you, but there is a shade nearby that has something to tell you," she explained.

"A shade?" he asked quickly.

"Ah, I feel it too," Tori chimed in as he placed a hand on the man's shoulder. "Perhaps if we work together, Etera, we can give it form."

Unsure of what all of this meant, Ben let the two seers touch him. They ran their collective energies through his body. At first he felt just a tingle, then on the edge of his sight, he saw something stir. It was a ghostly apparition. He wanted to jump but the two of them held him in place. The apparition began to take form and he immediatately recognized her. It was his long lost wife, Sylvia. She was standing a few feet in front of him washed in a glow of white light. All he could make out was her face.

"Sylvia," he cried out as he tried to move toward her, but Etera and Tori's hands held him in place.

"I am here, my heart," she said in the recesses of his mind. "And I will always be here for you and our children. You have done the right thing by coming to this wonderful place."

"But I have lost Hue again," he said with tears in his eyes.

"No, Ben, you have not lost him," she smiled in a way that only she could. "He is closer than you think. Trust Jul. He would not hurt our son."

"Then why did he take him?" Ben snapped before he caught his tone.

"Because for all the love that Hue has given, something wonderful is going to happen to him. You will see him soon and all will be well," she assured him as she faded.

"Sylvia!" Ben said as he burst to his feet, breaking the hold that Etera and Tori had on him. However, once he severed the connection, her image faded. She was gone. Ben was standing on the hot sands on the Red Desert, unsure of what to do next. There were tears in his eyes, but for the first time in along time, he had faith in something other than bourbon.

Back at the command tent, Royal and the others had finished praying. They stepped out of the tent into the stark heat of the Red Desert. Wisdom, Purcell, and Simon were at Royal's side as soon as he appeared. Reverend Monroe and Father Benedito followed him out of the tent and waited in the shadows to hear what was to be done next.

"I am going to go to the line and see exactly what we are facing," Royal said calmly. "I will not hide in the shadows while others put their lives in jeopardy for me."

"You are making yourself a target," Simon cautioned.

Royal smiled. "It is what it is."

However, before he finished outlining his decision, Maximus and Lethia came running up to him with a parchment.

"What is it?" Royal asked.

"The High Queen has asked for an audience with you," Lethia said flatly as she handed him the paper. "She wants to meet you in the Arcana village square under the White Flag of Honor."

"And what is that?" Wisdom asked suspiciously.

"It is a promise between two opposing forces to meet before battle and talk," Lethia explained. "It is a promise of non-aggression."

All those who were assembled looked at the parchment in shock, unsure of what to make of the gesture.

"Sounds like a trick to me," Wisdom said immediately. "I don't like it."

"Neither do I," Lethia admitted.

Royal thought about it for a minute. Since all of this had happened, he had heard so much about his mother but he had never laid eyes on her. Perhaps there was a way he could quell the rumors and find a sense of humanity in the dark High Queen. His mind was made up. He would meet her.

"Send word back to her that we will meet shortly, with only our Royal Guards at our sides," Royal said. "Perhaps this madness can be avoided."

"You are not thinking about sacrificing yourself?" Reverend Monroe said hurriedly.

Royal smiled at his father and took his hand. "I cannot sacrifice what I believe in or what we have fought so hard to gain. But maybe I can find the mother inside of her who would rather reunite with her son than see blood shed over this Red Desert," Royal said as he returned to his tent to meditate and prepare.

All those assembled looked at each other. They were shocked by Royal's words. Lethia took out a cigar and began to smoke. She hated to admit it, but the boy was definitely becoming a man and maybe even a High King.

# Chapter 29

Word of the meeting between Royal and his mother spread throughout the camp of rebels like wildfire. Most of the assembled troops respected their young leader for daring to stare down the most feared person on Acara. They all prepared themselves in the trench and set large watch fires. The CODA began to play a huge drum they had carried with them through the Gateway. They smeared red dirt on their faces and garments. The Lampourians watched them with amusement as they strung their arrows and checked their lances and shields. Everyone wanted to be ready at a moment's notice to protect their monarch, Royal, if the High Queen tried anything out of the ordinary. On Acara, it was against decorum to violate the White Flag of Honor in battle; however, all of the troops knew that the High Queen played by rules of her own. They expected anything from her and wanted to be ready just in case she tried something.

In his small tent, Royal looked at the few pieces of clothing that he had brought with him from Earth. He sighed out loud. There was nothing there remotely festive enough for this encounter. As he sat looking at his few garments, he scratched his head. He could not believe how much he wished Hue was there. Hue would know what to do or, at the very least, give him fashion advice for the meeting. Royal was about to settle on a plain white t-shirt and jeans when Ikin came into his tent holding a bundle. The small Arcana bowed his head and walked up to the High Prince.

"What can I do for you?" Royal asked hurriedly.

"I thought you might need something to wear into battle," Ikin said. "So I began to weave this garment for you. It is of the tightest thread we Arcana can make and knotted in a special way. It should protect you. There is also a cloak dyed from the sands of the desert. More than ample protection against the High Queen's trickery," he said with a wink.

Royal accepted the package. He was overcome by the gesture from the young leader of the Arcana. This youth was continuing to surprise him at every turn.

"I do not know what to say," Royal admitted humbly.

"There is nothing to say," Ikin cut him off. "Like your father, Jul, you came to the Arcana asking for nothing and respecting who we are, that is enough for me," he said as he reached up and hugged Royal with all eight of his arms. Royal let himself be held, taking solace in the young Arcana's embace. Though he wished it were Hue's arms around him, the genuinessness of Ikin's actions filled him with confidence. It was the tightest hug he had ever experienced.

"I will leave you alone to get ready," Ikin said as he exited the small enclosure.

Carefully, Royal peeled off his jeans and sneakers and donned the finely knitted garment that Ikin had made. He placed the red cloak around his neck and smiled at the form-fitting garments. Ignoring his reservations, he exited the tent into the full day light of the Arcana desert. To his surprise, all of his allies were standing outside of his tent at full attention. He looked from face to face with deep love, admiration, and gratitude. His court had assembled to see him off. He was about to take his first steps into the future when Princess Jane stepped forward with Lethia. In their hands was a simple crown braided from some sort of decorative twig. It was encrusted with the biggest gems that Royal had ever seen.

"Step forward, High Prince Royal Monroe," Lethia said, summoning him over to them. "Also called Von at birth by your mother, the High Queen Mora."

He did so with out hesitating.

"You have restored honor to the High Royal Court of Acara," Princess Jane said as she began to transform into her male self. "By the rights of royals, we of Lampour and the CODA support you to bear this crown of ashberry root. Ashberry is a root of truth and honor. You have earned that."

Royal knelt before Lethia and Prince Janis as they placed the crown of braided twigs and gems on his head. He rose with his cloak sweeping behind him. Looking at the faces of those around him and adorned in his new clothing, for the first time in his life, Royal felt like a true High Prince.

"You honor me with your trust," Royal said as he proceeded forward to his rendezvous. "I will not let you down," he swore as he began to move forward. "Whether male or female, we are all equal in the eyes of the God I know as well as the Avatar," he concluded.

Simon was standing at the end of the procession. Like Royal, he had also been adorned for the meeting with the High Queen. He was dressed in thick armor of hide and a long cloak. He bore two swords at each side. Their eyes met and they nodded at each other. There was nothing more to be said.

"Let's do this," Royal sighed as he began to make his way through the trench filled with CODA warriors and Lampourian soldiers. Seeing the new visage of the High Prince, they all bowed as he went by. Maximus and Peku met them at the top of the rope ladder that led into the Arcana village.

"I am ready to pounce down upon anyone who tries to harm you," Maximus swore as he licked at his freshly sharpened claws.

"Let's hope it does not come to that, old friend," Royal said as he began to descend the rope into the village.

On the other side of the grind, Althea stared across the expanse through a looking glass. She could see the young High Prince making his way into the village square. She gave the signal to Holi who was standing nearby her to alert the High Queen. Word traveled swiftly through the camp of the High Queen. High Queen Mora was resting when Quan entered her tent to tell her that her son was descending into the village for their meeting. The High Queen quickly placed her crown upon her head and lifted the Scepter of Monarchs. Her handmaidens tied a long purple cloak over her light armor. She emerged into the harsh daylight and passed her advisors with Quan lurking behind her. The elite force of Royal Guards bowed to their High Queen as she made her way through the camp toward the Arcana village. Freshly empowered by her dark touch of the High Queen, Quan loomed large over the biggest of the Royal Guards. He now stood nearly 11 marks tall, larger than any Moritan had ever had stood.

Ela watched her mate pass with grim remorse. She had spent her enire life with him but because of the Dark Queen's touch she barely recognized him. It left a sick feeling in her stomach. She had spent her entire life being true to her calling as a Moritan and as a member of the Royal Guard; however looking at her mate, she found herself questioning her allegiance for the first time.

--You are right to have questions--her gorda, Rambien, said in the back of Ela's mind--Though the Gorda are joined to the Moritans, we are of a different kind. Many of us find the High Queen's actions completely unworthy of support.

--Dear heart, Ela responded in the back of her mind,--But I am sworn to uphold the High Court without question.

--Think Ela. You are sworn to uphold the *rightful* heir of the High Court – Rambien reminded her.--Perhaps the time for this High Queen has passed. Remember the marking on Tisha's face -- he said as his voice trailed off.

As the High Queen and Quan passed her, Ela made an abrupt decision. She shrank back through the ranks of the Royal Guard to where Tisha's small tent was. She dismissed the guards watching her and entered the tent. Tisha was surprised at Ela's sudden appearance. She lifted one of her throwing darts defensively. When she saw that it was Ela, she relaxed and settled back down on her small cot. Though she was never truly called a prisoner, she was never outside of the eyesight of an armored battalion. Since they were away from Acara City, Tisha was truly feeling the pressure of her confined status. In addition, there was the pregnancy to consider. At first she thought it was stress that was making her feel so oddly. However, as days passed, Tisha knew that it was something else.

She had been pregnant before and it was not that long ago. The feelings that were coming from her womb were far different this time than when she had borne Little Wisdom. Though she expected there to be some difference because Simon was a Moritan and she was a human, she had to be honest with herself, these feelings were beginning to scare her. Upon seeing Ela, she began to relax. Though their relationship was other than ideal, she had to admit to herself that she was beginning to enjoy their visits.

"May I sit?" Ela asked.

"Sure," Tisha said as she slid over. She was not used to the mother of the Royal Guard being so polite.

"I have spent my entire life tending to the High Royals. I have done it without thought or reservation," she professed. "It was my duty. However, now that I see what the High Queen has done to my mate, I find myself questioning my loyalities."

Tisha was surprised by what she was hearing. Her mouth dropped open in surprise, but she could understand where Ela was coming from. Carefully, Tisha reached out and touched Ela's hand. Ela did not recoil. She interwined her fingers with Tisha's. For the first time in their relationship, they were feeling like family to one another.

"I do not like what the High Queen has done to my mate," Ela said frankly. "I look into his eyes and I barely see the man that I love and have spent my entire life with. I am afraid that if this continues, there will be little of him left to speak of."

Remembering their experience from the Grand Dark Temple, Tisha nodded her head in aggreement.

"Little Flower," Ela began, "in your womb you carry the furture of the Moritans as well as my grandchild. I fear that I can no longer trust the judgement of the High Queen. Therefore, I will help you escape to the other side of the grind. This maybe our best chance of getting you back to Keyton– I mean Simon– safely."

Tisha could not believe what she was hearing. She was elated! She was over joyed. As happy as she was about the possibility of being with Simon again, she could not help but feel sad for Ela. Tisha reached out and hugged her close. It was a long, tender embrace.

"Why don't you come with me?" Tisha whispered "I know Simon would be happy to have you at his side," she said. "And I would be glad, as well."

Ela rose from where she was sitting and sighed.

"Perhaps one day we will all be together," Ela said. "Though I abhor what the High Queen is doing, my place is with my mate. I cannot leave him any more than you can leave Simon," she explained. "When the moons rise over the grind, be ready. I will have Aspion brought to you and I will get you to the other side of the grind," Ela said with finality as she left Tisha's tent.

Tisha could not believe what she had just heard. Out of all the people who she hoped would help her escape from the High Queen, she would have never expected one of them to be Ela. However, as Ela was speaking, Tisha remembered the way she had reacted when the High Queen infused the dark energies into her husband. If Tisha had not intervened, Ela would have surely tried to take the High Queen's life. Tisha guessed that seeing someone you love contorted by powers beyond their will truly did change a person, even someone as dedicated to honor and duty as Ela. Tisha reached up and put her hand around the crystal arrow she wore and concentrated on Simon. She wanted him to know that it was just a matter of time before they were together again. She also made it clear to him that it was his mother that he had to thank for this good fortune.

Deep within the recesses of the Red Desert, Hue lay upon a stone altar, which now hovered high above the center of a pool of thick, silver liquid. Energy coarsed around Hue as his mind, body, and spirit were filled with the ambient energies of the lost priests of the Avatar. Hue dug his nails deep into the stone as he felt the power of countless lost souls fill the cells of his body. He reached up and tore open his shirt as his body began to shake. Jul floated from the edge of the pool to the head of the altar. He opened up his robe to reveal the Arc Light or Heart Stone. It was a huge, red gem that was embedded in the middle of his chest. The crystal was blood red and about the size of a full-grown man's hand. It was the oldest gem on Acara. It also contained the full power of the priests of the Avatar. Jul had been the custodian of it since he had come to live in the Red Desert almost twenty cycles ago. It was a burden he knew it was time to pass on to someone younger and stronger who could fully embrace all the Arc Light had to offer.

"Are you ready, Hue?" Jul asked.

"As ready as I will ever be," Hue said weakly.

"Do you accept the mantle of the High Priest of the Avatar by your own free will?" Jul asked.

"I do," Hue said as he began to shudder with unseen forces.

"Then, by the worth of your character, I pass on the Arc Light to you, the Avatar's Heart." Jul said as the two began to descend into the silver pool. The silver waters began to ripple and churn. The chamber took on an odd, ambient glow. After some time, Hue emerged from the pool. He stood naked on the shore. In the middle of his chest was firmly implanted the Arc Light. It hummed with power, renewed by Hue's youth and character. Hue stuck out his hands and the sands around him began to swirl. They leapt upon his body and solidified into the sacred red garment of the priests of the Avatar. Hue turned to leave the sacred chamber to the echoing sounds of the voices of countless generations of Priests of the Avatar who had come before.

Royal stood with Simon at his shoulder in the empty village square of the Arcana. Royal tried to focus on the happy sounds of the Arcana from previoius days instead of thinking about the impending battle that lay in front of him. He put a finger in his collar as he tried to loosen the tunic that Ikin had knitted for him. He was having a hard time adjusting to the new royal garb, but he guessed like everything else that had happened to him, it was just another thing to get used to. Royal looked up. He caught sight of the crown he had been given. The gems caught the light and cast a sultry glow. Royal was having a hard time bearing the weight of the emblem on his head. He had never worn a crown before. This was definitely going to take some getting used to.

"Are you ready for this?" Simon asked carefully as he looked over his shoulder. The line was lit up with huge cauldrons of fire. The CODA were playing their drum fiercely. The archers from Lampour lined the trench with their stygian arrows ready to fly. Simon smiled. They were making a clear statement of defiance akin to Royal's garb. They were supporting their High Prince.

"As ready as I will ever be," Royal declared as he reached up to adjust the crown on his head.

"Here, let me help you with that," Simon offered as he reached up and straightened Royal's newly bestowed crown.

Royal stood awkwardly and let Simon straighten the new headpiece.

"Well, just know I am here with you," Simon said as he put a supportive arm around Royal's shoulder.

"I know that," Royal smiled.

"Well, we won't have to wait for long," Simon said, pointing to the far end of the encampment. Royal turned and watched Quan descend the webbing ladder. Behind him, dressed in golden, light armor with a purple tunic, followed the High Queen, Mora. For the first time, Royal laid eyes on the woman who had given birth to him. He did not know what he expected, but for a person who was causing so much grief in so many lives, he had expected someone more ominous. However, as the High Queen approached him, he got a good look into her eyes. They were pools of unmitigated darkness.

Royal took a step back as he felt himself caught in her gaze. This was unlike any of the times he had seen her in his dreams. She was really here now and he could feel her presence. Part of him wanted to run simply at the sight of her. However, Simon's hand landed at the small of his back and he regained his composure. He took a deep breath and stood tall before his mother. As he looked at her, he could see traces of himself in her face. Yet, as she moved, he could see that they were nothing alike. Royal's eyes fell on the Scepter of Monarchs. She held it before herself proudly, as a baggage of honor. Royal could feel the power flowing from it. The ancient relic was almost vibrating with the spirits of previous old High Monarchs.

The High Queen looked at her son for the first time. She sighed out loud. She was not impressed by what her copulation with Jul had rendered. She expected him to be a much more imposing figure, not a scrawny lad, dressed up to appear regal. She smiled to herself as she thought about the force she had mustered to bring this child under her control. She was sure accomplishing her goal was going to be easier than she thought.

As the two High Royals sized each other up, Simon looked at his father, Quan. The sight of the man sent chills up his spine. He barely recognized him. The Assassin cube had changed him, surely, but it was clear to Simon that the High Queen had added even more dark energy to that. He looked more like a Marauder than Simon's father. Simon felt his anger rise in him as he looked at the High Queen. The spirits of the land around him began to rumble in response to Simon's call. Simon quickly shut down his emotions and eased the growing tension. He had to remind himself that they were meeting under the White Flag of Honor and it was against Acara law to break that seal with violence in anyway. Simon held his hand and his power.

Standing in the center of the empty village, the High Prince Royal and the High Queen, Mora, came face to face for the first time. Royal waited for her to speak since she had called this summit.

"Von," the High Queen said simply, intentionally ignoring his bloodline and crown. "We can avoid all of this unpleasantness. Clearly, you see that I have brought a superior force to what ever you have hidden in that little hole."

"And how could we avoid that?" Royal asked carefully.

"Your unconditional surrender and return with me to Acara Cityto take up your rightful place as heir to the throne. Let me teach you the ways of the Dark God. Forget whatever these fools have filled your mind with and take my hand," she said as she reached out to him.

"And if I did such a thing, what about all those who have gathered under my banner?" Royal asked carefully as he waved at his flag that was lit up by the torches set by his forces.

"There is no room in my kingdom for traitors," she said flatly. "I promise them a swift and painless death."

Royal was shocked by what he was hearing. He could not believe that this woman had actually given birth to him. He had hoped that in laying eyes on her he could find some common ground for them to standon, but listening to her, he knew that there was no reasoning with her. She had a heart of stone and it was going to be his life's mission to chip it away or die trying.

"I see we have nothing to discuss here," Royal said sadly as he looked to Simon and turned around, giving his back to his mother. It was a bold move, especially for Royal.

"You dare turn your back on me!" she bellowed as she raised the Scepter of Monarchs. The air around her immediately began to crack with power. Quan quickly grabbed her hand and whispered in her ear. He reminded her that she was being watched by the Royal Guard, the dark priests and other royals. It would be beneath her station to strike Royal under the White Flag of Honor, especially; that she had called for it. Quan reminded her that she could lose important support. Though she was seething with anger, she caught herself. She looked over her shoulder at all the eyes upon her. Quan was right. The support she had put together was too fragile a thing to lose over a slight. She quickly stayed her hand.

Royal paused for a moment and turned back to her. There were tears in his eyes. This show of emotion disarmed the High Queen.

"I did not come here to negotiate war. I came here looking for my mother. I have been looking for her all of my life," Royal admitted. "I only wish I would have found her, not on the other end of threats and swords, but with open arms."

The High Queen was stunned by her son's words. Her mouth dropped open. For a moment, her heart opened. She did not know what to say. Then, as quickly as there was an avenue of openness, it was gone.

"Then we will meet at dawn!" the High Queen shouted. "I may not be able to cross into the Red Desert, but I will break you," she insisted, "in half!"

"I have faith that the Avatar has not brought us this far to leave us," Royal said as he headed back to his allies. "I would rather meet my maker than embrace your darkness," Royal swore as he walked away.

The High Queen was livid at her son's bravado. She was the High Priestess of the Dark God. How dare he invoke the name of the Avatar in front of her! She thought he had lost his mind. She turned to Quan, who was looming over her.

"Tell the forces to be ready at sunrise," she said as she turned to leave.

Quan followed the High Queen as she went away without saying a word. However, as he followed her back toward her camp, he found himself looking over his shoulder, back at the son he barely knew.

Above the rift, while the legion of Royal Guard prepared for the assault, the High Princes Burton and Holi watched their niece meet with the young High Prince. As they watched the meeting, they made sure that they were far enough away from others so that their conversation could not be overheard. They both stared oddly at the standard that Royal had raised over his invisible forces lying in the trench the Arcana had dug. The look of the flag with the two suns haunted both of them. It was oddly reminiscent of the flag used by their older brother, Roman, the former High King.

"I feel like I am staring at a shade," Holi said as he motioned toward the flag. "That reminds me of our brother."

"I was thinking the same thing," Burton sighed as he kicked at the dirt. "As many years as Roman has been dead, I feel tbat I still can't be rid of him."

"We have done our best to make sure he remains a memory," Holi agreed.

"Now we have to watch the ebb and flow of this battle to find an opportunity to get rid of his daughter *and* his grandson," Burton said as he chewed his lip.

"Do you think this will afford us the opportunity?" Holi asked hurriedly, thinking of his need to get close to Tisha. It was beginning to cloud his judgement.

"Ahh, I think it will," Burton swore. "They are both so focused on one another, we might have a chance for them to do each other in."

"I know you believe that, brother," Holi protested. "But it is only Mora who is holding that Marauder, that beast, under control. I would hate for us to have to confront that monstrosity, too."

Burton turned to look at the huge hulking beast at the rear of the encampment. He had not considered that point. Neither he nor Holi were versed in the Dark Arts. He was not even sure if the two dark priests with them could control the monster; especially if there was a sudden shift in power. The only thing he was sure could possibly control the monster was the power of the Scepter of Monarchs. Thus he knew it was important for them to secure the relic in any potential transition of power.

"The Scepter," Burton said as he watched the High Queen make her way through the encampment. "It is important that we secure it, so we can keep that monster under control."

Holi nodded.

"Wise," Holi laughed. "You always have a notion of what we need to do next."

"We have been about this along time, little brother," Burton said as he gathered his cape behind him. "Now, it is time for us to act."

Holi watched his brother make his way through the encampment. He smiled to himself as he thought about Burton's plan. His brother always expected him to be a willing ally in his schemes. He shook his head. Up until recently that would have been the case. However, since Holi had seen Tisha, his willingness to follow his brother's agenda had changed. For the first time in his life, he began to envision himself as the next High King of Acara. Holi was used to being overlooked and staying with his experiments in the basement of the Grand Citadel. Spending so much time by himself, he had learned patience. Now he felt like that all he had to do was wait a little bit longer and he would have the woman he wanted *and* the throne he now coveted. Holi looked out at the trench and smiled. With any luck, they will destroy themselves in this endeavor; he alone would be left to pick up the pieces.

In the rear of the High Queen's encampment, the Marauder and its hounds were laying in wait by a broken tree. As fierce as the Royal Guards were, they stayed away from the massive visage of the Marauder and its pets. Only the priests of the Dark God, Danthor and Fildis, dared to be in the prescence of the beast. In addition, Agar often checked in with them, since he had been given the assignment of trying to find a way for them to break through the Avatar's energy that blocked them from crossing into the Red Desert. Neither Danthor nor Fildis said anything to this. They knew it was a fool's errand. It was the perfect errand for a fool who had gotten himself killed in the first place.

Danthor and Fildis fed the Marauder and its hounds fresh meat. Their lust for fresh meat kept them ready for battle. They also said prayers to the Dark God over the Marauder that quelled its aggression. It was a task that would have normally taken an entire legion of priests. They were both feeling the strain of keeping the massive dark entity in check.

"I do not like this," Danthor said softly as he fed the hounds again.

"Nor do I," Fildis said as he raised his hands and uttered a prayer to the Dark God.

"Does she understand what she has done?" Danthor questioned as he looked at the huge destroyer.

"I do not know," Fildis said quietly. "It is easy to conjure such an entity, but keeping it under control is another matter altogether. If it does not get blood soon, I do not know how much longer we are going to be able to control it with simple meat."

"This battle is going to be a slaughter," Danthor said, shaking his head.

"Again, my friend," Fildis said softly, "more than anything else, we need to make sure that the off-world female does not get hurt in this battle. What she carries in her womb is an entity which has never existed before. In this battle for supremacy, it maybe finally decided by whoever controls that very special child."

"I am not so sure I care about this battle anymore," Danthor said frankly. "Being this close to the Red Desert has my senses out of sorts. Dark Priests were never meant to be in such proximity to this place."

"I agree with you there," Fildis said as he stared out across the ravine at the Red Desert. "I do not know how the High Queen is holding it together."

"She probably is having an easier time than you and I because she does not have to keep this beast under control," Danthor observed.

"Be careful what you say out loud or think to yourself, my young friend," Fildis warned. "Mora is the High Queen and the High Priestess of the Dark God. We have to make sure that we do not end up on the wrong side of her fury."

Danthor did not say another word. All he did was shrink back in his dark robes and continue to tend to the Marauder. For the majority of his life, he had been in service of the Dark God. It had been an honor to his family when his gifts were recognized in his youth. Now that he was in proximity to the space most sacred to the Avatar, he silently found himself questioning his years of devotion and training, especially as he looked at the Marauder and its hounds. He found himself questioning his life choices for the first time.

Back in her tent, High Queen Mora removed her crown and put down the Scepter. She rubbed at her eyes. Though the battle had not yet begun, she found herself feeling strained. She did not know if it was because of her proximity to the Red Desert or the reality of seeing her son for the first time; either way, she was feeling tired. After almost twenty cycles, she felt odd to actually lay eyes upon Von. Seeing him reminded her of a simpler time in her life. But most of all, it reminded her about Jul. Though she had eventually found out that he wasn't what he appeared to be, she did believe that what they had was real. And out of that love, Von had been born. Seeing Von had also made her realize why she still had reservations about her relationship with Prince Gregor. She silently had the fear that he would disappoint her the way that Jul had. It also helped her realize why it was so easy for her to dedicate herself to the Dark God. It had been the one relationship in her life that she had actually given herself to that had given back to her. The High Queen sat down and rubbed at her face. Then she looked up and realized that she was not alone. Quan was standing before her.

"What is it Quan?" she asked quickly.

"What are your orders?" Quan asked.

"Orders?" Mora sighed showing a rare moment of a lack of certainity.

Sensing her distress, Quan walked up to her and grabbed her by both shoulders. He shook her gently, snapping her back to the grip of reality.

"This is not going to be as easy as I thought," the High Queen admitted.

Quan did not say anything in response. He reached down and replaced her crown on her head and handed her the Scepter of Monarchs.

"Focus!" he insisted." Your uncle, Prince Gregor, and the CODA woman are outside."

"Right," the High Queen exhaled. "Send them in."

Quan turned to show them in.

"Quan," the High Queen stopped him.

Quan turned.

"Thank you," she smiled crookedly.

Quan bowed his head and opened the flap of her tent. The High Prince Burton, Prince Gregor, and Althea came into the room. They all bowed before the High Queen.

"At sunrise, we take the trench," the High Queen commanded. "I will let the Marauder and its hounds go first. Then you will lead the Royal Guard in and capture the High Prince. Anyone who is left alive, we will take back to Acara City where they will be publicly executed. The Dark Priests and I will fall back, because we cannot get that close to the Red Desert, damn Avatar."

"Your Highness," Althea asked. "Can I have the head of the renegade CODA queen?"

"It is yours," the High Queen agreed. "And you can wear her entrails back to the Eastern Region as garland for your mount."

"I could ask for no more," Althea grinned. "And I assure you, when I return to power in the CODA, all of our secrets will be yours; including the Eternal Spring. With it, you can rule Acara forever, you won't need and heir."

The High Queen was stunned by Althea's words. She tried not to show her surprise, but she couldn't help from smiling. The High Prince Burton tried not to show his reaction to Althea's words. He bit down hard on his lip until it almost bled. This was a development he had not forseen.

"I will go get the Royal Guard ready," the High Prince Burton said as he excused himself, trying to regain his composure.

Seeing her uncle's discomfort made the High Queen smile. It confirmed for her in her mind that he could not be trusted. She had had her suspicions about him before, but no real evidence of his traitorous agenda. His reaction to the news from Althea was all the evidence she needed. And if she could not trust her uncle Burton, then that meant she probably couldn't trust her uncle Holi, either. They were always whispering amongst themselves and seemed to have an agenda of their own. Though they were members of the High Royal family, their deaths were of little consequence to her considering that she had already killed her father, Roman. Before this conversation, she had always believed that she needed to have an heir by her side to secure the plans she had made for Acara with the Dark God. Now with this revelation, Von's significance to her had been diminished. It would have been nice to have her son by her side as she followed the edicts of the Dark God, but now it was no longer neccesassry.

"Prince Gregor?" the High Queen called.

"Yes, your Highness," the blue skinned monarch of the Northern region responded as he stepped forward.

"Tell the Dark Priests to stop feeding the Marauder and its's hounds," she directed. "Have them bring the dark entity to the head of the rift. At dawn, we are going to set it free, and may the Dark God have mercy on their souls" she laughed.

"As you wish," Prince Gregor said, bowing as he exited the tent.

"Now tell me more about this Eternal Spring," the High Queen said as she turned to give Althea her full attention.

Royal returned to his side of the grind with Simon on his heels. He walked through the renegade troops quickly, trying not to betray any emotion. As he moved through the trench, the members of his inner circle fell in line behind him. Those who knew Royal best could tell that he was putting up a façade. He was trying to look more confident and sure of himself than he actually felt. Smelling the fear and indecision upon him, Maximus appeared out of the shadows of the trench and protectively took up point in front of Royal. He and Simon led Royal back to his command tent in the rear of the encampment. Wisdom and Purcell took up guard outside of the tent.

"I don't think him seeing his mother was a good idea," Purcell said as he checked his rifle.

"Yeah, me neither," Wisdom agreed. "I bet all she did was get inside of his head. Fucking crazy bitch."

"Come on, man," Purcell said, cutting him off. "That is still his moms. Ours wasn't perfect either, but she was still our mother."

"Yeah, I know you right," Wisdom sighed, remembering all the times he made heroin runs for his mother and saw her stick a needle in her arm or neck. "I guess I still have some anger issues."

"Ya think?" Purcell said as he jabbed his brother in the side.

"Forget you, man," Wisdom said as he took out a cigarette and lit it.

Once he was inside of his tent, Royal struggled to get out of the suit that Ikin had made for him. He was having a hard time with the ties. He knew that he had done a good job of sounding brave, but he really didn't feel that way. In fact, while facing his mother, it took everything in his power not to urinate on himself, turn, and runaway. Royal did not know what he had expected to gain from laying eyes on her. Perhaps he just wanted to put a face with all the horror stories he had heard about her. Either way, it was over now. He had met his birth mother and she had turned out to be as unreasonable as everyone had said she was going to be. In some Pollyanna-ish way, Royal had believed that he would have been able to talk his way out of the conflict. He was a trained minister. He was used to being able to reason his way out of anything. Yet, after meeting the High Queen, Mora–his mother– he knew there was no reasoning with her. Conflict was coming in the morning.

Lethia, Patel, Reverend Monroe, and Prince Janis all descended on Royal's tent. At first, he paid little attention to them. His mind was still consumed by his meeting with his mother. Then he slowly began to tell them about the general tone of the interaction. He didn't have to tell them how it made him feel, it was clear from his telling of the events. No one was particularly surprised by the posture the High Queen had taken. Most of them had been dealing with her for years and were used to her attitude.

"To be honest," Royal began, "I almost feel like I should simply turn myself over to her," he admitted to the shock of those assembled.

"You must be daft!" Patel chastised him. "You have gained the support of the CODA. For a man, that is unhead of. Now you would throw it all away because your mommy freightened you? Boy, you may be looking more and more like a High King, but you are behaving like a baby on the tit!" Patel was beside herself. "Lethia, give me one of those a.. . .a cigars."

"No, it is not that!" Royal interjected. "I would exchange myself for all of your lives."

Simon shook his head, No.

"Royal," he began softly. "This is not Earth. I understand what you are saying. And I read the same scriptures you did. However, Queen Mora is playing by a darker set of rules. Even if you gave up, she would do her best to slaughter all of us."

"I have to agree, son," Reverend Monroe conceded. "The High Queen has never been known for her compassion; expecially regarding treason. And look around you; Avatar or not, we have all commited high treason."

"Indeed," Princess Jane agreed. "I did not agree to help you to gain favor with the High Queen. In fact, my own father, the King of Lampour, is unaware of my actions. I do not know if I will even have a home to go back to after this."

"Fine," Royal conceded. "They may have us outmanned and even have more magic than we do. Then what we have to do is out think them," Royal smiled.

"Now you are using your head," Patel stomped her feet as she took a lit cigar from Lethia.

"The High Queen said she was going to attack us at dawn," Royal began as he looked up at the midday sky. "I say we don't wait for her to attack us. Let's attack her in the dead of night."

"Brillant!" Simon cried as he clapped Royal on the back.

"Deciteful and direct," Lethia agreed. "I love it."

"My obsidian guard thrive in the dark hours," Princess Jane agreed. "It is when we are at our best. You know what they say about Lampourians; we're nothing but thieves and renegades, liable to rob your mother's purse."

"Good then," Royal sighed, "it is decided. Lethia and Princess Jane, will you work out the particulars?"

"Gladly," the two women said as they bowed their heads and left Royal's tent. After a few minutes, he was alone. He sighed out loud and leaned heavily on his packs. He did not know if he was doing the right thing or hastening the inevitable. Eitherway, he was sure that he had to do something and waiting for his mother to attack was certain suicide. Royal sat down among his bags and took out his Bible. The binding was still sure, but the thick pages were beginning to discolor. Royal was about to begin to read one of the gospels, when the plastic-covered comic book that Hue had given him fell out of the backof the Bible. Royal picked up the vintage volumn of the Fantastic Four and smiled. Looking at the item, he couldn't help but think of his lovemaking with Hue from the previous day and whether his young friend was okay.

As Royal thumbed through the book, tears formed in his eyes. He began to wipe them away just as the flap of his tent opened. It was Mr. Lee, Hue's father. Royal quickly regained his composure and smiled at the elder Lee. Mr. Lee was grinning oddly from ear to ear.

"Mr. Lee!" Royal exclaimed as he cleared his throat. "Are you okay?" he asked.

"Royal," Mr. Lee began, "I think everything is going to be fine."

"What makes you say that?" Royal asked curiously.

Mr. Lee wiped at his eyes and smiled like a mad man.

"I think you better sit down for this one," he said as he directed Royal over to an empty chair.

"What is it?" Royal asked.

"I don't even know where to begin," Mr. Lee said as he rubbed his hands on his pants. "First of all, Hue is going to be fine."

"How do you know that?"

"My wife told me," Mr. Lee said as he exhaled. "I saw Sylvia. She has been with me the entire time."

Royal's mouth dropped open. He had heard the story of Hue's mother on more occasions than he could remember. He could not believe what seeing her after all these years must have meant to Mr. Lee. As Mr. Lee cried, he related to Royal the fullness of the visitation. Royal listened and smiled. He couldn't wait to be able to tell Hue about the experience. Though he knew he faced overwhelming odds, hope had come from the oddest place.

# Chapter 30

The suns went down over the Red Desert and the moons of Acara began to rise. The members of the High Queen's war party began to light torches to illuminate the camp. Tisha stood outside of her tent watching the Royal Guard prepare for battle. Tisha had been nervous since her last conversation with Ela. She was having a hard time believing that the Queen of the Royal Guard was willing to help her escape. However, Tisha recalled the look that crossed Ela's face when the High Queen infused Quan with her Dark energies. If it had not been for Tisha, Ela would have attacked the High Queen. Clearly, as much as Ela was a devotee to the code of the Moritans, she loved her husband more. Though they had started on opposing sides, Tisha understood the power of true love. It had been her love for Simon that had drivern her to take the actions she had – why would Ela be any different? It also became clear to Tisha that though Quan and Ela were staunch Moritans and Royal Guards, their children had been conceived with love. In Tisha's experience, there was no greater force than love to make someone change.

--I told you to have faith, Aspion said in the back of Tisha's mind.

--We still have to pull this off though, Tisha responded. --And I have to say that Iam scared to death.

Aspion laughed loudly in her mind and tried to use his psychic ability to ease her misgivings.

--As I told you before, many of the gorda do not approve of what the High Queen is doing, he reiterated. --And they have conveyed their misgivings to their Royal Guard in secreet. The once unbreakable cadre of Royal Guards now find themselves split in this battle. That alone maybe the anchor we need for victory-- he concluded.

"I hope so," Tisha mistakingly said out loud with a sigh.

"Ah, what is that you hope for Little Flower?" Burton said as he appeared out of the distance. "I am a simple man, but I maybe able to make all of your dreams come true," he said with much lust and certainty in his voice.

"Oh, fucking great," Tisha mused as she looked at Burton's goggling eyes framed by the moonlight.

Ignoring him, Tisha was about to go back into her tent when she saw High Prince Holi approaching. He had a gleeful look upon his face. He was also carrying a hand full of flowers. Tisha shook her head. She had no idea where he had managed to get flowers from in the desert. However, he clearly had, and was on his way to give them to Tisha. Tisha retreated into her tent trying to get away from him. However, as soon as Tisha got into the tent, Holi came inside with a huge grin on his face. Tisha thought about trying to move past him and get out of the tent when she realized that Holi's personal Royal Guard, Bilk, was positioned outside. Tisha sighed to herself. She felt trapped.

"I brought these for you," Holi began. "I know you like flowers. These are called Peterals. They do not have much of a smell, but they are only common to this area of Acara." he explained as he offered her the blooms. "Trust me, they were not easy to find."

"You looked for them yourself?" Tisha asked snidely.

"If it were only that simple," Holi laughed. "I sent Bilk to gather them for me. He is an apt Royal Guard."

Thinking of Bilk rummaging through the woods for flowers pissed Tisha off. She guessed that she was supposed to be impressed. She wasn't. Holi could at least have lied and said that he had foraged for the flowers himself. Tisha shook her head. He was a typical man. She guessed that on Acara, some things about gender remained the same.

"Thank you, I think." Tisha said as she reluctantly accepted the flowers.

"I thought it would be good to give you something beautiful," Holi continued. "We are attacking the interlopers in the morning. I will be glad to have this done with. I do not like all of this sand," he complained.

Tisha was shocked by Holi's directness about war. She also could not believe how arrogant the High Queen and her warriors were. From Holi's tone, she could tell that they did not entertain the idea that they might lose. Tisha was scared. In the short time she had been around the High Queen and the Royal Guard, she had come to believe that their power was overwhelming. However, Royal and his allies were proving that they were miracle workers and should not be underestimated.

Tisha was about to smell the flowers when she heard a thump from outside of her tent. She looked up just in time to see Bilk crumple and fall backwards into her tent. Holi swung on his heels and reached for his sword as he watched the shadow of the person who had knocked out his Royal Guard appear in the openin of the tent. But Holi didn't get the opportunity to see the person. Tisha picked up a water pot and hit him over the head. Like Bilk, Holi never saw the blow coming. The two men were passed out on the floor. Ela came into the tent. She was dressed in a full dark riding cloak which concealed much of her face. Ela looked at Holi's still form and smiled.

"I really don't like that man," Tisha confided with a smirk.

"Truth be told, no one does," Ela said quickly as she withdrew blindfolds and rope from her armor. "Now help me tie them up."

Tisha did not question her. She followed Ela's lead and helped her secure the High Prince and his Royal Guard.

"Your gorda, Aspion, is outside," Ela told her. "While the rest of the Royal Guard get ready for the dawn attack, I will lead you out of the camp. Somehow, Aspion has convinced many of the gorda to hide our escape. The wonder of the gorda never cease to amaze me."

--Did you think we would leave you to your own devices? –Rambien, Ela's royal gorda laughed in her mind—We have already charted a course to safety for you and Tisha. Some of the other gordas have planned diversions to make your escape easier.

--As always, thank you, my love, Ela smiled.

--You are making the right decision, Rambien assured her. --And before this is over, you may discover a new life for yourself and your mate altogether.

--I can only hope, Ela admitted.

-- Not hope, faith, my rider. Faith is the reason why there is a High Monarch and why the Avatar must rise in power once again-- he said as his voice faded.

"Isn't this dangerous for you?" Tisha quizzed quickly.

"It is," Ela said frankly. "But no one would dare question or supect me. Not even the High Queen. I will use this to our advantage. No one would expect treason from the Queen of the Royal Guard, not even my mate. I will hide in their assumptions."

"And why are you doing this?" Tisha asked as she gathered a spare cloak around herself.

"Because I do not like what the High Queen's dark touch has done to my mate. I barely recognize him anymore," Ela admitted. "Not to mention that I believe you belong with Simon. You need to be protected from the High Queen's darkness especially with a unique baby coming."

"I can take care of myself, ya know," Tisha said with a wink as she stared at the bound High Prince.

"I stand corrected," Ela said as the two women shared a rare laugh.

"Why don't you come with me?' Tisha asked but she already knew the answer.

"Thank you, Little Flower," Ela said as she put on the hood of her cloak, "but my place is with my mate. I may not like his support of the High Queen's darkness but he is a good man and the father of my sons. I will never leave him. Just let Simon know that I love him and his father does, too, in his own way," she concluded. "And if there is any way in this battle that I can redirect the outcome, I will.

"I will tell him that," Tisha promised her. "I will make sure he knows."

"Now come on," Ela directed. "Let us be like the wind."

Tisha followed Ela out of the small tent. The two women were cloaked from the prying eyes of others. Ela put Tisha on her gorda, Aspion, and began to lead her through the legion of Royal Guards preparing for the morning assault. No one took notice of them as they made their way toward the head of the camp where Wisdom's Jeep was parked. Ela expected to have to reveal herself when she reached the guards that were posted with the vehicle, but to her surprise, she found them in a daze. She could tell immediately that they were being controlled by an external force. She smiled to herself as she guessed that it was the young High Prince. The work had the smell of the Avatar's hand.

"That trickster," she mumbled as she turned to Tisha and explained to her what she was sensing. Then Tisha disclosed to her about Royal's power to control others. As the two women whispered in the shadows, Ela caught sight of Purcell and Wisdom alone in the village carrying strange weapons. She pointed them out to Tisha. Tisha looked at the Sims brothers carrying two sawed-off shotguns. Tisha swallowed hard and broke out into a cold sweat.

"We got to move!" Tisha insisted as she reached down and pulled Ela onto Aspion.

"I don't understand," Ela said, confused.

"You will," Tisha insisted as she turned her gorda down the length of the cliffside. The two women vanished into the darkness, while the Royal Guard that were under Royal's control moved out of the way of the Sims brothers' approaching assault.

"We only got one shot at this," Purcell said as he loaded his gun.

"Well then, let's make sure it counts!" Wisdom said as he loaded his gun.

The two brothers began to shoot at Wisdom's Jeep. The sound of bullets echoed throughout the High Queen's encampment. The Royal Guard was puzzled by the sound of live ammunition. They looked around confused. They rushed toward the edge of the cliff where the Jeep was, but were surprised to find a wall of their colleagues standing in the way with linked arms. There was a glazed look in their eyes, a sure sign of their being bewitched. The High Queen, Quan, Prince Gregor, and Althea came running out of her tent. The High Queen raised her hand and the air in the camp began to electrify. The bullets in the air quickly fell down.

"Now that we have done away with that," the High Queen said as she looked down into the village, "let's proceed with killing them all."

"What do we do with the Royal Guard who were bewitched?" Prince Gregor asked.

"Kill them for being so weak-minded that they allowed themselves to be mesmerized," she commanded.

"As you wish," Prince Gregor said as he withdrew his sword and approached the huge, lurking Royal Guards.

As Prince Gregor approached them, Wisdom and Purcell looked at each other knowingly. They had drawn the majority of the attention of the High Queen Mora's troops to the front of the camp. They smiled at each other. She was playing directly into their plan.

"Do you think you can hit it from here?" Wisdom asked his brother hurriedly.

"You forget, I used to be baseball player," Purcell said as he removed a grenade from underneath his Kevlar. "Piece of cake," he said as he withdrew the pin, looked up at the Jeep, and took aim. He carefully caluculated the distance and hurled the grenade at the SUV.

"Your Highness," Burton protested carefully. "They are Royal Guards. You do not have to kill them," he pleaded as he reached out and caught Gregor's arm.

"Uncle," the High Queen sneered, "do not let our blood association fool you. I am in charge here. And perhaps it was your softness that allowed the young High Prince to get away the first time."

Prince Gregor snatched his hand away. He was just about to deliver the first blow when Purcell's grenade hit the top of the SUV. Everyone's eyes shifted to see where the sound came from. However, it was too late. The grenade exploded under the rear tire. The Jeep exploded instantly. It scattered everyone that was on the far side of the grind. The remaining Royal Guards and the Dark Priests came running to the aid of their fallen comrades. They were struck by shrapnel from the SUV and their flesh was mangled. The first gambit had worked perfectly.

"That is what she gets for fucking up my car," Wisdom cursed as he raised a hand in defiance.

"Don't get cocky, fool!" Purcell shouted as he began to toss grenades into the disoriented Royal Guard. "We got a long way to go!"

"Now!" Princess Jane screamed from the shadows. The troops of Lampour came rushing into the encampment at full speed from the shadows. They scattered smoke bombs as they moved. It clouded the eyes of the already disoriented Royal Guard. Through the haze, many of the Royal Guard called for their gordas, but somehow the herd would not respond as it usually would. Though out numbered, the assassins pounced on the distracted members of the Royal Guard with full force. The Spiel was used to fighting in their man-made smoke. Their faces were covered with hoods and they wore goggles that covered their eyes. They were also more nimble than the hulking Royal Guards. They pushed them back toward the edge of the rift easily. Many Royal Guards fell to their demise, stumbling over the edge of the cliff, confused by the swords and the smoke of the gallant warriors of Lampour.

"To arms!" Quan yelled as he struggled to get to his feet. "To arms!" he commanded as he tried to cover the dazed High Queen with his body.

Out of the shadows, Lethia, Simon, Captain Sarison, and Tildon ran into the camp. They headed straight for the nobility with the goal of subduing them. Prince Gregor and Tildon immediately engaged one another in a duel. Lethia confronted Althea once again. The two women of the CODA rolled around in the sand, each trying to get the upper hand. Captain Sarison headed straight for High Prince Burton and knocked him off his feet. This left Simon alone to face his father, Quan, who was conflicted between facing his son and protecting the dazed High Queen.

Seeing the tide of battle drift toward the side of the young High Prince, the priests of the Dark God hesitated. They looked at each other and tried to drift away in the melee. However, as they turned to flee they were immediately confronted by an elite group of CODA that had appeared at the far end of the camp. They were stunned as they raised their hands and brought forth a torrent of dark fire. However, to their surprise, it never reached its mark. Patel appeared among the CODA. The elder CODA raised her hands and deflected the venomous blows, to the surprise of the dark-robed priests. Though she made it look effortless, it was a great strain on her. She fell to one knee. She was immediately surrounded by CODA women. Cree lifted her to her feet and stood guard over her protectively.

"Forget me!" Patel commanded. "Get them!" Patel directed the women of the CODA. The priests of the Dark God were at a loss. They were not used to having their energy rebuffed. They fell over each other as they tried to escape the CODA's blades and arrows.

"I think we have them on the run!" Purcell said gleefully as he checked his shotgun.

"Let's not let them have all the fun," Wisdom said as he tossed his rifle over his shoulder and headed to the rope that led to that side of the ravine.

"Yeah," Purcell said as he began to climb. "I want to see what this skin of yours can do in real combat."

"Man, you just want what I got," Wisdom said with a wink.

"Hopefully, I won't need it." Purcell said grimly, recalling his encounters on Earth with the Marauder and its pets.

"Don't worry, Big Bro, I got your back," Wisdom assured him as he reached the top of the cliff. "We got this."

Purcell did not say anything in response. It had been his idea to blow up the Jeep as a diversion before they attacked. It seemed like a really good idea at the time. As he got to the top of the bluff, he could tell that it had definitely given his side the upper hand in the battle. After the explosion, it was up to the others to attack from all sides and squeeze the Royal Guard into fighting in close quarters. They were supposed to be larger, more seasoned and probably better trained in the dark, but in a tight space, their stature would work against them. Before Purcell engaged in the melee, he could tell that the Lampourians and the others were actually winning this thing. A smile ran across his face as he ran to aid a fallen Lampourian solider with his shotgun ready and loaded.

At the rear of the camp, the Marauder and its hounds were straining at their bonds. It had momentarily been distracted and confused by the explosion. Now that its head was clear, it was ready to join the battle. It could taste blood. However, it still needed a command from its High Queen before it could engage the fight. After the death of its twin brother, it was waiting for the opportiunity to tear at the flesh of one of these treasonous cowards. As the Marauder watched the battle, it knew that this melee would be one sung about for generations.

From the other side of the grind, Royal waited impatiently with his other allies. Most of the CODA troops were left behind to guard Royal and the others. Royal would have preferred to have joined the majority of his force in battle with the High Queen. However, the majority of the members of his newly installed High Court suggested otherwise. They knew that he was the prize that the High Queen wanted more than anything else. If their bold gamble was going to pay off, it would have more of a chance in succeeding if they did not have to worry about his safety, but Royal did not believe that. He reminded them that he was probably the most powerful of them all. Yet, they had insisted that the success of this gambit was based more upon stealth than brute force. In the end, he had conceded and agreed to play a minor role from afar.

On the bluff, Royal was surrounded by Reverend Monroe, Ben, Father Benedito, Etera, Peku, Ikin and Tori. As they watched Royal, they had given up trying to say anything that would comfort him. They all knew that Royal hated the idea of others putting their lives on the line for him. It was an ache the young monarch was just beginning to learn how to endure. The only thing that he took some solace from was the vision that Ben had revealed to him about Hue. At the very least, he knew that Hue was safe. He had no idea what this wonderful thing was that his intimate friend was going through, but he guessed that it had something to do with his birth father, Jul, who was still missing in action. He had no idea what the Last Priest of the Avatar could do, but he wished he were here to find out.

The torch lights from the camp on the otherside of the grind made it very difficult to see exactly who was winning. Royal bit down hard on his lip in anticipation. Then, all of a sudden, twin explosions erupted from the High Queen's camp. They could hear the sound of Royal Guards shouting under the weight of Purcell's grenades. The members of Royal's party shouted out in triumph as the smoke from the grenades filled the grind.

"Adios," Father Benedito said as he crossed himself. "I think that Purcell was right. It looks like they have no defense against his grenades. I wish I had some binoculars so I could see." the priest remarked.

"Me, too," Ben said as he lifted his shirt to reveal two magnums. Purcell had left the firearms with Ben along with a lot of amummition, in case they needed it. Ben felt the weight of the guns around his waist and sighed. Silently, he hoped it would not come to a point where he would have to use them. He had never used a gun before in his life and did not know how useful he would be in a battle. However, he felt better having the cold steel at his side as a last resort.

Reverend Monroe walked up to Royal and placed a reassuring hand on his shoulder. Royal almost jumped at his father's familiar touch. Royal smiled at his surrogate father and leaned back against him. Royal knew intuitively that this was not the posture a monarch should take, but he did not care. His main concern was the idea of the others returning safely.

"Have faith, my son," Reverend Monroe consoled him. "The plan was bold, but I think it had merit."

"I don't know anything about war plans," Royal snapped. "I just wish there was another way. I wish I knew what was going on."

Hearing this, Etera stepped forward and reached out and took Royal's hand. Royal turned to face the young sea witch and smiled at her sadly.

"I can tell you what is going on Royal," she offered.

"How?" Royal asked hurriedly.

"Through Tildon," Etera said softly. "Though I am weakened here because of the lack of water, Tildon is my twin. We share an atural connection. I can see through his eyes."

"Is it dangerous for you or him?' Royal asked.

Eterashook her head, no.

"Then let me know," Royal insisted.

Etera went over to the edge of the cliff and stuck out her hands. Her eyes rolled back in her head until all that could be seen were the whites of her eyes. Ikin came up behind her and used his four sets of arms to steady her. After a few minutes, she began to speak.

"Smoke is everywhere," Etera's voice intoned. "My brother is fighting a blue-skinned Royal from the North. The others are actively engaged in struggling with the Royal Guard. The Royal Guard is not fighting as a unit. They were caught totally off guard. Princess Jane and her troops are pushing them back. Few of our troops are hurt, but more of theirs are falling,"

"The High Queen?" Royal asked warily.

"I do not see her," Etera said as she returned to her senses.

"This is a good thing," Royal said quickly.

"No, it is not," Tori said as he leaned into the conversation. "Do not under estimate her, Royal, or the Royal Guard," he warned.

"We need to end this," Royal said as he summoned his fire. Royal was surprised at how easily it came to him and how strong it was. Royal knew immediately that it had something to do with the Red Desert. This haven for the Avatar was amplifying his powers, making him stronger. Royal knew immediately that he had to join the fight, especiaslly if his mother was missing in action. He might be the only one with enough power to challenge her. Royal was about to take to the sky in spite of the protests of those around him when several CODA warriors came running up to him. Royal looked at the concern on their faces and hesitated. They spoke to Reverend Monroe in whispers. Reverend Monroe smiled and almost jumped up and down.

"What is it, Father?" Royal asked.

"It is Tisha," Reverned Monroe smiled. "She has escaped and is on this side of the grind."

The fire on Royal's hands faded instantly. Tears appeared in his eyes and he began to pace back and forth. Seeing the effect that this had on the young High Prince, Peku looked at him oddly.

"Who is this Tisha person?" Peku asked.

Royal quickly stopped his motion and explained to those assembled about the young woman whohad made it possible for them to get to Acara. Royal made it clear that she had been the hero in their fight against the assassin cube. He also reminded them that she was Simon's girlfriend and the mother of Wisdom's son. Peku seemed utterly surprised by this last fact. He could not believe that these two men had actually shared a mate. It was a foreign idea to the Opions.

Moments later, Tisha appeared on the edge of the bluff with her gorda, Aspion. Royal's mouth dropped as he looked at her. Royal stood with his mouth agape, surprised to see her without her characteristic hair extensions. He was not used to seeing her with a baldhead. On top of that, there was a warrior tattoo on the left side of her face. She was dressed inalight, hide armor that covered her from head to toe. Across her chest was a sash with numerous throwing daggers sticking outof it. Tisha looked at Royal and slid off of her gorda. She walked past the others and straight up to Royal. Looking at each other, they both began to laugh joyously. They had come along way since BaltimoreCity. They fell into each other's arms and hugged each other deeply. As Royal held her, he was surprised that he could feel the energy of her and Simon's unborn child emanating from her womb. Evenn thoughRoyal was hugging Tisha, he could feel the unborn child hugging him back. Royal put his hands up to his mouth in surprise as he pointed at her belly.

"He is something else, isn't he?" Tisha mused as she rubbed at her stomach. "He is called Dewa."

"How do you know this?" Royal asked. "Have you named him already?"

"No," Tisha said, shaking her head. "The baby told me. It is a long story."

"I have never felt anything like that before," Royal admitted.

"I don't think anyone has," Tisha admitted. "It was because of the baby that I did not wind up in a dungeon back in Acara City. I think the High Queen wanted to exploit him in some way."

"I am not surprised," Reverend Monroe said as he grabbed Tisha and drew her near. "Only someone like her would try and figure out a way to exploit an unborn child, no matter how special its lineage."

"How did you get away?" Royal asked.

Carefully, Tisha told them about her time in Acara City under the watchful eye of Ela, the Queen of the Royal Guard and Simon's mother. She explained to them that it had been her intention to brainwash her, but it seemed the opposite had happened over time. She told them about the scene from the Grand Citadel where she stopped Ela from attacking the High Queen when she infused Quan with more Dark energy. Tisha made it very clear to them that Ela was not the same person after that incident. It was a surprise to Tisha that the change in Ela had gone so far that she would help Tisha escape. Tisha was honest that this change in Ela made her look at the Royal Guard differently. Though they were sworn to protect the High Monarch, even their allegiance was finite in the face of clear evil. She explained to them that even the gorda, the dedicated mounts of the Royal Guard, were beginning to turn on the High Queen because of her actions.

"I tried to convince Ela to leave with me," Tisha admitted, "but she would not leave without Quan."

"What do you think she will do in our battlle with the High Queen?" Royal asked.

"I think at the very least we have an ally on the inside," Tisha guessed. "At the most, she might help us along the way," she added as she recounted how Ela had subdued Holi's Royal Guard and guided her out of the camp.

"What is that mark on your face?" Royal asked naively.

Tisha turned to Royal with surprise. It had not occurred to her that he would not know his own royal seal. Tisha did not reveal the specifics of her birthing in front of the others. However, she did tell Royal that it was his seal. Royal was about to ask her how she came by it, but thought better of it. Some secrets were not even meant to be shared with the most loyal members of his inner circle.

"I must go to the triage area," Etera announced. "We will be seeing wounded soon," she said grimly.

This announcement brought the members of the party back to the reality of the battle they were currently facing. Tori got to his feet and Peku began to help the elderly man move toward the makeshift healing station. Watching them leave, Tisha stepped forward.

"I want to help," she declared.

"Are you familiar with the healing arts?" Etera asked.

"My mother is a nurse on Earth, a female healer. I learned how to tend to the sick and wounded from her," Tisha said proudly.

"Do you think that is a good idea?" Reverend Monroe asked. "I mean, it may be stressful for you and the baby."

"I'm pregnant, but not dead," Tisha said as she sucked her teeth, leaving Reverend Monroe red-faced with embarrassment.

Just then, another grenade went off on the otherside of the canyon. It was followed by a barrage of gunfire. It was clear from the noise that Purcell and Wisdom were still driving to keep the troops of the High Queen off balance. As the group watched the smoke rise into the night air and blot out the light of the moons, they each silently wondered how long it would last.

Princess Jane and the other members of the Lampourian force had been prepped about what would happen when a grenade exploded. They kept their heads down and their faces covered. The Royal Guards, though bigger and better trained, were not prepared for the concusive blasts. They were disoriented and running away from the swords of the Lampourian mercenaries. Princess Jane made sure her darkly clad troops faded in and out of the plumes of smoke that were keeping the majority of the High Queen's forces off-balance.

Amidst the smoke and debris, Althea and Lethia were locked in mortal combat. Although Althea had been able to use her mastery of fire to fend off Lethia the first time, this time Lethia used her mastery of the land to even the playing field. Like Royal, she was empowered due to her proximity to the Red Desert. She was able to shield herself from Althea's flames with walls of rock that rose from the ground.

"Not this time," Lethia swore as she yanked the ground from under Althea.

"No!" Althea screamed as she fell into a pit.

"I may not get to snap your neck," Lethia swore, "but I will be done with you," she insisted as she poured a torrent of gravel down on top of her. Althea struggled to conjure a wall of flame to protect herself, but it could not hold back the weight of the ground. She was smothered to death as Lethia smiled. She was finally done with her nemesis.

"No!" the High Queen screamed as she watched Althea vanish beneath the rubble. With her vanishing, the High Queen saw her hopes of accessing the CODA's Eternal Spring vanish. She turned her rage toward Lethia. The two women's eyes locked. In that moment, they shared a wealth of unspoken hatred. The High Queen raised her hands and unleashed a torrent of dark energy at Lethia. Lethia was barely able to sidestep the energy and erect a wall to protect herself. She fell down but used all of her might to try and contain the brunt of the High Queen's attack.

Just when her energy began to falter, Simon appeared. He stepped in front of Lethia's shield and direcly in the line of fire of the High Queen's dark onslaught. Simon crossed both of his swords in front of him and called on the energy of the land around him. The pure force of the Red Desert ran through him and dispersed the High Queen's energy. She dropped her hands in disbelief.

"Get your Scepter!" Quan cried as he came up and pushed her behind him.

The High Queen looked at her Royal Guard for a moment, then transformed into a pillar of dark smoke. She vanished from the battlefield, leaving Quan to once again face his son. The two men stared at each other with disdain.

"You could not defeat me before, Keyton," Quan laughed as he licked his lips. "What makes you think you can defeat me now?"

"Where once there was doubt, Father," Simon declared as he began to swing his swords rhythmically," there is now only assurance," he insisted as he charged Quan.

Yet Quan did not budge. He threw back his cloak and revealed his wolf-like arm. He bent down into a squat and began to call upon the ambient energy that the High Queen had filled him with. He rose to twice his normal height. He towered above the battlefield. He caught Simon totally by surprise. Simon tried to stop his forward motion but it was too late. Quan slapped him with his lupine arm across the battlefield.

"By the Avatar," Captain Sarison shouted as he watched Simon sail through the air. As he watched Simon fly, he dropped his guard for a moment. Burton took full advantage of his lapse and knocked him off his feet. Captain Sarison held up his sword at the last moment, escaping a death blow the elder High Price had aimed at his chest. Tildon watched two of his comrades fall but he did not break form. He held his own against Prince Gregor. The two were evenly matched in their swordsmanship.

Wisdom and Purcell turned their attention away from the Royal Guards they were shooting at. They stared at Quan's immense form with reservation.

"That muthafucka is big," Purcell said as he struggled to reload his shot gun.

"The bigger they are, Brother," Wisdom said as he leveled his weapon, "the harder they fall," he shouted as he charged at Quan leveling a volley of bullets. Quan raised his hands to protect his face from the explosive ammunition. The gunfire stunned him, but he did not waver. He turned his attention toward the Sims brothers and charged them. He swung wildly, knocking them off their feet. As the other Royal Guards watched their leader begin to make headway against the attackers they began to regroup. They fell into formation and began to advance on Princess Jane and her mercenaries.

"Hold them back!" Princess Janis commanded as she waved her sword over her head and led her mercenaries in pushing them back.

In the tent that the High Queen used, she rifled through her things and lifted the Scepter of Monarchs. It immediately began to glow. She smiled at it as she came out of the tent. She ran to the edge of the encampment. The marauder and its hounds were there struggling at their bindings. She raised the Scepter and the bonds that were holding them fell away. The huge beast immediately got to its feet and released its hounds. The Marauder and its devil dogs charged into the battle. The hounds immediately engaged the CODA women and Patel, leaving them open to attack from the Dark Priests. The Dark Priests joined together and sent an array of energy into the CODA scattering them.

"Destroy them all!" The High Queen bellowed as she made her way into the center of the fray. From the edge of the battle, she released a volley of dark fire from the Scepter of Monarchs that burned the Lampourian mercenaries. They howled as the dark energy tore at their skin.

Lethia got to her feet slowly. She looked around at the state of the battle. Where they had once been in control of the melee, the tide was turning quickly. Their forces were scattered and losing ground. She bit down hard on her lip. There was only one thing left to do.

"Retreat!" Lethia yelled as she banged her swords together." Retreat!"

Hearing this, Tildon hesitated in his fight with Prince Gregor. He had never run from a battle in his life. However, as he looked around he saw the wisdom in Lethia's actions. He began to fall back and similarly sounded the call for their forces to retreat. Simon rose to his feet, hearing Lethia's yell. He was battered and bruised from his father's solitary blow. As he looked at Quan, part of him desperately wanted another round with him. However, the Lampourian forces were wavering under the onslaught of the High Queen and the CODA were struggling against the Marauder's hounds' bites. He quickly began to wave for the war party to fall back into Arcana village.

"We need to give them some cover!" Purcell screamed as he took out his last grenade and hurled it at the advancing Marauder. The Marauder caught the grenade and held it in its hand as it exploded. The huge dark beast was thrown off its feet and it fell back into the Royal Guard. It blocked the flames of the High Queen, just long enough for the war party to withdraw from the bluff. They ran quickly through the Arcana village back to the other side of the grind. The waiting CODA helped them into the trench. They carried their wounded as they went.

"They are coming!" Lethia screamed as she ran. "Form the line!" she ordered.

"Ready yourselves!" Princess Jane said as she struggled out of her charred armor and lifted a lance.

The Lampourian mercaneries and the CODA quickly began to form a line in the trench and readied themselves for the attack that they knew was coming. Royal watched these brave men and women form a line in defiance of the High Queen. He bit down hard on his lip. He looked at those around him and smiled oddly.

"Royal, don't," Reverend Monroe said as if reading his son's thoughts.

"You have all fought for me," Royal began as he took a step forward. "Now it is time I fight or you," he insisted.

"Royal, you can't!" Father Benedito cried as he watched the line of the High Queen's troops form on the other side of the grind.

"Father, I must," Royal insisted.

With that, Royal bent down and began to float over the trench. He flew through the air until he was over the Arcana village, to the sudden surprise of the High Queen and her forces.

"What is he doing?" Ben gasped as he watched Royal's floating figure.

"Being the High Prince!" Reverend Monroe cried out.

Behind him in the trench, all eyes fixed on Royal in awe. From the otherside of the grind, the High Queen came forward and raised the Scepter of Monarchs at the visage of her son. Royal did not move. He stared down the High Queen and her dark forces.

"This will end only one way," the High Queen insisted as she leveled her Scepter at Royal. "You will bow to me!"

"I bow to no one!" Royal cried as he closed his eyes and called out to the fire within him with all of his might.

Before the High Queen could act, the entire length of the cliff erupted in towering flames. The High Queen and her war party fell back as they fought to extinguish Royal's fire. The Marauder and its hounds howled in defiance as they tried to breach the wall of flames and get to the High Prince. The High Queen held up her Scepter, shielding herself from the onslaught but the other members of her war party were not so lucky. They fell back and ran from the tremendous attack trying to extinguish the flames that engulfed them.

"Hold the line!" the High Queen commanded as she tried to extend her shield to protect her troops but she was unable to protect them all. They fell back under the weight of Royal's attack. Only the Marauder, its hounds, Quan, and the Dark Priests seemed immune to Royal's volley. They slowly began to inch their way forward.

Royal hung in the sky for a second longer. Then he slowly began to descend to the village square of Arcana. As he fell to the ground, he did not move.

"By the Avatar!" Simon cried as he began to get to his feet and climb down into the Arcana village. Wisdom was directly behind him. "We have to get him!" Simon cried.

"He is mine!" the High Queen laughed as she looked at Royal's still form. "Bring him to me," she commanded.

"I don't think so!" a voice echoed through the grind. Everyone froze and strained to see where this voice was coming from. Then slowly, folk in the trench began to point toward a rock formation near the edge of the cliffside.

"Who dares!" bellowed the High Queen as she shook her staff at the figure.

"I do," the figure answered.

"And who are you?" the High Queen asked.

"The Last Priest of the Avatar," the figure answered.

"No!" the High Queen screamed. "Destroy him!" she commanded her remaining forces.

"I don't think so," the Priest said defiantly as he raised his hands to the darkened night sky. For a moment, there was an odd stillness that consumed both sides of the grind and the rift in between. Then the entire Red Desert behind the figure began to swirl. It rose up into a huge twister and leaped over the troops in the trench. It expanded into a huge vortex, cutting off the High Queen and her minions from the fallen High Prince. The High Queen raised her Scepter and sent volley after volley of energy against the wall of sand. The two Dark Priests did the same but their efforts were in vain. The wall of sand washed over the High Queen, her remaining emissaries, and the fallen Royal Guard. It lifted them all from the cliffside and carried them far into the distance to the cheers of the troops in the trench.

Simon and Wisdom were the first to make their way to Royal. They lifted him gently from the floor of the Arcana village and cradled his head. Royal slowly began to stir. He looked up at the night sky as his head slowly cleared. He was exhausted by his assault. He had never used his powers in such a way. He could barely move.

"Did we win?" Royal asked as he struggled to sit up.

"Yes we did!" Simon told him as he hugged Royal. "Yes we did!" he laughed.

"Alright big guy, let him breath," Wisdom said as he sucked his teeth and lit a cigarette. It was the best cigarette he had had in a long time.

"How did that happen?" Royal questioned.

"We had some help," Reverend Monroe said as he walked up with Lethia, Patel, Princess Jane, Ben Lee, Purcell, Tildon, and Father Beneditio.

"And it was right on time," Lethia smirked as she grabbed the match from Wisdom and lit a cigar. She gladly shared it with Patel who was beaming from the victory.

"I don't understand," Royal said, shaking his head as he struggled to his feet.

"Look there," Princess Jane said as she pointed to the red-robed Priest of the Avatar on the rock formation.

As the troops filled the Arcana village, the priest floated down from the rock and glided over their heads. Then he landed a few feet away from Royal. He folded his hands in his robe and walked up to Royal with his head hung low.

"I guess thank you is in order," Royal said gratefully. "We couldn't have done it without you, Jul" he added.

"I didn't think so," Hue winked as he removed the red hood of the robe to the sounds of awe from the crowd. Seeing Hue, Royal was speechless. All he could do was reach out and hug his intimate friend.

"Where is Jul?" Royal asked as they separated. "Where is my father?"

"It was time for him to go," Hue explained as he clutched Royal's hand. "His journey with us was over," he said simply "But his spirit will always be here among the dunes."

Royal looked around sadly, but he somehow understood.

"Well I'll be damned," Ben laughed as he ran up and hugged his son. "When did you decide to do this?" he asked.

"I think it chose me," Hue said as he shrugged his shoulders. "It chose me."

"We're going to have to discuss this, young man," Ben said with a wrinkled brow.

"Tenemos tiempo," Father Benedito smiled widely. "We will have time. I think we should celebrate now."

"I will break out the wine!" Ikin insisted as he clapped all four sets of his hands.

"After all of this, a drink would be good," Captain Sarison laughed as he raised his sword over his head to the cheers of the others.

Etera, Tori, and Tisha cared for the wounded in the triage area beyond the trench. They applied salve to burns, put on bandages, and wrapped wounds. As they tended to the wounded, Simon silently snuck in behind them and lifted Tisha in the air. She was stunned by his sudden appearance. She began to giggle as she grabbed hold of his neck. Tisha kissed Simon's face wildly. She never thought she would see anything that looked as good as he did. Simon put her down and placed his hand tenderly on her stomach. Simon could feel the energy of his child respond to him. It was the most powerful thing he had ever felt.

"I thought I would never see you again," Tisha sobbed as she hugged him.

"Nothing could keep me from you," Simon assured her. "You, Royal, and our unborn child are my sole responsibility."

"I hope you don't mind my new look," Tisha said as she lowered her head shyly.

Simon pushed her head up and kissed her lips.

"You look fine to me," Simon assured her. "As beautiful as always."

"You're lying," Tisha teased.

"No, he isn't," Wisdom said as he came into the triage area with Purcell on his heels.

Tisha looked at Simon. He nodded at her. She walked up to Wisdom and Purcell and hugged them both together.

"Girl," Purcell shook his head. "Don't you ever do anything like this again."

"I don't plan to," Tisha laughed. "How is Little Wisdom ?"

"Big and bad like his mother and father," Purcell told her. "He will be much better once we get you two home."

"I think I've had enough adventure to last me two fucking life times," Wisdom exhaled as he took out another cigarette and lit it up. Then he recalled Tisha's condition and put it out. He grimaced. It was a waste of good nicotine.

Just then, the air near Wisdom shimmered and the apparition of Malik Jones appeared.

"What makes you think it is over?" he laughed before he vanished again.

Late into the night, the CODA played their drums for the troops. The Arcana let their wine flow long and steady to alleviate the pain of battle. Everyone danced around the fire well into the early morning hours. Royal watched the merriment from his small hut with satisfaction. He never could have asked for a better outcome. However, he knew that this was just the beginning of his battle against his mother. They may have won the first battle, but there was a war ahead. Now he and his allies had to persuade five major monarchs to confront the High Queen in the Grand Citadel so that they could remove her from power. He had no illusions. He knew this was not going to be easy.

As he turned inside the small hut, Hue was lying on his side under a thin blanket. Royal could make out the shape of the crystal in the middle of his chest. He still could not believe that Hue had agreed to take on the mantle of the priests of the Avatar for him. He guessed he really did love him. Royal smiled and lay down next to Hue. He placed a hand against his face and slept better than he had in a long time.

# Epilogue

The red wind of the Priest of the Avatar swept the High Queen and her minions all the way across Acara, back to Acara City. It shattered the Gateway they had used to get to the Red Desert and made any other ineffective to dark energy. No one dared say a word to the High Queen once they were back in the capital. Under Quan and Ela's direction, everyone simply put away their weapons of war until it was time to take them up again. The High Queen was embarrassed beyond belief at her defeat. It was more than she could imagine. She had not only lost the heir, but access to a power the CODA had that would make him unneccesary. It was more than she could fathom.

Once she was back in the capital, the High Queen went directly to the altar of the Dark God. She fasted and prayed, looking for answers. She did not leave her knees until she felt the huge altar tremble with the promise of her victory and the promise of the death of her adversaries; even if that included her son.

# Epilogue II

Etera watched the celebrations in the Arcana village from the doorway of her little hut. As happy as she was that they had won, she was feeling awfully alone. Looking out at the night sky, she found herself severely missing her grandmother, Anna-Beth. It was the kind of ache she would get for her in the mines when she was being kept as a slave. Standing in the doorway, she watched as her brother, Tildon, approached. He was drunk from all the wine and merriment. Etera was glad to see her twin so happy. Looking at him, she thought he looked ridiculous in the cape that Prince Janis had given him, but he was wearing it like a badge of honor. She could not bear to tell him how she was feeling with all the good news flowing.

Tildon approached Etera's tent and climbed up the rope ladder into the hut. The two siblings hugged and settled down next to a set of hot rocks and snuggled as they did when they were children. It was something they had not done in a long time. They sat in silence as they listened as the CODA played in the distance. Snuggled in her brother's arms, Etera found tears forming in her eyes. She hid her face from her brother.

"What is it Etera?" Tildon asked softly.

"It is nothing," Eteralied.

"We are twins, Etera, and if there is one thing you can not do, it is lie to me," Tildon chided her. "We are one spirit cleaved in two. I feel you as you feel me."

"I know, Tildon," Etera smiled as she wiped her eyes. "I could never hide anything from you."

"It is the young High Prince," Tildon said carefully. "Your heart still yearns for him."

"I see how he looks at Hue and I try to respect their bond, but I am drawn to him," Etera admitted.

Tildon's brow wrinkled and he thought about his sister's words for a long time before he spoke.

"We are venturing into new territory, dear sister. I have to say I was not one to respect Royals, butI have come to respect High Prince Von. I also know that for as much as he may love Hue, Hue can not give him one thing that you can," he said flatly.

"And what is that?" Etera asked dumbly, missing the obvious.

"An heir," Tildon said as he kissed Etera on the forehead. "There will come a time when such a thing will be an issue no matter how much he loves Hue, and I do not think Hue can fulfill such a function, even in his new form."

Etera was shocked by her brother's word. They weren't treasonous, but they left an odd taste in Etera's mouth. She liked Hue and the last thing she wanted to do was undermine their relationship. However, she did know that one day the High Prince would need an heir, and who better to carry the next generation of High Royals than her. It was something she would have to think about seriously.

Just then Princess Jane appeared in the doorway of her hut. She was smiling widely.

"Dear Lady, may I steal your brother for a drink?" she asked politely.

Etera looked from Tildon to her with surprise. Tildon was actually blushing. This was a side of him she had never seen. He wore it well. Etera reached up and touched his face gently.

"Go, Brother, and make merry," Etera insisted.

Tildon rose quickly looking at Princess Jane, tripping over his feet. He looked back at his sister before departing.

"We will speak of these things again," he said as he reached down and kissed her forehead.

"Yes, we will," Etera agreed as she watched Princess Jane take Tildon's hand and lead him back toward the party.

Etera returned to the doorway and watched the moons in the sky. Her hands fell to her stomach as she thought about what her brother had said. It left her spirit lightened and her mind with much to contemplate.